INSATIABLE HATE

A Zach Miller Adventure: Book 2

INSATIABLE HATE

DENNIS A NEHAMEN

Golden Poppy Publications™
Los Angeles, CA

Every person has a path to success. Only a few stay
on it long enough to reach the goal.
Sarah and Craig Nehamen

Owing to that wisdom, I dedicate this book to
my son and daughter.
And of course to my dear wife, Bernice.

PROLOGUE

I THOUGHT IT WAS THE morning of my life. Past horrors had graciously bid me adieu. My shoulders were light and I had no cause to look over them anticipating tragedy. Then I sneezed. As I blew into a Kleenex, a ghastly smelling stringy substance streamed out of my nose, foul matter I imagined might flow from the bowels of evil.

I couldn't stop it. *What is this?* I shouted into an echo of irreverence. I had my answer even before I finished posing the question. It was hate. It was the worst sort of hate, the type that wants revenge, the type that won't be satisfied without a rampage of murder and the type that will kill millions to punish one.

Rueben Cloud and his wife, Josea Roth-Cloud, were causelessly buzzing back stage, trying to appear to be addressing last minute details in preparation for the lights to go up for the first time on their latest musical. In truth, they, as well as the remainder of the staff, were panic-stricken, gravely incommunicative like parents whose teenage daughter hadn't returned home on time from her first date.

The audience, composed of those privileged souls fortunate to have a ticket for the kick-off performance of what the couple believed to be their greatest work, was seated, impatiently waiting the unveiling—they would never serve as witnesses to the grand opening.

After fidgeting in their chairs for over half an hour, the announcer informed this eager group that due to an undisclosed tragic event they would all receive refunds, along with the right to see the work as soon as it was next scheduled. That would not happen; the piece would never be staged at The Center for the Performing Arts at Kuruk.

The lead female character, an eight-year-old girl taking the role of Star, had gone missing. The spokesman for the theater must have sensed a worse crisis than any participant of the show would have allowed themselves to imagine when he referred to a "tragic event." However, that is exactly what accounted for the conspicuous absence of the budding young prodigy. While resting late in the afternoon following the final dress rehearsal, she was lured out of her room and then abducted. The mystery of her missing the curtain call was solved at sunrise the next morning.

The killer had hung sweet Adina Bernard like Christ from a cross. He had driven the stake into the ground deep enough to support her limp body, drenched in blood from a visible puncture to the heart. The site where she rested was half way along the private road leading to Kuruk.

I recall the first time I drove the quarter mile stretch leading to what was then not only our restaurant but also my wife's home. The earth paralleling the road on both sides had been stingily landscaped by nature. Scattered randomly were a few large yucca, tall figures with their sword-like leaves shooting out in every direction like the frizzy hair of a mad scientist. The older, lower growth was thick and drooped downward from the trunk. The overall impression suggested that this family of cactus had been awakened too early and needed a cup of coffee to perk up. Less notable were clumps of mescal plants interspersed with Alaskan Ginseng, the latter creeping their dark green, maple-shaped leaves like tortoises across the blackened loam-covered ground.

Most memorable for me was the wooden gate that at some past time might have proudly permitted or denied entry. Yet as I passed it, I noticed that it was so badly eaten by termites that its miracle was having wrestled with the earth around it such that it had managed to stay standing upright. During my first fall season at the New Mexico Indian Reservation called Mescalero, an early windstorm finally terminated the stubborn structure like a bullet fired into its brain.

At first I felt like weeping but my wife, Preeti, consoled me that all objects, animate and inanimate, have their time. It was our calling to construct not only a new gate but also a fence of similar style spanning the entire length of the road. That wasn't all. She also surmised, correctly, that with the volume of traffic it now served, we needed to pave the entrance to our place of business.

I used to smile, reminiscing about the ticklish sensations I had stored like gems in a leather pouch from my maiden voyage to Kuruk.

Now, if any person by chance turned onto the road leading

to our restaurant the morning Adina's body was found, they would have been welcomed by a spiffy split rail open gate with matching fence. Resting under the crossbars were clumps of blooming coneflowers with their pink petals submitting gracefully to feature the perfectly round-shaped orange jewels cloistered in their center. These bursts of color were so bright that each possessed as potent an effect on the senses as a field of California golden poppies. Dandelions, in their supporting role, covered the adjacent ground.

That very morning the wonder of this precious and beautiful strip of earth was looted from the rooftop of my memory like tenderness from a warrior.

I was already, owing to the unsolved mystery of what happened to Adina, in a gloomy mood when I left home just before daybreak to address a number of business matters at the restaurant. I had proceeded only some two hundred yards before the grotesque figure of our lead lady came into view; the image burns eternal agony in my heart to this moment.

I slammed my car to a stop, sending my companion, the esteemed English Cocker Spaniel family pet, Henry Higgins, unpleasantly head first into the dashboard.

He yelped. I screeched. The next thing I recall was the sound of a damn fleet of pickup trucks roaring along the road. Then, I heard sirens. The noise of a procession of police vehicles racing toward me was deafening. Successively each skidded to a stop before the officers bolted from their cars. After the near fatal events I had lived through during the few years prior to this tragedy, I felt doomed.

It would not be until some time later that I would come to understand that this adorable little girl was savagely murdered owing to two crimes, neither of which she could have had knowledge of or averted. Putting aside that she was an unusually talented child who was going to bring joy to thousands of people during her career and had been a delight to all of us associated with her at Mescalero, she was sentenced to death for the offenses of being associated with me...and being Jewish.

This was not to be a common hate crime. The evildoer of this act was a rabid animal who had stuffed his belly with viciousness but could never be sated. He wanted me, and everybody and everything precious to me, to suffer or be destroyed. He landed in town with vengeance. He wanted to play with me like an alley cat with a field mouse, terrorizing me with pinprick impalements by his wicked incisors before releasing me to scamper away, but only to then mouth me with just enough grip to let me know that at any moment the fatal tightening of the jaw could bring about my termination.

Adina Bernard was only a warm-up exercise for this sick monster. I would soon learn that the man wasn't bred for the role of cold killer but acquired it out of irrefutable faith— the worst equation for the devil's work in that the horrors he commits in his demented mind are permissible, rational, necessary and justified.

The end game would come much too late for many innocent people. I'm not sure to this day what other acts of terror were on his agenda when we did finally meet. I do know that his enterprise was futile to him unless at some point he would be able to encounter me face-to-face. I surmised this to be the case as time went on but it wasn't until the moment he embraced me that my suspicion was confirmed.

After everything, he wanted to kiss me—twice on each side.

BOOK I
ACTS OF EVIL

1

NO FREE PASSES

SADLY, SHORTLY AFTER TURNING thirty, the sweet cradle of blessedness I had enjoyed up until that time brashly delivered a Dear John letter—it would be one crisis followed by another for the next several years before a brief respite leading up to the loss of Adina. I presumed this most recent tragedy would be an isolated event, one that would have to be grieved and then survived.

Sure, I knew there would be an aftermath to her murder. Yet how could I have imagined at the time that the epilogue to the horrid slaying of Adina Bernard would elasticize into a full blown yarn, the unraveling both inspiring and commanding this thought-to-have-retired author, Zacchaeus Miller, to finger tapping the blues on his computer keys?

This tale took its next turn on a Thursday afternoon in early March, only a week after the body of Adina Bernard was found. Inside a run-down apartment in the crime-ridden Tom Tenorio Park area of Albuquerque, New Mexico, Narsi Platta's body was found lying in a rouge-watered bathtub after bleeding out from slashing his wrists. If hatred toward me hadn't been fomenting before this event, the feeling had now stepped out of the mist of silence with a hissing sound, licensed by the owner to aim at me unrestrained rage.

I wish I could have asked the God of Revenge why I was selected. There was no need for dumb questions. The answer was obvious. My own God of Innocence—the teasing type—had laughed an all too familiar chuckle, anticipating that I'd appeal to His sense of justice. "I'm only half Jewish," I pled, blamelessly. But my words lacked prestige. Like it or not, I was fully chosen. All I recall hearing was a pathetic "tee-he." I threw up my hands as a prayer, making a last appeal to self-pity, a talent that I had mastered years earlier. Yet my pal turned a backside, abandoning me as if I were a shoddy beggar.

What credential did I possess qualifying me as an object of revenge? Part of the answer is that a couple years before I had assisted my father-in-law, Len Cloud, the legal guide of his tribe, the Mescalero Apache, to investigate the possibility of tribal funds being fleeced by the president, a man named Bernard Platta.

My role was innocent enough. I was asked to sniff the flow of money coming in to and out of the tribal trusts and investigate if contracts entered into by the tribe were on the up and up. With the help of my sidekick, Josea Roth, unfortunately we found the fiscal management of the tribe to be filthy.

The key character in this play of corruption was the senior Platta, father of two sons, Gopan and Narsi, both of which were living high off illegally attained wealth—and aware of it. Not only had the three Platta's sprouted noses longer than

Pinocchio's, there was a host of other actors who had gleefully signed on for supporting roles in the multi-pronged swindle.

Once the proof had been attained, and then bound in a tidy book of incrimination, an attempt was made to retrieve the assets without having the entire tribe humiliated by a trial conducted by the State of New Mexico. The effort failed miserably. What it proved, at least to me, was that you can deal openly and honestly with crooks, but expect at just the moment you think you have a deal to be congratulated with a knuckle sandwich smacked into your face.

Bernard Platta was swinging both fists at the same time— toss him a sling blade and he'd have severed my head from my neck like a weed.

2

BOUND BY REVENGE

UNBEKNOWNST TO ME, OWING to my diligence in amassing the evidence against these criminals, and then my participation in resolving the matter, I was identified as the culprit. Bernard Platta designated me as the loathsome villain; he reviled me.

At the time of Adina's murder, Gopan had been sentenced and had just begun serving time. Narsi was sentenced but a final appeal had postponed his incarceration for two weeks. Daddy Platta was still free on bail, battling with tooth, nail, hammer, chisel, drill and…lead pipe for a longer Stay out of Jail card.

Several times I was ordered to testify at hearings and on each occasion Platta venomously eyed me. While I had no doubt that he detested me, his rancor was all bluster…until after his son Narsi carved out his own punishment. Then my father-in-law's warning to me about Platta, that "he could be a mean son-of-a-bitch" came to fruition.

"I…want…him…dead!" Bernard Platta declared, his foot

stomping punctuating each word like a child throwing a tantrum. "You want to help? Then kill that bastard."

Bernie, as his few friends and many enemies referred to him during the trial, was a short man. He bore a remarkable resemblance to another dictatorial figure, Napoleon. His face was round with soft, light skin several shades lower than most of his fellow tribesmen. His hair had years ago backed off his forehead like an army in retreat, waging his fight against Old-Man Time by letting the strands on the center of his head grow long so that he could meticulously comb them forward. It was a defiant, and futile, attempt to challenge nature's ravaging way.

His belly protruded. As he stood with a perfectly erect spine, his shape might be mistaken for a proud soon-to-be mom showing off her pregnancy. He impressed you as being a kindly and sweet man…until he lowered his head. Vacuous swagger was not his game. When his chin started to work like a mallet—pounding on his upper sternum—and his teeth gritted with such ferocity that the lips and surrounding tissue stretched tautly, the man was expressing raging determination intended to scare the crap out of anyone thinking of testing him.

He presented himself in this posture when he instructed Mr. Fadi Abbas what service the man could be to him, pertaining to the termination of myself.

"I'm afraid that's not what I had in mind…at least not right away," Abbas countered with a demonic grin smeared widely across his face.

If Platta were accurate in his read of this man who was unabashedly proclaiming himself a killer, he would understand that the satisfaction of murder is not solely to eliminate the victim but equally to gratify the sadistic cravings of the slayer. Mr. Abbas was a hungry man—he's the second piece of the puzzle as to why I was selected for termination.

In a small office sitting across from one another were these two soon-to-be-partners-in-crime. Abbas was behind a desk covered with papers that had been taken out of a folder and dropped randomly. He was in the process of enlightening Platta on his vast knowledge of the life of yours truly, Zach Miller.

"There are many people from where I was born who despise this man," Abbas said as he glanced disdainfully at my photo that he was dangling from the tips of his fingers like a germ. "I have been honored with the assignment of avenging his crimes."

The room was dimly lit. The only light reflected from two lamps resting on one of a pair of oak wood tables. Other than the desk, chairs, a wooden bench and lighting, the interior was empty. The walls were void of decoration, their only sign of wear was several small nail holes revealing that at some time prior an occupant had been more attentive to the ambiance of the space.

Platta had noticed when he entered that adjacent to where they were talking, a grander office was more generously honored with ornaments pleasing to the eye and senses. On the desk of that space was a large photo of a couple. A careless cleaning person had no doubt turned the picture to face the entrance to the suite. Platta recognized the attractive female when he first arrived but didn't address his concern until moments later.

"Look, Abbas, what if your boss shows up unexpectedly?"

"She won't," he assured a fidgety Platta. "She's visiting our friend in Mescalero tonight."

Platta leaned back in his chair, emboldened by the disclosure.

"I'm still not sure why you're willing to help me with this. Whatever your motive is, let me make it clear to you that if you cross me I'll see to it you pay."

Abbas smiled. He took no offense from the explicit threat.

"You'll come to trust me like a brother." He paused to close his eyes while placing his right hand to his heart. "The betrayal of this man has lead to the death of many people. You have lost a son owing to his juvenile meddling and I know for a fact of many situations where loved ones have been killed, imprisoned or gone into hiding because of what he would suggest are his acts of gallantry."

Abbas stood, pressing the palms of his hands into the wood desktop, peering deeply into Platta's eyes. "My services will not be free."

"I told you when you contacted me that I was running out of funds, that defending my sons and myself has bled me—"

"Please, Mr. Platta," Abbas abruptly cut him off, but with a gentle, rhythmic voice that might be mistaken for lyrical. "I take offense at your mistrust. I told you I would not be charging you a nickel to dispense with Miller, didn't I?"

Abbas appeared to be in his early to mid-thirties, at least two decades younger than his new associate. He wore an armor of musculature yet it was apparent he'd laboriously superimposed it on a more fragile figure to bulk up a perceived shortfall of masculinity. His head was covered with a brown knit cap; his full beard was meticulously cropped at a length of half an inch and was coal black in color.

His eyebrows were thick and composed a perfectly horizontal and unbroken line above the eyes. The latter two organs appeared in a perpetual state of glint, as if his being was one of inner joyousness and playfulness.

"But you just said your services are not free, unless I didn't hear you?" Platta posed inquiringly.

"No, you heard me perfectly. I want you to be my partner."

"And I want that bastard dead before I'm no doubt sent to prison for most of what is left of my life," Platta hurled back at him with the potency of Zeus firing a bolt of lightning to smite an enemy.

"As you know, while I'm not a licensed private investigator my boss is," Abbas continued, ignoring the outburst. "I've learned a good deal over the past year working with her."

"What does that have to do with me?" Platta questioned impatiently.

"I knew that you would hate Miller. No different than the detestation you hold toward your father, I assume."

Platta's face tightened as he reflexively gripped his brewing anger.

"My father has nothing to do with this," he stammered. "And it's no business of yours."

"To the contrary," Abbas pleasantly disagreed. "Your father was a Jew, no?"

"He was out of my life by the time I was seven," Platta retorted dismissively.

"Thankfully, for you. He was a monster, isn't that true?"

Platta shifted uncomfortably in his chair. Abbas was forcing his new partner to dredge up memories from a cesspool of childhood horrors that the man was never able to conquer but was successful in hiding from anyone else intimate to him.

"My mom was a gorgeous woman. He raped and beat her," Platta admitted. "He was very wealthy and thought he could do anything he wanted. When she finally got away from him, she came back to her birth home. She raised me after that on the reservation. I'm a Mescalero Apache," he proclaimed. "

"You're also as passionate a Jew hater as I proudly label myself," he smirked, well aware of disclosures on the subject made by Platta. "I know of your past associations with the most respected anti-Semitic groups in this country," he informed Platta as he was leaning forward to punctuate his point by whispering. "You need not have secrets with me. As I said, you can rely on me like a brother for we share identical goals."

Platta impatiently interrupted. "These people are responsible for—"

Abbas, still speaking in a lowered voice close to the man's ear, knowingly filled in the answer for him. "Everything evil on earth? Is that what you're about to say?"

"Well, yes."

"Then we're agreed? I'll help you with Miller and you'll help me make war on the Jews…and Miller as well."

Platta nodded agreement, but with bemusement. He still had no idea what role he was to play.

"I want you to have a clear alibi any time we deal with Miller. It's too transparent that you might want to harm him."

Platta nodded again. Abbas rose and started for the door, motioning his partner to follow. He lead him to his car, a dilapidated old snot-colored Toyota Camry, the right passenger door secured shut with a piece of wire and portions of the top and front hood exposing raw metal—the vehicle's condition was an angry compromise between necessity and disdain.

They traveled silently a short distance to an apartment building mimicking the low esteem of Fadi's wheels. He parked in front of the structure. There was no landscaping other than randomly scattered rocks. Volunteer weeds were proving that spring holds no prejudice against drifters; they were grabbing the otherwise nude grave-like earth and encroaching on a loosely defined path composed of broken steppingstones.

Platta followed Abbas up a narrow stairwell. The banister was secured by one bracket on the upper portion but the bottom hardware hung listlessly out of the wall, allowing the metal rail to rest on the concrete steps. A door opened to a hallway with a filthy carpet of unrecognizable color leading to several entrances on each side. He asked Platta to wait behind the hall door until he called him.

Out of sight of Platta, Abbas stopped at the fourth unit on the right. He paused to carefully inspect the door, eyeing it closely to be sure that the hair-thin clear thread he had placed across it hadn't been moved. He inserted two separate keys into the locks and opened it. He entered and similarly inspected the single street-facing window to be sure it hadn't been jarred.

He went back to get Platta. Then he motioned for the man to come along, waiting for his guest to enter first. Abbas' living space was dingily decorated, and small. The studio apartment had an unmade mattress on the floor and in a corner was a frayed couch. The kitchenette revealed neglected dishes and pots, the only interested parties several flies feasting on the stinking remains of meals likely digested by the master days or even weeks earlier.

Abbas was shameless. His dwelling was obviously inconsequential to his esteem. In the corner of the room was a closet. He swung open the door. A gleeful smile stretched his cheeks. His rounded face redeemed the despair of his abode. He invited Platta to behold the numerous weapons and objects looking like explosives carefully set out on a series of shelves.

"I'll supply all the materials we'll need from now on," he informed his guest. "I think it's time to get to work Mr. Platta," Abbas noted, waving his arm as if calling the deadly equipment to attention.

There was a small wooden box sitting on the floor in the closet. Abbas picked it up. While holding it open, he took out a single pill and a small plastic pouch. He replaced the closed box where it sat seconds earlier, dropping the pill into the bag. He then handed it to Platta.

"Take this an hour before you finalize the assignment," he said with a coy smile. "Trust me, you'll feel like a saint."

Platta looked at him with bewilderment. Abbas had already anticipated an objection by Platta.

"You'll be alone. This will help you overcome any last second hesitation." Still reading uncertainty—possibly fear—in the man's glance, Abbas continued. "Don't be a fool. I need you alive."

Platta nodded, signaling he'd do as he was told.

3

THE ECSTASY OF MASS MURDER

IN THE HEART OF Central Phoenix, just north of Camelback Ave, is an upscale neighborhood with an unusual inner city treat. Murphy's Bridle Path is made up of 2.5 miles of a tree-lined urban trail. Previously, it had been an equestrian path. More recently, as it meanders up Central Ave, it invites the exercise enthusiast for a beautiful jog as well as strollers to amble along while viewing the natural setting lined with luxury homes and attractive olive trees planted late in the nineteenth century.

The corner of Central Ave and Bethany Home Road might be seen as the tip of the park. In fact, the North Phoenix Baptist Church rests on that precise location and down the block, the Beth Israel Temple.

Three days after the meeting between Abbas and Platta, while under the instruction of his Arab partner, the soon-to-be-convicted Platta drove to Phoenix. He had left Albuquerque at nine in the evening and arrived at his destination, the outer border of Murphy's Bridal Path, at four in the morning.

He parked on an isolated street behind both the church and temple. In the trunk of his car were three identical objects. They each appeared like large serving platters that were several inches thick. These canisters were soldered closed by the hand of a skilled craftsman. Inside each of them were several sets of high explosives designed to go off sequentially. They would fill the air with liquid chlorine and tear apart the flesh of anyone in the area with shrapnel composed of tiny razors.

They weighed almost forty pounds each. Visible on the outside was an activation switch. The genius that manufactured these improvised explosive devices (IED's) had cleverly used old mobile phones and garage door openers to devise the electronics required to set off the charges by remote control.

Each apparatus had been placed in a material pouch so that Platta could carry one over each shoulder and the third draped around his neck. He didn't have far to walk so the weight was not a factor.

He moved in the direction of the Temple Beth Israel, but only after surveying the area and determining that nobody was around. He had been prepped to know exactly where to place the bombs. He was also informed that the portion of the building he was most interested in was constructed on a foundation with a crawl space beneath the first floor of the two-level structure.

He placed the parcels on the ground and opened the trap door to gain access to the space below the building. He then reached out to pull each of the bombs securely on to the cold dirt surface. He took a small pen flashlight from his coat pocket and crouched down so that he could move to the locations where he wanted to place each explosive, dragging them along the ground behind him.

As he left each of the packages, he set their respective switches.

He turned off the light as he approached the door and carefully looked around before opening it and exiting. Since he was comfortable that he had not been observed, he strolled away. He moved intentionally in a direction away from where his car was parked. In fact he walked several blocks, backtracking and observing the surrounding area until convinced he had attracted no more attention than that of a spider he noticed spinning a web between the branches of a Chinese Elm tree. He recognized it as a juvenile version of the giant parent elms he had in the back yard of the house he was raised in after birth in Los Angeles.

He finally made his way back to his car and drove several miles before pulling into a rest area where he fell asleep for a couple hours. When he awakened, he used a drive-through window at a McDonalds to purchase breakfast. He then drove back to where he had parked earlier in the morning when he set the bombs. He exited his car and began walking to the bridal path where he found a vacant bench to sit on while eating.

He finished his meal at ten in the morning. Spring was expressing an unusual indolence, leaving the air crisp and sharp, with the sun moseying out from behind a thin sheet of white streaky clouds. Platta was wearing a tan nylon windbreaker with black pants of a similar fabric. On his head was a bright yellow baseball cap. He looked like any other hiker out for a walk. In fact, the smell of pine was faintly perceptible and lured him deeper along the path. His conditioning was poor and he stopped to rest several times.

Diligently monitoring his watch, he took the pill Abbas had given him precisely at ten-thirty.

He knew that it would not be until eleven thirty that the facility he wanted to inflict terror on would be fully occupied. Not long after taking the pill, he perceived a feeling of immense calm. That was followed by the loss of a sensation of weight, as if he might have unwittingly uncovered the elusive elements to create the feeling of anti-gravity.

He then noticed his mind burst out from the confines of his cranial cell, expanding to fill the eternity of universal space. Beams, like visions from giant diamonds with infinite facets piled as high as a mountain, bright and wondrous, shot in every direction. At their distal point the rays began to warp, looping back upon one another to form what at first appeared to be a tangle of yarn. Yet as he visualized the miracle, he noticed that each strand was distinguishable and had ended its voyage by aiming for a particular point. The end product might have been a tapestry, the picture representing what looked to Platta to be a likeness of the resurrection of Christ.

Had God invited him into His private chamber of ultimate peace, he wondered. For at that moment all the conflict, fear and hate he had suffered during his conscious existence dissolved into a blissful awareness that life had order, and he was merely a passenger in the cosmic plan. The apprehensions he might have admitted minutes earlier were comical. He sat playing with them. He tossed worry about death in the air like pizza dough and watched the discs take off like space ships on a celestial journey.

Abbas had honored him to complete a task. It was so obvious. He was doing nothing wrong. To the contrary, he was doing the ordained work of The Creator.

As Platta sat, he couldn't help noticing the parade of people passing him. Soon they would be grateful for what he was about to do. Thank God. Bernard Platta was now the chosen one.

To his surprise, at the same time these miraculous insights were unfolding in a continuum he was able to draw on his normal senses and perceptions. He could hear the yells of children playing in the distance and notice the grey roots of strands of hair on a lady's head seated on another bench close to him. He was fully oriented to time and place. He knew where he lived, who his family members were, and the need for caution with respect to his upcoming duty.

He glanced down at his watch. It was still only five after the hour of eleven. He stood and began walking slowly out of the wooded area, thinking about the act he was about to commit. It was as vile and cruel as could be conceived. Yet the bitterness he harbored for all that had gone wrong in his life at last would be vindicated through the torment planned for others.

With the little present Abbas had given him, he was void of common human conscience. He laughed to himself thinking about the burden that he and the rest of mankind had pointlessly hauled along in their psyche. Conscience? Superego? Shame and guilt were foolish games...played mindlessly by the foolish. He no longer would have to shoulder responsibility for becoming a murderer. Bernard Platta was no more, and no less, than a thread in the fabric of human destiny.

As he made his way back to the car, a feeling of exhilaration overcame him. He picked up the pace, as if not wanting to be late for a special lady. It was quiet where he had parked. He started the engine. Owing to a slight decline in the level of the street, the car rolled forward about two hundred yards without him engaging the gear. At the precise distance he was told he needed to be from the bombs to transmit the activation mechanisms, he stopped.

He reached into the glove compartment. There was a device with three buttons. He took it out with his right hand and fondled it erotically. He glanced over at the temple, now only about a hundred and fifty yards away. A breath exhaled in slow motion, lacking sound or movement, sponsored his transcendence to an ultimate yogic trance. With a smile on his face he pressed one button after the other, three in total.

The feeling reminded him of the successive pulses of a splendid adolescent orgasm.

4

BAD NEWS

NOTHING SEEMED TO BE able to harm business at Kuruk. We had survived murders of tribal members, threats and attempts on the life of people who were family and friends of mine, and then the inexplicable killing of a little girl so beautiful and talented she would have been looking forward to a long life of fame and accomplishment. Yet we thrived.

If our establishment were being evaluated for investment purposes, the steady stream of profit, regularly increasing sales and revenue, and growth potential, would have a great buyout story. Our chef—who insisted on a low profile—was world class, our service was impeccable, and vacationers coming to the Mescalero reservation for winter skiing, summer hunting and hiking, and year round gambling, generated an inexhaustible stream of customers.

For a man priding himself on being anything other than a businessman, the moneymaking story was a joke. To take the ridiculous to the level of the absurd, there were now four Kuruk restaurants under franchise in Beverly Hills, New York, Boston and Chicago. My friend—and the ex-FBI agent who worked on the murder cases at Mescalero that I just mentioned—along with his chef brother-in-law were inspired to take the Kuruk sensation and recreate it multiple times. They did so with immense success and, as a result, they were tossing royalty fees our way like lollipops.

Thus, while Bernard Platta was enjoying a drug-induced celebration during his ride back to Albuquerque, I was in my office at Kuruk talking on the phone with our accountant. We had purchased a new set of freezers and refrigerators, an expenditure requiring decisions regarding depreciation, amortization, and interest expense. These were all the subjects that I was as fascinated with as electroconvulsive shock therapy.

I had just hung up with the man my best friend, Preston, referred to as the "ceppa poppa alpha" (for Certified Public Accountant), Martin Crowell, when I received another call. It was close to noon. My discussion with the money counter had been much lengthier than I anticipated and by the time we hung up, my coffee cup had cooled to the point that the fresh milk I poured in it had curdled to tiny icicles. In fact, I had just tested the temperature with my lips and was in the process of putting the cup on the saucer when one of the servers peeked in on me and placed a bowl of my favorite soup, Mulligatawny, on the table.

I silently expressed appreciation to her, as I clicked to receive a new call. On the other end of the line was Nadine Street, a woman who had, during an illustrious career as senior investigator for the Washington, D. C. Metropolitan Police Department, run into a most intriguing yet personally impairing serial murder case. In fact, she came to Kuruk to detail the story to me so I could write it as a novel. Along the way, this fascinating and indomitable lady fell in love with Preston. To my surprise, they both wanted to stay in New Mexico.

By chance, our local theater needed a sound engineer and Preston took that position, plus a part-time gig that simultaneously came available at the university in Albuquerque—he was a perfect fit. Then Nadine decided to start up a boutique private investigation firm in the same city. When she called me on the morning that Platta had performed his first hideous assignment with Abbas, she had been operating for just over a year. She was also at the time of that call, engaged. She and Preston were living together. She had become a close friend not only of mine, but my wife as well.

"Zach, I was thinking you've never seen my office."

"You're right," I acknowledged, a bit perplexed how that could be the case after such a long period.

"So, what are you doing for lunch?" she asked in the breezy fashion she used when she was in a gay mood.

"Nothing. I'm finishing up a couple projects here at Kuruk. I'll shoot down there as soon as I'm finished."

"Good. My treat."

Within ten minutes, I was on the road. I had left behind my cherished soup to cool next to a full cup of cold coffee.

We were still in a tentative temperature cycle in Mescalero as we peeked into spring. The weather was capable of behavior that would land a man in an institution. One day the sun was smiling a full mouth of white teeth, the next day his lips descended over chattering that might crack a denture. None of this was troublesome to the people living in my region, unless they were to leave home without a coat and hat.

It was dark outside when I walked out of Kuruk. The surrounding mountain peaks appeared to have been chopped off by the sovereign clouds that were sweating a fine mist. There was no wind but the icy cold air exploited every exposed surface of the body. It reinforced the sense of gloom that hadn't let up for a moment since the killing of little Adina Bernard, a crime still with no known motive and not a single clue who might have been responsible.

Just as I hopped into my car, I noticed the sky illuminate for an instant. The light was coming from the north but lasted only portions of a second before it darkened, as if suffering from a power failure. Then it burst a second time, now lingering for moments as its energy assumed the role of master over a magic sword drawing white stick figures on the horizon.

As I was making my way down the hill, my cell went off.

"Zach. Don't come if the weather is too bad," Nadine volunteered.

"It'll be fine. But thanks for the concern."

"Drive carefully. It looks ugly here."

"I'm used to it; I'll see you soon."

Lightning strikes, like temptresses calling seductively from a distance planet, lured me down the mountain and then all the way to her office. By the time I arrived, massive groans, clashes and grating sounds were belligerently trailed by fractions of a second by bursts of light. I might have arrived at the doors of hell and in a few minutes, I was sure that I had.

Nadine had elected to place her office in one of the oldest areas of the city, ingeniously called Old Town. It was recorded as the first neighborhood settled in Albuquerque, back in the early 1700's. Organized in the traditional pattern that could be found to this day in Spain, there is a central plaza, which is surrounded by businesses and homes.

Nadine fell in love with the authentic adobe brick structures and wouldn't consider placing her business anywhere else in the city, although in truth she was in a small, newly constructed building that mimicked the original adobe design but had employed modern techniques and materials.

I parked in front of her building, only a couple blocks from Rio Grande Boulevard where the center of town is located.

I walked up to the second floor. The door opened to a small reception area with no staff in attendance. As I gazed to my right, I noticed a creamy-skinned man close to my age in a small room with a desk. He glanced at me for an instant before averting his attention to the assignment he was working on.

Staring at his now downturned head, my attention was quickly diverted as Nadine came out of the adjacent office to the left. I could tell something had spoiled her mood between when she invited me to visit her and the instant she looked at me. Whatever it was, she muzzled voicing it for long enough to greet me.

I noticed immediately that her long brunette hair that traditionally famously descended in several dangling layers had been straightened and now did a free fall below the shoulders, half resting on the right and half on her left breast.

She was wearing a grey felt hat with such an enormous brim that as she approached to hug me it softly poked my forehead—the vastness of the piece made her face appear to be seeking subterfuge. I knew she was dying to have a baby and I wondered if she purchased the contraption with birth in mind; it reminded me of a far more practical setting to cradle a newborn than to shelter an adult head.

After we disengaged, she resumed a grave stare. She grabbed a jacket she had hung on an oak coat rack near the front door. While putting it on and simultaneously opening the door, she called out to the man in the other office.

"Going out to lunch, Fadi. I have my cell."

She then swung the door wide open and waited to follow me out. Before we fully descended the stairwell, she burst out with what was bothering her.

"Zach, my Lord, didn't you hear the news on the way here?" she inquired frantically.

"No. I use CD's to listen to music. But what news?"

"Somebody bombed the preschool at a Jewish temple in Phoenix." She paused, clearly disturbed by what she was about to disclose. "At least twenty children are dead."

It was dim inside the staircase. I'm sure she couldn't have noticed that my already light skin had turned to an ashen shade of white. There was a long silence while we made our way into the street.

"They were babies," she cried out, her eyes moist. "You were in Israel. Would those people resort to something as vile as this?"

I noticed my emotions freeze. It was everything I abandoned like an unfaithful lover in Israel: Insatiable hate, the kind that feeds on itself, is never satisfied unless it's sucked every atom of goodness out of man's essence.

My head was bobbing. Sure, during my journey to that region of the world I had encountered people—only a tiny fraction—who would kill the innocent and who would rejoice doubly if the victims were children. But after my intervention was employed to arrest a potential tragedy in that country, those capable of evil had been subdued, had been brought to their knees and had been forced to make peace—so I believed.

Now these just murdered children would testify to a pathetic truth, that man was saddled with a violent nature no different than a stone plagued to live eternally with no volition over its shape. It was more likely that nothing lasting had been accomplished from my participation in the affairs of that region.

Why couldn't I respond to her question? It was instinct, a deeply buried awareness that the horror I had experienced during that period of my life had followed me home—but none of this pierced my consciousness at the moment.

"It's senseless killing," she muttered, shaking her head in disbelief.

I still said nothing. Nadine must have computed that the news struck me like a hot pin being shoved into one of my nerves and that I was screaming silently.

"I know this isn't a pleasant subject…especially for you," she said uncomfortably, as though she had thoughtlessly imposed her emotions on me. Then she attempted to erase what she saw as insensitivity on her part. "It's not directly related to our lives but it just upset me. Let's talk about something more pleasant," she proposed.

"I can't run away from reality. I would have found out regardless and then been just as upset." I stood silently for a few moments. "I know these people who did this," I mumbled as if in a fog.

"You know them?!" Her exclamation forced me to clarify my comment.

"No. I don't know specifically who did it but I know the mentality. Nadine, I lived with people who would do this sort of thing and then compliment themselves for the accomplishment, as if they had sponsored the cure of cancer."

"Sick!" she cried out.

"I think it's a bit different than that…no, it's not sickness."

"I don't understand how you can say that," she wearily challenged.

"It's worse. They believe."

"Believe in what?" she asked urgently.

"Does it matter if you believe in something that can't be verified, that has no rational basis for truth, but that you are convinced is absolute and incontestable? Does it matter when based on mere prejudice you grant yourself the justification to act with impunity, and worse, to undertake killing with what you're supremely sure is God's will?"

"So a sick person," she paused to carefully compose her thinking, "is acting because they have no choice, because they are diseased by something they have no control over? But then there is—"

"Right. Then there is warped, wicked belief that breeds evil," I affirmed. "Nadine, as a peace officer you've dealt with demonic minds capable of harming innocent people; rapists, sadists and brutal murderers. They're wayward, damaged, tragic and twisted souls; they're people with regrettable and suffered pasts, but they're not evil. I've looked evil in the face. Its blood is frozen, its heart pumps acid and its mind is a razor blade. It believes…unquestionably."

"It may be different but I believe too," Nadine retorted, wanting to defend the goodness of faith. "I believe in god. I believe in faith and in the commandments."

"Of course. So does Preeti. So does Josea. So does most of mankind," I countered.

"I don't think I'm evil, and I don't think you or any of them are either."

"Surely not. I'm only trying to define that point where belief morphs into evil."

"And where is that?"

"Where belief jettisons doubt, where there can be no other truth."

After a few minutes she smiled. "Well, I still believe—it helps me."

"Sure you do. My simple point is that you don't 'believe' like a fanatic, like a true believer. That's what has been worthy about religion for millions of people," I proposed. "I think that's why there are so many religions and variations of each system of belief and why throughout the history of mankind there have been so many approaches to faith. The secret is they all believe, but with doubt—most adherents can never be true believers, the type who kill to defend the indefensible."

I gazed at the people passing by. Each was on a mission. It might be to win a contract, sell a quota of cars, develop the next strain of life-saving antibiotics, defeat a spouse in a divorce court or threaten a neighbor for letting their dog bark at all hours. Their most powerful motive is to survive. I'd have bet that each of those souls crossing my destiny at that second believed.

They want to avoid needing miracles or having to resort to gambles to live in peace. Their beliefs are merit badges that they earn for behaving with decency and common regard for their fellow man. True believers? Hah! Few are endowed with the simple twist of fate permitting them unqualified hate.

"Nadine, the doubt is what allows for tolerance and respect. It's only when uncertainty is eviscerated, blasted out of the conscious mind like gas farted from the guts of the earth, that we encounter profound lack of conscience—that's how evil is born and it's an un-Godly force so potent we have no choice but to smite it."

Nadine started laughing, more a giggling sound than comical expression. "I never heard you talk like that. Very heady." She looked at me kindly. Then she hugged me. "Give me about a week to think it over."

"Take a month," I generously offered.

All the while we were standing just outside her building. Nadine touched my arm and gently led me down the block.

"Zach, I have a question for you. It's totally off the subject of what we're talking about."

"Good. Ask away."

"How do you think your friend will be as a father?"

"Why? Are you telling me you're pregnant?"

"No," she responded with a wily smile. "But I am getting ready. I want this taken care of by the time I hit four zero."

"Preston will make a fine dad," I assured her. "And I know you'll be a great mother. You love each other. You can't miss with that in the bank."

"Thanks. I knew I could count on your support."

"Every man is frightened about beginning a family," I volunteered free of charge and without invitation. "It's one of those forever moves that scares the daylights out of us.

"Preston said you were excited from the beginning."

"My situation was a little different. I didn't have time to be fearful until afterward," I explained. "Preeti was probably pregnant as soon as we were together. Then I was dealing with the aftermath of Israel, losing Jivin ("the little dude"—Preeti's son), adjusting to being married and living in Mescalero. Trepidation seeped into my psyche gradually following Souche's (my firstborn, a daughter) birth."

"What are you scared of, especially considering everything you've gone through?"

"It's just the responsibility, the uncertainly about the future...it's more a free-floating worry that might attach itself to whatever errant thought pops up at any moment. It's similar to a fickle free electron in space hitching up with one atom's energy after another, still never losing its force."

"So in the end you conquer the fear...by believing in something, right?"

"I guess you could say that. But I've never been able to categorize my belief system. When it comes down to it, I think what I believe in is the capacity of every person to do everything possible to increase the probability of living a healthy, worthy and honest life," I posited off the top of my head. "If we do that, we reduce the likelihood of bad, and that's the best we can achieve. Even with everything that has happened and is still happening in my life, that's all I have to hold on to."

"You are in a zone today," Nadine mentioned with a grin. "I'll take two months to deliberate on all this, thank you."

"While you're doing that, the simple answer to your question is that it's a big thing for me having children." I paused, the lingering thoughts of murder were shouting in my mind. "It's a forever deal, even for those people who just lost their child."

I observed her unwittingly pick up the pace, striding down the block like a speed walker heading for the finish line. I recall several times in my study when writing her Washington case experience into a fictional story watching her behave similarly. Spontaneously, she'd rise from where she was sitting and begin pacing back and forth, faster and faster. Typically the burst of energy would be stimulated by an emotion of fright or terror on the one hand, or, on the other, defiance or bravado. It was as if movement was a tonic used to empower her to battle feelings intent on bullying her into retreat. One of her problems was that Nadine Street was a force with no reverse gear.

"The finality for those families...I think that's what's upsetting me so much about what happened in Phoenix," Nadine cried out just loud enough for me, galloping three lengths behind, to hear.

I knew Nadine well enough to understand that, in this instance, the rapid movement and the stomping of her feet to the ground, was her method of attempting to shun sin, dusting it with exhaust like a Ferrari spitting on a Prius.

I pounded on my own accelerator enough to reach Nadine's side. As I was astride with her, an errant image popped into my mind. I didn't know Nadine had an employee; she had never mentioned anything about the man she called out to with the name, Fadi.

"The man in the other office works for you?" I asked.

"He's been with me almost from when I opened," she informed me, decelerating to a mere walk as her mind processed a thought. "I should have introduced you. He's a doll. He's not an investigator but he's my assistant and he's as loyal and devoted as my own blood relative."

"Strange," I said. "What did you say his name is?"

"Fadi Abbas. He's from Egypt."

"Really. My father's first name was Abbas," I reflected.

I dwelled on a strange familiarity I sensed with this man. I even made the mysterious Mr. Abbas the topic of my discussion with Nadine as we continued our journey to the restaurant.

Grateful she had continued backing off from the prior grueling pace to settle instead for a stroll, I noticed at that wonderful moment that the storm had decided to take a break. Without need for umbrellas I could see upward through the blackness of the sky. A lone crack shot an arrow of light that beamed down on us, brightening our figures like stars in a stage production. The street lit up circularly around us and we looked at each other, knowing we were both thinking similarly and that good would prevail even when surrounded by evil. Sure, we were resorting to hope—a most dangerous enterprise under even the best of circumstances—but it was comforting just the same.

"This man working for you, does he have family?" I innocently inquired.

"Only a mother in the Middle East. It seems his father was a successful surgeon in Egypt and left enough money for Fadi to go to college. He's trained as an engineer in his country."

"And he came here…with no relatives? Why?"

Nadine smiled proudly on a topic it was apparent she had discussed with him at length in the past.

"He loves America. He wants to be free."

I knew Nadine to be devout in her belief of her country and everything it stood for. She could find forgiveness for the most demented and sadistic human criminals but would banish without regret unpatriotic citizens enjoying the rights of a free society without appropriating deserved loyalty and fidelity.

"Fadi Abbas would fight for our country. How many of our own people can we count on to give their life to defend what we so often take for granted?" She emphasized her point with a sharp bow of the head. "We'll find who's responsible for the slaughter of these children."

"I know. It's just that your employee…it's funny but that happens for me occasionally. You know, when you see someone for the first time and would swear you've known them but can never place how, where or when?" Nadine didn't comment. "It's okay. Besides, I probably knew Mr. Abbas in a prior life." My statement momentarily permitted me to laugh off the pestering vision of the man.

Within minutes Fadi Abbas had strayed from my mind. But he would linger on the perimeter of my consciousness, sneaking in and out of my thoughts during the coming weeks. Had I known then what I do now…but it was useless, whatever we would at a later time understand about this man would come at a great price.

"Ever eaten at *Antiquity*?" she asked, breaking into my thoughts.

"No. Anyplace is good by me."

"If you want Spanish…but this is the best French food and since I'm paying, it won't bother you that it's pricy."

"I'll be on my best behavior."

"You can be on any behavior you want but I'm ordering so if you're thinking about saving me money, forget it."

Nadine and I had a lot in common. We had side-stepped death like a child playing dodge ball, even kicked the frightful beast back in the face of the enemy on occasion. We had overcome crisis, suffering the ill effects of a post-traumatic reaction like a soldier returning from battle. In the end, we both managed to salvage our souls. I needed her in my life and she needed me around her as well. There were only a few people close to me that I could laugh tears with. She was a bright woman, once philosophizing to me that the only way to not lose faith in your fellow man is to never ask the question, "why."

During lunch, Nadine and I talked about the plans for her upcoming marriage to Preston, the assignments she was taking at work, her impression of a competitor named Farley who had assisted me in the past with investigation work, and…eating.

There's a lot to be said for food being the route to a man's heart. There was a piece of Nadine that was no doubt driven to gastronomic excitation owing to scarcity during childhood, but beyond that, the male aspect of her personality kicked in—a tasty meal was a panacea to her.

She would now routinely dine at Kuruk and I'd witness the thrill that she'd experience tasting the preparations of our chef's creative genius. Yet at the same time, she was a disciplined lady, vigorously and religiously exercising, and when not indulging in an exotic meal careful to prepare healthful and organic dishes at home.

She had experienced loss early in life. Her mother was killed in a car crash that left her father vegetative. The responsibilities imposed on her during her formative years set the stage for a no-nonsense approach to life, and there was no doubt that her childhood rigors accounted for the success she had as a detective. At an age younger than any that had preceded her, she rose to the lead position in her department.

She had been set back by the parental tragedy, to the point that fear of abandonment had repeatedly short-circuited intimacy for her. In spite of her beauty and generously proportioned figure, loneliness stalked her like a predator. But as often happens, when one is in the most fragile emotional state, they are most likely to experience the weakening of inhibitions and defenses. It's then they can be conquered by love. Preston will testify to this as a truism. He seized that crucial moment to impale her heart with the passion she was desperately seeking.

As we were finishing our lunch, our discussion focused on Preston, and somehow, as well, again on the subject of her assistant, Mr. Abbas.

"Preston is proud of you. He talks about you all the time. If he wasn't constantly telling me how much he loves me, I might be jealous," she lightly expressed.

"It's not often you have a friend for life," I said appreciatively.

"The other evening when he picked me up he was talking with Fadi, telling him all about what you did in Israel."

"That's how he keeps getting me into trouble," I jested. "He talks me up and the next thing I know I'm in the midst of high adventure…that's how you came into my life!" I reminded her, referring to Preston's cousin in Washington who was a friend of Nadine's making the connection.

"Well, Fadi was impressed, I'll tell you that. He said you did a great thing for his part of the world."

"The truth is I did nothing. It was all done through me or for me. To this day, I don't understand it all."

"I doubt most people would agree with your humility. Anyway, Fadi is an educated man and prides himself on being a pacifist. The killing and violence in his part of the world sickens him."

Nadine had seen the horrors produced by demented and tormented minds for years during her work as a murder investigator. She was now relieved to at last have retired from having to console families of murdered sons, daughters, fathers and mothers, having to forge bonds with wicked murderers to tame them into submission, and needing to capitulate to the demands of politicians and administrators who ignored her safety while using her to further their selfish ambitions for power and wealth.

But it wasn't only the ugliness of man's acts or the consequence of harm done which finally sidelined her, and nearly snapped her like a tree trunk in a hurricane. Instead, it was breach of trust. It was deception, corruption and heartbreak. Sure, the force of steel couldn't crush her. But she was no different than the rest of mankind, possessing a point of vulnerability, an intersection where adequate pressure will cause the edifice to cave in.

When a person arrives at this juncture, if they are lucky they might suffer temporary mental defeat, a loss of faith, a sense of betrayal, and the agonizing pain of psychological identity deterioration. If, on the other hand, they are less fortunate, death might greet them before they are able to muster the strength to begin the journey back to health. Nadine was one of the fortunate ones, but still her being was dramatically altered as a result of the horror she went through.

She now described her work as benign and peaceful. She once again found that she enjoyed coming into the office. As she free-associated about her new career and her relationship with Abbas, I came to understand the bond that had developed between them. Her employee was a smart man—cunning, if necessary—possessed gem quality character, was willing to work hard, had a good sense of humor, and was also charming, humble and gracious—and a lot more than that.

After eating, I walked back to the office with Nadine. Then I headed to Mescalero. The weather had resumed a pissed mood, beating the daylights out of everyone and everything in its kingdom. At the same time, Phoenix was deluged with tragedy. I wanted no part of any of it.

I cranked up the volume on my speakers and let the music delude me into invincibility. I heard my own lyrics over the sound of whatever piece was playing. *Don't even try to stop me. I can hear the sounds of my heart racing ahead, of the road inviting me to where I once have been,* I shouted. *I'm fueling up my own asteroid, and I'm about to scoot blazing hot through the sky; I'm lickety split, chop-chop, a supersonic dude, indestructible.*

Hell, I had been imprisoned, tortured for crimes I could have never committed, accused of being an enemy agent by both sides of a bloody battle, yet I endured. To accomplish this improbable feat, I traveled to distant galaxies where I watched newly birthed stars tossing cosmic debris like a dog shaking water after a bath. I witnessed the aging parents and relatives of these tots inhaled like laughing gas into the mouth of black holes. I was fondled by legions of ladies who knew no purpose in their universe but to love, and on stars of distant galaxies I met communities of people with no gods, and no concept of killing or hate.

While I'm proposing that these space adventures contributed measurably to my survival, in the safety of my new life, I rarely had the need to revisit these spectacular places. Yet journeying home on this day, I was inexplicably inspired to travel. I yelled out to the passing cars, *I'm having the time of my life. It's so good, so good. Out of my way, out of my way. You can't stop me, not even if you try, not even if you try."*

I thought I was my own little planet, for I aimed to blast into the cosmos on my way to far off stars. But in my haste, I had mindlessly breezed through any admonitions warning me that I might have gone out of control or that I was on an about-to-collide-with-other-objects-of-greater-size-and-force path. Any foreboding lyrics I might have written would have been for anyone other than me. Murdered youths in Phoenix, dear Adina dead and faint recognition of Fadi Abbas, were subjects that I buried where I wished to never dig again.

It was then that I noticed there was a break in the sky, a close relative to the one that earlier that afternoon had put Nadine and me on a lit stage. It was time for take off. I sped toward it, launching myself upward and through it, to the outer limits of infinite space.

I would soon return. Shortly after that, I would learn that the gap in the heavens permitting that sample of rays was surrounded by blackness. It was a dark endlessness intent on swallowing me within its viscid pus. I was to die. Fadi Abbas and Bernard Platta willed it, but my ignorance of what was coming granted me the spirit to exalt, and I did.

I'm in bliss out here. There's no traffic or congestion. I have lots of empty space. Come visit me on Mars. I'm more powerful than a million nuclear bombs about to explode. It's a beautiful world. I had defied gravity. *Hey, mom, I can outrun bees.* It was good to be alive and I couldn't wait to get home and see Preeti and my children.

While I was day tripping, Nadine headed back to her office. Her only lyrics were speaking to the *Motherless Child* now snugly tucked into her soul—getting pregnant was a huge subject for her, perhaps too consuming and blinding. Somehow the master detective's sense of circumspection had been befuddled—she'd laid out a red carpet for the cat to enter the henhouse.

Fadi Abbas, a man who would kill her as soon as spit on her, was sitting in the office next to hers while Nadine Street, ex-crack detective, was dangerously clueless that her assistant believed...doubtlessly. I was equally ignorant that the generals of augury were forecasting heavy downfalls of evil for yours truly.

5

HORRORS FROM ABROAD

I AROSE VERY EARLY the day after I met with Nadine. As had been the case every morning since losing Adina, I had to battle to overcome the long shadow of sorrow that dragged after me like the train on a wedding dress. It was still dark when I quietly rolled out of bed. I lumbered into our kitchen to boil a pot of water. Preeti and the children were lights out and would be for at least a couple of hours. As I became cognizant of the first breath I drew, I sensed a tightening in my chest. The air was rough and resisted traveling freely to my lungs. I tensed and at the same instant, I noticed my larynx close as if a surgical clamp had been affixed around it.

Needing fresh air I bolted for the front door. It was near freezing out. It wasn't until I was able to resume the flow of oxygen, that it dawned on me that the front door was not locked. I knew I had shut it and then turned the dead bolt before I retired. I did it every evening though it was a routine hardly necessary given the safety of where we lived. Still, owing to spending the early years of my life in Los Angeles, I did it out of habit.

I assumed Preeti must have awakened out of her sleep. But why would she subject herself to the cold in the middle of the night unless she was distressed? Furthermore, if that were the case she surely would have awakened me to talk. Besides, we were in some respects a single being—I always sensed when she left our bed and would wake instinctively on those occasions.

Standing in the front yard contemplating the odd circumstance, I could hardly see in the dimness. But after a few moments my eyes began to focus and whatever night vision the human eye is capable of came to my service. That's when I saw what looked like two posts with signs about the size of standard copy paper stuck in the ground next to one another at least fifty feet from the porch where I was standing.

I hadn't put on slippers or shoes and my feet were already icy, but the peculiarity of these stakes in my yard demanded I inspect immediately. I walked along the brick path leading toward the front gate. Only half way there I froze, sadly not from the outer cold but from an arctic blast flash-freezing me from deep within—so fast was the halt to my breathing that had I died, ten thousand years later I might be defrosted with every molecule of my biological self perfectly preserved. The dissection would then determine that I had passed from horror, a surge of hormones from the adrenal glands instantaneously wrapping my organ system in a death grip.

While my body stood immobilized staring at the ghastly sight, my brain activated. The first object was a thin wooden pole with a rectangular drawing. There were two thick horizontal bars bordering the upper and lower area in sky blue on a white background. Centered, in the same shade of blue, was the Star of David, a perfect replica of the Israeli flag.

What distinguished this atrocity? What could produce a profusion of sweat soaking my body in the bitter cold of morning? There was a black swastika drawn slapdash over the star.

Had this been the only piece I might have tried to dismiss it as somebody's sick idea of pop art. Not many people in Mescalero knew of my Jewish heritage. I never thought of hiding it. My background was frankly insignificant to the people who were now my friends and family. Sure, those closest to me knew but none cared.

It was what was mounted on the second identical post that confirmed this was an act intended to teach me a lesson. A person may do goodness for millions of people but there will always be one who wants to kill you for it. If you ever take your eye off the enemy, you just may die. The problem is that sometimes we don't know who the adversary is until they proclaim it.

The drawing juxtaposed to the Israeli flag had a half square in red cut diagonally into the left side of the rectangular shape. The remaining space was filled with three horizontal bars of equal size, top to bottom, black, white and Islamic green—the Palestinian flag, constructed in pristine order.

I can't attest to having shouted, but Preeti will. She later described one of those classic blood-spewing types. Must have been. She was standing next to me at a few minutes past four in the morning as I began a slow thaw, staring at the two images that together rose to iconic significance, representing to me more than the epitome of everything gone wrong with civilized man. What I saw was a missive announcing my past had just blown in like a foul draft, the spearhead of a deadly storm aiming its mighty force with me as the target.

Most people might be inclined to judge me a bit of a hysteric, overreacting to what might have been an adolescent late-night prank. I knew that was not the case. When I looked at my wife, the grief in her eyes confirmed she understood as well that we were in for trouble.

I ventured the remaining distance from where I stood to the signs. I then tore them out of the ground. Holding both in my left hand, I lifted my arm in a rare display of militancy, a male calling to service the full armament of weaponry required to do battle with a sinful foe. The feeling of might that shot through my veins could have downed the Ultimate Fighting Champion or knocked an undefeated football team out of contention—it was short lived.

I wouldn't consider myself to be a coward. I had faced enough challenges to know that I had guts. But volunteering for danger and electing to fight an enemy, was as appealing to me as wearing sanitary napkins. I raced into the house. I leaned the two sticks against the wall before sitting on the couch. My neck went flaccid, my head dropping between my knees where my hands served to keep it from free falling to the ground.

"It's Amir," I said in a resigned manner. "It has to be."

"You told me that he and Bahlya adored you," Preeti responded.

"Call Josea," I insisted.

"You sure, honey? You'll wake her."

"Please! She'll want to know."

Thirty minutes later, I sat mute on the couch, Preeti with her arm draped over my shoulder, tightly pulling me toward her. I heard a car speed into the driveway. A second later, Josea ran into the room.

"Let me see them," Josea said excitedly, referring to the signs.

I pointed to the corner where they rested against the wainscoting. She went over to inspect.

"Before we jump to any conclusions let's think this through." Her words provided a brief reprieve from an obvious conclusion neither of us wanted to believe. "Zach, Amir never knew your role. The last time he heard of you probably was when the Palestinians turned you over to the Israelis." Then, cautiously she added to an argument she wished could be verified. "Amir is probably dead. Bahlya is dead for sure."

Josea is a girl that I knew in high school. She was considered a mental giant, of such esteem that at a young age she was sharing conversations with some of the greatest philosophers and scientists of our generation. At just a measure over five-foot and with a figure even after birthing her first child not much more than a twig, her brain had to be transported in a rail container.

I lost contact with her after my grad night. Then by chance, after I ran into some problems in Israel, she was working for their government. She was able to intervene on my behalf: I owe my freedom, if not my life, to her.

After taking a sabbatical for her own self-discovery, she expanded her interests more toward the arts. Then she met our chef and fell in love. That's how it happened that she settled in Mescalero.

"I'm sorry, Zach. I didn't want to tell you," she confessed, knowing I'd be upset that a young lady I had cared for deeply was killed.

I looked at Preeti, a silent inquiry if she also knew about Bahlya's death.

"Josea told me. I suggested not letting you know," my wife acknowledged sheepishly. She knew her motive in keeping Bahlya's death a secret from me was to spare me unnecessary pain but she still carried a shred of guilt.

Preeti was still in her pajamas. She was nervously playing with her long dark hair. Finally, she braided it into a single strand that rested over her left shoulder. She was fidgeting with it, taking the end and suckling it. I'd seen her do that before, but only when she was tense.

"What happened to Bahlya?" I asked Josea.

"The Israelis knew she was harmless but she and Amir were inseparable. They traced them to a terrorist camp in Pakistan about a year ago. She was killed during a raid."

"You've been in touch with the Israelis?" I asked.

"Every so often, yes," she confessed. "Zach, I didn't want to burden you with it. You've had enough to deal with."

"They found her body?" I pried.

"It was awful. They never identified her remains but they did find the jewelry she was wearing…there's no question she's dead."

"Amir too?" I asked.

"They believe he was killed during the same operation but none of his personal possessions were discovered to confirm the kill."

"Then, he could be alive." My voice was emphatic so that rather than posing a question, I was attesting to a fact.

"It's unlikely, Zach," Josea responded, leaving more room for uncertainty than she wished there to be.

"Who else could be orchestrating this?" My voice elevated. I was in disbelief that there was an explanation other than Amir. I volleyed the question to Josea as a demand. "Nobody knows of my involvement over there other than the Israeli and American presidents, and the other five officials we met with in that room, plus you and I. Isn't that correct?"

"Okay, that's right. But Amir had no way of knowing," she argued.

"I've never found you to be anything other than brutally objective in matters of this sort. Josea, don't let me down. I'm in trouble and you know it."

"I won't, Zach. You know that," she shouted with uncommon irascibility. "Is there something you're not telling me? Because it doesn't compute to me that if Amir...and I don't believe it...but if he's alive, that he would have figured out your role. He had to believe that he was fleeing from The Palestinian Authority, not the Israelis. He couldn't have even known that the Israelis were on to him working with Jawiris." (Jawiris was the man who had crafted a plan of destruction against Israel and parts of America, and who had enlisted Amir as his chief operating officer.)

"Josea, the day he was to take me to the airport, when I was going to leave Israel, before we left the house, he did something odd. He called me into his bedroom and started questioning me if I had ever been in his room before, which I hadn't until my stealth operation the prior evening. He then mentioned that he had noticed something was out of order. Amir was obsessive. Every article in his space was meticulously organized," I informed her. "He suspected something but didn't want to openly confront it because he already had been instructed to turn me over to Hamas, who as you know at that time was convinced of my duplicity in working for the Israelis."

"Then you're saying he discovered that you found the safe in his room?"

"All he had to do was question it as a possibility. Then after Jawiris' plot fell apart, and after the Israelis had hauled in each of the participants, it would all come together. What I mean is that by the time he was on the run, he would have had to conclude that I had betrayed him." My mind raced on to new territory as I surmised what I believed happened.

"Josea, he must have assumed that his lover was correct in designating me as an Israeli spy. The next logical conclusion for him would have been that I had put myself into his life from the beginning with the intent to harm him and his family. How could he even conceive the improbable circumstance that brought us together? Nobody would have believed it. Nobody could imagine the unlikely events leading to me even ending up in Israel either. None of it was supposed to happen, but it did. Amir had to come to the answer that made sense—I'd have done the same."

Josea stood with her mouth agape, not sure she wanted to agree that my position had merit and at the same time certain it couldn't be dismissed as idle speculation.

"Imagine how his adoration for me turned to hate for my perceived villainous acts. Then his sister is killed! He wants me to pay," I stated, with meek resolution.

Preeti sat listening, aware of every detail I disclosed, but in disbelief there could be an aftermath to my Israeli travels as horrific as I was proposing.

"Then where is Amir?" Preeti wondered. "Wouldn't he have showed up to do the dirty work himself?"

"Amir has a huge network of people in the Middle East. Josea just said the Israelis tracked him to a terrorist network in Pakistan. He doesn't have to be here to orchestrate violence," I answered my wife.

"You're right about that. Really, he couldn't be here," Josea stated emphatically. "He's not stupid enough to try. Between the Israeli and U. S. security, they'd pick him up the second he tried to get on a plane."

Josea was correct. My silence spoke agreement. With the pause in the conversation, I noticed camping out on the fertile grounds of my mind a progression of new thoughts. From thousands of miles away, Amir must have been stalking my life, learning about my wife and children, friends and family, pursuits and activities. He must have been biding his time, waiting for the right moment to begin his revenge.

He had to have employed somebody to drift in and out of Mescalero to do the surveillance that Amir needed to chart my activities? I wondered if that were the case, and if I identified that person, then would it preclude any further acts of hate Amir had to be planning for me? Josea, who must have been formulating similar questions at the same time, interrupted my thoughts.

"Adina? It couldn't be that she..." Her words trailed off. The idea that somehow Amir had been behind her murder was too forbidden to be permitted expression.

"It could," I affirmed hesitantly. "He had to know how precious she was to me...to all of us. You know the rest."

"She's Jewish." Josea filled in the answer. Then she offered a perplexed look. "But so am I."

"One hundred percent Jewish, both of you. We have to get help with this...or he'll try to have you killed too."

"The hate just never stops does it?" Josea reflected solemnly.

"For Amir, it's just shifting into second gear." I stopped to reflect on another troubling thought. "The door to our house was open when I went out this morning, Preeti. I presume you never unlocked it last night?"

She shook her head side to side, a definitive negative. The person who planted those twin pillars in my front yard also entered my home. He was intentionally leaving no doubt that the prizes left were not random signals which might as well have been planted on a neighbor's property.

I knew without question that there was no running from this. I could have Preeti take the children to my mom's home but would they be safer there? Amir knew about my mother. I'd talked about her many times while living with the Hamdallah family. He'd figure out where they went before they even reached Los Angeles.

I stood up for the first time. My destination as I began walking was to inspect my children's rooms. I opened the doors to be sure they were safely sleeping. Then I went to the back door and made sure it was double locked. On my return to the living room where Preeti and Josea were, I stopped a second time to look in on the children.

Amir had no children. He had to hate mine. They were a quarter Arab, a quarter Jewish, and half Apache—he couldn't eviscerate the Jewish quarter only but he would have no hesitation killing the whole to punish the deserving portion.

As I arrived back to where Josea and Preeti sat, I had to chuckle as I looked at Josea. She had rushed out of her house without even getting dressed. She was wearing a pair of bright red PJ's. On her feet were slippers, but they didn't match. In the darkness of her closet while hastily preparing to leave, she must have grabbed one from two different pairs. The left had a blue Cookie Monster on it and the right was a fluffy padded plain green. On her head, she had thrown a red cap with a long crown dropping like a ponytail to the left side of her neck.

"What is it you find so funny?" Preeti asked innocently.

"Take a look at your friend," I instructed with a tone of disbelief. "I'm relying on her to help?"

The tenseness of the moment had thoroughly blinded all of us to how we appeared. Josea must have realized that she looked ridiculous. She began parading around the room like a stage model. Then she pointed at me. "What about you?"

As her words came out, Preeti began laughing too. My hair hadn't been combed but since I was having it cut short it required little grooming. I didn't wear makeup and I had shaved the night before I had gone to bed. I had on my bathrobe. What could be so humorous?

"Okay, I give up."

"Go look in the mirror, dear," Preeti suggested.

I walked across the room to the dining area where we had a breakfront with a glass backboard. When I posed myself in front of it, I saw what they were making fun of—to me it was more an omen than comical event. A bird, rising early with a mission, had discharged with laser-guided precision a large wet turd on my left shoulder. I wanted to cry.

I slipped off the soiled robe, rolling it into a ball and throwing it on the ground. "What else can go wrong?" I said with disgust. "I know what I have to do. I'll get in touch with Kershaw later today. He'll tell me who to call at the FBI."

"Right. And I'm going to Israel as soon as I can get a flight," Josea said as casual as announcing she was buttering toast.

"For what?"

"Zach, you don't understand the Israelis. They'll never give up avenging an evil act…and they'll also never forsake a friend. They owe you and they will help."

"There's no hope unless we find Amir," I mumbled.

"The only thing we have going for us is time. If it's him, he's not ready to kill you. This is all about suffering and he wants that the most."

"I have children, Josea," I bellowed. "Suffering is even thinking he might try to harm them."

Josea was silenced by my retort. Now that she was a mother, she understood that nothing could cripple a person for life, turn them into an abandoned shell of a being, faster than harm coming to their offspring.

"Then let's work fast." I could see Josea's mind churning. "I think Nasir should go with me," she announced.

My initial reaction to my mother's new husband journeying back to the region where he was born was objection. What could he accomplish, especially since it had been two years since he had served as an acclaimed and respected journalist on the Middle Eastern region? Then I understood. Josea, being Jewish, could never travel freely through Egypt, Iran, Iraq, Syria or Pakistan, which were all the places where Amir might have left a trail leading to his current place of operation. Nasir would be welcomed wherever he journeyed and had contacts to call on literally in every country in that part of the world.

I reached for my cell phone sitting on the table in front of me. "Mother, is Nasir there?" I tentatively asked.

"Israel?" Her voice was helpless to conceal consternation. "I knew some day it would come back." I had to have awakened her but her wick had been lit. "Don't worry, son. We beat those assholes once and we'll do it again" she spewed with bravado that she could have inherited only from her pugnacious Zionist parents. Her tone then changed, as if victory was a fait accompli. "Hold on. I'll get Nasir."

6

THE FOX GUARDING THE HENHOUSE

DURING THE NEXT TWO hours, before Mr. Sun began peeking his luminous smile through the ominous darkness I had awakened to, I was in and out of my children's rooms. My little one, Abraham, was only five months old.

If Adina's murder was orchestrated from afar by Amir, and if he also used a ghost killer to do his dirty work in Phoenix, then he had to be planning an assault on one or both of my children before coming after me directly.

In between glancing into their rooms to satisfy myself they were secure, I sat in my office contemplating. I had no physical picture of Amir to refresh my recollection of his appearance but the images of the man who had been my close friend were vivid.

Amir was not a person easily forgotten. My mind went back to the first time I met him, as my seatmate on the plane to Israel. He couldn't stop yakking about his artistic pursuits yet he was so charming, actually seductive, that those hours we spent together passed in what seemed like moments.

He wasn't a large man. Frankly, he was several inches shorter than me and at no more than five foot nine he would have had to take a large meal before weighing in as a lightweight in if he aspired to a career as a boxer. I always perceived his figure as rather fragile, lacking the muscular bulk most women droll over.

Amir Hamdallah may have been short on physical force but his presence was powerful, particularly when espousing his dedication to the cause of the Palestinian people rising above the Israeli "oppressor" by exterminating the "rabid Zionist dogs" from his land. Amir was unwilling to settle for any solution to the conflict between his people and the Israelis other than the complete destruction of Israel, the elimination of every Jew from the region, and if possible from the planet. Still, at that time, he was arguing that he had no prejudice against the Jews per se.

That said, what always baffled—and intrigued—me were the inconsistencies he presented. Those pertaining to race were only one example. Mr. Hamdallah, his father, was a fabulously wealthy man. He lavished opportunity on his children and provided them freedom to reward themselves with endless gifts and adornments. Names like Armani, Versace, Gucci, Boss and Fendi were tossed around their home like beer cans at a Super Bowl party. Amir was sent to America for his Ivy League education, advancing the mental powers he would employ later in the service of terror.

Staring at him in the mirror of my mind, most remarkable to me was his perpetually kind smile. He was always gentle, seemingly genuine, and most exceptionally gracious. In spite of what I now know that he was and remains capable of, there is still a part of me vulnerable to his allurement and enticement.

I see his innocent face gazing at me. The elongated jaw accentuated the ruddy, manly, very short-cropped beard he wore. His crown was trimmed ever so slightly longer than the facial covering. The overall effect was a dark mystery easily approached but impossible to decipher.

While the ladies found him appealing, Amir had eyes for only one of the opposite gender, his sister. No. It was not carnal love. Rather, he idolized her. Bahlya was without doubt a remarkably beautiful woman, the true Arabian Queen. Men gaped at her ungovernably but for Amir the lure was that he was dependent on her for approbation, like a grade school child seeking the teacher's attention.

My reminiscing about Amir was cut short when for the tenth time I stood to recheck my family. Then I returned to my desk. I began formulating once again the list of people I could count on for my team—it was the same group. Preeti, my mom and Nasir, Preston, Josea and her husband, Preeti's dad, Len Cloud…I had quickly passed the fingers on my right hand and knew I was a rich man. I hadn't even counted Nadine, or my friend and business partner, Gabe Kershaw.

I highlighted emotional support and undying love after several names. But my resources ran deeper. Kershaw had retired after fifteen years with the FBI. Most importantly, he was still intimately connected with people in The Bureau, up to the highest level. Being a likeable man who was also respected as a dogged agent when it came to investigating misdeeds, he had earned his prestige. He also mimicked my policy, making it known to his professional friends that when they dined at one of his Kuruk restaurants they paid half price—he had lots of chips of his own he could cash to assist me.

Then there was Nadine. While writing the book about her serial murder case, I had several times contacted associates of hers at the D. C. Metropolitan Police Department. If the streets, buildings and houses were a jungle, Nadine was the gorilla commander. She was reputed to be able to woo killers out of hiding, psychologically intimidating and frustrating them into submission. If anyone could provide security for my family and me it would be Nadine.

Josea had enough brainpower to whip the best computer chess program while yawning herself to sleep. Her husband, while "only" a chef, had in a prior life been a very successful man, amassing a fortune calculated easily into the hundreds of millions range—his dream was cooking up exotic dishes and he does it out of love. Regardless, I had some money of my own. Yet, if more funds were needed for protection, I knew where to go for a loan.

My mother—along with Nasir—while I was helplessly imprisoned in Israel handled an unimaginably complicated research project to provide proof that the plot Amir was knee deep in was not a ruse. Kate Miller succeeded by summoning an animalistic drive to save her innocent son. Nasir's contributions were investigative diligence and an army of loyal reporters willing to assist him.

All that was on my side of the ledger! Only one enemy was on the other! How could I lose? I knew damn well I could.

Amir had his own army, and money to recruit more troops if needed.

Preeti cooked breakfast. I sat with her and the children, trying to find an appetite hiding in a sea of fear. The kitchen faced east and lit up brilliantly when the first rays of morning interloped on my agitation. I could tell Preeti was tense but she wouldn't address it. Her style was similar to my mom's: worry if you lose.

The phone rang and we looked at each other. It was going to be like this for some time, until this ended one way or another. I answered. It was Preston.

"Josea called," he shot out as if reprimanding me for misbehaving.

"What's the problem? I have you on my list…somewhere here," I retorted like a brat.

"Very funny," Preston countered, in no mood for comedy.

Preston was like a brother to me. If I was in trouble, he wanted to be the first to know; I'd insulted him by not waking him at four fifteen in the morning.

"Zach, you know damn well I'll do anything," he unnecessarily assured me. "Nadine wants to talk with you also. She's already organizing security."

I stood up and walked into the living room. Why? I really had no idea until after I had sat down sobbing on the sofa.

"My Lord man, I'm on my way."

I knew there was no stopping him. Even had I explained that my tears were more owing to the outpouring of affection than even fright, he still would have come to be with me. A minute later, the phone rang again. I answered.

"Hi, it's me," Nadine informed me as if she was three moves ahead of the game and had no time for chit chat. "I've got Abbas on the way there now. He'll be staking out your place round the clock." Then she proceeded to calculate the rest of her plan. "Well, he along with other people I'll be bringing in to help. There's a man in town here I met, Farley… right, right, of course you know him. Anyway, I talked to him last night about another matter but I'm sure he can assist. "

"I was about to call Gabe Kershaw. Don't you think we should get the FBI involved first?"

"Zach, you need protection this minute," she adamantly expressed. "I don't want you, Preeti or the children stepping outside the house right now."

"We can't live like that," I protested.

"Just for the moment, until we put together a more permanent plan. Zach, I've done this many times, so let me handle it."

"Okay. I'll instruct Preeti what the rules are."

"Good. Now I imagine Abbas will be arriving any minute. You're not going to know someone is watching the house but don't worry. I'll have you covered at all times."

"What if Amir's people know your guards are there and kill them?" I asked, the worst scenarios budding in line to keep my mind fresh with angst.

"Just stay in," she commanded.

I can't say that I felt relieved. But at least I was comfortable that nobody was going to enter my home and slaughter us. Still, my father-in-law had brought over a Westchester rifle the prior year when the murders of three tribal girls occurred. I went into the closet where I had stored it and took it out. I even loaded shells into it and placed the weapon on the shelf above my desk.

I had only shot it once. Len had taken me on one of those male bonding trips into the woods outside of Mescalero to teach me how to fire it. I recall pulling the trigger the first time, the kick bruising my shoulder and landing me on my derriere. It was so powerful I'm sure it could fell an elephant with a single shot.

While I was lying on my butt, my father-in-law laughed until he ached. Then he asked me if I ever used a shotgun before. When I responded I hadn't, he chortled louder. That was my first and only glorious lesson. Fortunately, I never had occasion to use it, but it was clean, loaded, and…

"What does Kershaw know about this Israel business?" she questioned.

"Nothing…less than you."

"Great, because I don't know much."

"Josea's the only one with all the details," I informed her. "I'm not sure what to do. Both the Israeli and U. S. governments would deny publicly that they even know of me. But I'm sure they'll be interested, especially after Phoenix."

"I'll leave Israel to you and Josea."

"You can leave that to her. My wish is to never hear about that part of the world again."

"Too late for that," she said sympathetically. "I'll tell you, with all this going on, in a wink my business is booming."

"What do you mean?"

"I probably shouldn't tell you this but I'm sure you'll keep it to yourself. A man named James Cortez, Cortez Bail Bonds in Las Cruces, called yesterday. He's the one who posted the bail for Bernard Platta. Zach, it is a million dollars. He's scared that Platta is planning to split. This is not Walmart Corporation. A million bucks breaks this guy. Anyway, he's got three other bail people willing to do what the insurance industry labels reinsurance; basically share the risk.

"The only glitch for Cortez is that they won't come in unless Platta has surveillance to be sure he stays put. Yours truly has the job. That's why I called Farley. I'm going to have Abbas supervise both operations and bring in a few other people."

"It's good for you. I'm glad you're doing well."

Abbas had outfitted himself with night vision goggles. He was loping unsuspected around our wondrous country while the whole universe of his opponents was in a blackout—most important, Nadine was clueless. Making matters worse, we were to find out that he owned the Bank of Good Luck.

The phone was ringing off the hook.

"I'm leaving in an hour," Josea briskly informed me. "Hazut (her ex-boss, Major General Uri Hazut, director of an independent agency handling military intelligence and reporting only to the Israeli Defense Minister) sent a car for me and they're flying me to Los Angeles. I'll be hooking up with Nasir there. Then we're on El Al together this evening." I said nothing. "Zach, I love you. Take care of my man."

The phone shut off. I felt as if I was a child, dependent on a host of moms and dads to keep me breathing. What could I do for myself? It was maddening. I was mad!

Piss off the wrong person and look what happens.

7

ALL IN THE NAME OF GOD

THE FOLLOWING MORNING BERNARD Platta and Fadi Abbas met at the Rio Grande Botanic Garden in the northwest area of Albuquerque. Abbas was at the time being employed to coordinate both the surveillance and protection of my home and the monitoring of Platta. He had notified his boss, Nadine Street that their new associate, a woman named Bernadette Raymond, was on duty in Mescalero watching my family. He promised he would be on Platta like "stink on shit," the exact words selected—perfectly phrased I might add.

Abbas was a fan of the unique park where they were conferring. It housed one of the most outstanding collections of butterflies in the world. In fact, he insisted before getting down to business that they take a stroll through the pavilion. While stopping to quietly observe the varieties of specimens, Abbas poked his buddy with his elbow.

"Look over there, Bernie" he instructed, pointing to an unusual type. "I've never seen one before; it's the Common Buckeye."

Platta had no interest but did observe the remarkable creature. On a limey green-shaded background was a bright orange pattern. Toward the outer edge of both wings were two deep blue circles surrounded by a cream color, the overall effect being a pair of eerie eyes on each wing. Below the lowest eye on each side was a smaller round white spot, filling what could be seen as a face with a nostril. The made-for-Halloween masks seemed to be staring outward. A partner joined the lone butterfly, the two pausing to flutter in front of the men.

Abbas was delighted with the entertainment. In an instant, a full flock of another variety swarmed in to take the place of the Buckeyes.

"These are Red Admirals. I see them all the time," he mentioned to his indifferent guest. "What do you think of when you see them?"

"Nothing," Platta sharply responded. "Can we get on with our business?"

"All work and no play?"

"This may be good sport for you but I've run out of time to play."

"Not to worry. I'm going to let you go. That's why I brought you here," Abbas gloated.

"What the hell are you talking about?" Platta countered with hostile impatience.

"You're going to flicker off like a rare butterfly—never to be seen again," Abbas chuckled shrewdly.

"And my wife and son? What happens to them?"

"I have many friends here and around the world," Abbas bragged. "You'll all fluff your little wings and flee," he jubilantly proclaimed. "Now, try a little imagination. The Red Admirals want to introduce themselves."

These butterflies he was pointing out to Platta were black aviators. They had parked in mid-air, seeming to be awaiting Platta's answer. A thin orange band looped circularly around the center of this variety, the perimeter line leaving the tips of each wing to distinguish themselves with several small white sphere shapes. They had the appearance of planets exploring the vastness of the cosmos—they belied their name in that while they were indisputably beautiful, their shading showed no sign of red.

"They look like butterflies to me. But those over there," pointing to several yellow ones with a black pattern unfolding symmetrically on both wings toward the outside, "remind me of one of those psychology test things—one of my kids once took a course and brought them home."

"Bernie—"

"Damn it, Abbas, stop screwing with me…and don't call me Bernie."

"Bernard," he corrected with derision, "it's called a Rorschach card. But the task of the subject is to interpret it, which you still fail to do."

Platta turned and started walking away. Not insulted, Abbas followed after him.

"You didn't see the little puppy faces? That's why they call the ones you were pointing to Dogface butterflies," he burst out laughing. "Okay, let me take care of your need now."

Abbas had a distinguishing tonal pattern. It was as if he were perpetually suffering sinus infections. His voice made a raspy sound. It must have been that the vocal cords tired easily. If taxed, they would eventually cause hoarseness. One could surmise that the abnormal shortness of his lower jaw accounted for the uniqueness of his speech…and to a degree they would be correct.

The two men walked a short distance after leaving the exhibit. They entered another area of the park called Sasebo Japanese Garden. Passing over a wooden bridge straddling a slow running stream they came to a waterfall. The sound of rushing water muted their voices, the perfect place for the conversation that followed.

"You never told me how you liked the little treat I gave you last time," Abbas teased.

"I'll admit it was amazing. I really don't know if there is a word to describe it," Platta remarked. "What was it anyway?"

"Some day I'll explain more about it," Abbas responded evasively.

"I have to tell you, the stuff is addicting. Just tell me what I need to do to get it and I will," Platta pled unabashedly.

"Not a problem. You'll have plenty," Abbas comforted him. "Did you see how many different varieties of butterfly there were at the pavilion? I have at least that many types of pills."

"What do they all do?"

"You'll see."

Abbas took out of his pocket another plastic baggie with a single pill.

"Now, here's your magic potion for the next assignment."

He handed it to Platta. With his free hand, he reached into his other coat pocket, extracting a small glass bottle.

"It doesn't look like much but I promise it's sufficiently concentrated that this fraction of a dose will put a thousand brains on furlough indefinitely. If their heads wake up they'll have flashbacks for the rest of their lives," Abbas commented cheerily. "I warn you, this is one you do not want to sample."

Platta soaked in the admonition, contemplating the upcoming act of wrath.

"All in the name of God, is that it?"

"I know you don't see it that way," Abbas answered kindly. "But yes, it is God's will. He never intended one group to terrorize another, to spit on their pride, to attempt to acid wash away the fingerprints of their history, to shame them to their wives and children, to enslave their offspring or to cheat them of their right to live as human beings. I take my orders from people in my country, they take their orders from God, and yes, this is willed, by Him, by Allah."

"You're a lucky man to believe as strongly as you do. That clarity is a blessing." Platta then made a confession. "I don't see God, He doesn't speak to me and I don't take instruction from him. For me, it's about getting even. It's an eye for an eye. I'd kill Miller on my own but it would be too obvious. I don't want the spotlight on me when the time comes for you to arrange my disappearance. I'll have to suck up what I'm doing for you in exchange for my future payoff."

Abbas walked further, directly over a pond filled with koi. He then took a piece of bread from his pocket that he had picked up as he passed a snack bar. Rolling a small portion between his fingers into a ball, he tossed it in the water. A white skinned fish with red markings on the top rushed to snatch the bread into its mouth. In an instant, a large group of relatives congregated, sticking their mouths out in anticipation of food.

"Would God punish us if these beasts were starving and we teased them with the promise of nutrition while we planned all along their extinction?" He paused for a response that didn't come. "Imagine His judgment if instead of fish, it were humans. Whether you care to see it this way or not what we are going to do is God's verdict."

"My people ate, they got fat!" Platta shouted, Abbas' faith setting in motion an outburst of impious disgruntlement. "I made them rich. Every venture brought them wealth. If not for me, they'd be eating dust."

Abbas had no interest in Platta's rationalizations. Nor did he care to pass judgment on the man's actions.

"You'll have to leave soon. It could be a seventeen-hour drive. You have to be in San Francisco by ten in the morning. As soon as you finish, turn around and come directly home. I don't want any suspicion of you being gone."

"And what will you be doing?"

"Don't worry about me," Abbas mischievously responded. "I'll be working away on the report I have to submit, describing every move you've made in the last 48 hours." He smiled at Platta. "Then I have a little plan of my own."

"I can imagine," Platta said with repugnance.

"No, you can't," Abbas chirped. "And don't forget to take your medicine; exactly one hour before. It'll make your trip home an amusement park ride."

8

BOBBY PERSKY COMES ON STAGE

AFTER THE MURDER OF Adina Bernard, Bobby Persky, the FBI agent designated to handle federal affairs at the Mescalero Indian Reservation, for the first time visited tribal land. In all fairness, he had only been in the Albuquerque field office for three months. Still, it would have been customary for him to introduce himself.

The tribe had their own justice system, along with the authority to handle a range of crimes and disputes in accordance with tribal law. However, the book had been written outlining what illegal acts would fall under the jurisdiction of the U. S. government, to be investigated by the FBI, and if necessary prosecuted by either the Justice Department or the State of New Mexico.

While the 1994 Crime Act expanded jurisdiction to the tribes in Indian Country in a number of areas including drugs and domestic violence, acts of murder had long before been defined as falling outside of the tribe's legal reach.

Thus, with the death of Adina, Persky had no choice but to begin an investigation.

He hadn't avoided contact with the reservation and Indian population due to irresponsibility. It was because his predecessor had apprised him that the Mescalero resented the "intrusion" of outside influences, especially by the government of the United States. He was even advised that as long as no matters of urgency came up, he could comfortably neglect the reservation.

That was fine with Agent Persky. His interests were not in American Indian affairs. In fact, he took it as an affront that the assignment had been imposed on him and he was particularly offended that he had been sent to New Mexico. His goal was to be placed in Los Angeles, a priority he intensely lobbied to accomplish.

What was so compelling about The City of Angels was the entertainment industry. Persky was in his early thirties. He stood about six foot-two inches tall, had the build of an NFL outside receiver, and had actually finished a mediocre career playing for the New England Patriots. In all likelihood, he might have eked out another two or three years of inferiority as a pro had it not been for one mean hit by the meanest linebacker on the Green Bay Packer roster, Mel "Meanie" Mack.

Mel was a gentle, kind, soft-spoken, respectful man… unless you met him on a football field. Meanie hit Bobby so hard he busted his patella into several pieces, causing severe internal derangement of his knee. After surgery, the question was not whether or not he would play in the future. It was whether or not he'd ever be able to walk.

His career ended like so many of his colleagues' had. The good fortune Bobby had was that juiced-up-Mel hadn't cracked him in the head, in which case he might have spent the rest of his life trying to figure out how many toes he had on his feet.

As his recovery from surgery progressed, he demonstrated that he would be able to ambulate without support of a cane, but he limped severely enough to agonize anyone looking at him. Still, his goal was fame and to break into the acting field. The Los Angeles field office would have been perfect but instead he was handed a two-year sentence in New Mexico—the dream of seeing Rob Persky on the cover of *People Magazine* in the supermarket had at least temporarily been crashed.

I had been called beforehand to let me know that Agent Persky was coming. Frankly, I was shocked that I hadn't been contacted before for an interview regarding Adina. I had been the first person to find the body. In addition, she was on my land. What I was soon to learn was that Persky was handling the matter without assistance since the staff at the Albuquerque office was only a skeleton of what it once had been. Despite the jurisdictional authority, historically the FBI obliged the unspoken wish of the tribe by shunning matters occurring on Indian land.

When Persky knocked on my door, I had never met him. After insisting that he hold up his identification, I finally let him in.

Men don't spark my hormones but this specimen was dazzling in appearance, even I could tell. I thought of screaming to Preeti to stay in the other room until he left. Most males would commit crimes to keep this agent away from their wives. No doubt he was the best looking man on The Bureau's squad.

His hair was thick and blondish in color. His complexion was ruddy, an outdoor appearance that fit the New Mexico lifestyle perfectly. An exercise freak, he never let the injury deter him from a vigorous routine that kept his body "buffed."

"Sorry that I wasn't able to get to you before, bud, but I'm playing QB without receivers or running backs." His word selection was juvenile but his tone of voice was grave. "You ever face eleven of the toughest and roughest boys in town, all at once, wanting to bust you up?"

You're the FBI guy who is going to solve this case…and protect me? I shuddered.

"Knocked me out of the game," he shrugged. "Now let's get on to this young actress, Adina. I talked to one of her friends in Los Angeles, a girl named Julie Pedrus. She phoned Adina an hour before the time we estimate she was murdered. The little girl told me Adina sounded like her normal self. She was excited about opening night and planned to rest, have something to eat, and then perform—nothing out of the ordinary."

"Don't you want the security camera tapes? We don't have them for the restaurant but The Center for the Performing Arts records during every performance. We do have a video of the theater for that evening, as well for the housing facility where all the cast stays."

"Until I get some help, I don't have time for fishing trout in a frozen pond. The asshole that did this was not about to be seen on a security camera. Let me tell you more, to see if any of this triggers a recall for you…and don't worry I'll get to your situation in a moment.

"Only minutes before Adina left the compound, she received a call on her cell. That had to be the trigger event leading her outside. But why would she go? Her mom was in the room next to her and she never told her she was stepping out. I'm informed the little lady wasn't permitted to go anyplace unaccompanied, and without the permission of her mother. Any thoughts on what would lure her to voluntarily go out, presumably to meet someone?"

"I really have no idea."

"I don't either…yet," he said with conviction. "Our Washington office at first couldn't trace the call. Finally, they determined it came from a cell phone belonging to a girl named Tony Cruz, a student at the University of New Mexico. I checked. She had reported her phone stolen several hours before Adina disappeared. She was with two of her friends having lunch when she assumes it was picked out of her backpack—the girls all corroborate the story and there was a report filed immediately for the missing object.

"The killer, therefore, had to take the phone knowing he was going to contact the girl, had to know her number, and had to have a carrot at the end of his stick to draw her out alone," Persky noted with disgust. "The killer knew precisely what he was doing. He took a hunting knife, slid it into her heart, and let her slowly bleed to death." His anger was too real for acting.

"Was there any sign...? I started to ask hesitantly.

"No sex play, no torture, no secondary scaring or indication of resistance—Christ, she never had a chance. Closest we can get is she was killed near five in the afternoon but not placed in the field where you found her until close to two in the morning."

"I think it's related to what's happening with me."

"I'm not ready to go there yet," Persky snapped. He was going through a progressive thought process. My role was to sit and listen. "Now if you were motivated to simulate a Christ killing, would you use plastic straps to tie the victim to the cross? And by the way, I found where the sign came from. There was a home listed for sale down in Ruidoso. He pulled the sign out. But there were no clues near that house and not a shred of evidence suggesting mischief anywhere near the compound on your property. Tells me he had to bundle up the package, take it somewhere to store it, and then when he felt safe, bring it back to where you found her.

"At first, I thought this was some sort of bastardized attempt to denigrate Christianity. Can you think of a better way to insult the largest religious group in our country than to substitute a female child for the male adult Christ? Says your religion is inferior to mine. Was that the message?" he rhetorically posed.

"Adina was Jewish. You know that?"

"I do. That's what blew some wind through my argument," he quipped. "Now let's get to you."

"Right now, I have protection 24/7. My friend, Nadine Street—"

"I know all about that. So, there are three events to look at. Adina is killed and she's Jewish. A Jewish temple is blown up and kids are killed. Then you receive hate material with Jewish, Israeli and Palestinian messages—and you're, what is it, half Jewish?

"I will tell you this, there are over a hundred agents and all of the FBI resources working on the Phoenix matter. They're dubious about a connection with Mescalero. The crimes are so distinctly different that it's not feasible to bundle them. On the one hand, you have a single murder by impalement and hate paraphernalia left on someone's property. On the other, you have detonation devices setting off massive explosives. Where's the similarity?"

He went on to explain that regardless of the unlikeness of the crimes, the FBI was proceeding with both investigations classified as hate crimes, defined as a criminal offense against a person or property motivated in whole or in part by bias against a race, religion, ethnic group or sexual orientation. He also informed me that what the FBI calls their "Fly Team" had been sent to Arizona. This group is a small, highly trained cadre called first to any possible act of terrorism.

After the incident at Temple Beth Israel, the Jewish community went into high alert. Every synagogue in the country implemented code-red security measures and the vast influence of the Jewish population in America bore down on the national security system with all its might. The FBI was put on notice to spare no resources on the Phoenix investigation. As a result, Mescalero had limited personnel and was nearly being ignored.

"I read that there were a few clues regarding the temple incident." I mentioned to Persky.

"Right. An elderly man walking in the dark of the morning saw a figure carrying objects close to the temple and then a few minutes later, walking away without them, toward a car on the street behind the temple. He later reported that he thought it was a small truck of some sort but it was dark and he couldn't testify to the color. It gets worse. His eyesight is terrible, even with his glasses...and he was out without them.

"More promising was another report by a woman who witnessed the explosion in the morning while she was driving. She panicked, hitting the gas petal on her truck to get home and check on her children. The attraction of the bombing was so remarkable that all vehicles had stopped or were pulling to the side of the road. But to her left, was what she described as a dark blue Ford pickup accelerating past her. Besides the speed, what caught her attention was that as she glanced toward the other driver, she noticed that he was gleeful, as if he had an invisible lady friend giving him a hand job. It happened so quickly that she never thought of getting the license."

"That's what I heard on the news," I noted suggestively, wondering if there was more.

"If there are details that weren't reported, you can rest assured I'm not telling you," Persky promised.

"All I care about is the safety of my family. This is pretty stressful for us."

"I can imagine. Right now I think you're not in danger. If you are connected with these other tragedies, then whoever is behind it will assume by now that you're under heavy security. They'll also surmise that you're too dangerous because you could be used as bait. If anything he, or they, will want to stay away from you."

"Makes sense," I acknowledged, adding, "But really, would you feel any better?"

Persky couldn't answer with confidence and was kind enough not to say anything on the subject.

"If there's another incident coming up, we may have our answer about all of this being connected. We're going to have to wait," Persky lamented.

After he left, I locked the door, went over to the Westchester—which I now carried from room to room—and checked that it was loaded and ready to fire. What a joke. I could hardly control the recoil—had the agent(s) of Amir invited me to an unobstructed shot at him, I most likely would have blown off my foot.

Still, in a curious manner, it empowered me. For the first time, I understood what the American Rifle Association members were fighting for. It wasn't their fault that the gun manufacturers were marketing rifles capable of blasting through foot thick concrete walls to the average citizen.

That's empowerment! What a bore my father-in-law is. He gives me a lousy sub-cannon Winchester.

9

FUNNY FLUID

IF YOU WAKE UP in the morning and find the plates on your car missing, it's a good idea to report it immediately. Chances are decent that they've been put on another vehicle and then used for a misdeed. Later, the original plates for the crime car are replaced with the correct ones and the police might be looking for a late model dark blue Ford pickup that belongs to you. If the wrongful event was a serial act endangering the lives of over forty young people, expect to see more federal and local law enforcement officials surrounding your home than show up for a riot.

Bernard Platta left for San Francisco shortly after the excursion to the botanical garden with Fadi Abbas. He was driving a 2010 dark blue Ford pickup, a yellow plate with red lettering and a yucca pattern defined it as a New Mexico registered vehicle. The license number was BRD 361. It designated the truck as coming from the Land of Enchantment and belonging to Wasa Brook in Socorro, New Mexico.

Platta arrived in San Francisco at nine-fifteen. He parked nearly a block north of Howell Street, on Hawthorne. His good fortune to have had very little traffic, afforded him an extra half hour to sit for breakfast and use the bathroom. There was a small café conveniently located right in front of where he found a place to park his car. It was quieting down after the early morning rush. He sat alone at a table and ordered a ham omelet with wheat toast—grumbling that there was no white bread. He heavily buttered the wheat English muffin before applying a satisfying portion of jam. He also ordered a cup of coffee.

He noticed something unusual as he took one bite after another. There was a full body to the food with an exceedingly gratifying taste. When the waiter came over to fill his coffee he couldn't help commenting.

"This food is remarkable. It's not even like food," he chuckled, "but in a good way."

"I'm glad you appreciate it," the waiter responded while sneaking in a speck of hauteur. "We only use eggs from chickens that are free-range raised and fed a diet of sprouted grains and seeds. The ham is not real meat. We use a soy based product."

"I see." Platta was hardly able to mutter the reply, not versed on meat substitutes.

"I'm sure you do or you wouldn't have said anything," the young server commended. "It's different eating real food, isn't it?"

Platta acceded with a pleasant smile. "Can I get a check please…and a glass of water?" he requested.

"Filtered, of course," the waiter chirped as he walked off.

Platta remembered that he'd been instructed to take the pill Abbas had given him a half-hour earlier. From his coat pocket he took out his tiny capsule. When the waiter arrived with a glass of water and the bill, he quickly drank down the delightful medicine.

Inspired after eating one of the healthiest breakfasts of his life, he haplessly made his way up the block. On the southwest corner of Hawthorne and Howell was an old Victorian home that had been remodeled after the earthquake of 1906. It was a three-story structure, the large wood front door accessed by three steps shielded by a small, extended roof held up confidently by two bold columns. Atop the doorway was a sign, *Mogen David Temple*, and just above that was a large glass window cut in the shape of the Star of David, the center eye inlaid with a stain glass picture of a Torah.

Platta passed the front entrance at five to ten. It revolted him. He recalled the several occasions when as a boy he or his mother, or both, would be brutalized by his father on a Saturday morning, and then he'd be taken to synagogue to pray. His desire at the time was for his father to die, and for him not to be punished for the sin of his forbidden wish.

He walked around the rear of the building where a small door opened to a kitchen. He went inside, finding the space precisely as it had been described. Several platters of food were placed out and in the middle was a bowl with a drink, cooled by a large block of ice.

There was nobody present, the food having been prepared ahead of time. Before being served for the festivities soon to take place, it needed the blessed command of the religious leader. Rabbi David Dosa was a man in his late sixties. He had served as the spiritual head of the congregation for the last forty years.

His grey hair was never seen without a kippah, the longer strands falling carelessly to the neckline. His face was drawn in; matching deep crevices stood out as they wrapped from the lower nostril around the outside of the cheeks forming perfect circular cups.

Rabbi Dosa ran his temple with the earnest discipline he insisted for his personal life. Every Thursday morning, snacks were served for the Bar and Bat Mitzvah students, usually numbering in the forties. It was his time to get to know each of them on a more personal basis so that when the time came for them to take the sacred ceremony to become men and women in the Jewish faith, he would be able to speak about each of them from his first-hand experiences.

The food was always waiting in the kitchen. The volunteer staff would leave after laying out all the items. The students at precisely ten would bring the food into a homey meeting room with old red brick walls and the furniture made of even more elderly spruce. Each of the platters and bowls would be placed on a round center table. There were also three long tables with chairs where the children would sit.

Platta's assignment took under thirty seconds. He twisted the cap off the glass vile, poured the liquid into the drink, covered his hand with a piece of Kleenex and used the large spoon to give two swift mixes, first clockwise and then counterclockwise. Then he walked out.

In less than three minutes, he was back in his car. He thought of getting some food to go from the "real food café" but instead headed for the freeway to begin his "trip" home.

He wondered how long it would be before his pill would

kick in. He also wondered what plan Abbas had for him and his family to escape. He knew prison was in his fate in the near future, and that his sentence could be far more severe than that delivered to his son. Then he contemplated the murder of Zach Miller, and how refreshing a feeling it would be knowing in the end he had prevailed—beating his nemesis, Len Cloud, by having the man's son-in-law murdered. Wily old Platta would then disappear, never to be seen again.

Such delirium. It especially tickled him knowing his funny pill would need another half hour before it would begin working its magic…and he was already in a spiffy mood.

Platte drove home, never having inquired exactly what would be the consequence of the act he had just performed. By that afternoon, the world would know.

10

I'M DECLARING WAR,
YOU IDIOTS

PLATTA DROVE IN A southward direction. He would make a sweep deep into California before turning due east into the vastness of the Arizona and New Mexico deserts. Not more than thirty minutes out of San Francisco, he imagined himself zooming in a chauffeur-driven stretch-Ford pickup. He envisioned that he was sipping a McCallum 25-year Anniversary glass of scotch, while his two buxom lady friends were massaging him top and bottom, his only care in the world being that the voyage home was going to come to an end too quickly.

It amazed him when every so often an infidel thought would scamper through his mind, reminding him that it was all a fantasy. The astonishment was that he was aware he was living in a bubbly state of his own creation. Yet at the same time, he was conscious of the fact that he was operating perfectly attuned to the real world of asphalt highways, streams of gaseous trucks and cars, and blaring sunlight, the beams upon which he believed he could ride like rockets to undiscovered planets in still uncovered galaxies.

He had calculated that he would arrive home close to five in the morning. His mapping of the trip also estimated that he would cross the border into New Mexico close to midnight. The instructions given to him by Abbas included stopping in a discreet spot after entering his home state and replacing his true license on his truck, then tossing the stolen plates. Thus, it was about one in the morning when he completed the simple assignment, folding New Mexico license BRD 361 into a quarter of it's original size and then burying it in a dumpster at a filling station.

Fate had been at Abbas and Platta's service on this occasion. Within an hour of Platta hitting the road out of San Francisco, sirens were descending from every direction toward the *Mogen David Temple*. The waiter who served Platta saw him park in front of the restaurant and noticed the New Mexico plates on the car. There was something suspicious about Platta in the mind of the server, but he couldn't figure out what. He did write down the license number of the out of state plate.

Subsequently, the waiter was called for a family emergency and left moments after Platta finished paying his bill. Thus, it wouldn't be until that evening he would hear on the news of the events that took place later that morning just down the block from where he had been serving food.

By the time he reported the license and vehicle type, Platta had already made the switch and was heading homeward. New Mexico State Police vehicles sped up from behind Platta on two occasions. Noticing that his license not the one they were looking for, they backed off—had Fadi Abbas known how fate had tossed him a prize, he surely would have high-fived his God.

Concurrently, Wasa Brook, an associate at a nearby Staples store, was shocked when a team of FBI agents crashed through the door of her tiny apartment with rifles drawn while she was using a neti pot to clear mucous from her clogged nostrils. The ceramic piece cracked on the floor, beating her to the ground as she passed out.

She had been home for the last two days trying to outfox a flu bug. During that entire time, she hadn't visited her dark blue Ford pickup parked in front of her apartment. After the agents revived her, she accompanied the men outdoors. She was about to be delivered her second shock in only a few minutes, when she discovered that the license was missing. The agents were understandably disappointed but for the inconvenience to Wasa, one of the agents offered to reimburse her for the broken neti pot.

While Ms. Brooks was healing her illness, Abbas was presumably diligently watching over Platta. In reality, he was in the process of implementing his own mischief. His line of thinking was similar to that of Agent Persky in that he knew Zach Miller would be too hard a target to get to, and regardless, it was too early in the game for the cat to pounce on the mouse. Why not first drop the little rodent in an aquarium with a hungry viper and let him shit himself?

Approximately two years earlier, The Center for the Performing Arts at Kuruk was built. Before that Kuruk had been only a restaurant. Preeti owned and operated the establishment to support her and her son, Jivin, until I came along and married her. The many acres of land surrounding the business were also her property, though it was worthless on the open market.

After Josea married and began writing musicals with her husband, their dream was no different than any other aspiring artist. They wanted their creative endeavors shared with the world. But, there was one difference. Neither yearned, nor needed, the mainstream fame that necessitates front-page spreads in the Star or Vanity Fair magazines, television appearances with late-night hosts, or performance tours around the globe. They eschewed it, in fact.

Their vision was a small and intimate space, limited to seating just over a hundred people. From change clanging in his pocket, our chef was able to construct what would soon be referred to as "the compound" of The Center. It was composed initially of a state of the art theatre with one hundred thirty-five seats and a housing unit sufficient to provide living quarters for the full staff and cast during rehearsals and staging. A separate building with food service, meeting rooms, social space and entertainment for the theater group was later added.

The productions ran for several months at a time. There would then be a "dark" period, during which time the next piece would be getting ready to light up the stage. Since Adina's death, the entire compound had been draped in black with all of the personnel racing down the hill out of Mescalero as if escaping the blast wall of a volcanic eruption. With the exception of a small maintenance crew, the facility two hundred yards down the road from the restaurant was abandoned—but not on the evening when Platte was driving home after executing his horror in San Francisco.

Abbas could have been found poking his way into and out of the three buildings of the compound, strategically placing in several locations of each structure, materials of the highest caliber of flammability. Certain that he was unobserved since the skeletal staff had taken the day off, he comfortably completed the task at four-thirty in the morning. He doubled checked that everything was in place.

Finally, he took two poles he had brought along and with a hammer pounded them into the ground, just far enough from the upcoming heat that they would not be destroyed. Once everything was in place, he left to wait for Platta to arrive from his San Francisco mission. It would not be until minutes after that when Abbas would sneak back to the theater and begin a sprinter-like performance, dashing from one building to the other, setting off the combustible material that would leave the wood trimmed sites nothing more than collapsed steel beams and ashy debris.

There was no pyromanic erotic excitation for Abbas. He considered his calling of a higher order, falling into the category of god-ordained business. He didn't stick around to witness the ejaculatory thrill generally associated with acts of this sort, nor did he show up in the crowd of spectators rushing to witness the remains of what was once a proud and culturally enriching addition to their community.

Abbas, instead, vacated the scene to finish his "thorough" report on the activities of Bernard Platta during the first

102 I INSATIABLE HATE

48-hours of observation. In his car some miles away, outside the apartment where Platta would be if he were home, he sat confidently and mightily, thinking what idiots he was dealing with.

The authorities, with all their resources, would be compiling profiles from their data banks, looking for prospective individuals or groups inclined toward the type of acts he was orchestrating, never understanding that in truth Fadi Abbas, on behalf of his people in the Middle East, had begun to wage a full out war on foreign territory, an opening salvo he envisioned leading the enemy to be comically chasing their proverbial tails.

A sense of rejoice came over him, as if he had just completed a revival. He knew that Platta had successfully conducted his assignment and it was only a matter of time before he'd be arriving home. Abbas could then deliver a glowing report of good behavior on the man he was assigned to follow.

Acting with foresight and prescience, Mr. Abbas went so far as to build into his report an explanation in the event that something unforeseen occurred with Platta, such as being discovered as the madman responsible for the acts against Jews. He had to account for how Platta could have been gone for such an extended period of time while he himself was assigned to do the surveillance.

The answer to his problem worked out brilliantly. Abbas had been bringing in assistance. Mr. Farley was cooperating in terms of leads for competent people to help. A young man named Jason Nance was hired. Abbas scheduled the man at precisely the times covering when Platta left for San Francisco and returned home. That way, if it were ever to be calculated, based on when he had to be in San Francisco to conduct his project, at what times Platta had to have left and returned, it would be on the shoulders of Nance.

Abbas instantly recognized young Nance as the right man. The choice to hire him was based on an admonishment by Farley to Abbas that Jason had just recovered from a drinking problem. Farley was invested in his rehabilitation in so far as he liked "the kid" and wanted to give him an opportunity to redeem himself. What Nance didn't know was that while he was being distracted by Abbas during the moments both Platta had left, and then precisely before he returned from his journey to San Francisco, he was in the position to be the perfect fall guy in the event the operation went awry.

When Platta arrived back home from his trip, he drove directly to the underground garage, hit his horn gently two times, and then went inside and parked. It had been agreed between Platta and Abbas that they would have no direct communication. The twin blasts from the car, however, was a prearranged sign to alert Abbas that Platta had returned. After getting the message from Platta, Abbas left Nance to continue the remainder of his shift.

On his way back to the theater, where he would inflict his own act of destruction, he called Nadine. "Nadine, everything is perfect here. The subject rarely left the house."

"Look, you must be tired. I'll cover you while you get some rest," she offered.

"Not necessary, but thanks," he responded jovially. "One of Farley's people was on shift."

"Good. I'm sure you're aware. Hell is breaking out all over," she said tiresomely.

"What do you mean?"

"You haven't heard the news," Nadine questioned.

"No, I've been busy. Besides, the news is too depressing."

"You're right on that point, Fadi. And it's getting worse."

"What are you talking about?" Fadi inquired calmly.

"There's a Jewish temple in downtown San Francisco. Yesterday, the entire class of Bar and Bat mitzvah students were drugged by a strange strain of hallucinogenic substance."

"This has to be related to Phoenix," Abbas asserted with alarm. "Thank god, it sounds like nobody is dead this time."

"That's the good news. The bad news is that not one of the children has come out from under the effects of the substance."

"Those drugs can last a while, I hear, Nadine."

"Not like this one. Owing to the extreme potency of the chemicals, each of the youths is stuck in a psychotic trap. It's really scary."

"We'll have to pray for their recovery," Abbas voiced reverently. "By the way, I'll be finishing up a report on Platta's surveillance. Do you want me to email it?"

"Sure. So you're covered now with help on Platta?"

"Right. I'll use this same man Farley referred."

Nadine shook her head approvingly, never imagining that her trusted associate was headed in my direction.

11

FIRST THERE WAS FIRE...

I WAS AWAKENED BY the sound of sirens. I could hear one after another roaring down the road a quarter mile from my front door, heading in the direction of Kuruk. Then within minutes the phone rang. A person I didn't recognize was on the other end.

"Do not go outside your house," the voice shrieked at me. "Do you hear me?"

"Who are you?" I demanded.

"Bernadette Raymond. I work for Nadine Street. There's been a fire at Kuruk. Let me make sure it's safe first. If it is, I'll pick you up in a few minutes."

When she finally came, both Nadine and Josea's husband had already called me. They also had advised me to stay put and informed me that the restaurant was miraculously undamaged. Still, with the rapidity of tragedy unfolding, my instinct was that something far more horrific was jetting my direction—I have no idea what lead me to believe it was traveling by air, even less that I could anticipate it moving at a fast pace.

I should have recalled based on prior lectures by Amir that the Arab concept of time was nothing like that in the West. Therefore, from my perspective, what I expected happening could have been nothing but wrong. The Arabs believe Allah controls time, as opposed to the assumption we in the West adhere to, that we are empowered to order our clocks. Thus, I would be expecting a rhythm to the attacks, a progression with a planned frequency building toward a final encounter.

But it was not Amir pulling the strings. It was the will of God, and events would unfold according to His wish. I might have to wait, agitate on what was coming, even for such a long period I would begin to wonder if indeed the threat was past and life could resume normalcy. Had I kept the temporal differentiation between the cultures in mind, I might have better computed what the future was to bring, a slow roasting of my nerves. God was angry, willful for my suffering.

Bernadette did arrive at my home a few minutes later. I ran out of the house and into the car, mindlessly leaving Preeti with the children. A moment later, while I was gaping at the remains of the theatre, Josea's husband, who had built the facility, pulled up and ran from his car directly to me.

"Screw them!" he shouted while glaring at the charred remains of the theatre he had built to bring joy to the people of Mescalero. "We'll rebuild in no time. I want the new musical up by late this year," he declared.

I stood facing the smoke-belching structures, this outraged man to my right and my bodyguard to the left. The smoldering materials were insouciantly burning the crisp spring early morning air but the radiant heat couldn't warm my chilly skin.

I looked in the direction of Kuruk. In spite of Bernadette's assurance that the restaurant was undamaged, I was relieved not to see any flames or smoke. But the disburdening was short-lived. Directly in my line of sight were twin poles, similar ones to those I found in front of my home. Each stake this time was holding a round sign, about ten inches in diameter. They were black with yellow printing, the still glowing embers in the background, lighting the area in oranges and reds, made the circular objects look like a pair of eyes staring out from a fiery devil's face.

Walking closer, I was able to read them: MESCALERO HATES JEWS and GO HOME. I knew they were evidence but I pulled them out of the ground with a fury and hurled them. My outburst was curtailed by the sound of more sirens.

It was overwhelmingly sad looking at the once beautiful playhouse. The wooden building that had appeared much like a giant mountain cabin lay in ruin. In the past, I had loved approaching it to see a production. It was a single story building with a simple gable roof that rose gradually to double the height of the first and only floor. The eaves jutted out fifteen feet, providing a covered area in the front where people could stand waiting to enter and not worry about getting wet, if it were a rainy evening.

The woods were chosen to match Kuruk's warm mountain feel. They were composed, inside and out, of natural firs, honey pines, golden oaks, red mahogany and traces of ebony.

At night, the three large chandeliers dangling under the overhang lit up the entrance. The upper area of the building contained a large plain window, but the lower floor space housed a ceramic mosaic of dancers. There were double doors leading to the foyer on each side of the picture.

The fire had caused the peak of the roof to fall backward and inward upon the stage area. The random pattern of destruction left the front wall with the dancers soot covered and darkened, but standing defiantly. It had a message to deliver to the handful of spectators witnessing the disaster, as well as to the world not yet aware of what evil was raining on little Mescalero—that man is united in holding his imagination and artistry sacred, and that the will of humankind cannot be defeated.

My chef had personally selected the signature piece. As I glanced at him I thought I read his mind: his words suggested that I did.

"We'll keep the art work as it is and build back around it. Nobody will ever be able to tell, except it will forever remain charred to symbolize we cannot be vanquished."

"I know," I responded with unhidden melancholy.

"Security round the clock. This will never happen again. The only way you stop people like this, is to shove it in their face that you can't be intimidated."

"I'm intimidated," I said, the words easing out unabashedly.

"I guess I would be too."

"I don't even know if it's about dying anymore," I expressed. "It's Preeti and the children mostly. Why should they be harmed because of my past?"

Before he could respond, another siren was blaring up the road. It was Agent Persky in his vehicle, followed by two additional cars and a truck. He opened his door and jumped out, as did the other six agents with him. They immediately began to cordon off the area, making sure that only the fire fighters were allowed access.

After securing the space surrounding the buildings, he noticed my presence and came over to where I was standing.

"Don't jump to any conclusions, Miller. We have to sort out what happened here first."

I could hardly hear his words. My mind flashed on Preeti and the children: I realized they were home alone. I panicked. The monster had lured me out and was at the house, having his way with my sleeping family.

"Shit! They're all at home with nobody there to protect them."

Persky yelled to the other agents he'd be back soon and motioned for me to follow him. We hopped in his car and he sped down the road and back to my house. It was quiet and nothing seemed disturbed…until I charged in the front door like a lunatic.

"Preeti," I screeched at the top of my lungs, "are you okay?"

She had been standing guard over the children. The abruptness of the car speeding up startled her. Instinctively, she ran into the living room, the shotgun in her hands was poised to fire.

"What is it?" she shouted, holding the weapon pointed at my heart.

"You okay?" I gasped.

Preeti looked over at Persky who was now standing just outside the porch. She rotated the barrel enough to aim it at the agent.

"It's all right, Ms. Miller. You can put it down. I'm Agent Persky."

Preeti glanced one more time in my direction before letting the barrel tip drop to the ground.

"You sure that's a good idea?" Persky stated, referring to Preeti with a deadly weapon.

"You don't want to come in my home and try to harm my family," my wife informed him in a manner she might have used purchasing tickets for the movies.

My wife was more comfortable with shooting than I was. Her father had schooled her on self-defense from when she was a little girl. A petite lady, appearing womanly by any definition, her ferocity and fearlessness would better never be misjudged. If the bad guy wanted to enter my home and harm her or her children, he better bring a lot more than a handgun.

By now the baby was crying and Sousche came drowsy-eyed into the room. She said nothing. The unusual scene clearly had frightened her to silence. I was so thrilled to hear my son crying and see my daughter unharmed that I took my little girl in my arms and squeezed, hard enough to bolt my eyes shut to arrest the tears dying for attention.

Bernadette had followed us to the house and peeked in.

"We good here?" she asked tentatively.

I nodded affirmatively.

"Great. I'll be around. I'm not going anywhere, you hear me?"

I would learn later that Farley had used Bernadette for jobs for many years and there was a good reason: she was reliable, courageous and tenacious. Except for her physical size, she reminded me of a girl I met on a river raft trip some years before. Preston and I were in a small boat with a guide who had been assigned his own craft for the first time. We were on the lower Kern River, in California, a stretch of water known to be extremely challenging when running high.

It was early summer and the currents were at full strength. Unfortunately, our boatman was not up to the task and we were repeatedly in trouble. We had swung full circle out of control on several occasions and had taken unsafe amounts of water that had to be bailed constantly. Finally, coming through a hazardous stretch called Pinball, we were jammed against a huge boulder, our guide having been thrown out of the raft. After we were rescued, they put us in one of the other boats. This time the guide was a girl who had to weight all of ninety pounds…soaking wet. But she moved that pontoon so smoothly through the most dangerous rock strewn currents, we thought we were floating in a tub.

Bernadette was a hefty thing but shared the characteristics of confidence and competence with the girl in the boat. She had brunette hair that she wore in a ponytail. I never saw her with a brush of makeup but her skin was smooth and flawless. She dressed like a country girl in jeans and plaid blouses. She was also licensed to carry a weapon. When it was called for during a job, she wore hers on a belt around her waist. You might have imagined her walking into a western saloon—I never saw her without it.

Over time, we came to know her more intimately in that Preeti would invite her into the house for snacks. I learned that she was the daughter of the most prominent neurosurgeon in the state, and a bright girl in her own right. Her father was irked she went into investigative work. It was his dream that his only child would follow him into medicine.

Her interests were actually in the sciences. Had her father been endowed with both more patience and cunning, he may have had his wish fulfilled. But he badgered her to the point of developing a rebellious spirit that turned on itself and refused to allow her to pursue a career likely closer to her highest capability.

I'm grateful to her father. Bernadette was vigilant in her assignment.

So was Persky. After the firefighters completed their work, he had a team of experts brought in to determine the cause of the fire. I could have saved him the trouble, knowing for certain it was intentionally set by the same person or persons responsible for all of the other violent and vicious acts taking place. For reasons I couldn't compute at the time, Persky insisted on calling for a professional investigation of the matter.

It took several days during which time a team of pros (chemists, electrical engineers, fire brigade staff and laboratory scientists knowledgeable in extraction methods employed to determine materials used to cause a fire) studied the scene. Persky delighted explaining in detail how ultraviolet, nuclear magnetic resonance spectroscopy and infrared are used to identify accelerants, components used to quicken the pace of fire, adding to my edification that these accelerants, if present, are one of the key elements that can be used to determine arson.

I was hardly interested in attaining a working knowledge of setting fires but Persky seemed to be enjoying lecturing me just the same. Thus, I tolerantly listened until he finally summarized the findings of their scientific exercises. It was concluded that the fire had been set by someone strategically placing petroleum soaked rags and igniting them. The individual had likely studied methods to best speed the combustion in that the sites where the accelerants were placed were perfect to increase the likelihood of maximum damage.

The arsonist had thoughtfully placed the materials near specific passageways—ones he intentionally left open—to assure a steady flow of oxygen to feed the blaze. He had also determined what the most flammable material would be given the components of the building itself.

"Sure, I would have pegged my next year's salary on it being arson," Persky proclaimed. "Still, don't you think it's worth something not only to confirm it scientifically but also see what we can learn about the criminal from his execution of his act?"

"We know who it is who did this," I countered with a tone of defiance. "We're simply back where we started."

"You're back where you started. That's the difference between us. I didn't start anyplace except uncertainty. What if you're still wrong and the arson is not connected in any way with you?"

"Can't be," I argued impatiently.

"Well, as it stands, I agree with you. But until this comes to a finale we could both be wrong. Anyway, I will tell you this much. We know now that an educated person planned this. We also know that none of the people showing up to see the damage were the arsonist, meaning we're not likely dealing with a professional pyromaniac. It's not petty vandalism or the firefighters would have been able to save most of the structure of each building."

Persky stopped and shook his head back and forth as if dumbfounded by a fact.

"Damndest thing. Do you know that the owner had no property insurance? Who owns buildings of that size today and refuses to protect it in the case of fire, flood or other disasters?" Again he expressed his confusion by wagging his head. "His answer to me was that he just never wanted to be involved with insurance companies…he's an eccentric fellow who just took a bath in kerosene…but that's his problem."

"He's more like a relative to us. He is a bit different but can afford the loss without hurting," I assured him.

"Lucky man. Well, the point for me is we're not dealing with insurance fraud either."

"It's precisely what we all knew from the beginning," I said exhaustedly. "Hate. Revenge. As you've discovered, there's no other motive left."

"Sure seems that way, coach. Too bad I'm not a writer. By the time this is over, I might have myself one hell of a story," he quipped.

"I'm a writer and I'll make you a deal."

"We'll have to make it informal; it might violate agency rules."

"Gentleman's agreement. How's that?"

"Let's hear."

"Keep my family alive and once this matter is settled I'll write the story and when I sell the movie rights I'll stipulate that you get to play a role, your real life character if you choose. I think I can pull it off."

"You couldn't have given me a finer motive to secure your loved ones," he grinned.

Unbeknownst to either of us, two days later the plot would be coming to a starchy thickening.

12

MORE MURDER

IT WAS REPORTED TO Nadine that during the time spans Abbas and Nance were responsible for watching Platta, his only time out of his place was to take a few local excursions. On one occasion, the man went to the market to buy food and then stopped at the drug store. On another outing, he went to visit his wife who was living temporarily two miles away with her sister. On the surface it might appear that the couple were tightly bonded. Still, due to the trials, and knowing he was likely to be under surveillance by the prosecutor's office, Bernard deemed it better to keep his wife as much as possible on the periphery.

There was another entry denoting him going to the park and sitting alone on a bench and then watching children flying kites. But, for the most part, his life was humdrum. This especially was the case when Nance logged his hourly reports—Platta never left the house.

What was certain was that Platta's recorded activities did not reflect that he was a mass killer of Jews, as well as responsible for drugging an entire synagogue's Bar and Bat Mitzvah class, all while he was supposedly under the diligent eye of his guardians.

Shortly after his trip to San Francisco, and on a biting cold Thursday afternoon, Platta had arranged to meet with Abbas. Due to the frigid conditions they agreed it would be best to choose an indoor forum. Each purchased tickets to the movies, purposely selecting different features but later joining one another in the same theatre. Whispering in the back row of a nine-tenths empty auditorium, the conversation turned adversarial.

"I have a right to know exactly what this plan is to get me out of the country. I want to know where I'll be going, when and how my wife and son are going to be brought out," Platta barked in a muted voice at Abbas.

"Everything is being arranged now, my friend," Abbas responded in a hushed voice. "Sometimes I get the feeling you don't trust me. Yet, we are bound now by the highest service to God."

"I'll take your god and shove it up your rectum so far you'll be gagging on it if you keep jerking me," Platta warned. "Push me you little towel-head and I'll expose you in a second."

"I doubt that," Abbas retorted, indifferent to the slur. "Besides, we still have work to do."

"I want him killed. That's the next work. Until that happens and you show me the proof for how I'm to be rewarded, our business is over," Platta protested in a slightly elevated tone as his foot firmly kicked the backside of the empty seat in front of him. "Listen, you have two days. Don't test me."

Platta stood up and walked out, leaving Abbas. The latter proceeded to sit through the rest of the flick: he couldn't have recounted to a soul the name of the movie, the star actor, or what the theme was.

That evening Abbas arrived unannounced at Platta's apartment. He was about to make his first mistake.

He parked in front of the building. On his head was a cap that he had pulled down tightly. On his hands, he wore a pair of leather gloves. He knocked at the door, Platta questioning through the partition the identity of the visitor. Abbas announced himself, notifying his friend in an excited manner that it was urgent.

When Platta opened the door he must have assumed that Abbas was about to inform him that Zach Miller had finally been or was about to be properly punished. Instead, Abbas took a Glock 26 revolver with a homemade silencer on the end of the barrel out of his pocket. The six bullets that he unloaded into Platta's heart and neck sounded like a succession of rapid spits.

Platta grabbed first at his neck as he tried to move in the direction of Abbas who was standing directly in front of him. But the force of the bullets thrust him backward, his hands now flinging wildly in the air. His body continued in retreat, finally landing in a perfectly seated pose in the very chair from which he had just risen to greet Abbas.

Nadine's faithful assistant put the gun into his coat pocket and pulled the door closed. He then made several successive trips to his fully packed car, carrying numerous parcels into

Platta's unit. After unloading the cargo, he carefully organized the contents in strategic locations. When he finished, he gently shut the door and left.

It so happened on this day that Nance didn't feel well and Abbas had employed another assistant to help with the surveillance. The log kept by Abbas and the new man under his supervision, pertaining to his subject's coming and going over the next two days, would read that Platta was highly inactive, not once leaving the apartment.

On the third day, perplexed why her husband was not returning her emails or calls, Mrs. Platta came and knocked on the door. Not getting an answer, she tried the door handle. As her hand turned without resistance, she sensed trouble. Then as she swung open the door, she witnessed her husband coated in his own dried blood. Her screeching was sufficient to attract the attention of several residents who were home at the time.

It was Abbas' fill-in assistant who was on duty when the wife came to check on her husband. As soon as Robbie Hart heard the scream, piercing even outside on the street where he was strolling to exercise his legs, he ran up to the apartment.

When he gazed inside, his eye caught sight of explosives placed within the unit. Wisely, he grabbed the grieving wife, forced her downstairs, and then had one of the other tenants call the manager and order everyone out of the building. While that was underway, he called the FBI office in Albuquerque, and then Abbas, the latter, in turn, calling Nadine.

With the mention of explosives, the FBI descended on the building. Persky had to valet his car; there were so many vehicles vying for a parking spot the area looked like a jammed freeway.

The scene was everything agents of the most prestigious bureau of our government could dream. In a single swoop, they were hauling one of the most notorious serial madmen out of a building, stone cold dead, solving the case of multiple deaths of Jewish children at a temple, bringing closure as to who had used a highly dangerous hallucinogenic substance to mentally damage numerous other young people, understanding who the monster was that had lured an innocent little girl, Adina Bernard, to her death and determining who was seeking revenge on an innocent man.

All that…and not a shot fired.

It was ecstasy and the Bureau's own brand of drug. The proud men and women wearing their navy blue nylon jackets with **FBI** in large bright yellow lettering on the back, breast, shoulders and arms—advertising like NASCAR driver suits—were in their glory. In no time, the Director of the branch office was in front of the cameras, making cautious but optimistic statements.

What was all the excitement over? Platta's apartment was packed with evidence. Explosive materials identical in type to those used in Phoenix were shelved neatly in a closet. Several commando type rifles and handguns with thousands of rounds of ammunition were stored in boxes on the floor of his bedroom.

There were maps with driving instructions to San Francisco and Phoenix, with detailed drawings and pictures of the two synagogues where the atrocities occurred. Then, most amazing, two small glass bottles with a substance seeming to be similar in chemical composition to what was used on the teens at the Mogen David Temple in San Francisco were found.

Stakes similar to those planted in my front yard and drawing materials coinciding with what was used to create the signs were found as well. They conveniently discovered structural plans of the buildings of the compound at Kuruk, plus research articles regarding combustible materials.

There was also the phone that had been stolen from Tony Cruz and used to call Adina Bernard with Platta's fingerprints—even her last name shared in common with Platta's first earned the child no reprieve. Finally, typed notes answered the mystery as to how he had seduced Adina out of her quarters.

The phone call placed to her had informed her that it was Zach Miller's birthday and if she wanted to gift me with the most beautiful flowers ever bloomed, she could come out to the side of the building and into the small grove of pines. The "dumb puppy," as he referred to her, "took the bait."

"Holy shit," was the mantra of the day. Agents catalogued the contents and scientists examined the evidence. Where had he attained these hitherto unknown substances, capable of altering, apparently permanently, the synaptic functioning of the brain such that a new, immutable order of thinking ransacked the mind? Who supplied him with the explosive materials he used criminally to kill innocent children?

Yet, there was more to be answered. Why, for one? What motivated him to such extreme acts of hate? Those taken toward me were obvious and rational. But the others, projects he had clearly been planning for some time and executed with diligence, made no sense at first.

His life had been destroyed as a result of the trial he and his sons were enduring. There was no doubt that there was nothing he could do to rebound from what had been taken from him. Then, on top of that, he lost a son. Sure, it could drive a man mad. Yet not to the extent of evil that Platta had performed. There had to be a better explanation...and there was.

Persky stopped by Kuruk one afternoon about a week after Platta's body was found. He and his men were clearing out of the area, their investigation concluded. His boss, Vince Packard, had ordered Agent Persky to end his involvement on tribal land, expressing to his agent that the Mescalero Apache people had suffered enough and the sooner federal agents were gone the better relations would be between the tribe members and The Bureau.

I doubt it was the informal pact he had entered with me regarding his acting career that influenced the skepticism he experienced. Persky didn't believe the violence was over, or that Platta had worked alone to accomplish the nightmares he had inflicted on innocent people. There were nagging inconsistencies he kept regurgitating like a rancid meal.

"Well, Miller, I'm out of here...for now, anyway," he informed me, combing contemplation through his golden locks with both hands. "Everything is perfect, too perfect, don't you think?"

"I'm not sure what you mean but if you're referring to Platta being the sole agent for this obvious assault on myself and Jews I agree, way too perfect."

"Platta was under prosecution. Why would he stash all the evidence of his crimes in a small apartment where it could have been found in a minute? Sure, you could argue he had nothing to lose and decided to declare war. But I also question why the hell, even if that were true, wouldn't his prints be on any of the objects we found other than his personal toiletries and possessions?"

"He was set up?" I replied with the obvious answer.

"No. He's guilty," Persky assured me. "The woman who reported seeing the man leaving the scene in Phoenix made a definite identification that it was Platta. The waiter in San Francisco was absolutely sure that Platta had come into the restaurant just minutes before the crisis at the temple occurred—he distinctly recalled Platta commenting about the food and the eerie feeling he had serving him.

"Then one of the State Troopers who pulled up behind Platta's car and checked to see if his license matched the one they were looking for told us that by chance he decided to write down the licenses of all the dark blue, late-model Ford pickups he saw that shift, a total of eight. Platta's real plates were on the list, clearly after he had changed it back from Wasa Brooks'.

"No. Platta is the man responsible for these ugly actions. And there's more to support it. His wife, after she settled down, went into exhaustive detail of her life with Mr. Platta, including what she knew of his past. Turns out he's half Jewish, would you believe that? She described it as an identity that he rued bitterly. He would never talk about his background but by chance one time a distant relative came looking for him—some sort of inheritance issue whereby money was coming to Bernard from a deceased relation.

"Platta refused to see the man. Still, before his wife called him to let him know that someone was looking for him, the visitor shared with her the hidden secret of her husband's Jewish roots. It was all about his father being an abuser. It seems Bernard had a bit of a tough youth and long before he met his wife he had anger control issues. For a number of years, he was in and out of institutions for one cruel act or another.

"As a father, she described him as heartless, similar to his own father. He was physically abusive with both of his sons, as well as his wife—her expressed devotion to her husband was a cloak to conceal the awfulness of life within their marriage and family. To her it was fear and constant terror of a man she knew capable of brutality that kept her in silence."

"Persky, my father-in-law, Len Cloud, is a fairly bright man. He's doesn't have a whole lot of formal education but he's the legal authority within the tribe. He quotes passages from Canby's American Indian Law off the top of his head like you provide your email address and phone number.

"Platta was tribal president and Len told me that, in his opinion, he attained his position by intimidation. More important, he knew him well and always marveled at his ignorance. His opinion was that Platta was academically deprived."

"That's what I think. He's too damn stupid to have orchestrated all of this on his own. Besides, I hate it when things are too neat. It tells me that the tale is incomplete."

"Then why is your bureau buying it?"

"They're not. But if you're asking why they want to make it seem like they do, I'll answer. First, it's a matter of practicality. Quantico, our main facility, and our 'data campus' in Clarksburg, are overwhelmed with a number of even more pressing issues. They're hoping to get some time. Then, they've got all the Jewish organizations in the country to deal with. They've taken the position that reassuring them the threat has been terminated is the best approach—at least for the time being."

"Persky, somebody killed Platta. Don't they want to know who did it, and soon?" I posed with amazement. "Doesn't it make sense there was a falling out between Platta and whomever he was working with?" My confusion had graduated to consternation.

Persky paused before answering. "Sure, it makes sense. But there's a bigger issue here. Those drugs. That's a spike shoved up our rectum. The Bureau is more worried about that than anything. So far, all they know is that the two vials found in Platta's apartment contained the same elements used on the youths at the Mogen David Temple. The problem is the lab people are coming up with definitely different chemical compositions from any known type of hallucinogenic substance."

"What does that mean?" I asked to draw him further along his line of thinking.

"Look, LSD is a semi-synthetic drug. It was discovered back in the thirties. It came from some sort of fungus that, if I remember correctly, grows on rye. One of the pharmaceutical companies actually introduced it with a trade name in the forties, and in the fifties the CIA was experimenting with it for mind control. Then came all the counter-culture stuff of the sixties, and for the most part that stopped the research.

"Experiments are going on today; ones that are known to the public. I'm sure there are lots more that are not publicized. Many scientists believe that these drugs can have positive therapeutic value. The problem is there's also a high risk involved in using them due to their unpredictable effect.

"That brings us to the children in San Francisco. None of them are coming out from the influence of the drug. This is something totally new. It means that somebody, somewhere, is conducting research that is far more sophisticated than anything we've done. This is definitely a new substance. That's why The Bureau is not taking the matter lightly. But so far… they haven't even sorted out where Platta got it."

"Sounds scary. It really does," I gravely responded. My alarm level shot up, focusing on concerns I knew I couldn't and shouldn't shake. "Where does that leave me…my family? Let's say Platta hated me more than imaginable. How could he have known about my past history? How could he have pinpointed in on my Israel experience and known exactly how to warn me that he was coming to get me?"

"I'll be around," Persky smiled. "I have a stake in keeping you and yours well, remember?"

Persky limped off to his car and I sat in a stew. Amir was behind the madness, had to have orchestrated Platta's murder, and he was operating on God's clock. Sure, after Platta's killing everything quieted down. However, in my gut, I knew that the moments of peace were only a hiatus dangling deception like laughter between tears of heartbreak. Yet even with that awareness, hope offered a teat, and I sucked. Was I going to be forgiven once more for crimes uncommitted?

My cell chimed. It was Nadine.

"Zach, if I come up there in about an hour will you have some time to talk?" Her voice sounded distressed.

"Sure, I'm free. I'll be waiting."

About an hour and a half later she arrived. Her hair was pulled back and pocketed neatly in a tan knit cap. I recognized immediately that she was tormented by something, the right side of her cheek defenselessly sucked into her mouth. Once in a while she would nibble on the interior wall with her teeth if troubled by a thought or circumstance she couldn't resolve—she wasn't biting down, yet.

"Let's walk," she proposed.

I went to my office and grabbed my coat. We exited the front door. To the right of the parking area Preeti kept a large fruit and vegetable garden, most of the crop used at the restaurant. Rows of newly planted squash, carrots, eggplant, watermelons and cantaloupes were craning their necks out of the ground, awaiting stronger beams of sunlight before shooting limbs from which they would birth luscious edibles. Behind the garden was a path leading into the surrounding forest.

We strolled silently a short distance before she started talking.

"It's about Fadi Abbas…"

BOOK II
RETURNING TO THE SOURCE

13

SETTING THE STAGE

LANDING IN ISRAEL, JOSEA perceived the mission she and Nasir were to undertake being to find and terminate Amir so that he would be incapable of harming me in particular, but other innocent people as well. The Phoenix incident had alarmed her. She had taken off as quickly as possible with the hope that the matter might be resolved before any other disasters were inflicted.

Shortly after her arrival in The Middle East, however, she was confronted first with the Mogen David Temple incident in San Francisco and then the destruction of the compound that she adored at Kuruk. Thus, within a brief span of less than two weeks in March, an Armageddon she prayed wouldn't happen was underway.

Only a few years had passed since the near crisis in the Middle East that both Josea and I were involved in. The outcome for the combatants had been that the Palestinians had settled for a near worthless swath of desert land running from the southwest tip of the West Bank to the northeast edge of Gaza, land that did connect the two regions they already called their own. The prize was a wide strip that might have looked like a giant runway on a map.

It was a victory, however, in the sense they were now a recognized state. Still, it was perceived as a pathetic capitulation. It had been their goal to drive the Zionists out from the entire land mass of what had been included in Israel's state mandate of 1948, plus what was "stolen" from them in wars thereafter—in other words, put an end to what had been carved out of Arab land that had become Israel. They came up shamefully short of their goal.

The rest of the Middle East swallowed hard accepting the new truce; they were still choking on cud that Sadat had spit in their faces, the recognition of Israel's right to exist as a nation.

Thus, while it was hoped that the settlement would bring a lasting peace to the region, nobody believed it. All of the parties involved knew that enemies could fight wars as non-nation states, rogue entities, just as easily as they could if they were nations and neighbors. Being forced into an ugly resolution, both sides of the Israeli-Palestinian dispute, if anything, had greater hatred toward the other side—the crisis I had inadvertently helped to avert was waiting like a stick of dynamite for a match, with a man like Amir a likely candidate to apply a torch.

When Josea and Nasir were settled in Hazut's office, the high-ranking officer wasted no time commencing his orientation. Given the frightful news from America, raising concerns that Amir could be alive, he focused on the reputation Amir had attained in the Middle East and on Israel's own efforts to find a man they considered a great national security threat.

Josea would soon report to me the Israeli version of the story of Amir Hamdallah. Shocking to both of us was that Amir's name in the Middle East had risen like property values in a bubble; he had become a titanic figure, the hopes of a whole region placed on his puny shoulders.

The seeming organic growth of his reputation and influence had apparently been gradual at first, but exponential over time. I certainly wouldn't have been shocked to hear of Amir becoming a leader, even before uncovering his role in the planned atrocities. At the same time, subsequent to me identifying him to the Americans and Israelis as the vicious terrorist he was, I would have anticipated him running for his life before the Israelis, in pursuit, finally killed him.

The truth is that prior to Josea's arrival in Israel, my first-hand awareness of Amir only went as far as shortly after the prison I was held in was taken over by another faction of the Palestinians, an event that took place months before the above referenced peace accord was imposed on both sides.

Nevertheless, it was at that point in time, when the Palestinian Authority took over control of the prison previously held by Hamas that both Amir and his sister fled. They were certain that the Palestinian Authority had earmarked them for elimination. Under that assumption, brother and sister grabbed hands and went into deep cover. At that point, Amir had no idea that the scheme he had worked on diligently for two years had just been uncovered. He could also not have had knowledge that the PA never cared to harm them but it was the Israelis that were giving chase.

Bahlya had nothing to fear regarding the Israelis but it wouldn't have mattered if she had. She was closely bonded with her brother due to both blood and her shared hatred of Israel. The sister would have had to journey along with Amir, if for no other reason than to try to protect him.

The Israelis, from the beginning, were relentless in their pursuit of Amir. They tracked him tenaciously, but to no avail. Finally, on a fateful day several months into their pursuit, after Amir had already assumed a near mythical image, the Israelis were certain that along with his sister, he'd been killed.

"After that raid, which was orchestrated by the Americans, we rested a lot easier," Hazut went on. "That is until these recent events in America, especially those involving Zach. I think you need to know the entire story of what happened from the time we began pursuing him."

"So we're going backward, right, all the way to when Amir and Bahlya fled?" Josea clarified.

"Well, not exactly. More accurately, we'll begin when Zach enlightened us regarding Amir's role in the planned attack— still, close to that time."

Hazut and his people had been able to detail every step taken by Amir and Bahlya, up to when they were presumed dead, after which everything went dark. Hazut narrated the story as best he and his sources could reconstruct together.

I must digress at this juncture in the unfolding of what to me is a nearly unfathomable excursion into fate, fortune, folly and fanaticism to point out that I have relied on many sources in reporting what I believe to be a full and accurate accounting of the tale of Amir Hamdallah and all the people, events and circumstances associated with him.

Documents shared by Israeli security with Josea, captured terrorists who after being "rehabilitated" disclosing their discussions with Amir, associates of Amir who had been bribed to provide information, Nasir's first-hand experiences in collecting clues while traveling through the Middle East, and of course the investigative genius of Josea all contributed toward my being able to author this portion of the story.

To be forthright, I should also confess that some passages and descriptions of events outlined in the first section of this piece—as well as a number to be included in the final book— were not attained through my direct involvement. I was again fortunate to have had first hand narratives by truthworthy and observant witnesses who helped me fill in material that otherwise would have remained unanswered mysteries—and even then I had to draw on logic at times to embellish on motives, actions and thoughts of some of the characters in this drama.

With my heart and soul cleansed, on to the fleeing from Israel by Amir and Bahlya.

Hazut noted that the journey for brother and sister began with them traveling by cab to Eilat. Eyewitnesses described them as being in a jolly and untroubled state. One suggested a tone of cockiness for Amir, perhaps the only clue that beneath the surface there might have been apprehension.

When they arrived on that warm spring afternoon at the marine blue waters of the Gulf of Aqaba, the gentle breeze ruffling the surface water randomly shot out red, orange, yellow and green reflections from the sails of boats in the harbor. A cargo ship was unloading a fleet of newly arrived BMW vehicles and hoards of tourists were vacationing on the beaches of swanky hotels.

Neither Bahlya nor Amir had much interest in commerce or luxuriating. They paid the driver who left them off at the station and then proceeded to purchase tickets on Bus Number 15 to the Taba Border Crossing, the only point open to travel directly from Israel to Egypt. It was a short drive as they made their way south, the Red Sea on their left. Bahlya elbowed her brother, pointing out a school of dolphin riding atop the water, each reaching ahead with their noses similar to racehorses dashing to cross the finish line ahead of their fellow contestants.

When they reached the terminal on the Israeli side of the border, they each paid ninety-one new Israeli shekels for the privilege of entering Egypt. Along with hundreds of other travelers, they entered unmolested into a country both more easily identified as theirs than where they were born.

They paid for bus tickets to…their plan went no further than to get out of Israel.

14

ON THE RUN

THEY ANTICIPATED THAT THINGS would in no time calm down and that the PA would lose interest in them. The siblings concluded that they would soon be able to return home to their parents and other pursuits. In the meantime, the cheery couple would do what most rich kids might do if they had nothing but time on their hands…vacation, visit with friends…and fantasize schemes to destroy countries and peoples. They chuckled as they made their way south, appreciating the ease with which they dodged the perceived enemy.

That foe, again the Palestinian Authority, reviled for its inglorious willingness to be pandered to by the Israelis and Americans, in their estimation would no doubt in due time follow the misfortune of many predecessors. This included loss of prestige with their people, and subsequent privation of power. Their organization narrowly had resources to operate, let alone try and find Amir and Bahlya.

Nevertheless, while in hiding from the presumed foe, the siblings had been living in a two-bedroom suite at the Four

Season Cairo Nile Plaza Hotel, registering under their given names. It so happened that the Cairo Physician's Union was having a meeting of their executive committee. Dr. Jawiris, who might be recalled as the mastermind behind the plot to punish Israel and America, was the head of the Union, as well as the most renowned physician in Egypt. Mysteriously, he had disappeared the day before the gathering was scheduled—that puzzling fact accounted for by the Israelis, who unbeknownst by Amir had taken Jawiris into custody.

Dr. el-Erian was filling in for Jawiris. This gentleman had been introduced months before to Amir by Jawiris, but had no idea as to the nature of the relationship between them. In particular, he did not know about the devastating assault they were planning against their enemies. By chance, el-Erian had run across Amir earlier that morning in the hotel lobby and mentioned that oddly Jawiris couldn't be found. In fact, he asked if Amir had seen him. He assured the doctor that he hadn't.

It was likely Amir's assumption that with the attack scheduled for September 11, in just two days, Jawiris was busy. He thought nothing more of it. However, another coincidence later that morning dramatically altered the situation; but played in Amir's favor.

Dr. el-Erian had stopped at the reception desk, checking to see if he had received a message from Jawiris. An agent speaking English had just walked up to one of the clerks at the desk and the doctor overheard the other man's furtive conversation.

"Mr. Amir Hamdallah is staying at this hotel, I believe."

The agent then pulled out an identification badge and flashed it. When the hotel employee saw the title of the man he was dealing with, he realized he wasn't being asked a question so much as being delivered an order. He glanced at his computer screen and then typed in a few characters. Looking back up at the agent, he nodded his head affirmatively.

"I would appreciate you calling his room to see if he's in. If he answers, apologize for intruding, tell him it was a mistake and hang up." The agent's head leaned forward to reinforce his demand and to be sure he had the clerk's full attention. "Remember," he asserted in a hushed voice, "if he answers, tell him you made a mistake."

"I understand, sir," the clerk said dutifully.

After placing the call and making the suggested excuse, his chin dipped almost imperceptibly, but enough for the agent to record his answer. Amir was in his room. The agent took off swiftly toward the elevators, followed by two other men.

Sensing danger, el-Erian, who Amir had given the room number to in that they thought they might meet for lunch, ran to a house phone in the lobby. He had Amir on the line in an instant. In an excited state, he conveyed every word he had heard. He hardly finished before Amir hung up.

Rushing down the stairwell, eight stories, with nothing but the clothes they were wearing, the twosome caught a cab and disappeared into the tangle of Cairo's congested city streets.

This time as Amir reached back to pull his sister along with him, there was no smugness or smirking. They went immediately to the train station and bought tickets to travel further south.

Goodbye Cairo.

It wasn't long before Amir began to worry that the troubles they were facing exceeded any mischief the Palestinian Authority could stir up. He made several calls, including to Jawiris. Unable to contact his mentor, he reached out to others in Egypt he knew would help.

It was determined that they would make a stop in Asyut before being smuggled out of Egypt. This modern city, located approximately midway into Egypt, was the perfect place for a pit stop. It was not only home to an educated Copt population but also some of the more fundamentalist radical Muslims—new identities could be purchased and travel plans covertly arranged for their departure.

Only a handful of the population of Egypt lives more than a few miles from the Nile River, the largest flowing waterway in the world. The cities of Egypt built on its banks are flooded with millions of people dependent on the river to fill their lungs with the essential ingredients for life. These populated centers serve much like a myelin sheath to the axon of a human neuron, insulating and protecting the pulses of liquid life as they creep northward along the giant waterway.

As I studied the area visually, especially the full span of the river, increasingly elements reminding me of human anatomy came into my mind. Like the dendrites of the human neuron, the two arms of the Nile stretch mightily south and east. By far the greatest eastern tributary begins at Lake Tana in the highlands of Ethiopia, where a tight-fingered hand paddles fast-flowing water along what is called the Blue Nile.

The phalanges of the other upper extremity, reaching southerly half way into Africa, channel waters from still undiscovered sources. But the White Nile, as it has been named, eventually begins to gently glide along a path through Tanzania to Lake Victoria and past Uganda and South Sudan before the powerful currents of both siblings (the Blue and White Niles) join to thread like nerves through the center of a series of spinal discs and then move on as partners up to Lake Nasser. That giant pool is like a mouth of a whale in Upper Egypt, swallowing water, filtering it through its baleen, and then gushing it out so it can drive northward to the Aswan Dam.

From there, like the esophagus channels food and liquid to the abdomen, the main axon of the river now drifts through Egypt. It seems in no hurry to complete its journey, which ends with the two lower members splitting at the groin and then sprawling lazily as distributaries to nourish the Mediterranean, the Rosetta leg to the west and the Damietta to the east of the giant Nile Delta.

As an award-winning specimen of nature's colossi, the Nile River was undoubtedly the elemental ingredient serving to nurture a once great Egyptian civilization.

Moving counter-current, the train transporting Amir and Bahlya tugged laboriously to reach the succession of destinations along its path. With each stop, Amir was attaining more frightful and disturbing information. By the time he reached

Asyut, he was aware that all had come to doom. In fact, as he tried to make contact with the financial backers of the scheme and several other key players in the plot, he easily calculated the danger that he was in.

When they disembarked from the train in Asyut, the temperature was extremely hot, and equally humid. Neither Amir nor Bahlya had suitcases but they were each carrying a small knapsack with a few items they had purchased along the way. Amir had pocketed his Patek Philippe watch, and the fine diamond studs he routinely wore on each ear lobe were hidden as well. Bahlya was also toned down. She wore a plain blue burka. There were no signs of the designer clothing she typically paraded in at home. No doubt these had been left in the hotel room in Cairo.

A man named Sayyid el-Adli was waiting for them as they stepped onto the station platform. He was a very slender man in his fifties. His right eye was glass, glowing like a mirror reflection in the bright sunlight. The left cheek was also memorable. It looked like an aerial view of a crater left after a meteor strike had dug deep into the earth's crust. The flesh was darkened frightfully as it caved in toward the core. It was a defect inflicted on him courtesy of the Egyptian military—he had been shot twice in the face.

He was a shy man, the type who needed to warm up to people before he talked, but once he did couldn't stop. Still, his voice always had a tone of prayer. He conversed slowly, each word earning a pause as if it were of divine creation. One communicating with him might wonder if the meaning of the sentences was subordinate to the sounds, his utterances mimicking a communion with god, stating that a theological connection was the higher purpose of human articulation.

The story of his facial abnormality, an unsightly scar he wore as a badge of honor, he disclosed to Amir and Bahlya later that evening while at his home.

"It was 1981. There were tensions between the Coptic Christians and the Muslims...it was nothing new; these people have no faith in anything but money, like the Jews," he expressed contemptuously toward the Coptic sect. "A clash broke out and many people were injured or killed. Sadat's thugs believed we were responsible and they came after us harshly. I was shot for doing nothing," the bitterness in his words not evident by raising his tone but by him elevating from a seated position to continue his account while he walked in a circle unconsciously clenching his mandible.

"Sadat did everything in his power to eliminate us as a force." el-Adli now aimed his true eye at Amir. "A month later Sadat was dead, assassinated. He deserved it."

"There were lots of stories about what happened," Bahlya commented, hoping to entice him to make a disclosure about what really took place in terms of Sadat's murder.

"Yes, we were blamed. Did we do it? My dear, some questions are best left unanswered. We must be grateful that God was just, Allah always brings truth."

When el-Adli showed up at the station earlier that day, on his head was a white gallabieh, the remainder of his body robed in mud-colored clothing matching the surrounding buildings. Without a word spoken, he led them through many blocks lined with apartment buildings that were crammed with humanity. The smell of gas fumes from cars and garbage rotting on the ground commissioned the olfactory gland to wish it could call a strike.

People were densely packed in the maze of narrow passage-ways. Their tan monotone stick figures seemed bundled like bales of hay. As tenacious was the sense of smell to defend against the stench, one couldn't help breathing the exhaled air of a neighbor or feeling their clothing as it brushed another human's arms and hands.

el-Adli was a member of gamaa al-Jihad. It was a group he would later infer might have at least contributed to Sadat's murder, and an association now stamped a terrorist organization by many Western countries. It was also a group that had established some type of informal connection with al-Queda. Most importantly, they could supply Amir and Bahlya with the necessary documents to leave Egypt.

They took a taxi to what was called the northern portion of the city. On the way they passed a few open spaces with garbage piled so high that at a short distance during dawn or dusk the peaks might have been mistaken for mountaintops. Young boys moved like ants carrying to their agents, the collected trash they had picked up from the designated sector of the city they were assigned. As they unloaded their goods, their employer would pull out any materials that could be resold or redeemed at a profit.

The area of the city that el-Adli took them to had for centuries been home to mostly Coptic Christians, the largest Christian population in the Middle East and the largest religious minority in that region. It was also a group suffering oppression and discrimination, especially by fundamental Muslim groups. People like el-Adli held contempt for the Copts. Still, these outcasts had their uses.

The taxi left them off. Again they walked, but this time only a short distance. The air remained scorching to the lungs and the dull and dusty landscape of densely knotted buildings presented nothing to cheer over. The shuffling of human limbs, barking of dogs, and loud voices of vendors and children playing stole quietude as rapaciously as fire breathes air.

The home of Abanoub Hilmi showed no signs of wealth, though he was reputed to be a man of some means. The living room he invited the visitors into had no screens on the windows. Hundreds of flies buzzed so loud they near muted the hum of a single fluorescent light hanging from the ceiling.

In the corner of the room was the kitchen with the appliances old and corroding. Rust had been feasting on the hinges of the refrigerator, slowly eating away at the enamel—the brown color seemed to be drooling down the sides of the door. The floor was covered with dirty carpets, spotted with cigarette burns.

On a small wooden table were several pictures of what were most likely family members. On the wall hung a bas-relief of Jesus Christ. It had a large fracture in the plaster that neatly severed the miraculous saint's left arm at the elbow, what might have been an intentional impressionistic twist if not for the fact it was obvious the piece was cheaply made and no doubt had achieved it's abnormality due to an accident.

Mr. Hilmi, like so many of his fellow Copts, was an educated man, as well as industrious. In addition to the business he ran repairing rail cars as they limped into the station, he specialized in the finer art of forging and creating papers of identity. His work was known to be precise and his clandestine services carefully parceled out by referral only. He worked under the protection of the local Muslim leadership—and at a steep price in terms of payment for the privilege to operate.

"What is it you'll need, sir?" he directly asked Amir.

"Computerized National Identity Cards as citizens of Pakistan, passports and drivers' licenses issued out of Karachi and signed by the provincial police chief," Amir recited like the alphabet.

"The identity cards are no problem," Hilma answered flatly. "Passports and drivers' licenses," he shrugged, "are not so simple."

"Whatever it costs, Mr. Hilma," Amir assured him, "I'll be in your debt."

"How soon do you need it?"

"Tomorrow. We must leave Egypt immediately," Amir disclosed.

"Come at two in the afternoon, my friend," Hilma instructed. "Everything will be in order."

"Good. And the price?" Bahlya queried.

"Twelve thousand pounds (roughly two thousand American dollars)," Hilma answered without a flinch. "These materials are not readily available. I'll be up all night."

"We'll be here tomorrow," Bahlya assured him.

On the way back by cab to the southwestern section of the city where el-Adli lived, the host filled in the details regarding the documents being purchased for the siblings.

"Don't worry about Hilma betraying you. He knows if he does, he'll never see his next birthday. There's a flight leaving tomorrow evening at seven for Karachi. I've already booked two tickets."

"Thank you, Abanoub" Amir said demurely.

Ignoring the mild show of affection, el-Adli continued with the orientation. "You'll be picked up at the airport in Karachi. Arrangements are being made as we speak to get you to a safe house."

"I never imagined this could happen," Amir muttered dolefully. "I feel that I failed Allah."

el-Adli kindly patted Amir on the shoulder.

"You will do great things for our people, for all Muslims, and your Palestinian brothers."

"I hope that I have the opportunity."

"We have God's eternity on our side. We can only win," el-Adli wearily assured them.

That evening Amir surmised how the Israelis and Americans must have twisted Jawiris' hand to call off the operation—it was all about threats to Jawiris' family. Vowing to never be in the position where loved ones would get in the way of his devotion to God, Amir swore to never have children. He also pledged that he would be the architect and agent of the next battle. Before retiring in preparation for a day of travel, he chatted with el-Adli, a discussion that included the above disclosure of how the man's face was damaged.

"You are right, Abanoub. As soon as I get to Pakistan, I'll carry on our work in honor of Jawiris."

The elder man hugged him and left for his room.

His last words before drifting to sleep pertained to me. "Zach betrayed me. He betrayed all of us."

They were sleeping on a thin mat laid on the floor. Hearing his words, Bahlya pounded her fists twice to the ground and sobbed until she feel asleep.

The following evening on Air Arabia flight 2847 a young man in his early thirties, Aban Gurmani, was sitting in the third row. A female about the same age was in the seventeenth row. Her name was Harata Jafuzai. The former was returning home to Karachi, Pakistan after a holiday and the latter from visiting a relative. Both had purchased one-way tickets.

15

THE BIRTHING OF MYTHS

"AFTER THE EMBARRASSMENT OF being confronted with the fact that Jawiris, an Egyptian of high standing, had been the genius of such a heinous plan…one who many of his Egyptian brothers would have endorsed in a blink…" Major General Hazut smirked, "we requested that the Egyptians pay with more than exhortations of regret." Speaking to both Josea and Nasir, he stopped to clarify a point pertaining solely to Nasir. "Danish, you understand all this so I'll speak frankly in your presence."

"I'm not involved in politics," Nasir stated respectfully. "Zach is my wife's son. I have none of the juvenile faith conflicts that have historically fueled violence in this region. My allegiance is to people I love. I want Zach to live…my motivation is simple."

"Okay. I'll go on. We were working very closely with the Americans at this time and they were in a better position to handle the operation in Egypt. The local government lent support. Basically, they gave our partners free reign to locate Amir and then bring him in…we nearly had him in Cairo."

"It was never addressed in the papers that you gave me," Josea interrupted, "how Amir got out of the hotel. I would have always included that type of material in any summary I prepared."

Hazut's head drooped downward, casting a shameful eye toward the tabletop.

"We had them. It was the desk clerk who gave us the lead to figure it out...they left everything except their billfold and purse. After that, as I'll explain, we tracked him like a dog." Hazut's consternation was visible as he looked up at Josea while at the same time he rhythmically hammered his right hand on the wood table to demonstrate his frustration. "But we kept landing a step behind."

Hazut went on to relate that they had no problem finding out that the couple had finally arrived at Asyut, and then were taken under the guardianship of the gamaa al-Jihad. As expected, the latter denied ever having had awareness of either Bahlya or Amir coming to the city. Still, the Israelis easily uncovered the lie.

Two days after Amir and Bahlya departed the city, an Egyptian intelligence officer in that city led them to Mr. Hilma. It was a known fact, one typically ignored by the Egyptian political leadership unless they themselves had need for his services, that Hilma was an expert in matters of creating new identities for prosperous citizens who for one reason or another were, or anticipated they might be, in need of subterfuge. It was assumed that if the couple left Egypt, it had to be out of Asyut in that there was no reference to them anywhere else in Egypt during that time frame.

The Egyptian official and three American agents paid Mr. Hilma a visit. Hazut explained that the man was "persuaded" to disclose the new names Amir and Bahlya were using to travel. Indeed, Hilma had no idea where they were ultimately headed but could convey his efforts to get them out of Egypt and into Pakistan.

As soon as the officials left Hilma, he placed a call to al-Adli, hoping the admission he made under duress would earn him sympathy. A call was placed by al-Adli immediately to Karachi, notifying them that the couple was hot. He frantically warned that both Amir and Bahlya needed to be hustled out of the city under new names. An hour later, he visited Hilma and thanked him for the warning…and then gifted him with a single bullet through his brain.

My once friends had been in Karachi only a couple days before Hilma's fateful disclosure was made. During that timeframe, they had been placed under the security of the Al-Suley Trust. Described as a welfare organization, it did operate a collection of mosques, as well as providing food, medicine, drinking water and clothing to the needy. That was about five percent of their mission. The remainder was to defeat the infidel. The Trust, like so many other similar entities throughout Pakistan, received most of its funding from very wealthy donors in Saudi Arabia.

Pakistan, "Land of the Pure,"—an appellation freely dispensed by wealthy intellectual Muslims from India when independence was granted in 1947—was consecrated at the cost of millions of lives of innocent people at the time living in the region. From its inception, Pakistan marketed itself as an ideological state, most accurately the land of Islam. The mass of ethnic and cultural traditions with the two dozen languages representing distinct geographic regions, are melded together as a nation unique unto itself in so far as its cohesion is based exclusively on religion. The country is often described as a divinity whose intolerance is unsurpassed in any other nation.

The documents reviewed by Josea, ones being referenced by Hazut, referred to the sad reality that the political elite in Pakistan was being supported largely by illegal drug money. Worse, it was an accepted fact that the Pakistanis had a nuclear device, and that their father of nuclear science had sold the secrets to the Iranians. These weapons of mass destruction were only a handshake away from being placed at the discretion of terrorists, making Pakistan the ideal home for Amir.

A metropolitan area with a population of over eighteen million, Karachi is a bustling metropolis, one that adds more residents each year than it had in the 1950's, about 400,000. The tony areas of the massive city mask the depravity and poverty oozing from a landmass that is in size ranked in the top ten urban areas in the world.

It might seem like the ideal place to get lost and not found, but as it turned out it was a better one to be diagnosed with hepatitis for Bahlya—the beginning of chronic illness for Amir's sister. Within a day of getting off the plane, she began running a fever and shortly after that her appetite was waning. Furthermore, when she did eat, she'd experience nausea and bouts of vomiting. In short order, skin rashes were irritating her and her body was aching.

They were brought to the home of Mullah al-Kurdi in the fashionable community of Clinton where he owned two entire floors of a twin tower building facing the Adriatic Sea. That evening the sunset blanketed orange fire over the ocean and sand as the small radiant yellow ball prepared to cloak itself behind the horizon's fortification. On the beach, a man was seen leading his camel through the surf at the speed jelly squeezes from a needle hole, neither man nor beast appearing impressed by nature's show of grace.

Amir had traveled to Karachi on two prior occasions, each time to meet with one of the donors of the project willed by Allah to terminate Israel as a nation, Asif Pervaiz. As the gentlemen fronting the money for Jawiris' plan were identified to Amir, he was initially disillusioned. It seemed as he talked to each, he identified personal gains accounting for their interest in striking Israel. He had hoped they would all share his pure vision of an act ordained by His decree.

Instead, one by one he was told stories of land allegedly confiscated by the Israelis belonging to family that wanted to reclaim it for personal wealth, or perceived acts of dishonor carried out by the Israelis pertaining to business investments for which these men wanted repayment.

Jawiris was aware also that the interests of his financial backers were driven in large part by greed or personal revenge. However, he was a man who understood that God acted in strange ways. As a result, he was more willing than Amir to subordinate his ideological purity to a few hundred million dollars here and there. In fact, he convinced Amir that if these wealthy men were opening their hearts—and pocketbooks—to Allah and behaving in His behalf, that was all that mattered.

Pervaiz, however, was the only one who shared with Amir and Jawiris the dream of The Middle East void of the usurpers. He believed that Israel was a danger to the region and at all cost needed to be deconstructed. He also hated Jews and made no excuses when expressing his prejudice. Amir cared for the man. Coming back to the city where he had dined with Pervaiz and his family saddened him in that by the time he arrived, he was apprised that his co-conspirator had been abducted and then imprisoned by the Israelis.

Mullah al-Kurdi knew Pervaiz well. He also shared the same attitude as Pervaiz regarding the Israeli "problem" and was more than eager to assist Amir, a man who al-Kurdi was certain had been sent by Allah with a divine purpose.

That afternoon while Amir and al-Kurdi took a long walk, a doctor was called to look in on Bahlya. The examination determined she was ill with hepatitis. "No need to worry," was the message given to the patient by the physician. There was no treatment for the transient condition that she likely picked up during the visit to Egypt. In a matter of a few days, the symptoms would lapse into remission and she'd be good as new. In the meantime, she was physically weak and lacking motivation, highly untypical for this energetic woman.

During their outing, Amir and the Mullah moved at a brisk pace, covering a large section of the safe sector of the city. The first resting spot was across from a small roundabout in the middle of a congested intersection of three main roads. Dominating the inside space was a monument reminiscent of the Arc de Triomphe. It is called the Three Swords Monument; a white marble piece is inscribed with the code of the founder of Pakistan, Mohammed Ali Jinnah, Unity, Faith and Discipline.

Each of the three separate pommels anchored the grips, covered by rain guards. Then they each shot giant knife-like blades skyward in identical and parallel position, the view from where the men were seated having the impression of a huge letter "W" with a deep sweeping circular bases. Amir loved to gaze at the trophy. It was not only because the artistry was perfection of form but also because he imagined holding one of the weapons in his hand, whisking the blade to symbolize the Conquest of Mecca brought about by Allah.

The Mullah interrupted his fantasy.

"It's a great honor you have come to help us. Your feats are heroic."

"I had planned to do more but Allah was not ready," Amir expressed with lamentation that al-Kurdi quickly tried to dispel.

"Last night I had a dream. I could hardly wait to tell it to you." al-Kurdi's excitement was evident.

My own research on Islamic culture enlightened me to the fact that dreams are very important to Muslims. They take one of three forms: first truth, then greed or personal desire, and finally evil, the latter coming from the devil. Great

Muslim scholars had studied and written about dreams for centuries, usually cautioning in agreement with Freud that the practice of dream interpretation is usually a messy enterprise, best left with vague "may" statements, rather than absolute conclusions.

Somehow, however, my experience was that in practice the admonitions were carelessly flicked aside, permitting gross examples of wild analytic process—both in The Middle East and West. In the case of the former region, these excursions into the equivalent of Muslim dream casinos could, under the worst of conditions, result in horrid injustices and even death.

Al-Kurdi had a dream, an interpretation, and a guest just beginning to entertain the idea of himself as an apostle of his beloved Allah.

"Amir, you were in my dream. You had wings and as you flew higher and higher, first small, and then large and larger objects like bullets were shooting toward you. But each time your beak would open and with great breathes you would blow away the projectiles.

"Each of the missiles fell to the ground, littering the earth like a huge graveyard. Then you dove down and as you passed over the piles of fallen material you emitted heat, thousands of degrees; everything on the ground melted and dissolved into the earth. Not until the soil was clear did you land, perching yourself on the top of a date palm tree.

"Beneath you were clumps of deep purple fruits. In an instant, they ripened to dates the size of softballs. You looked at them and then you flew away, high in the sky until you disappeared."

Amir said nothing, imbibing the nectar of what he sensed was a prophetic reverie.

"It's a dream of rahmani (truth). Jawiris—and I hear many others—have been taken by the infidel, but you alone Amir are free. Allah has chosen you to melt away the enemy's weapons and nurture the fruit of our people," al-Kurdi concluded.

"I will do as He has ordered," Amir reverently bowed.

"May I ask you, Amir, what happened? What was it that you and Jawiris were planning?"

"When Allah is ready you will know. What was done will not be in vain," Amir assured him.

al-Kurdi's interpretation of the dream may have been accurate. The only problem was that it was his dream, a creation as likely reflecting his personal wish for the arrival of a symbolic leader that would return glory to the Middle East.

Ah, but the dream was the beginning step in the making of a myth, a phenomenon whereby legends are born bigger than the reality they lived. Typically these iconic figures are conjured from the waiting wick of wishes never bound to— nor answering to—truth, but always expected to grow larger and larger.

The myth of Amir Hamdallah was still in the chrysalis stage, snug in its cocoon, but destined to evolve into a full blooming iron butterfly. Ironically, had any of the individuals who ordained him to such lofty status known of his aversion to straight love, they would have gladly performed the Israeli's wish, and after severing his head used it to practice kicking extra points for football games.

Fortunately for our blooming hero, the only one who could betray his sexual preference was a young lady unlikely to have any knowledge as to how Amir's life was unfolding, and even if she did, wouldn't have risked the consequence of disclosure: expressing what she knew would have earned her a severe punishment for betraying a male.

For the remainder of the afternoon, Amir and al-Kurdi enjoyed the beautiful weather as they ambled through Jehangir Park, and beyond, nearing the center of Karachi, a full seven miles from al-Kurdi's home. They then turned to head back.

Bahlya was sleeping, alarming Amir who had never seen her ill. By contrast, he had always marveled at her inexhaustible energy. Nevertheless, after al-Kurdi's wife explained the doctor's diagnosis and treatment plan composed of "lots of rest," Amir eased into a comfort zone. It was one that would prove to be narrower than a pencil and shorter than the arc in a boys' pissing contest.

The two men where having tea when al-Kurdi's right hand man (al-Kurdi was left handed, as was his "right-hand man," but the boss insisted on the right-handed title for Kamal Akbot to avoid the implication of gaucheness) dashed into the room. He asked if he might have a moment with the Mullah alone. al-Kurdi sensed trouble and quickly followed his assistant.

"Your guests have been uncovered. A call came in from Egypt saying that a loose end was handed to the Americans and they now know the names being used by the couple and where they went after leaving Egypt. They must be moved immediately, out of Karachi."

The dogged pursuit by the Americans and Israelis served to magnify for al-Kurdi the stature of Amir, and to convince him that his dream was of oracular pronouncement.

"Plans are being made now for their safe passage. They are being picked up within the hour," Kamal notified his employer.

The "right-hand-man" opened the door using his left hand for al-Kurdi to go back to his guest and inform Amir—he dismissed himself with a swift deep forward bow. He would never see Amir or Bahlya again. However, this loyal assistant to a man known to be part of a fist-sized collection of individuals in Pakistan wielding the greatest power and influence would be monitoring their movement and play a crucial role in their lives.

Kamal, the left-handed right-hand man stood about five foot eleven and was slender as a stick. His pious face was perpetually in atonement for wrongdoing he had never performed...but believed he had—a condition legitimizing the worst of punishment under the cruelest of masters, oneself.

He was a Sunni Muslim, by far the largest group of his religion with the authority of the Sunnis coming from the Wahhab family in Saudi Arabia. It so happened that this meek and fragile young man passing his twenty-fifth birthday two months before, was a Wahhab heir which was a birthright that guaranteed him respect from even the most esteemed Muslims—bin Laden and Al-Qaeda also share Wahhab roots.

His skin was boyish, having a thin and pure tone. The eyes were small, with long dark lashes that flicked as he unconsciously obeyed a nervous habit of blinking. He wore his hair short but it was straight and long enough to fall naturally in perfect order to the right side.

For reasons only Amir might be able to expound on, Kamal reminded him of his murdered lover, Faisal Alwari, a man sharing none of the delicacy and tenderness seen in al-Kurdi's assistant.

He was schooled at the finest educational facilities in Riyadh. Always proving himself to be a bright pupil at the top of his class, he memorized most of the Holy Qur'an before he would have been Bar Mitzvah had he been born Jewish. As his education continued, he was instructed on how all authority was vested in God and in order to serve he would have to follow the same path of bin Laden and so many others who had turned to jihad.

His father, a Sheikh, early on anticipated great things from his only son. Sadly, it was not long into the boy's development that his father recognized a jagged fault line running through little Kamal's temperament. It unnerved the Sheikh that his son didn't gravitate to sports, and while excelling in the classroom, his social development seemed retarded. He preferred spending time alone and rather than relate to the stronger and larger males in his immediate universe, when in the company of his peers he'd gravitate toward the girls.

His father wrestled with his perceptions, initially trying to repress them but later beginning to assault the boy with insults and ridicule. The son couldn't imagine what he had done to fall into disfavor with the man he loved and wanted nothing more from than a return of affection.

By the time he was eighteen, he had embraced Islam as his faith. He had thrust himself toward a jihadist mission. He prayed five times a day and followed the most rigorous devotion to his faith. He even manufactured a male persona, dedicating himself to the study of terror. He found that he could compete with his peers in terms of executing acts of violence. Better still, his powerful will permitted him to exceed most of them.

He obediently committed any acts that were ordered by his superiors. Even then, however, his father eyed him with suspicion. But within the terrorist organization, he earned respect, and that along with his standing as the son of a Wahhab Sheikh finally landed him the position as second to al-Kurdi.

It was not long after his assignment with al-Kurdi began that he fell in love. By chance, a new houseboy arrived not long after Kamal took his assignment. He was a wiry, frail boy of fifteen. Kamal imagined staring in the mirror and seeing the boy's reflection glancing back at him. He thought that young Aban was his perfect likeness. His face was innocent and sweet. Kamal began to have fantasies of them together.

They both knew that when they were in the other's presence they could think of nothing but the warmth they imagined they would experience wrapping their limbs around one another.

The amorous attraction between them was never consummated in a carnal love, but still warranted severe punishment in Kamal's mind. The entranced state he found himself in while sharing the company of Aban left him feeling as unworthy as if he had taken the young boy to his lips.

The trust that did develop between the two, allowed Aban to admit to Kamal he was inclined toward gay love, something he knew would endanger his life if it were to ever come out. In return, Kamal—who was never willing to admit his lust for males—confirmed for Aban that his life was a sham, that he hated his father, that he hated al-Kurdi for his complicity with the Pakistani government that proclaimed itself a partner with America in the eradication of terror, that he hated the acts of violence and cruelty he had committed and was rewarded for, that he hated the wholesale intentional killing of innocent people he witnessed innumerable times on the part of his fellow Muslims and that he hated all acts of evil carried out in the name of Allah. Kamal final disclosure to his friend was that he had at last found peace in his declaration that Allah represented love, and love alone.

It was in this mixed up and possibly lethal state of mind that young Kamal found himself when Amir arrived. Amir was being groomed for a top leadership role with the Muslims. To Kamal, this new player was just another radical jihadist with no interest in life other than destruction and death.

Money would have never lured Kamal to commit treason. But the conversion away from jihadist radicalism that had been steaming through his veins for some time was the perfect condition for treachery. Thus, when he was approached one afternoon while sipping tea at a local café, he was fruit-falling-off-a-tree ripe to hear a message with a purpose of higher Godliness than what he had seen himself living over the past few years.

Abu Mazari, a Pakistani, was a spy. In his forties, he had long before renounced devotion to any god but money. His fortune came in hundreds of thousands of dollars paid by the CIA. The services he performed varied but were known to the Americans to include everything from assassination to extortion to theft. In this case, the assignment was to snoop and to see if by chance there was a crack in the Karachi elite network protecting Amir and Bahlya.

It was a known fact that a harsh or cruel employer might alienate a person to betray a secret overheard in their household or office, that a falling out of faith, love, health or finances might incline a person to divulge information for a price, or that the thrill of operating as a sleuth might entice a person to hand over data of value to a third party.

Individuals gathering information for pay were wise to the fact that human beings were common animals, all with the same drives regardless of their tradition, culture or ethnicity. All that was necessary to turn them into traitors or informers was to have the skill to listen. Then one could ascertain what would motivate a person to unthinkable actions, and at what price.

The Americans by this time had tracked Amir and Bahlya to Karachi and also knew that they had been residing with al-Kurdi. However, for the second time, somehow just as the noose was about to snap the desperado's neck, Amir disappeared. It was the warning dispatched from Egypt that resulted in the swift action whereby brother and sister were shuffled out of al-Kurdis home and placed under the protection of another esteemed member of The Trust, Zahid Chutani.

Thus, by the time Abu Mazari, the CIA funded spy, was attempting to set up bribing information from Kamal, Amir and Bahlya had been snuck out of Karachi. They were now on their way with entirely new identities, headed to a more remote, and what they thought was safer, quarter.

Kamal had been sitting alone in the café. Abu scooted over to him, introducing himself. Kamal must have been in a sour mood because he carelessly expressed his sentiments to a stranger. Abu would later comment to his superior that he could have never imagined how easy it would be to earn his money.

He typically carried a recording device when engaging in this type of operation, mainly so that in the event he thought he might have overlooked something in the exchange that might be of value, he could listen a second time. The taped conversation was included in the file that Josea reviewed. A portion of the transcript that took place after Abu had been able to establish a rapport with Kamal is shown below.

"I had the same experience as you, Kamal," Abu confided. "Many of our jihad fighters are earnest in their faith but they are led by men who are corrupted. As a result, many fine men are forced to defile their love of Allah."

"Allah is love!" Kamal proclaimed as if he were the first man to discover fragrance.

"What can we do to express our devotion to God?" Abu innocently asked. "How can simple people like us who see truth do something to stop hate?"

"What if we could stop evil from happening, and do that without committing violence ourselves?" Kamal questioned. "Is there a way, praise to Allah, to do it?"

"Only if we know what hateful people are planning and we…it sounds extreme, but could we report these acts before anyone is harmed?"

"To whom?" Kamal eagerly asked. "Who can stop terror? Who can neutralize the force of violence?"

"I know people who could but I have nothing to offer them," Abu gestured his impotence with a slow wiggle of the right index finger.

"I do! I have much to offer," Kamal volunteered.

The young traitor first oozed the already known fact that Amir and Bahlya had been guests of the prominent al-Kurdi. Then Kamal flowed with new information. He offered that the twosome was now traveling under the names of Imran Durrani and Abida Qalat. They had been flown out on a private jet to Islamabad and then were headed to a yet undisclosed camp. At the time, he had information confirming that they were traveling along the Karakoram Highway. He assumed al-Kurdi would be kept abreast of their journey. Kamal offered to meet again with Abu with the express purpose of updating his new friend on further details regarding Amir's whereabouts.

The information was invaluable to the Israelis and Americans. They had drawn a circle encapsulating the possible geographic area where Amir might be found. They could now begin shrinking the size of the landmass they were exploring.

There would be several ensuing short chats between Kamal and Abu during which time a final destination for the couple would finally be confirmed. By then, a plan would have been set in motion that was to be operated by the Americans. It was hoped that at last they would bring justice to a man doggedly pursuing destruction to his perceived enemies, Israel and America.

Once Abu had sucked from Kamal the essential information to hone in on Amir, the young man would have no further role to play in the drama. He discovered that fact when to his surprise, Abu failed to show up for any future meetings. Kamal gave the loss little attention. At the time, he was in too much emotional pain, a consequence of an unquenchable thirst for male love, a satisfaction he knew could never be realized—out of desperation, he turned to technology, specifically the internet.

It was a pathetic choice for Kamal. He was using sites that were being monitored by the government. As a result, ironically, it was not the gross crime of treason that would be punished, but one equally serious, homosexuality. When the young man's solicitations were brought to the attention of the authorities, Kamal was arrested under the most unsympathetic circumstances. Referred to as a "sick faggot" he was roughed up on the spot by government officials at the home of al-Kurdi.

Had it not been for the fact that his employer was aware of his esteemed status as an heir of the Wahhad family, he might not have survived the evening with the local police. Instead of the more severe treatment that another of lesser standing would have been awarded, he was shipped back to Saudi Arabia where his father, disgraced and shamed, placed the confused son in a special rehabilitation facility.

Two years later he emerged. The institute declared Kamal to have successfully converted to a straight lifestyle. His father then arranged a marriage to be sure that the treatment was effective. He was with his wife all of two weeks, before he disappeared. A week after that, he showed up in San Francisco's Castro District.

Due to the service that he unwittingly provided to the Americans (sedition that would never be discovered or suspected by his employer or the Pakistanis), as well as the wealth he brought with him (over fifty million dollars), he was permitted to stay in the United States. Tragically, he was never able to do more than fantasize the lust he yearned to share with another man—Kamal Akbot would remain loyal to the one love that he knew was pure, the praise of Allah.

I had one question that I would have loved to ask Kamal. "What happened on your wedding night?"

16

ON THE ROAD AGAIN

AS THIS INFORMATION PERTAINING to Amir was being fed to me, I sat home deliberating how and when my life was to be terminated. It was apparent to me that Amir's journey had placed him in Pakistan, and that it was from there he was likely directing his jihad against America and me.

Knowing little about the country, I thought I'd begin by studying the geography. I grabbed my atlas and opened it to the page on Pakistan...then I swallowed. As I gazed at its shape, an ominous image shot out, the drawing of a dragon.

Was it a joke?

Was my imagination playing a game? I'm sure others might have perceived in the outline of the country the figure of a duck...or Santa? Not me.

The northern part of the country formed a head with the snout jutting into China and India. Through the olfactory organ, it appeared to be sucking in fresh air while poised to exhale blasts of fire, especially into the highly contested, and gorgeous, Kashmir area, a region considered more combustible than a drought-suffering forest. Then as I focused on the city of Gilget, the location I was soon to learn was next on Amir's journey, it stood out as the country's right eye—convincing me that I was looking at a prophetic image.

Further scanning the outline of Pakistan, I noticed that their new capital, Islamabad, was positioned close to where one would expect to find the Adam's Apple. From there, the chest thrust forward with bravado, now into the belly of its worst enemy, India. Its spine was concave, the weight of Afghanistan bearing down mightily on the long bony structure. Finally, the tail had two wings, both knifing into Iran, the upper to grab near worthless desert and the lower greater access to the Arabian Sea.

The atlas imagery I stared at froze my senses, leaving me woeful that I had undertaken the exercise of edifying myself further on Pakistan. I slammed the book shut, tossing it aside. I had enough to worry about without feeding feasts of serpent tail chimera to an imagination famished for a mental beating.

*****

The plan to secure Amir and Bahlya out of Karachi was handed over to a man named Zahid Chutani. He was in his fifties, a remarkable achievement for a gentleman who was a career terrorist for Islam. During his three decades of service, he had established his reputation not solely through faith, but faith fortified with brutal force, unconscionable ruthlessness, and irrepressible revenge.

He had early in his study of religion imbibed the incompatibility of Western values and Islam. Muslims were devout only to Allah, and were expected to sublimate personal drives and needs reflecting individual identity or ideology. Each person was to dissolve their sense of self like crystals of sugar in a glass of hot water, the sweetness of the whole of Muslims praying to Allah the highest order of man.

The contrary belief in freedom, personal achievement and individual potentiation was perceived to be a seductress cloaked by the marketers of Western values in racy movies and song lyrics, unhealthful food, and movements to promote the rights of women, gays, animals, the disabled, pregnant women seeking free choice to abort, and any other group collecting themselves into a mass with a voice.

It was war. Not the type where people shoot each other on a battlefield. This was a war where geographic terrain was subordinated to the tissue of the mind. Allah was speaking truth to the people of Islam but the infidel was busy trying to pervert the Muslim population for no purpose other than to convert more souls to the enterprises of capitalism.

McDonalds, Starbucks, IBM, Goldman Sacks, Caterpillar, Procter and Gamble—and hundreds of others were symptoms of a sick culture trying to infect healthy beings. The sight of any of these pillars of perversity was cause for jihad, to strike at the heart of the enemy—at their wallets.

No doubt a powerful warrior at some early point in his career, Zahid's physique had begun to deteriorate. In truth, his entire body presentation was a shadow of the frightful figure he had once paraded menacingly in front of peers. His six-foot height had lost at least two inches during the past few years and his white hair was dry and covered with tiny specks of dandruff.

Still, he was a bright man who had been called upon many times in his service to Allah to protect important people. In this case it was his decision to book two separate flights, one for the couple under the names they assumed after leaving Egypt and the other using the new names they had just acquired. Furthermore, the couple out of Egypt would allegedly fly to Rawalpindi, near the new capital of Pakistan, Islamabad— Zahid had arranged for shells to fill the seats of the absent Amir and Bahlya, who would instead be on a flight to Peshawar.

Once in Peshawar, Zahid rented a jeep, stopping in the city only long enough to purchase provisions for the journey. It was late afternoon and the sky was beginning to darken before they were ready to leave. They were set to travel eastward along what is called the Grand Trunk Road, headed in the direction of Islamabad. Zahid decided it prudent to stop and camp off the road.

First, he was fearful that resting the night at a hotel might draw unnecessary attention to the threesome. Second, he knew this region of the country well and understood that it was not the volume of trucks and passenger vehicles that made this a treacherous strip of road, earning the reputation of a "suicidal highway." Instead, the famous designation was the result of people living and working along the roadway always being in a great hurry, traveling at obscenely dangerous speeds. They were also prone to test the nerve of other travelers by passing, dodging and weaving through traffic like figures on a computerized game board. The number of deaths on this road was unpublished but everyone was aware that if they had a few extra bucks and wanted to go into business, a hearse service was a sure winner.

They slept poorly, Bahlya moaning through the night. Unfortunately, she'd had insufficient time to begin a recovery from the illness that began in Karachi—weak and feverish, she was rushed off to the airport. By morning, she was physically depleted, forcing Zahid to make a dangerous deviation in a plan he had settled on before leaving Karachi. He hadn't revealed to anyone other than al-Kurdi where he was headed—a practice in caution and secrecy he adhered to in the same fashion as his daily prayer.

It was only a couple hours driving time to Islamabad. Zahid determined that he needed to take Bahlya to a doctor. He knew no medical people in the city. Assuming one was as good as another, he pulled into a parking area in front of an office building. It turned out the whole facility was medical so he randomly selected one of the suites, going into the office first to make sure the doctor was in, and then informing him that it was urgent and they needed his consultation without delay.

The physician agreed. After the examination was complete, his diagnosis was similar to the doctor in Karachi. He did offer a suggestion, however. If Bahlya felt uncomfortable she could use Tylenol. "A couple days and you should be fine," was the doctor's verdict.

From Islamabad they headed north on Highway 15 before continuing in the same direction on Highway 35. They were headed toward Karimabad, but that was not their final destination nor would they be able to reach the city that day. The driving time varied depending on the condition of the road and the journey might take up to 24 hours.

The potential problems along the road were not traffic or construction. Rather, they headed northward into a region of unparalleled geologic instability, a zone where radical shifts of the earth's crust were unceasing. These titanic forces of the earth's plates crushed, pounded and pressed such that they were over the course of millions of years responsible for the emergence of the vast and immense peaks of the three nearby mountain ranges, the Himalayas, the Hindukush and the Karakoram, monsters of nature still hiccupping surges of energy pushing upward.

These convulsions might at any time send boulders downward, pellet vehicles with small rocks, shower particles of debris blinding to the driver, or cause avalanches, mud or landslides—all this the travelers might encounter yet they were still on the periphery of a more precarious area. It was quite a distance from where they were travelling, yet where they were ultimately headed, the Karakoram Highway. On that stretch of roadway, they were sure to face glacial masses moving not by feet or inches per day, but sixteenths, eighths or quarter miles in a twenty-four hour period.

That day the trip to Karimabad was slow, forcing Zahid to stop and set up camp about two-thirds of the way towards their destination. Bahlya had always avoided drugs but under the circumstance of her illness she relented to use the over-the-counter remedy. It helped. As soon as she took a dose, she perked up a notch, but she still lacked appetite and energy. She slept more peacefully, taking additional pills during the night. By the next morning, Amir assumed the worst was past.

That day they successfully reached Karimabad. To their right was the over 25,000-foot Rakaposhi Mountain, a massive sight of white. This colossus is so magnificent that it was easily visible to the naked eye a hundred miles away. Zahid couldn't resist pulling off the road and parking to sightsee. This was his land, the earth of his family and friends, and Rakaposhi ruled as its benevolent master, ethereal, pristine and elegant, but uncompromising and, if necessary, punishing.

"I remember as a boy," Zahid recounted as if in a reverie, "the Mother of Mist (name given by locals to Rakaposhi) was angered. A girl in our village had been raped, an act so vile we had no word to describe it. That mountain shook for days, coughing one breath followed by another of freezing air and dew, blanketing us ceaselessly, terrorizing and tormenting us until the perpetrator of the crime confessed."

"You were a young boy, Zahid," Bahlya retorted. "A child's imagination can play tricks with reality," she reminded him, but without the seduction she commonly employed in safer company.

Zahid took offense. "So you deny Allah works miracles, speaks to us through the land, sea and sky?"

"No, I am devout to our God as you." Bahlya, feeling a bit spunky answered with a chuckle. "I can't apologize if my faith leans toward rationalism at times."

Zahid was an educated man, being sent to school in Karachi as a child and later training for two years at the Pakistani Military Academy in Kukuk, not far from his home. His philosophical course work was limited to Islamic study. This contrasted with the higher education attained by Bahlya, who studied abroad at the London School of Economics—she would brag that coercing her father to send her to university was a greater challenge than graduation, a feat she accomplished with honors.

To Zahid, her disclosure was repugnant. He felt compelled to reprove her.

"A lot of effort is being devoted to keeping you safe. Allah is lenient with you, but I wouldn't test his generosity."

Bahlya knew their lives were in this man's hands. She had listened carefully along the way to his exhortations of terrorist acts, recognizing him as a dangerous and volatile type. He spoke openly of working his way through the ranks, insisting in spite of his education that no privilege was ever granted to him.

He listed among his occupations cleaning bathrooms and shoveling human dung, making explosives, assassinating traitors, planting bombs, cutting the throats of infidels— "hundreds, perhaps thousands, if you want to know the truth," he conveyed with no vanity.

She easily calculated that the humiliation she would inflict on him by arguing to his ignorance was a fool's gesture—

wisely, she went mute rather than attempt to explain further her position on irrationality muddying the interpretation of Allah. It was the right move. Zahid would have never shared with her the conflicts and tensions that had recently compelled him along a new path of faith, one he saw as an evolving face on the Islamic panorama, a fledging movement shrouded by the religious shield of the majority of fighters intent on inflicting terror in the service of Allah. His disclosure would be to Amir, but not for some time.

When they started up again, Zahid informed them that it was only another two or three hours of motoring before reaching Gilgit. However, while it was Zahid's intention to venture further north, he also mentioned to his guests that after fueling the vehicle he would first be heading south, the detour necessitated by him needing to pick up another man. He referred to him only by his nickname, Eppy.

Zahid knew the areas well but had not worked there for a couple years. Eppy, on the other hand, was in direct contact with many people in the region. It was Zahid's goal to deposit Amir and Bahlya at a unique and safe site, but he could not gain entrance to without Eppy.

By this time, Zahid assumed that the Americans and Israelis would be threatening and intimidating people in Islamabad to get a clue as to the whereabouts of Aban Gurmani and Harata Jafuzai, the names used when they exited Egypt. He trusted that the new identities of the couple, Imran Durrani and Abida Qalat, would hold up for some time, and with prudence, permanently. Once exhausted from one failure after another to locate Aban Burmani and Harata

Jafuzai in Islamabad, he was sure the enemy would shift their search to Afghanistan, particularly to the safe Tora Bora area that had sheltered bin Laden for so many years.

"We go now to the Hunza Valley," Zahid announced like a tour guide. "Have either of you been there?"

Both Bahlya and Amir motioned they had not, allowing Zahid to proudly provide a lecture he wouldn't have passed up even had they responded affirmatively.

"I vacationed here with my family as a child. Look!" He shouted as his body shot upward in reverence. "Those gigantic peaks to the east are beautiful, are they not?" Both smiled in agreement, allowing Zahid to continue. "But notice which one is still dominating the landscape."

"Yes, it's amazing," Amir responded in awe. "Rakaposhi is like a momma bear."

"No matter where you are, her shadow and light will intimidate you. I urge you to try to escape her watchful eye," he challenged with a boastful laugh. "She never releases her subjects. She is a marvelous feat of nature and exists as a perch for our God to sit and rule."

Amir noticed all the mountain peaks, each rising well over twenty thousand-feet, seemed to collapse at the base, dramatically yielding from pure white to verdant greens within the measure of a yardstick. The valley then took command, enriching man with a fertile surface upon which to work, play and dream.

"This is an area, young people, where you can be protected, where the local population is cooperative with those seen as friends. Nobody can approach us in this valley without being detected, and strangers are not encouraged to trespass," Zahid added. "And that goes for the whole region. But where we are going is an even more secured area where nobody is permitted to enter without authorization, right, Eppy?"

The man didn't reply. In fact, he never said a word during the entire trip, a behavior in no way diminishing him in Zahid's esteem. Eppy was the authority needed to enter a world intentionally missing from promotional materials used to lure tourists. They were headed toward an inner sanctum that no vacationer would care to visit.

They drove another two hours, Bahlya twice having to get out of the car to do a bowel movement, not announcing to the all male cast of characters accompanying her that she was now suffering diarrhea. It seemed that every three to four hours she'd take Tylenol, being relieved for only brief periods before her illness would stick its tongue out in a tease, whipsawing her into an even more severe state.

In a flash, her energy level would dip like a gas gauge whose tank was being siphoned by a thief. The undulation of her symptoms kept the party constantly unnerved—none knew that while the dual identical diagnoses were correct, both doctors had been too eager to accept the first condition as a full explanation, careless in that an obvious simultaneous, and more pernicious, disease was never considered—she was suffering from a secondary kidney infection, one that if untreated might lead to abscess, Septicemia, and possibly death.

Along the way, she would want to die. But I knew Bahlya to be as tough a lady, physically and mentally, as any. Her otherwise healthy constitution would have eventually conquered the invader, and she was just showing signs of rising from the death ward when another far more lethal assault challenged her.

In spite of her weakened condition, the group was at last traveling the final leg of the journey, headed to one of the few terrorist camps in northern Pakistan. It was a most unusual place, more a campus than camp, yet a more virulent facility than probably any on earth. You'd never know it going in. It looked so innocent, like…

17

CAMP APRICOT

THE JEEP FINALLY TURNED on to a dirt road, hardly wider than the vehicle. Thick, lush shrubs canopied the path. Two hundred yards past the entrance was a gate, a lone guard droopily coming out of a kiosk to greet the visitors. Eppy jumped out of the car and walked up to the man, who instantaneously recognized him. They exchanged a few words. Eppy re-entered the vehicle and it proceeded.

The next mile presented gradually rising hillsides, left and right, as far as the eye could see. Doting the space were trees with pink shading similar to cherry blossoms. They were standing at ease, the branches, like college kids, enjoying the aftereffects of a few too many beers or a smoke of forbidden leaves; the currents of warm air appeared to relax the blooms.

The landscape then opened to a couple miles of neatly planted orchards, the dark green leaves sharing the branches with tiny brown swollen buds in an infantile state of growth. The valley then sharply narrowed, the walls of two high rock formations sternly herding the trees to a halt. It was within this pass, that several structures had been constructed.

"This you will find to be like no other terrorist camp in Pakistan," Zahid laughed. "It trains no terrorist."

"I don't understand," Amir retorted irascibly, his mood suffering from the long journey and worry about his sister. "I know we need protection but I have work to do. What is this, a fruit garden?"

Zahid was in the mood for humor, his chuckling turning to bellowing.

"It is exactly as you said, a fruit garden." Zahid slowed his speech to articulate each word. "The proud owners of this farm raise apricots; we believe they're the sweetest in the world."

"That should frighten the enemy. We'll get them inebriated on sweets and then kill them." Amir's sarcasm attested to his single-minded determination to bring horror to his foe.

Zahid couldn't stop the funnies. Eppy was still not talking but a broad smirk across his face was testimony to the fact he was delighting in the same thoughts as Zahid.

"You'll be very happy when you get to know the true nature of this enterprise. In the meantime, both of you have to get settled."

"What do you mean, 'true nature'?" Amir questioned impatiently.

"Just that the Apricot Camp is full of surprises."

"If there's anything I detest it's dealing with the unexpected." Amir sneered.

Bahlya took to bed as soon as her quarters were prepared. Her fever would spike to 104 degrees as soon as the medication wore off, leaving her sweating and listless. There were no women at the camp and she was left alone, except for Amir who was faithfully looking after her.

Following two days of instruction by others at the camp, specifically teaching him what the bud-bursts on the orchard trees was going to look like, Amir became irate. More to his consternation was that Zahid initially evaded him, then outright disappeared. Boredom then set in, which coupled with Bahlya's worsening condition, didn't ease the tension.

When Zahid did finally show up, Amir was ready for a showdown.

"Where have you been?" Amir demanded.

"I took Eppy back to his home."

"We need a doctor to come and see my sister," Amir barked at him.

"I'll look into it," Zahid responded as he walked off unfazed by Amir's anger.

The following day brought bad news. Zahid was informed that a leak—owing to Kamal—of undiscovered origin had compromised the identity of Amir and Bahlya. The ISI, the Pakistani Inter-Services Intelligence—the country's powerful security agency—secretly cooperating with The Trust responsible for Amir and Bahlya's safety—an entity known to be terrorist—had reported that the Americans were requesting assistance in locating a male and female traveling under the names of Imran Durrani and Abida Qalat.

It was related as an urgent matter. The level of "demand" by the Americans ranked not a sliver less than that for any other subjects on their list of wanted terrorists. Before the American's petition could be assigned to a lackey officer who would run them around in circles, the ranking Pakistani general who had first been contacted took it upon himself (after receiving an advance token of appreciation) to report that they had flown to Peshawar.

That would have been as far as the Pakistani officer could assist them had it not been for the fortuitous illness of Bahlya requiring medical evaluation in Islamabad. While examining the woman at his office, the doctor casually asked her name, which she reported as Abida Qalat.

It was Kamal during one of his sessions with the spy Mazari who mentioned that Bahlya had been ill and a physician called to treat her. The Americans embraced this potentially insignificant piece of information, passing along to The General that at some point in their travel in northern Pakistan, medical services may have been requested.

The instincts of the doctor who evaluated Bahlya raised suspicions, but it was due to the gruff and demanding attitude of Zahid that his mistrust was further elevated. Taking no chances that the matter could come back to him with negative repercussions, and motivated to act as a good citizen, the physician reported both to the local medical bureau and the police that he had seen a woman who might have been a foreigner traveling under illegal or questionable circumstances. It took all of two seconds for The General to make a match on the name, Abida Qulat.

There was additional information provided that was potentially more damaging, although Zahid would never know this fact. The same doctor eyed Zahid and Bahlya into the parking lot, witnessing them getting into a jeep with another man, who of course was Amir. He jotted down the license number.

Even without awareness that the vehicle they were using for travel had been identified, Zahid went into a defensive posture. Thus, when Amir confronted him regarding calling in a doctor for his sister, Zahid flatly and emphatically refused. Further, he chose not to inform Amir regarding the increased danger of him being uncovered. It was Zahid's position that the Americans could still not advance their knowledge of where Amir was being held, especially with them presumably not knowing how they were traveling. Thus, all Zahid needed to do was make arrangements one more time to secure new identities, which he did—these would never be used.

It was on the third day at the camp, when the nature of the facility was first explained to Amir. He had again pestered Zahid with questions and expressed his objection to being "imprisoned" with no understanding how he was to be planning to reach his goal of avenging the injustice served on Jawiris and the other men he had worked with.

"Tomorrow you will begin working in the orchard, Amir," Zahid calmly informed him. "Then, your education will begin."

"Am I being punished? If I have done something wrong in the eyes of Allah, then I will gladly be beaten or killed."

"To the contrary," Zahid said affably, but with a measure of derision. "You are most revered, in a position to lead at the highest level."

"Then what am I doing working with trees?" Amir asked,

still irritated, but more than that nonplussed by the bizarre assignment.

"There are only a handful of people here," Zahid explained. "This farm is the most highly kept secret in our nation. Just a few in the Pakistani military and ISI know of it, and even fewer in the various terror groups. It looks like any of hundreds of apricot tree farms in the region, except the people operating it are the most treasured and respected in our movement. They are all here for one purpose, and they meet regularly to discuss and study how to execute a plan to accomplish their goal."

"What is that, may I ask?"

"Nuclear bombs," Zahid answered matter-a-fact. "As you know, Amir, our country possesses an arsenal of these devastating weapons. The problem has been that our leaders have been accused of timidity, unwillingness to if not use them against our enemies, at least put them in the hands of those with more…guts?"

"The leaders of Pakistan have always been patsies to the Americans," Amir shot out venomously. "This is an accepted truth."

"It's also a false one," Zahid countered. "Later we can talk more on that subject but for now be assured that these leaders you call 'patsies to the Americans' are also making fools of those same Americans, taking billions of dollars to battle the Taliban, al-Queda and the other hundred or so terrorist groups in our country. What they are doing in truth, is sheltering those entities so they can aid in the struggle in

Afghanistan against those same Americans—and also fight the Indian menace to the east."

"So why won't they cooperate in handing over a portion of the weapons? Amor wondered out loud. "They can always claim they were stolen?"

"We're getting ahead of ourselves, Amir, but I'll say for now in answer to your question that there is more money in playing one side against the other than taking one side and sticking with it." Zahid smiled like a knowing mentor tutoring his student. "The Americans seem stupid, do they not?"

"They are stupid," Amir affirmed. "I lived with them, studied at their great university…I know how depraved and ignorant they are."

Zahid was willing to leave Amir for the moment with the view that he understood was comforting to the hero. But he had hopes that further discussion with the young man he wanted to enlighten might be more bountiful in terms of convincing him that there was a lot more to the puzzle than Amir had considered. The younger terrorist, however, was too busy lusting over images of atomic bombs ordered by Allah falling on Israeli and American cities to permit lessons.

"So what we're doing here is scheming to get those weapons, one way or another?"

"Yes. This is more a campus or what the Americans call a 'think tank.' Most of the people here are quite knowledgeable about the workings of our government. Shall we say that a coup is being discussed?" Zahid glanced slyly at Amir.

"Why am I honored, by Allah, to serve with these people?" Amir posed reverently.

"The name Amir Hamdallah has spread throughout the Islamic world. You are considered a great man. Nobody knows what you did or planned to do, but isn't that the stuff of which heroes are made—more rumor than actual deed?"

"So I'm to be a poster boy—"

"Much more than that," Zahid interrupted. "We know you have been involved in operations more extensive than anyone here has participated in. It's your organizational skills, experience...and education that are valued."

For the next two days, Bahlya remained under the domination of an oscillating body temperature, the Tylenol plunges yielding to feverish elevation no different than the outside giant peaks surrendering to valleys and in turn the valleys rising grandly to meet steep ascents. She might get up for a spell, but mostly she was bedridden.

Amir found inspiration working with nature, especially knowing there was a sacred project needing his assistance. He was eager to help the elite group assembled at the farm but at the same time did not lose sight of the fact that he had his own personal agenda, one he had not mentioned to a soul.

It was a new program of terror he had been cradling for some time, a sort of back up plan he left in incubation with the intent of birthing, if things never materialized with the Jawiris project. In fact, all along he had focused his interest on meeting one man.

Having been shipped to Pakistan for protection was just one in a series of god-ordained miracles in that the man he was eager to meet, one his brother-in-law—another of the conspirators now in jail in Israel—had mentioned to him as a brilliant scientist, was presumed to be in Pakistan. It was this gentleman's specialty that stimulated Amir's juices, setting his mind to work on a delicious thought.

18

ZAHID'S CONVERSION

IT WOULD BE TWO days before Zahid would get back to Amir. He had insinuated that he had further material to discuss with him and knew soon he'd have to disclose the need to again move him and Bahlya for their safety. But before he could address that, a new development had taken place, a single grave matter demanding immediate attention—there was bad news from Karachi.

"Amir, I wish I didn't have to be the one to tell you this." The mournful expression alerted Amir that something terrible had happened. "It's about your father".

"What? I just talked to Bahlya about a dream I had last night. My father was bathing in a cool pool near a gentle waterfall. He was repenting to Allah."

"I'm afraid it's worse. Your father had a heart attack three days ago…it was major. He didn't survive it, praise to Allah."

Amir appeared unruffled by the terrible news, acting as if he expected it.

"My father, whom I loved and respected, was an infidel and an atheist," Amir reflected. "He has now been delivered to Allah. The calamity of his life has been redeemed. I feel relieved."

"When will you tell your sister?"

"Not until she feels better—she'll take it hard."

Zahid made no further comment, wanting to provide time for Amir to absorb what he thought would be a shock. But without hesitation, Amir proceeded with the conversation.

"You had other things you wanted to discuss with me?"

"Tell me first, what do you think of this little place?"

"Truthfully, so far it is a bit frustrating. Are you sure we can't get a doctor now? My sister is not getting worse, but she's not getting better either—she's suffering and perhaps something else is wrong or she needs medication."

"I'm going to look into that when we finish." Zahib paused. He was about to take Amir on a journey—it was one Amir would have never anticipated, nor willed, to travel.

Why Zahib chose to reach out to Amir, seemingly the least likely to embrace his message, is a mystery. The older man was reputed to be the most ferocious officer in a vast army of soldiers fighting first for Islam to be the dominant world religion, and second for Pakistan to be the true Islamic state. Did he imagine his high standing would impress Amir, and then because of the younger man's intellect, he would have a receptive ear? Or, could it be speculated that he perceived in Amir the same fires of hate that burned in his soul at the identical age, the blazing odium that resulted in what he now, later in his life, believed was a betrayal to Allah?

Did Zahid believe he could save the sinner? Or might it have been nothing more than a confessional, the man's final attempt to cleanse his soul and achieve forgiveness through an act of giving? That is one question, I regret, which can never be answered—Zahid had been targeted to die.

"Let me emphasize first, Amir, that from the beginning my mission was to give my life for God. The feeling that compelled that quest enslaved me like a debtor to a creditor. No different than the love of a teenager, I lost reason and never looked back," Zahid said, but without a sign of the emotional suffering that in the end was strangling him. "Look at me carefully, Amir. What do you see?"

"A great man who serves Allah."

"Take another look! I'm hardly fifty. After three decades of violence and hatred, my neck is boring downward, exposing me as a pathetic portrait of contrition. I limp, my body aches, and my heart hurts from a spitefully irregular pattern of beating—even after a surgery that nearly took my life. I have one child and I hardly know him. My wife fears me, as does my boy. I'll never live to see a grandchild." Zahid punctuated his regret by looking straight at Amir before proceeding.

"Interrupt any time you wish," he offered but without a response from the intended pupil. "I've found duplicity in the Pakistani leaders. It's not one or two isolated individuals; it's endemic of the whole government. But that's really off the subject; every official of every country is a crook, to one degree or another.

"More to the matter that I want to discuss with you is what I've studied first-hand by serving the highest levels of leadership of our faith. That's right, I've been bodyguard and driver for people as powerful as presidents, and more so. They ordered me to kill, and I killed. They ordered me to train soldiers to fight our enemy, and I trained. They ordered me to blow up a shopping center, and I blew up a shopping center.

"When you are a soldier, you learn that the system breaks down when anyone along the line of command doesn't follow an order. My soldiers followed my instructions or they were removed. If one of my privates even expressed doubt, he was punished. I thought nothing of taking a life to prove to the rest of the group that rules were immutable, and delivered not through man but by God.

"I knew as gospel the ribbon-tied conspiracies perpetrated by the filthy Jews around the world to crusade against Muslims, and I believed if God instructed me—through the word of my emir or general—to avenge them, I was obligated to do so.

"Amir, I was good. I was the best. Am I still the best? Answer that," he tossed to Amir, not as a question but as a confession. He smiled wryly. "Look at me again! I'm assigned child's work now. People who would have sent me on jihad missions ten years ago, now smirk at me."

"If Allah mocks you, you've been a fool." Amir's words were sharp and derisive.

"Agree on that, we do."

"You have lost your way, Zahib."

"Oh, have I? Why don't you permit yourself to hear the rest of my story before you come to a conclusion?"

"In God's presence, I'll sit for your confession," Amir conceded.

"As you wish; then we shall call it a confession," Zahid retorted shamelessly. "It wasn't long ago when my epiphany took place. It wasn't that a novel experience came my way. The breakthrough aspect was that actually I, for the first time, tried to consciously swallow the injustice, indignity, dishonor, deceit, lying, stealing and corruption I had been ignoring for decades.

"There's no point mentioning names. It's the same story over and over regardless of who is the subject. Our Muslim leaders, in charge of our nation, of our mosques, the people who represent Islam to the world, who profess like socialists that nobody is entitled to more than the average man, have two faces; one they wear openly at home and the other they use for masquerading around the world.

"I can tell you this for certain—I've seen with my own eyes the accounts that prove it—that while these people who are trusted to represent our people internationally, who wear robes and preach piously, who speak of death to the infidel, who proclaim to support the destruction of Israel, who vow to destroy the American dream owned by the Jews, who proclaim that we are all equal in the eyes of Allah—those faces our people look to for guidance are flying off to Switzerland, Paris, yes, even to America, and dressing up in Armani suits, lunching in Beverly Hills at Spago, and shopping for jewelry while their wives are in salons and beauty spas.

"Shopping sprees and fancy vacations? Big deal, you say? That is the tip of their cunning and greed. They send the billions they steal to banks in Switzerland or America, send their children to be educated abroad, and buy homes at fancy ski resorts in Europe or on Hawaiian beaches. These gross swine do it all while Zahid Chutani sweeps his prayer mat clean of dust with his lips and then gets up to plant a bomb on a train or bus."

"Zahid, you're admission—"

"Don't interrupt now, Amir. I want you to take it, like the man you are," Zahib raised his voice, but respectfully. "Have I lost my way? Soon you can answer. Sure, I'm angered. I've been used, and it's my own fault. What I have done in the name of God is unforgivable—I'm not looking to be pardoned. I'm not seeking absolution. I know what acts I am responsible for having committed and they are mine alone to own.

"But I found my way at last...and no, I have not lost my devotion or soul! I discovered mine. I am more than ever in the embrace of Allah. Many of us, in the name of God have created hell on earth, but alas I will go to Heaven. I am at peace...and I am free.

"You and your sister are my last act of obedience. I only accepted you as an assignment because of the reputation that has now shrouded you in a cathedral of the divine. My last service to our people is inspired by my wish to raise your consciousness so you might use your newly acquired authority to do good."

Amir sat obediently, though unfazed through the entire expiatory speech. Once he was certain that Zahid had finished he stood up; he was seething. He realized this would be his last conversation with the disgusting man. He was aware that there was no purpose in responding to the substance of Zahid's speech. He did pose a question he had been waiting to ask since he first arrived at the farm.

"Mr. Chutani, do you know a man named Fadi Abbas?"

Dumbfounded by the request, especially in the context of what he had finished sharing with Amir, he could only mindlessly shake his head to let him know that he did know this man.

"Where can I find him," Amir asked flatly.

"Had we stopped in Karimabad when we first arrived, I might have been able to pick up a lead to him. He's not an easy man to reach. He may be in Syria"

Amir's face tightened; the glare in his eyes, the suctioning of his cheeks and the clenching of the forehead could never express the degree of hate he felt for Zahid. His parting words rang out like a school bell signaling a fire drill.

"If I find you here tomorrow morning, I'll kill you with the flesh of my hands."

19

UNDESERVED LUCK

AMIR WAS A PRIVILEGED man. All of his life he had been free to spend money in any way that he wished. He'd never admit he loved the wealth he enjoyed, but he had to. It could buy him almost anything. After his father died, it was like owning an oil field in Saudi Arabia.

One of his first purchases at the Apricot Farm was an afternoon of freedom. Zahid had sequestered Amir on the farm and objected to his early requests to even take a daytrip. Now, disgusted by the man, Amir was hell bent on taking an excursion.

As far as he knew, Imran Durrani had as much importance to the world as any other joker. So, when he bribed one of the staff to sneak him out for a few hours he assumed he was safe. What would have set him in a more prudent frame of mind would have been the awareness that the Americans—still handling the direct search for Amir and Bahlya—with the assistance of the same Pakistani general who for his services was earning a down payment on a flat in London, were hot on Amir's tail.

The jeep used to transport him and Bahlya to the Apricot Camp had been traced to the precise location where he and his sister were now being sheltered. In fact, the famous snitch, Kamal, pouring his sweet heart out to Abu Mazari during their last meeting, confirmed that he had taken updates to al-Kurdi on the fugitives' location.

With certainty that at last a fatal strike could be delivered, the CIA went into action. Operating out of Shamsi airfield in Pakistan, two men were leaning back in their comfortable leather entertainment chairs, each watching two large colored screens on panels in front of them when an order was received.

Both men were wearing headphones and dressed in military uniforms. Their workspace would have made any adolescent think about joining the military. It was not only the screens lighting up like Blu-Ray players but there were several other instruments to be manipulated, plus enough joyous joysticks to whack off for the rest of a teenager's life—and that's a lot of masturbation.

Not only that, the MQ-1 Predator drones flying aloft miles away, scanning the sky and ground below, were carrying Hellfire missiles capable not of mass destruction but enough damage so that anyone on the ground near where one was aimed would definitely think in terms of "mass."

The assignment the two military men had just taken was to implement a full strike on the coordinates coinciding with the area between the two rock formations where Amir and Bahlya were presumed to be hiding. The fascinating scoop here was a point the CIA was oblivious to: they were about to miss their key target but would score an incalculable victory, killing some of the most notorious terrorists operating within Pakistan.

It was only about five in the afternoon but darkness was descending and all personnel at The Apricot Camp were indoors. The tranquility of the moment was interrupted by missile blasts, so intense they not only demolished every structure in the area but they also awakened the already unstable rock walls that nature had left in a not-so-peaceful state for millions of years. As the formations heaved giant boulders atop all matter inanimate and living, they assisted the explosive devices to guarantee there could be no survivors. As the munitions landed the interior ground screeched, sending a shock wave so intense that anyone within miles would swear god had ordered the most severe earthquake the land had experienced.

Testimonials were unnecessary. Viewing the live pictures from the UAV's (unmanned aerial vehicles) rejoiced the operators. The collateral rock damage was like nothing they had seen, causing both of the men to jump out of their seats and high-five one another as if they had just teamed up for the winning touchdown at a frat football game. They eagerly reported their success to their superiors and within an hour a full team of operatives was brought in by helicopters to verify that the intended targets were taken out.

The entire bombsite was in chaos. Owing to darkness, it wasn't until the next morning's sunlight when they would have an answer. As far as they were concerned, there was no chance that anyone had escaped. There was no sign of life, every vehicle was reduced to unrecognizable rubble and the buildings were completely blown to fragments. As the investigation ensued, they found no body parts belonging to Bahlya, but a necklace known to belong to her was located two hundred yards away under a tree—none of the other people present, including Zahid, were identified.

The Israelis breathed a sign of relief. The Americans patted themselves on the back. Amir vowed to turn Israel and America into living hells.

The lucky kitten had no interest in superstition. Cats with nine lives? That was a manifestation of Western thought, the arrogant, profane belief that one could further their time on earth by employing caution disgusted him. He wasn't counting, but I did my arithmetic.

I was certain he had used up at least four just in the space of time up to him sitting alone on a plateau miles away from the destruction where he was peering down on the belching fumes shooting flames from the distant canyon—had he not taken off against Zahid's instruction, it would have been his final resting place.

If I had known him while he was growing up, no doubt there had to have been another two additional lives squandered...at least. What boy during his active years doesn't do something stupid about a thousand times with at a minimum two that would have surely killed him had it not been for some inexplicable and unimaginable circumstance of fortune sparing him?

I had to be conservative in determining that six was as high a number as I could reasonably go. Then nine minus six is three. Okay, three more. The way Amir was living was that so many? It would have felt better if it were nine minus eight, even better still, nine minus nine. Nine would have been like hitting a jackpot—I would have loved it. I never wished anyone dead but...

Amir must have been receiving first aid from angels sent by God. How could he observe a disaster he knew killed his sister—but had to have been aimed at him—and at the same time be digesting the death of his father, and not be crushed? Amir loved his sister. As adults they argued like children but his respect for her was immense. While he never confided in her pertaining to his project with Jawiris, it was Bahlya he typically turned to for advice.

From his perch he sat for hours, first fuming over the senseless killing of his sister, and then realizing that for the first time since leaving Israel he was alone. To make matters worse, the bribed day trip to Karimabad, where he had hoped to find a lead to a man named Fadi Abbas, had been a total failure.

Now as the air temperature cooled and the sky darkened, it dawned on him that he had no place to sleep. In order to inspect the destruction at the Apricot Camp from a higher elevation he had climbed well over five thousand feet above sea level, above the floor of the valley; he needed to descend and then try to find warmth.

It took over two hours before he was able to hike back to the main highway. He noticed when he did that he was close to a fence demarcating a farmhouse. He had seen several helicopters entering and leaving the campground and worried that troops might be patrolling the area looking for him. He reasoned it was too risky to contact the family living in the home, assuming with daylight he would be able to assess the situation more favorably.

He noticed as he studied the area with the aid of the small amount of moonlight filtering through a thin cloud cover that there was a tiny shed about a hundred feet from the main structure where no doubt the farmer and his family made their home. At least it would provide safety from a chance encounter with a deadly creature.

Amir had heard stories of a giant lizard called the Bengal Monitor. This species was known to inhabit the region where he was. While it was near impossible that one would come upon the monster reptile where he was in the valley, the thought terrified him. He believed these huge creatures were venomous (which they are not). Being out alone in the darkness of night, he envisioned two giant lime green eyes closing the distance between him and the monster poised for attack. It was all myth. Still, it served to enhance the irrational fear driving him to risk exploring what he assumed was a storage area for tools.

He approached from the trees to the east, about twenty feet of clearing separating him from the camouflage of the forest and the wooden hut he hoped to borrow for a night. As he crept out in the open, he noticed first that his shoes sunk deep into the moist glacier-fed pastureland. Then as he trudged only a few short steps to grab the door handle that had just come clearly into his sight, he heard a voice.

Had it been from within the main house, a sound of normal volume, he would have rejoiced that the family was enjoying time together. But this was the sound of a human with their tongue trained on the soft palate, talking in a raspy voice, and directly at Amir. The man spoke only the regional dialect of Arabic and Amir could barely understand his words.

"What do you want?" the man who Amir could now see aiming a rifle barrel at his heart shot out at him.

"I need help," Amir carelessly admitted.

"You were at the farm that was attacked today?"

"I had gone out for the afternoon but was headed back when I learned what happened," Amir explained. "My sister was there…she was killed."

"Who brought you?" the man demanded.

Amir had to make a quick choice. Being a stranger, the owner of the house might have decided it best to keep his nose clean and contact the authorities, in which case Amir had no idea what might have happened. If the matter was put in the wrong person's authority, they may have validated Zahid's warning and for a big price sold him handsomely to the Americans—either way, as I learned how the situation unfolded, I felt justified to chalk up another cool cat life lost for Amir.

The only thought Amir could generate while being questioned by the man holding the weapon was to try Eppy's name. "A man named Zahid Chutani brought me, but it was another man named Eppy—"

"Come with me." The man lowered the snout of the weapon and reached out in the near black of night to hug

Amir. "My name is Hamoush. I am the closest neighbor to the Katoosh Apricot orchard. I know Eppy well."

Hamoush then did a strange thing, in an instant he used his hands to cover first his eyes, then his ears and then his mouth, gesturing a little monkey who sees no evil, hears no evil nor speaks evil.

"Are you hungry?"

Amir indicated he was. The man lived in a single story house painted white with what looked like a dark brown trim around the flat roof. The outside shape was rectangular and the walls stone bricks but with a few long planks of wood at the base and below the short eaves.

When they entered, there was no fire burning but the thick walls kept the temperature warm, a relief to Amir who by this time was chattering from near hypothermia. He noticed on the front door as well as interior doors, and on several pieces of furniture, that Swastikas had been carved.

Hamoush recognized that Amir's eyes fixed on the familiar figures.

"Do you know why we employ that symbol?"

"I only recognize it as the Swastika used by Hitler for the Nazis," Amir answered.

"It originates from India, where it was first associated with Hinduism and Buddhism. It was used to represent shakti, you've heard of it?"

"Yes. I've read about it as a primordial cosmic energy... bringing empowerment?"

"Right. We are not Nazis—they were thieves even stealing the symbol," he smirked derisively.

The Swastikas at Hamoush's home differed slightly from the Nazi version in that there were dots in each of the quadrants close to and around the core. They gave the impression that this was a toy to be spun by a child.

There was nothing else remarkable about the home except that it was composed of only a bedroom, living space and bathroom; and that it was warmer than outdoors.

Still shivering, the woman of the house brought a sweater and helped him put it on. She then sat him at the table and proceeded to serve him the remainder of what had been there dinner. The soup, a hot and sour broth that might be expected in a Chinese restaurant in New York, was still warm. As he spooned it into his mouth Amir noticed the peppery spices calmed him from within. In a matter of moments, she had warm bread, vegetable biryani and yak meat in front of the guest.

Hamoush sat across from Amir, but politely refrained from speaking while the obviously hungry man ate. When he finished, and after his wife served a cup of tea, Hamoush broke the silence.

"You will sleep here this evening. We can talk more in the morning." He paused and looked down at his wrinkled hands, then up at Amir. "You'll need my help. Don't worry. I can reach Eppy. He'll know what to do."

He then motioned to the bedroom, suggesting that Amir would be honored to sleep in their bed. Understanding it was a gesture of friendship that would insult Hamoush if refused, he bowed to the wife and entered the room.

The next morning…

20

DUSTING OFF AN OLD FILE

"THAT'S WHERE THE TRAIL ended," Hazut explained lamentably, after hours of orientation, spanning two days. Speaking to an intrigued Josea and Nasir, he went on with his address. "We've worked very closely with the Americans on this. Caplow (U. S. Secretary of State) and the people at your CIA put everything they had into it. Hell, after that bombing we hit a wall. I don't need to tell you, Josea, we do a damn good job with this sort of thing, so there was only one logical conclusion."

"So you're saying you were satisfied at the time that Amir was killed along with everyone else that happened to be with him?" Josea paused, more to add a variable to an equation than to attain his response. "Seems logical, except—"

"Oh, we're not that stupid. You know that," Hazut grinned to his former assistant. "I wanted to see his remains to confirm we had taken him out. As you can see, we could have tested that site for ten years and never found a human cell. We really had no choice but to slow the search and see if anything showed to suggest he was on the loose—every other person involved with Jawiris we've accounted for."

"As far as I'm concerned, he's alive," Josea stated doubtlessly. "My bet is he's still in Pakistan. With the aid of some of our fine Pakistani friends, and under yet another name, he's safely orchestrating his personal vendetta."

"The file was getting old, a little dusty, I would say. I'm sorry we have to open it again, Josea," Hazut lamented.

"Okay. I didn't come here for nothing, and neither did Nasir. I want to get this clear. We have free reign to take a shot?" Josea petitioned.

"I'm not saying we've completely called our people off. But if you two have a plan, Josea, you know I'll back you," Hazut assured her.

Hazut was a tall man. His figure was large and broad. Josea standing next to him shrunk in stature, but size never registered on her intimidation meter. In fact, knowing her as well as I did, the only time I ever was aware she was threatened was when confronting issues of either cosmic enormity or subatomic minuteness. It was the biggest and smallest that tormented her, the questions nobody had ever answered that she imposed upon herself to understand.

There were occasions when I would see her sorrowful. When I would pester her for an explanation for her mood, she'd finally share with me that for weeks she had been trying to map distant space and had become lost in galaxies far from ours. She'd explain that a time warp had taken an unanticipated arc, causing her to think she might not find her way back—she was serious, and nuttier than that, I believed her.

Now that she had stood up and was standing next to her former boss, looking up at him, she was intent on reading his eyes, discerning if, indeed, he was going to be faithful to his promise. What she feared most was the Israelis mistrusting Nasir. They might use their agents and network to rubberneck to the point they interfered with his activities. They might also monitor him and just when he was to accomplish his goal, step in, reducing his efforts to insignificance.

She had witnessed this first-hand working with Israeli intelligence many times, even organizing operations of a similar sort on her own. She understood counterintelligence but wanted a guarantee that her ex-employer would not be implementing a campaign of this sort.

"Uri," she snapped out, "I'm counting on you. I don't want Nasir out there having to dodge your agents."

"I told you. We'll be doing what we can. The Americans are on alert and will be helping." Hazut now glanced toward Nasir. "We know your network of informants is different than ours. If you can find him, all the better."

Hazut reached down to the table in front of him, picking up the file he had been browsing. He opened it and stared for a second at a picture. Then he tossed it on the table for everyone to look at.

"Josea, you never met Mr. Amir Hamdallah, did you?"

"Only through the pictures we have in his dossier, and, of course, from what Zach has told me."

"Nasir, I'll get you a complete portfolio with multiple views of him if you need them. We suspect by now he's altered his appearance as much as possible. We've taken the liberty to do some renderings of our own; changes of hairstyle or color, clothing types or glasses. You know, whatever a person can do to modify their physical presentation."

"That will be helpful," Nasir responded.

"I do have one demand. I hope you'll take it as a matter of gravest importance." Hazut's stared sternly at Nasir. "If by chance you are able to find him, or even think you've found him, you are to have Josea let me know immediately…you back off and don't do a thing."

"Without question we'll—"

Hazut cut into Nasir's intended promise. He knew how people in situations of this sort were prone to do precisely as they were instructed not to. It was equal to an adrenaline rush for an athlete. They would be prone to thrust themselves into competition while injured, risking damaging themselves worse. He was worried that Nasir, a novice in these sorts of operations, might actually succeed. Then, while in the process of approaching Amir, blow the whole project—and be killed in the process.

"Believe me, you may find yourself in extreme danger if you get too close." Hazut now glanced at Josea. "I want updates on everything you two are doing. I hope I'm making myself understood." Hazut warned. "Keep a leash on him, Josea."

"I understand. The last thing I want to do is come home without Nasir," Josea expressed.

"That I will double ditto," Nasir laughed.

There was no humor for Hazut. He disclosed to the couple that the Israelis were concerned that Amir wanted to begin his campaign in America as a decoy with the real jewel Israel.

"Nasir, it's not that I doubt your will and sincerity. Your hands and heart are clean. Do yourself a favor and keep it that way. Nobody wants you to kill him. Even a lead will be a great contribution," Hazut said kindly. "The other thing is we would prefer if possible to take him alive—I repeat, don't do anything to alert him that he's in danger."

It had already been explained to Hazut that Nasir and Josea would be working together, but it was Nasir going into the field. He would be calling on his extensive network of fellow reporters and tipsters that had provided him inside scoops about news in the region in the past.

As a local reporter, integrity was a badge Nasir wore with honor. Those who knew him understood that they would never be betrayed. Another asset working for him was grit and determination. Danish Nasir never backed down when he was confronted with dishonorable or illegal activities. In a region like The Middle East, where so much of politics, human rights and business is conducted informally, and frequently shadowy, his standard could be dangerous.

Nasir's pet area of reporting, where he placed his greatest effort, was pertaining to justice. He abhorred the wholesale slaughter inflicted on innocent people for behaviors only the most primitive types could even conceive labeling as criminal. His most cherished goal was to enlighten Arabs that punishment should be equitable to a given crime, and that conviction of wrongdoing required more than the whimsy of a tribal leader or misguided prejudice of a gang of hoodlums.

He was now to embark on a different journey than he had ever in the past. There was a madman on the loose. In the vastness of a landmass as diverse geographically as anywhere on earth, he was hoping to poke a thread through a needle hole spinning in open space.

Nasir was a tall man who I considered very handsome. I recall after first meeting him being impressed with his hair. Bright silver in color, it spiked into thousands of peaks that looked like pins lit at the tips, the effect being to elongate his frame.

He was meticulous about his dress, maintaining a strict standard of formality. Yet I had noticed after he and my mom married, that he started to mimic her fascination with casual clothing, and in particular with Lacoste shirts—of every color made. I had to laugh because Kaye Miller was not a big spender on clothing but every time the company released a new color, she went on line and ordered it—I think they had her on alert status so she might be the first on the block wearing the new burlywood shade.

One afternoon I was in her closet changing a light bulb that had gone out and there they were, carefully folded and sitting on shelves in several piles. I couldn't help but notice that each stack was a different color type, reds, blues, yellows, oranges, greens, and then they were ordered in a progression by hue. It was hysterical to me, especially since the remainder of her large-by-my-standard closet was sparsely filled—she really didn't give a hoot about wardrobe and most every day she'd wear one of four pairs of pants, all jeans.

"What is so funny, Zacchaeus?" She rarely addressed me with my formal name.

"Your Lacoste shirts," I clowned. "It's amazing."

"You're just going to have to accept that much less of an inheritance," she chirped at me.

Fortunately, by that time she knew I really didn't need the money. She was also aware I had encouraged her to travel and enjoy the wealth she and Nasir had. But her response was always the same: "I love my life right here. I'm in love and I have everything I could ever imagine."

"But you will be buying the new goldenrod Lacoste coming out next month?"

"How do you know they're coming out with a new color? Are you serious?" she questioned earnestly.

"No, mom, just teasing. But I do love you."

"Oh, if you did you wouldn't joke about things like that," she smiled. "Besides, take a peek into Nasir's closet."

I did. I found it stuffed with suits, dress shirts, slacks, ties, leather belts and loafer shoes, most of which he rarely put on now that he was a California boy. But there in a corner was a collection of Lacoste shirts rivaling my mom's. It was comical. This man was a grown and confident creature, yet in marriage a part of him had turned into a tail-wagging puppy. I think it had to do with living in a new country, with few friends or relatives.

When Josea and Nasir arrived in Israel, they checked in to the fancy Carlton Tel Aviv. After Hazut had bestowed upon them his lengthy summary of the Israeli's attempts to capture the villainous Amir Hamdallah, they spent the next two days studying the material with the intent of crafting a strategy to launch their investigation.

Being Jewish, they understood that Josea would not leave Israel, but would provide back up research and intelligence support. It was obvious to both of them that Nasir would have to begin his project in Pakistan, precisely at the location of the bombed out apricot orchard.

What needed to be created before Nasir took off was a pretense for him to have returned to the region. Josea almost immediately hit on the perfect justification. After the attack at the Apricot Camp, there was an outrage by the local citizens, people highly loyal to the factions prone to terrorism. Their contention was that the Pakistani government permitted the Americans to use their drones to bomb innocent civilians. They couldn't settle on what infuriated them more, the government's complicity with a force they saw as an enemy, or the unjustified military operation that as likely could have been on any of their farms, killing their families.

The government tried to appease the locals by telling them that the Americans had acted without authority. Their appeal to the farmers and townspeople was that they were as upset with the U. S. military operating on their land as were the people living in the region. The rhetoric rose to a level of ferocity, everyone in agreement the American action was another example of foreign powers coming to Islam to insult Muslims.

The Pakistani leaders had secretly authorized many interventions by the Americans, mostly against terrorist groups of little or no consequence. It was the same old game. The Pakistanis pacified the enemy by handing them delinquent individuals or organizations that they wanted removed because they were seen as a threat to the Pakistani authorities—thus giving the Americans the sense of partnership—while sheltering the entities whose terrorism enhanced the wealth and power of these top officials.

It turned out that due to the rogue general who generously cooperated with the enemy in their effort to find Amir, a fiasco of untoward dimension resulted. The "campus" at the apricot farm operated with the protection of a cadre of Pakistani officials that were intent on gaining control of their country's nuclear arsenal. They were stunned that the treasured residents living at the orchard perished.

The point is that the aftermath of the bombing led to a giant publicity gaffe, as well as a civil war between the elites of the country. As of the time when Nasir would be arriving, there were still aftershocks, although very few top Pakistani officials ever understood the prestige held by the group of people who had been killed at The Camp by the Americans.

Danish Nasir, reporter, would be the perfect man to venture into the region, seeking the true story behind *The Apricot Camp Bombing*. All that was needed was an endorsement that he was on an official assignment.

Nasir had worked under direct employment—and on occasionally on special assignment—for Al Jazeera for years. He had many friends who were both administrators and reporters on staff at the news outlet. He placed a call to Goldi Savpara, managing director of the Middle East bureau. After explaining why he hadn't been working for the past couple years, and catching up on a few items of gossip, he anticipated making a proposal to the chief. He would never get the chance, and was delighted that he didn't.

"I'm sure you've followed this mess we had in Pakistan," Savpara's exasperation evident by a note of disgust in his voice. "All this time and it's still a lightning rod."

"It is odd that you mention it because I've had a couple calls recently and both times the Pakistani bombing by the Americans came up," Nasir responded indifferently. "What do you have on it?"

"The story keeps going in circles. We know there's something big there but we can't get close to what it's about," Savpara admitted. "Frankly, to me the whole mess stinks. I only wish it would do us a favor and die." The conversation then shocked Nasir. "Why are you calling?"

"I can't call an old friend to say hello?"

"You can but you don't," Savpara quipped. "I have known you since you were a kid. It's all business for you."

"Maybe it was too much business," Nasir agreed. "I have to admit I might have sacrificed camaraderie when I shouldn't have."

"Everyone is entitled to his own brand of fanaticism. Yours was being the best damn reporter on the block, and you always were."

"Thanks, Goldi."

"But back to my question. Are you ready to go back to work?"

Nasir never needed to employ the strategy he and Josea had worked out, to tip toe around the subject and then suggest he was thinking of coming back to work and had a brilliant idea for a story. Now all he needed to do was to nod his head agreeably.

"Actually I miss it, but I've been away so long I haven't a clue what I'd do," Nasir beseeched.

"Take a crack at this Pakistani business," Savpara suggested. "It's a perfect come-back-to-work beat; everyone has failed, so what's to lose?"

"I'm a little rusty," Nasir responded with intentional hesitation.

"Where are you?"

"I'm visiting my cousin in the West Bank in Israel," Nasir informed him—the little white lie was unavoidable.

"Catch a flight and meet me tomorrow. I'll have the whole file ready for you."

Josea was in the room while he placed the call and the two were giggly after he finished talking with Savpara.

"He's giving me everything they have to date on the subject. Who knows what Al Jazerra has put together over and above what Hazut gave us," Nasir smirked. "If this whole project is this easy…I may actually survive."

"Stop it. Kaye Miller will never forgive me if I lose you."

The following morning Nasir left for Doha, Qatar to meet Goldi Savpara at Al Jazeera headquarters.

Nasir didn't object to visiting Doha, the capital city of the wealthy emirate, Qatar. He was born in Dubai, a neighbor state, and knew, or thought he knew, the city well. As a child, he recalled his father taking him to visit with friends and seeing tumbleweed friskily dancing on the sand, unobstructed for long stretches. Small buildings and homes were scattered randomly, as if they were confetti that had been dropped out of a plane.

That was then. Now, there was no room for weeds. Petrodollars had turned the country into one of the richest in the world. Giant malls, giant hotels and resorts, giant homes, giant new developments were under construction, even a giant man-made island—everything in Doha was giant-sized.

This giant-of-a-tiny nation was scheduled to host the 2022 World Cup, was home to a campus of Northwestern University, and had invited the U. S. military Central Command headquarters in the region to operate on their soil.

Yet as Nasir sat in the hotel lobby on Pearl-Qatar, the island built by the state to ingeniously increase the footage of oceanfront, and where Savpara had arranged for a room for Nasir, he couldn't get a drink. No alcohol had been the decree just a day before his arrival. Why? That's what Nasir asked his waiter.

"Most of the residents of Doha are Wahhabi Muslims. They objected to the riotous parties by foreigners, which they considered disrespectful to their strict prohibition against drinking," the man responded with notable disgruntlement. "Since the temporary restrictions were set in place, our bookings have dropped," waving his hands to point out the scarcity of customers. He continued. "And how is a man to support his family when the tips he is used to have ceased?"

"How long will it be like this?"

"We have no idea, sir. Our country was to be a bridge

between Middle Eastern culture and the West. How can that be when something like this happens?"

Sipping on a soda water and snacking on a bowl of fruit, Nasir listened to the man's theory. Bridge? He laughed silently. Even this ant-sized experiment where expatriates from around the world living side-by-side with an indigenous population adhering to a strict code of Islam was a loaded pistol in a baby's crib.

This was Doha. If the same thing happened in Islamabad it would make sense. Nasir wondered if he had been away from his home territory too long. *Culture shock in Doha?*

21

BACK TO THE SCENE OF
THE CRIME

NASIR SAT IN THE glitzy hotel lobby for a bit before going to his room. He spent the remainder of the evening scanning prior stories and supporting research on his new project. He then sent the file, including what he had been given by Savpara, to Josea.

The next day, while Nasir was in flight to Islamabad, Josea was carefully organizing, categorizing, dissecting and analyzing the contents. She sent a coded email to Nasir, the two having agreed that they would be as careful as possible with communications that might be intercepted.

"Subject of our investigation never mentioned by name. Suspicion was that somebody important was at the location in question, but not one article speculates who it was—emphasis almost entirely on illegality of foreign power intervening in internal affairs of another country causing suffering to the private citizens and property loss. All stories contradict one another; none conclusive and all run circuitously." The email ended simply with, JR-C. (Josea Roth-Cloud.)

There was probably nobody who had traveled as extensively throughout the Middle East as Nasir. He spoke several languages including French, English, Spanish, Arabic and Russian. When he arrived in Pakistan, he reached out to a friend who had been chief of Geo-Jang Group, by far the most powerful media conglomerate in Pakistan. Condemned by American and Western sources for using its television, radio and newsprint clout to promote Islamic radicalism and anti-American loathing, its official position was objectivism, smearing their critics as shameful weaklings who couldn't tolerate scrutiny.

In spite of their invectiveness toward America, the U. S. government paid the company to broadcast segments of Voice of America several nights a week in hopes of neutralizing the vitriolic speeches against American interests and veering the press toward "a more accurate and responsible type of reporting."

It so happened that when Nasir arrived, Ibrahim Sani had retired from his executive position and was living in Karachi. They chatted for a while before Nasir explained the nature of his call, after which he informed Sani that he wanted somebody local to assist him while he was in the Islamabad area.

"I have just the man for you, Danish. Perfect, I'd say."

"I need somebody who knows the people, you know, can break the ice so I can get the type of statement here and there I wouldn't be able to on my own," Nasir explained.

"Understood. This fellow came to Geo about three years ago—reminded me of you." Then Sani crowed. "Got himself fired."

"Right. I did that once myself," Nasir confessed with the pride of a man who knows that anyone without an enemy has no courage, and anyone who hasn't been bounced out of a job or been unsentimentally tossed out of a friendship at least once is a coward fearful to express his beliefs.

"Wajih Mirza, that's his name. He decided not to test his luck again," Sani joked. "He's been working freelance since."

"Why was he let go?" Nasir inquired.

"Insisted the edits his boss wanted were damaging to the authenticity of his story and refused to let it be published with those changes. By the way, it was on the same subject matter you're looking into." The coincidence added to Sani's enthusiasm putting Mirza together with Nasir. "The kid was right to object but was too inexperienced to understand that you have to be careful about painting big shots black. His boss had the good sense to be scared of what Mirza wanted to report. He also lacked the balls to change the color of Mirza's work to white, and then add just enough black spots to keep it interesting."

"Black is black and white is white. Gray is confusing for the average person," Nasir injected. "His boss didn't want to take a chance on his job...or his life.

"That's not how you played it."

"You're wrong. I was simply lucky enough to steer away from situations that might have endangered me. I'm really a fraidy-cat at heart."

"Have it as you like, but there are lots of people who would dispute that."

"Now, what about this kid?"

"I can give you his number. Call him up. The two of you will get along famously."

Nasir phoned Mirza immediately. By chance the man was living in Islamabad and agreed to meet that evening. They came to terms easily but Mirza had business he couldn't put off which delayed them leaving by an additional day. When Nasir mentioned he might take in a round of golf, Mirza was quick to inform him that the Sheraton Resort had Pakistan's first internationally recognized course and Nasir was welcome to use his set of clubs.

Thus, after completing an humiliating eighteen holes, Nasir swore he'd never use anyone else's equipment, play on a course with so many rocks and sand traps, tee off if there was wind, go out on a course with strangers, hit drives in mountainous brisk air, or wear rental golf shoes—he was content to disgrace himself with scores in the high nineties at home, but one hundred eleven—in Pakistan?

The following morning, they left together for the Hunza Valley. They traveled on N-5 until meeting N-35, carving their way toward the Karakoram Highway. It was a different route than Amir had followed with Zahid. As they made their way to the city of Thakot, the highway began to parallel the Indus River. Nasir had never been on the Karakoram and several times along the lengthy drive he stopped in an observation area. Otherwise, he insisted that Mirza pull over if he was driving so he could gape at the brilliant landscape.

They spent the night at Chilas, having made good progress but not wanting to drive into the large stretches of isolated highway at night. In the morning, they took off, within a couple hours reaching Bunji. The geographic uniqueness of this area did not fail to excite Nasir. In fact, he was brought to speechlessness by the exceptional beauty he was beholding—unaware that still greater sights were awaiting him further ahead.

Where he chose to rest next was a juncture. The Indus River hooked up with the Gilgit River at that exact point, and then clutching one another they flowed southward before emptying into the Arabian Sea near Karachi. Better still, and commanding his attention most, was the view of the three mountain ranges merging together. The focal point was the westernmost peak of the Himilayan range, Nanga Parbat. This ninth highest mountaintop in the world served as the intersection for these three distinguished ranges. Nasir found them enchanting.

In one breath, he vowed to return and spend leisurely time exploring the enthralling land. With the next exhalation of CO_2, he was already leveling with himself that it was unlikely he'd ever have the opportunity to come back. Thus, he soaked, sucked and swallowed what he could at the moment.

Within hours, he was to be treated to the Karakoran peaks to the east as they made their way upstream against the Hunza River—oblivious to his prior vow, he made a second identical one about returning to vacation in the region at a later date, the fantasy pleasing enough he saw no reason to destroy it with reality this time around.

"Nothing has been touched since the bombing—nobody even picked the fruit. Isn't that odd?" Mirza informed Nasir in preparation for presenting his conspiratorial theory. "Who owns the land? Not a clue. Imagine, there's no deed or record of ownership for this parcel—never has been according to the government."

"That can't be, Mirza. You sure?"

"In Pakistan anything is possible. That's why I was fired... I'm sure Mr. Sani mentioned it."

"It didn't depreciate your stock to him."

"Because he knows I was right. But our chief hadn't the strength to stand up to the people we know actually run the media, the generals," Mirza shot out like spittle from the extra wide space between his two front top teeth. "They wanted the Americans in the villain role, case closed."

"And you don't think they were responsible?"

"Of course, they were," Mirza admitted. "But this nonsense about them acting illegally and unofficially is a lie."

"I'll ask the question I'm supposed to, why?"

"I've seen drone attacks before and typically I don't find anywhere near the level of destruction that occurred where we're going. They used at least two of those pilotless babies, both with heavy munitions, more powerful than they routinely put on these craft." Mirza waited to let the thoughts settle in for Nasir. "Furthermore, most of the terrorist groups are quite a distance to the south. There's actually little if any activity in this area. What you have here is basically general farming, mostly dominated by apricot groves."

"And—"Nasir questioned, noticing Mirza pausing.

"And nobody in the area ever knew the people running that piece of land. There was more going on there than anyone was willing to disclose, a lot more," he stated with conviction.

"Why else would the government go to so much trouble to convolute any attempt at an investigation? When they step in, it's not because they don't care," Mirza said sarcastically. "They cared big time."

"But you have no idea what was taking place there?"

"Never got that far...and I doubt you will either—I'm coming along to see how a legend in my field works."

"I'm not that old," the mid-fifties pro laughed. "And I'd be careful with the legend business."

They arrived at the front gate where Amir and Bahlya had entered with Eppy and Zahid. This time there was no guard or any type of barrier to obstruct their entry. They passed the canopied section of the road before proceeding through the two sections of trees. At the very end of the orchard the paved road gradually dissolved into increasing sizes and amounts of debris until it came to an ominous dead end.

Wreckage from buildings and rock pieces ranging in size from footballs to small aircraft, natural landscape that had once been portions of larger boulders, blocked the entrance to the area. They stopped the car and got out. Both men attempted to climb further into the passage between the remaining rock walls. It took only a few steps to realize the futility, as well as the danger—there was a high probability of injury due to the instability of the rubble.

Nasir sat on a rock, staring at the scene. He was rehearsing some of the conversations I had with him about Bahlya, contemplating how sad it was that she had died as violently as she did at this very location. Then as he glanced to his right, where Mirza was standing, he saw a quick flash coming from a distance deep into the orchard. It happened too quickly to calculate the delay before light was followed by sound, but in the tiniest subdivision of time what he knew was a bullet had ricocheted off a rock.

Mirza, instinctively sensing danger, dropped to the ground. Nasir stooped down behind the rock he was sitting on. It was only one round, but enough for both men to know they might be in trouble. They waited at least ten minutes, neither moving. Finally, Mirza peeked out from behind the car where he had managed to crawl for protection.

There was no additional aggression by whoever had shot at them. Gradually Mirza further exposed himself, Nasir doing the same. Without a word, they cautiously entered the car. Nasir started the motor and in an instant wheeled it around and gunned the engine, propelling the car full speed down the long single lane road upon which they entered.

"You think someone didn't want us here?" Nasir posed to his younger associate.

"Why now, after all this time? I just wanted you to have a visual map of the site—the place has been investigated a hundred times," Mirza reasoned. "We shouldn't make too much of it. Everyone here has weapons and it's probably nothing more than a kid out randomly shooting his rifle. When he saw us he panicked and took off, which explains why there was only one shot fired."

"Still, not a good start, is it, Wajih?"

"We didn't even get to lift a few apricots. They're famous for them here. Did you know that?"

"Apricots?" Nasir questioned.

"It might be the only crops my people grow profitably besides those used to process drugs," Mirza quipped. "They're better than the Turkish ones, sweeter and more intense in flavor. We sell them all over the world now. Most all of them are grown in this region. Typically the farmers in the Hunza Valley have various crops, but apricots are dominant."

"Hunza Valley Apricots..."

"That's what they're called," Mirza confirmed.

"Let's go back to town, get rooms and dinner, and then we can return early in the morning to talk to some of the neighbors," Nasir suggested.

Mirza recalled once staying at the Hunza Baltit Inn in Karimabad, only a short drive away. When they arrived, Nasir was again overwhelmed.

"All the travels I've had over the years and I don't think I've ever seen breathtaking scenery like I have today."

"Not many people will ever see this. Come, let's get settled."

The hotel was built into the west face of a cliff about eight thousand feet in elevation. The rooms faced easterly toward the valley. The distant peaks sloped precipitously downward a couple thousand feet before beginning a more gradual descent to the base of the mountain.

The men were sitting on grey wicker chairs on the balcony of the restaurant having a drink. The expanse viewed from the balcony stretched out for miles, yet the clarity of the air created an illusion: it was as if they were using binoculars to hone in on the distant slopes.

Between the base of the peaks and the hotel were lush greenery, grasses, wildflowers and trees. Patches of white clouds dove downward, landing gently on the lower surfaces like surfboards riding smooth waves atop a deep green sea.

"You have a spectacular country, Wajih."

"The serenity you're looking at is deceiving. Besides, nobody who lives here pays any attention. It's only the tourist who ever enjoys it, and with our politics most don't want to chance coming here when they can get the same in Nepal, Bhutan, India or China."

"You disagree with the government?" Nasir asked to lead Mirza along in the discussion.

"Let me say that being in my company is not always the safest place to be," Mirza shifted his posture while grinning mischievously.

"Are you proposing a new theory for the shooting today, that someone was aiming at you? After all, you were already canned for not backing off. Is it possible they think you didn't learn your lesson?"

"No. I'll stick with my first conclusion. But you are right that they know I didn't learn a thing other than how vicious people are when it comes to defending their lies," he proudly proclaimed. "I'm fortunate that I don't need a job. I'm free to express my views," Wajih revealed while sipping a beer.

"Liberal ones, I presume."

"In Pakistan we need them more than anywhere," Wajih asserted. "Besides, anything counter to the radicalism of the government's view is liberal."

"And you don't need work for what reason, may I ask?"

"My family is wealthy. I have money of my own."

He stood only a hair over five seven. His posture was impeccable. He may have been lenient with his politics but his erect stance suggested that he'd quibble over a fraction of an inch in height. His chest protruded upward. If there was a cheat in his demeanor it was beheld in the labor devoted to holding his body upright.

"I hope you won't take this as a criticism but I've always found the combination of wealth and youth to be suited to an emancipated attitude. I'll admit that I know this from experience. From an early age, I also enjoyed the benefit of freedom that money provides."

"Right, Mr. Nasir. I always heard you had the reputation as a sort of a maverick, a man who speaks his mind," Mirza shared with admiration.

"I had the luxury to do that. But I've become more of a pragmatist than a liberal. It's most important to me to contribute to a tiny achievable change than advocate for reforms that are unrealistic."

Mirza was in his thirties and old enough to listen first before attempting to beat down beliefs that conflicted with his own. His round gentle face with dark short hair dropping bangs on to the top portion of the forehead looked pleasantly at Nasir.

"Just a thought," Nasir continued. "Your country is slow to change. There are reasons for that. Do you have children yet?"

"None. I'm a bachelor."

"Well, just the same. If I may offer a piece of advice," Nasir voiced paternalistically. "Think of your country like it's your child. Remember it has a temperament, a unique character, a history, and a future. Inch by inch it will evolve. Try to be a good model for her to follow."

Mirza still made no comment. He crossed one leg over the other, his golden-colored leather square-toed loafer revealing a portion of his sockless ankle and leg. He was wearing a long tan collarless shirt with white slacks. He reached in his pocket and took out a picture, showing it to Nasir.

"It's horrible," the elder man said sadly as he stared at the photo that had been taken of a woman who had been stoned.

"I want it to stop. We are not all barbarians."

"Everyone knows that. Remember, though, you have to love the child. The last thing you want is rejection. A child's disrespect is the worst thing you can permit to happen— especially for the child," Nasir offered as a final portion of advice.

"Your children are fortunate to have you."

Nasir glanced with a rascal's smile. "I have no children."

Mirza broke into unrestrained laughter. "Yes, you do. You're teasing me."

"I'll let you have it as you wish."

After dinner they went to their rooms. Nasir had a strange, inexplicable sensation as he approached his door. As he began to open it, instead of the jam providing a firm resistance to keying the lock, it slipped freely solely from the pressure of engaging it. Then as the door swung open he noticed his suitcase that he had left lying on the right side of the bed had been moved noticeably toward the center.

He was also certain that he had zipped it shut before dinner because he had taken out a sweater and slipped it on with Mirza waiting at the door. It was now sitting open with the items that were contained exposed. As he inspected the contents of his case, he recognized that the neatness he adhered to in managing his clothing had been tampered. Somebody had inspected the inside and then likely in a hurry to finish the job, forgot to close it.

He was certain that his briefcase, where he kept his computer and incidental papers, had been gone through as well—the computer was coded so that it could not be accessed without his permission and to his relief, he had turned it off. Before leaving, he and Josea agreed that he would carry no papers identifying the true purpose of his travel, but the computer would have the relevant files as well as access to his emails on the subject.

The hotel had full internet service and after inspecting the room and then locking it he sent an email message to Josea to keep her abreast of his experiences that day, including the shot that was fired and someone snooping in his room. She had placed an alarm on her cell to inform her any time a call or message came in from Nasir. After receiving his missive, she immediately instructed him to halt the mission until receiving further instruction—the professed coward ignored the order.

Nasir stayed up reading for over an hour before falling asleep. The next morning there were two additional emails by Josea, neither of which he responded to. It was the exact case he had been admonished about, adrenalin pumping excitation leading to dubious decision-making.

During breakfast he said nothing about the break in to Mirza either. The twosome sat for a quiet meal and left early for a trip back to the scene of the crime. Neither spoke of the rifle shot. Nasir had already placed his bet that Mirza was correct that the single bullet fired was a youth out target practicing who was startled when he realized humans were in the vicinity. He also doubled down that the uninvited visitor to his room was a not uncommon event in a region where strangers were always under suspicion.

His devotion to my mother had unconsciously turned him into a zealot willing to risk unwisely for the purpose of finding Amir and removing potential harm to me. What he failed to account for was the fact that when you gamble you have to know that the house stays in business by winning.

22

BAD BOY

BOTH MEN KNEW THERE was no value in going directly to The Apricot Camp. But the area surrounding where the American drone attack had occurred was the destination Nasir was aiming for. It shocked him that with all the attention the matter had attracted there was not one referenced interview with a local witness, particularly a neighbor.

Nasir was behind the wheel and several times as he checked the road behind him, he noticed a cab. It would at times trail by quite some distance and then close the space between them. One time when he pulled off the road to stretch his legs, he saw the vehicle turn off on what looked like a farm road. But then moments later when he resumed driving, the cab would again appear.

Finally, he informed Mirza. He confirmed Nasir's impression. Waiting for a moment until the trailing car was at a good distance behind them, he instructed Nasir to pull over. He jumped out of the car and told Nasir he'd take over driving. After the switch, Mirza drove only a couple miles before the other car was again closing in on them.

Mirza then did the unexpected. He spun the car around one hundred eighty degrees and began to accelerate full speed directly at the other car. Nasir, describing himself later as "scared crapless," was befuddled by his partner's recklessness. As he zeroed in on the intruding car, at the last second in the game of chicken, Mirza sharply skidded his car to the right, the other car veering off the opposite direction before sliding into deep mud that brought his car to an abrupt halt.

Mirza had already swung open his door and was racing toward the driver of the cab. When he reached the car, the startled man did nothing to disguise his fright. The more aggressive Mirza dragged him out from behind the wheel.

"You're following us, you flat-breasted termite," he screeched at him. Holding the cab driver by the lapel of his coat he pulled him upright. "What is this about and I don't want any of your vulgar lies."

"Sir," the startled cabbie pled. "I'm to pick up Mr. Sosooli. I'm early," his voice trembled.

"You're a lying mouse," Mirza yelled still louder and without regard for the man's obvious terror. "Where is your phone? Tell me who called you to do this?"

The man said nothing, still anguishing from the unexpected behavior by Mirza.

"Turn that car around and if I see you again I'll beat you senseless," Mirza threatened.

Mirza ran back over to where Nasir was standing witnessing the hostile exchange. They went back into the car and took off, Mirza still driving. Nasir looked back as the cab driver's vehicle remained stuck off to the side of the road.

"He's no threat to us now. We'll wave to the little cretin when we pass him on the way back—he'll still be dug into the mud," Mirza chortled as if the encounter was a scene in a comedy.

"What if he wasn't after us?"

"Don't be foolish, boss. He would have never told us the truth because whoever put him up to it would have warned him that if he were to be caught and then confessed the truth, his wife and children would be slaughtered."

"Why are we being watched?"

"I told you, they want this story left alone. You're a foreigner and a reputable reporter. That's the last thing they want so they're trying to intimidate you."

"Mirza, they're starting to do a good job."

"Not to worry," Mirza answered brashly. "I'll know if we're in real danger."

Nasir hardly felt confident but was drawn more than ever into the situation. He sensed that all the hoopla might mean that there was a loose strand connected somehow to Amir and he might have the opportunity to pull it. Still, he contemplated the importance of proceeding with caution.

"If something happens to me, just by chance, call her. She's my assistant and will know exactly what to do," he informed Mirza as he handed him emergency instructions including contact information for Josea.

"This is how things are done here. You're taking it too seriously and worrying too much," Mirza gestured with a shake of his finger, dismissing outright Nasir's concern.

"I fear I'm not taking it serious enough," Nasir countered his partner's seeming disregard for trouble.

"Nasir, now that we're free of that rascal, let's enjoy the rest of the day."

They spent what was left of the morning and the whole afternoon contacting neighbors of The Apricot Farm. The way the parcel was carved out, there were five other farms that had contiguous boundaries. In his notes, Nasir would later write that the first four contacts were "fruitless." He designated his comment as a "funny," making the point that these farmers, all growing apricots, had none of the famous crop at the time to harvest. No relevant information...and no fruit... warranted the "fruitless" label he thought was humorous. I adore Nasir, but the man has a sense of humor as witty as a cold sore.

The fifth stop happened to be to the home of Hamoush, the man who caught Amir about to bed down with his gardening tools. When they drove down the gravel road toward his home, they noticed a man working in a field of barley. They stopped the car. The man, who clearly was not used to unexpected visitors, strolled hesitantly toward them.

"I'm Mirza and this is Nasir," he said to the man, intentionally choosing the informality of first names.

"I'm Hamoush. You don't look Pakistani." The man delivered his words to me like an indictment. "Just the same, if I can help you I will."

"Nasir is a reporter doing a story for Al Jazerra. He wants to ask you a few questions about the bombing back some time ago."

"About time somebody asked me—"

"Nobody has ever interviewed you about it?" Mirza asked with bafflement. "All the other neighbors we met with today were contacted."

"Not me. Probably because they know I'm riled. The far end of my orchard sits right up to the rocks and when that part of the cliff came down it ruined an acre of my trees." The man appeared to be reliving an old wound. His anger was evident as he swung his right arm to point to the location of his loss. "I kept trying to find out who was going to compensate me but I couldn't get an answer—I'm still short the land."

"I'm sorry, Hamoush, I really am," Nasir expressed with genuine compassion. "Was there anything else you recall? I know it's after the event, but anything you know might be valuable."

"Not a thing comes to mind."

"Did you know who worked that farm? Could you lead us to any of the people, by chance?" Nasir probed.

"Nobody ever knew what was going on there. I doubt they were even harvesting their crop," Hamoush mumbled contemptuously. "It was probably owned by some rich city people."

"If it is, nobody knows who," Mirza confirmed.

Hamoush stood. His head bobbed forward and back, as if a thought was whizzing through his mind like a fly begging for a swat. "There is something," he proclaimed triumphantly. "Now I remember."

"What?" Nasir asked excitedly.

"Later that night, I caught this young fellow about to go into my shed. I should have shot him or let the police do it, but he looked like he was freezing. All of us living here have been instructed to report any unusual events or strangers coming close to the area. I know I would have turned him in except—"

"Who orders you to guard the area?" Mirza questioned with a tone of accusation.

"That's not your business."

Recognizing that Mirza's aggressiveness might inhibit the man, Nasir stepped in to salvage the interview.

"That's fine, Hamoush. Whatever you feel comfortable telling us is appreciated."

"It was the way he said he needed help."

"You felt sorry for him?" Nasir was determined to keep the discussion going.

"Not so much that. Just with the destruction earlier on, I wanted to see if by chance he wasn't a stranger and I could assist him."

"How did you help him? What did he look like?" Nasir impatiently rattled off questions.

"Hold on, I'm trying to remember." Hamoush paused to refresh his memory. "He told me he was living on the farm next to me and that he had been out when the bombing happened. When he was returning he witnessed the destruction and then knew that his sister was killed—"

"His sister!?" Nasir could hardly contain his astonishment.

"Right. I guess that kind of touched something in me. It was strange. I guess I did feel sad for him."

"By chance did he mention the name of the sister?" Nasir asked the man.

"I'm sure he didn't. I would have let the police sort out what this stranger was doing here but somehow he mentioned knowing a man named Eppy. He's a very important person around here. He's always been right by everyone living in our area. If this man at my home was a friend of Eppy, I was sure he was a friend of mine. I knew the right thing to do would be to get him to Eppy and let him decide how to help the man."

"Did you find Eppy?" Mirza chimed back into the conversation.

"Of course. My wife fed the fellow a fine meal and put him down to sleep. Then in the morning, I drove him to Gilgit to meet with Eppy."

"Is it possible he told you his name but you can't recall it? Or, when he met with Eppy, did a name get exchanged then?" Nasir asked.

"Never heard his name, I'm sure. I never asked him either. That was the last I ever saw of him."

"How do we reach Eppy?" Nasir asked.

"Go to Gilgit and ask around; everyone there knows him."

"Thanks. You were kind to take the time with Mirza and me."

Hamoush turned to go back to his work. Mirza and Nasir went back to the car, Mirza getting in the driver's side. Nasir hesitated just long enough to be sure Mirza was buckled in and had the engine running. Then he told Mirza to wait. He ran after Hamoush while reaching in his back pocket to take out a piece of paper. He palmed it so Mirza couldn't see.

"Hamoush, one more thing," the out-of-breath Nasir called out. With his back to Mirza he held out the picture for Hamoush to look at. "Is that the man?"

Hamoush's smile of recognition revealed a large vacancy where two top front teeth were missing. "Sweet kid—that's him."

Sweet kid? That's like meeting serial killer Ted Bundy for a soda and thinking it might be dear to set him up for a date with your daughter.

Nasir hopped in the car and they drove away. Mirza couldn't contain his curiosity about what Nasir asked Hamoush; it wouldn't be satisfied. Mirza could never know the true nature of the investigation. Nasir knew it would soon be time to cut his assistant loose—but first my step-father-in-law needed a spanking.

23

NOT SO QUICK, BUDDY

MIRZA WOULDN'T STOP PESTERING Nasir all the way back to the hotel. He agreed from the beginning that he would have no rights to any information they might attain, and furthermore that his name would not be attached to any articles that might be published as a result of the work they completed together. He was to be employed solely on a contract, work-for-hire basis for this single assignment.

Even with those stipulations, Nasir was wise and experienced enough to know that a reporter could never get a hot lead and play catch-and-release with it. Add to that the fact that since his disappearance, Amir's reputation had become as esteemed as any single individual in the region. Mirza having nearly irrefutable evidence that Amir had been on that farm, and then escaped, would have been grounds in his mind to claim improbity by Nasir, and thus negate the contract they had agreed on.

By the time they reached the hotel, Nasir was making plans to go it alone. But first he'd have an unexpected little visit to address.

He was finishing a pre-dinner drink with Mirza when three jeeps pulled up in front of the hotel. There were nine rifled men who with militant discipline jumped out of their cars. They had obviously been briefed on their assignment because no words were exchanged as the men rushed into the lobby.

Nasir was within earshot and heard his name barked by a man who might have been the leader. He marched directly to the front desk. The question was where Nasir was. The receptionist craned his neck out from the desk enough to eye Mirza and Nasir on the balcony. Hearing his name snapped by an army officer produced a profusion of sweat under his arms. During all his encounters as a reporter, he had never been arrested or run afoul with the authorities—that was about to change.

The platoon charged over to where the two were sitting, aiming their rifles like they were about to arrest a notorious outlaw.

"Mr. Nasir?" the leader shouted. "Come with us."

Nasir hesitated, hoping to explain that a mistake had to have occurred.

"Now," the soldier asserted, jabbing the tip of the barrel into Nasir's rib.

As he rose, Mirza's hot temper rushed into the fray.

"What do you think you're doing?" he yelled, standing and putting his forehead menacingly close to the officer's mouth. "This is a respected reporter who has every right…"

That's as far as he was permitted to go. The same man, presumed to be leading the group, harshly shot the butt end of his rifle into Mirza's abdomen. He keeled over in pain while Nasir was led at gunpoint into one of the military vehicles and driven off to…

The jeeps screeched as they swerved briskly away from the hotel. Nasir estimated that they drove about twenty minutes before they reached an open field where he was sure he was going to be shot. He was ordered out. The officer in charge took out a cell phone and was talking, glancing intermittently at his prisoner.

Finally after about ten minutes, a loud sound approached from the south. As Nasir looked up—the noise now deafening—he saw a helicopter circling above and then landing. Another man without a weapon jumped out and exchanged a few muted words with the officer in charge on the ground.

The man who exited the copter went up to the prisoner and grabbed him by his arm, forcing him to follow under the whirling blades. Pushing from behind, Nasir had the idea he was to hop into the bird. Within seconds the craft was in the air, shrinking the soldiers on the ground as it rose straight up before darting to the south to take Nassir…

The poor man had no idea what he had done nor where he was being taken but understood that the down comforter he was paying for at the Hunza Baltit was not going to be warming his chilly body that night.

Mirza had still not recovered by the time Nasir was flown off. It took a half hour before he could breathe normally—it would take a month before the black and blue rectangular design on his stomach would fade.

When he recovered sufficiently to gather his senses, he pulled out his notes with the number to call for emergencies. He reached Josea immediately. Receiving the bad news set her into emergency operational mode.

"You're sure they were Pakistani military and not local police?"

"You sound American."

"What's that have to do with it?"

"This is my home country. Local police are like your meter maids. Does that answer your question?"

"So they could be holding him anywhere?"

"Most likely at the capital in Islamabad or at The Academy close to there."

"What do you think they could be charging him with?"

"Nothing! If I had to guess, all they want to do is scare the crap out of him and have him leave the country."

After milking Mirza for as much information as possible in a minimum of time, she instructed him not to take any action on behalf of Nasir.

"Mr. Nasir deserves better than this. It's what I despise about Pakistan—"

"Mirza, if you respect Mr. Nasir, leave this to me. I'll get back to you."

Nasir was in danger. She preferred not to get the Israelis involved unless she had to. A diplomatic solution, she was sure from her experience dealing with similar matters, could be reached but it would be costly. She had another idea that if successful would be cheap and efficient.

"Is Mr. Savpara in?" Josea asked his personal secretary. "Tell him I'm Josea Roth, close friend of Danish Nasir."

Within seconds, Savpara came on the line.

"Ms. Roth, what's wrong?" he asked, recognizing her name and knowing she wouldn't be calling to chat.

"It's Nasir. He mentioned to me he was taking on an assignment for you. I don't know much except he was picked up by the Pakistani military. I have no idea why; he had every right to follow a piece fifty people have done before him."

"What? He's a reporter under our authority." Savpara authored a shout followed by a fist pounding loud enough on a table for Josea to instinctively pull the cell away from her ear. "Let me make some calls. I'll get back to you shortly."

If roughing up Nasir was their way of evoking fear, they succeeded. For the first time along this journey, the grown man wanted mommy. He couldn't reach the next best thing, Kaye Miller, but Josea had to. My mom detested Middle East politics as much as the thought of bathing in a tub of neem oil, but her first reaction was to let Josea know she was on her way.

Thank god Josea was able to convince her that she needed to stay put. My mother did as instructed. She immediately called me with the news. I couldn't help feeling it was my fault, but she'd have no part of it.

"It's not only you, Zach. We're all in this together—forget Nasir for a minute, do you think I'm sleeping any better knowing Amir is out there? I'm careful myself. He wants to hurt you, and I'm part of you, as are your children and Preeti."

An hour after speaking to Savpara, he called Josea back. The news was bad, but not terrible. The Pakistanis were alleging he was in truth under the employ of an American government agency but masquerading as a journalist working under the protection of an Arab media company. Essentially, he had duped his old buddy at Al Jazeera and was being held as a spy. They also inadvertently disclosed that of all the reporters they least wanted snooping in their country, it was Danish Nasir. They referred to his style of investigating as, "damaging to Islam."

"You know, Josea," Savfara explained. "We have the same story here as anywhere else. Don't you sometimes perceive your mother, sister, neighbor or good friend speaking a different language? These are Pakistanis. They have their own culture and political agenda, and sometimes I don't even get it."

"Are you saying you don't think you can get him out of there?" Josea asked, trying to read his message in case she needed to move on to the next strategy.

"Not at all. I will settle this. If I have to I'll sing a song to them that'll have their ears dripping. This is freedom of press. We sent Nasir and I'll foul the odor around them so badly that nobody will be able to breathe the stench. Not one reporter from anywhere in the world will step foot on their land. They won't have a voice left to lie on their behalf. They'll come to reason," he asserted. "I have already made it clear that if they harm one hair on his body they'll be showering in a shit-pool of international condemnation."

"I appreciate it. I'll thank you in advance on behalf of his wife too."

"It's not for you or her. Nasir is working for me!"

Josea shut her trap. God forbid Savpara knew the full truth about Nasir's mission. Was he a spy? The Pakistanis "sort of" had it right.

The negotiations between Savpara, on behalf of his employer, and the Pakistani government proved to be complicated. Savpara was backed into a corner. To agree to bring Nasir home without free reign to conduct his investigation would have been a defeat for free press in the region, and internationally. Yet the Pakistanis had arrested a man they earnestly believed was a spy. They didn't want him hanging around—at the same time they were not indifferent to, nor ignorant of, the highly damaging actions that Savpara could take against them.

What worked favorably toward an agreement was that the Pakistanis didn't care a whit about The Apricot Camp issue. They had vacuumed the residue of the losses from the bombing long before. They also actually had no idea that the focus of the investigation was Amir.

To the sober leadership of the country, Amir Hamdallah was a man who had vaporized into the ethers of the universe, leaving behind a fiction embraced by common Muslims in need of allegorical inspiration on their journey seeking Allah.

It was actually the brainchild of Josea who, in discussion with Savpara, found the sweet spot that all enemies or combatants seek when trying to back out of a bloody battle. The Pakistanis were to release Nasir immediately and allow him one week to complete his work. During the short period that he remained in Pakistan, he was to be left unmolested to complete his business, free to travel at will, and communicate as he wished with anyone.

After the allotted week, Nasir would be expelled from the country and the Pakistanis would be free to capitalize on the situation. They could announce that an Al Jazeera reporter was instead a spy working for the Americans. What sealed the deal was the plum Josea crafted to assure that all parties were coming out with winning hands.

Magnanimously, Pakistan would announce they decided to release the foreign agent rather than prosecute him. Why? First, no harm had been done to the internal security of Pakistan. Second, and equally important, they considered the matter one best handled by Al Jazeera and the Qatar authorities in that they had suffered greater loss of prestige as a result of being tricked by the "traitor."

The Qatar news agency had full confidence in the innocence of Nasir and had no intention of doing anything other than letting sufficient time pass for the matter to die—while Nasir was living with his wife in America.

So it happened that an unharmed Nasir was released. After talking with a relieved Kaye Miller, and then taking a stern rebuke from Josea for disregarding her entreat, he pulled himself together for the second phase of his trip. He had only a week. With the guarantee he would not be hassled, he felt compelled to yank with all his might on that strand he had picked out of Hamoush's memory that could lead to Amir.

It would prove to be a quick tug. Nasir was able to wrap up his business in Pakistan in under forty-eight hours, fleeing the country while definitively renouncing all prior vows to return for a sightseeing vacation.

He had been held in Islamabad. His first stop would be Gilgit, requiring a long northern drive. Having made the trip with Mirza, he felt comfortable travelling alone. His mind was consumed with trying to find a man named Eppy.

Knowing the time allotted to him was limited, he left immediately the morning of his release. Luck was with him in that the travel conditions were unusually favorable. He was able to reach the town by early evening. He recalled what Hamoush had told him, that Eppy was a man well known to people in the area—he was correct.

Relying on his journalist status and field experience, he stopped in at the office of the leading newspaper in the area, Baad-e-Shimal.

When he asked the man at the desk if he knew a local who went by the name Eppy he smiled. "Who doesn't?"

"Actually, I don't. But I have important business I need to discuss with him," Nasir informed the man. "How can I reach him?"

The man studied Nasir. His dress and manner assured the receptionist that Nasir was not a hoodlum aiming to bring trouble to a man he revered.

"Where will you be staying?"

"If you'll refer me to where I can sleep tonight I'll check in and wait to hear from you," Nasir responded, handing him a card.

"It's rather late," the newspaper clerk commented, hugging Nasir like a treasured friend.

Nasir noticed the man hesitate, not moving a muscle. He reached in his pocket and pulled out his billfold. He counted out several pieces of paper currency and placed the rupees in the clerk's jacket pocket.

"I'm hoping to leave early tomorrow morning back to Islamabad. I'd appreciate your help as soon as possible."

"I'll see if I can get a message to him immediately," the man answered like a soldier proudly taking an order from a general.

The man had written the name Gilgit Serena Hotel on a piece of paper. Nasir went there directly to register for a room. He was planning on taking dinner at the hotel as well. He had little time to do either. In fact, as he pulled in front of the building he noticed a tall, lanky man nod his head in an acknowledging manner—he also noticed several feet to his right, another man, the companion broad and heavy set. The second man turned about-face and walked into the hotel as Nasir was parking.

The other man waited for Nasir to get out of the car before he approached him. "I understand that you have business with Eppy."

"I want to talk to him, yes," Nasir confirmed for the man, handing him a card referencing that he was a journalist. "If you could tell him I would be in his debt if he would be kind enough to meet with me. You might mention to him the subject is a man who contacted him after the bombing some time ago, the one at the farm not too far from here."

The man left Nasir standing in the parking area next to his car. Two minutes later he came out, instructing Nasir to come with him. He then led him to a café where the same large man he had witnessed on the steps of the hotel was sipping a cup of mud-thick coffee. When he arrived at the table, the man sitting stood to address Nasir.

"You're looking for Eppy. I am Eppy."

Nasir noticed that he had to be in his fifties but his full head of thick black hair and matching bristly beard birthing only random tufts of grey made him look several years younger. Standing close to him, Eppy seemed huge. He was only an inch or two above six feet but the massiveness of his build increased his physical presence.

He was wearing a white shirt that buttoned down the front but had only a tiny rounded collar. Over the top was a maroon-colored silk sleeveless vest with a pattern that looked like bright lanterns. His pants were an old pair of Levi jeans that might have been purchased at a used clothing store on Hollywood Boulevard. On his feet were brown rubber beach sandals without socks—Eppy admitted that he occasionally would make a shopping trip to Karachi. He went so far as to openly proclaim himself a Walmart customer, though he would with equal candor admit he might have blown up the place ten years earlier.

"Now, what is it you want to talk about?" he ordered while motioning for Nasir to sit down, where a cup of Turkish coffee awaited him.

"I'm working for Al Jazeera. They want a fresh take on that bombing. I don't need to tell you there are many rumors suggesting that what happened that day has a big story that nobody has been able to flesh out yet."

"Rumors are good for editorials and movies." Eppy brashly dismissed what he saw as an aspersion. "If that's what you want, I'm afraid this will be a short discussion."

"I'm not here to explore hearsay," Nasir assured him. "The evening after the incident a stranger presented at the adjacent farm owned by a man named Hamoush. He stayed the night and then Hamoush brought him to meet with you the next day. Am I speaking fact, Eppy?"

Eppy stared mutely, a signal that Nasir had permission to continue.

"I know that man to have been Amir Hamdallah," Nasir announced, knowing he was taking a great risk mentioning the name.

Eppy's creamy skin darkened several shades as the blood rushed to his face. He jerked his body up, an intimidating gesture not unnoticed by the grayer haired Nasir. He stood looking downward at Nasir who by that time was wondering if he had grown wiser or dumber as he'd aged. He glanced up at the man, aware that the mention of Amir's name had struck a nerve.

"I apologize, Mr. Nasir, for you are only doing your job," Eppy stated as he sat back down. "I will give you a story now that you will never wish to publish."

Nasir sat waiting, knowing Eppy had nothing to be concerned about for he had no intention of publishing another article for the rest of his life—he had retired.

"This man," Eppy literally spit on the floor, "whose name I will not even mention is no more than a spoiled brat. I don't know if he used his money to spread lies like an American branding manager or my people are so stupid and desperate they'll bow to rodents because they're too lazy to look at the truth.

"Every day there's another fiction created about where he is, what's he's going to do to the infidel…if he's alive. The fascination with his life never stops and frankly I'm not sure anyone knows what is factual. To me, the answer has less value than maggots eating at a carcass." A defiant expression lingered on his face. "Ask me what you wish, Mr. Nasir."

"Why did he come to you?" he questioned cautiously to a man he could tell had explosive potential.

"The person you are asking about I had met briefly, when I arranged for him to be admitted to the farm where the bombing took place. Anyway, when he sought me out later, he was looking for another man. He also needed papers to conceal his true person—he had no identity at the time, He was flying with his ass in a frost."

"Let's start with the papers. Did you get them for him?"

"Of course, I did. You see, Mr. Nasir, I have an odd sense of honor. I would have killed him myself and never missed a meal over it. That said, my brother had taken on the assignment of protecting him. It was out of respect to my brother that I took care of his papers and arranged to get him away from here as far as possible. I never want to hear of him ever."

"May I ask the name he assumed at that time and where he went?"

"I'll get to that in a minute. Don't you want to know the name of the man he was looking for?"

"It would help."

"That you'll have to discover on your own; you are an investigative reporter so I'll point you, and then you can investigate," Eppy laughed perversely.

"If I may ask, is there something personal you have against Amir Hamdallah?"

Eppy tilted his head downward, lamentably staring at the floor before speaking.

"My brother, Zahid Chutani, was killed senselessly in that bombing. It was senseless because the little shit he had vowed to protect never deserved the attention he received and was never worthy of the reputation bestowed on him. I knew it. My brother knew it. But to the last minute, my dear brother behaved with nobility and integrity while in the employ of a troop of men he knew were the worst scoundrels on earth. He had already lost trust in the people he was reporting to but he had to be faithful for that one last job—it's called honor."

"I don't understand." Nasir's curiosity had peaked as a result of Eppy's disclosure.

"How could you? Zahib is my brother. He was as extreme a jihadist as any. What he did for the cause was unimaginable. He believed in what he was doing, but then he saw the dark side of Allah step out into the fresh morning dew. You know what I'm talking about. A conversion. Enlightenment. Whatever you want to call it, his spirit became free as an angel. I agreed with him. The violent brand of Islam he—and I also—had lived was a bust. Zahid thought he might talk sense with this little imp in order to get him to help use his undeserved authority toward good. I told him the enterprise of turning the kid in the right direction was futile. He insisted on trying, and it cost him his life. " Eppy's voice softened. "I'll never get over the loss."

"I'm sorry."

"Now you want to know the name I granted him, along with his worthless life? He left as Ashur Tayyeb al-Atassi. His destination was Damascus, Syria."

"You sure you can't tell me the name of the man—"

"Mr. Nasir, if I told you that I would ruin all your fun." As if negotiating a contract Eppy stopped to deliberate. "When you get to Syria, contact a man named Ahmad Yosf. I'll give you his number and you can tell him I sent you."

"Thank you, Eppy."

Eppy was writing the information for Nasir on a piece of paper. He paused to glance up at his guest. "If you find out this man you're looking for is dead, let me know…please."

Nasir notified Savpara that he had completed his mission. He was then ordered back to Qatar for a debriefing. Savpara felt compelled to play angry daddy and whip the bad boy a hundred lashes, then take away his free pass to Jannah, the heavenly place where in their afterlife, Muslims' every wish is granted.

"Isn't that a bit extreme?" Nasir queried his cruel employer, appalled that he'd be banned from ever attaining eternal peace.

"You've been a naughty boy," Savpara chuckled.

Had he? He'd deceived one friend in an attempt to save another.

24

LOOKING FOR A COOL CAT
WITH TEN LIVES

QATAR HAS ITS OWN airline, Qatar Airways. In contrast to American domestic carriers, it claims to be making a profit. This is a dubious statement likely permitted by generous subsidies from the ruling emir, Sheikh Hamad bin Khalifa Al Thani—a man with that many names surely can afford to keep a lousy airline flying.

Still quivering from his frisky fanciful encounter with Savpara, Nasir hopped the first flight he could get to Syria. He arrived in Damascus without any glitches. It was a city he knew intimately.

At the time, rumors were circulating in private circles pertaining to the country's esteemed leader, President Hassim al-Abitz. A brief history might explain the nature of the gossip.

Hassim was thirty-four years of age when his father, Fallez, died. He was next in line to inherit leadership of his nation but…the damn constitution stipulated that the leader of the country had to be forty. Hassim is reported to have at first yelled invectives at his mother, followed by going into the bathroom, locking the door, and crying.

It was while sitting on the royal throne that he had a royal epiphany, his first of many royal breakthroughs. He called for his servants to wash his hands and face and dry him. "No problem," he celebrated to a group of plebes with no idea what he was rejoicing about.

In the snap of the finger, presto, a new constitution dropped from the sky. It was perfect. When spread out in plain Arabic, it was clear to anyone with eyes to see that the president had to be thirty-four. As the new President put it to his those lacking a sense of humor, "Like it or lump it!"

When Nasir's plane set down on the Syrian runway, lots of people in the country had decided to lump it, and al-Abitz was in a rotten mood. While that meant lots of "lumpers" were going to die, Nasir's business was not to deal with internal politics.

In his pocket, he carried the single sheet of paper Eppy had given him with the name he hoped could finally answer the question of how to locate Ashur Tayyed al-Atassi. The man he was sent to see was Ahmad Yosf. Eppy had written the name, along with the man's phone number and address in Damascus.

Nasir knew where to stay, calling ahead to book a room at the small but exclusive Beit Zafran Hotel de Charme in the old historic district of the city. The owner, Basel Al Hallak, was awaiting his arrival and greeted him with a warm hug.

"Danish, it's been how long?"

"Too long to have not seen an old friend."

"Old?" he laughed. "A few aches, but my wife doesn't complain. I'm still as virile as a lion," his intonations sounding like a Brooklyn Jew. "And you?"

"I'm married."

Al Hallak threw his arms up as a gesture of celebration. He jogged without lifting his feet off the ground to a counter. He stepped behind it and took out a bottle and two glasses.

"To this we drink. You are living proof it is never too late," he smiled jubilantly.

"Yes. And she has a son which makes me officially a stepfather."

"What's the story that brings a man as famous as you to this…" the owner whispered, "shameful country?" After posing the question, he poured the glasses and took a healthy gulp.

"It's bad, I understand."

"We live in troubled times. In fairness, I'm not sure it's much different anywhere today."

"You may be wrong," Nasir commented solemnly, leaving no time to delve further into what he knew was a topic that would embarrass his friend. "But the answer to your question is that I'm looking to talk with a man named Ahmad Yosf. I have his number and address."

"Where does he live, Nasir?"

"He's a wealthy man, I can tell you that," Basel expressed as he perused the address Nasir showed him.

"Basel, I'll reach him tomorrow. Now, did you reserve a nice room for me?"

"Come, I'll take you up myself."

Basel called to the bellman sitting at the front of the lobby, motioning for him to take Nasir's suitcase.

This boutique hotel was one of Nasir's favorites in the world. His best description was elegance at every level. No room was remotely similar in size, dimension or décor to another. Tiles, woods, bricks, stones, fabrics of every imaginable shade, texture and type were jumbled to create an unimaginable visual display so soft and pleasing to the senses that it defied reason.

All the rooms were built around an interior open courtyard. Nasir was taken to the third floor. When the proprietor opened the door he beamed proudly. "Your favorite."

"You're too kind to me."

The room was huge. While every detail was to his taste, there were two items he loved most. In the sitting area was an old wood-framed chair with a chartreuse fabric he delighted resting in while sipping a fruit drink and reading a book. When he glanced to be sure the old relic was still in place, he noticed a strawberry-colored glass filled to the top with a cute green umbrella protecting the foamy liquid from particles of dust that might otherwise rain down.

The bathroom, however, was truly his favorite. It looked like a medieval dungeon. The walls were decorated with large grouted bricks of dark grey and dirty rust color. Chocolate and tan tiles formed the tub, and the floor was polished mahogany. The only bright item was the off-white sink.

He had talked about the hotel to my mom. I recall her "yuck" face when he described the bathroom. He tried to convince her it came off much different than she could imagine. She respectfully acknowledged perhaps it did—she was less respectful when he suggested proving it to her by redesigning their bathroom at home as a replication.

I know it was the only time that I overheard them argue, but I'm sure not the only time they did. What fun is it being married if you forfeit one of the great benefits of a permanent union, having someone to battle with who shows up the next day ready to do it again?

That evening Nasir was served dinner on the outdoor patio. He was feeling refreshed. He watched as darkness was proving that if given enough time, it would turn pure blue to black. He didn't notice when the lights were switched on. By then he was elevating his spirits with a rare second drink. He sensed good fortune was coming his way and soon he'd be home reunited with his wife, and I would be safe again— alcohol will do that to you.

The next morning he placed a call to Mr. Yosf. The man was out for a walk but the party answering assured him as soon as he returned in roughly a half hour he would get back to Nasir. He waited in his room for the phone to ring. When it did Mr. Yosf identified himself. Nasir mentioned that he was a friend of Eppy. Hearing the name, Mr. Yosf warmly greeted him. Immediately, he said he would be pleased if Nasir came at once to his home.

The visit was very short, yet extremely productive. Mr. Yosf, at the request of Eppy, had arranged for Ashur to get settled in Damascus. In fact, Ashur stayed the night with Yosf. He wanted to get in touch with another man that Yosf did not know. After making a few calls, however, Yosf told Ashur that another man, Suhail Abdo, living in the north, in Homs, would definitely be able to help Ashur find the gentleman he sought.

Yosf then looked at his desk to see if he could find the contact information for Abdo. He successfully located it, scribbling the information on a piece of paper that he gave to Nasir. Nasir thanked him profusely and left. He then emailed Josea that he believed he was a giant step closer to the objective of the trip. Indeed he was, Amir was using the name Ashur and had reached out to a man that Nasir was about to meet.

He headed north in a rented vehicle toward the central part of the border between Syria and Lebanon. It was only a hundred mile trip; he was told it would take no more than two hours. He reasoned he'd drive the first half before trying to reach Suhail Abdo—when he called there was no answer.

Nasir kept abreast of current events and had read extensively on the unrest in Syria. Anti-government protests had resulted in the leader-dictator calling out his security forces to quell the angry mobs that had the audacity to tear down images of he and his family.

Homs had been referred to as The City of the Revolution with tens of thousands of citizens gathering in the city's main plaza—"Liberty" Square—to voice their opposition to the iron fisted rule of the president's regime. More than sixty of those citizens didn't make it, but that's the highly dubious government estimate. Other sources reported deaths closer to the one thousand mark once the riots began. The area was unstable but

Nasir checked before leaving and was assured that at the time it was safe.

The Orontes River splits the city of Homs east and west. The east is flatlands, the portion of the city housing most of the old buildings and establishments. The more modern parts of the city are to the west. Nasir had mentioned to his friend, Al Hallak, at the hotel in Damascus that he had only traveled to Homs once in the past and that was years before. Al Hallak called ahead and booked a room at the Safir Hotel.

Eager to pursue his goal, he checked in and then called Abdo a second time. This attempt would result in an answer—it was not Abdo.

"What do you want?" a man named Sahi grunted.

"I'm trying to reach Abdo. I was given this number."

"Call me Mush," the man on the other end of the line curtly instructed Nasir.

Nasir said that when he heard the name he had to suppress his laughter. *Call me Mush? Did you lift your nickname from a character in a mafia movie? What about Benny Eggs, The Scrambler, The Ant, Meat or Vinny*, Nasir tittered inaudibly?

"Well, do I have the wrong number or do you know this man I'm trying to reach? I'm a reporter and I would like a few minutes of his time."

Sahi (Mush) at first refused to acknowledge if he knew Suhail Abdo, but instead informed Nasir that he'd call him back. It was not until late that afternoon when Nasir heard from him. "I'll be at your hotel in thirty minutes," he brusquely related to Nasir.

When he arrived, Nasir was sitting in the lobby. Sahi went to the desk and after a short talk the receptionist pointed to Nasir. The man approached. He was wearing a loose-fit tan Didiashah (robe) that fell almost to the ground. On his head was the summer white Gutrah wrapping the face. It was held in place by an Ogal, a black band formed around the head.

Only his hands and face were visible; he had a full beard partially hidden under the Gutrah. His eyes were a story to be told, but one that a wise soul would have the good sense not to probe. Their intensity was frightful, not owing to him seeming dangerous as much as him appearing to be in mortal yet unidentified peril. They popped forward, scanning, screening and scrutinizing like a madman.

"Come with me," Nasir was ordered.

He followed the man outdoors to a jeep-like open vehicle. Nasir noticed as he entered the car that laying on the floor in the rear was an assault rifle. The man took off without a word. They drove about a half hour toward the east, entering the Syrian Desert. As they proceeded the temperature was heating up, but still not rising to a full summer bake. Nasir had no hat with him. The man, recognizing the sun might burn him, handed Nasir a black baseball cap with NY in white lettering. Putting on the hat, he had to laugh.

"You a baseball fan?" Nasir questioned in an attempt to break the ice.

The man still hadn't formally made an introduction but Nasir assumed by voice recognition that he had to be Sahi or Mush. In response to Nasir's question, he carefully diverted his eyes from driving to look at Nasir, who was seated next to him. "It belonged to an American newspaper reporter who was found to be working for the CIA."

Nasir swallowed down the inference, noticing that despite the relief from the hot rays of the sun his head broke into a sweat—he knew better than to ask where the reporter was now.

"Don't worry. We know who you are and won't harm you."

Finally they stopped in a small town. There was a café and as they entered the proprietor nodded to Sahi. They sat for only a minute before two cups with rich dark coffee were placed in front of them.

"You are a reporter from Al Jazeera and you were investigating the Pakistani matter. You want to know what was happening there and who was killed, am I correct?"

"Yes, that's right," Nasir confirmed, shying away from mentioning the name Ashur too quickly.

"You want the story of what happened to Ashur Tayyed al-Atassi. Is that correct?" Mush questioned directly.

"A man named Eppy in Pakistan informed me that he prepared papers for this person you refer to as Ashur. He used them to come to Syria," Nasir explained. "Yes, I want to know what happened to him."

"And you know the true identity of this man?"

"I believe I do," Nasir answered tentatively.

"Then you must tell me his name."

"Amir Hamdallah."

"We really don't care why you are interested. It seems that lots of people are looking for him, especially the Israelis and Americans. He was a great man—"

"Was?" Nasir interrupted, unable to repress questioning the use of the past tense.

"Allah called him. He is dead."

"But he's not dead. Everyone in the region knows he's in hiding."

"If it were true that he was alive and hiding under our protection, would we be inviting you to report his story?" Sahi picked up his cup and sipped, while habitually surveying the other men sitting at tables.

"I presume not." Nasir agreed, but with notable bafflement. Irrefutable evidence spoke to Amir being alive, but now this stranger was insisting to the contrary that he was dead. "If you know he was killed—"

For the first time what Nasir interpreted as a smile creased the man's face.

"You assume he was killed, but that is not what happened."

"Then what happened?" Nasir paused, squinting from light shining through a shade partially covering the window next to him. "Before that, why would you even let me have the story? It makes no sense you would want it reported...I mean given his esteemed status."

"I will tell you, but truth is sometimes harder to believe than a lady's promise."

"I've had a few of those go sour," Nasir laughed.

"After you have the story of Amir Hamdallah's death, you will publish an article describing what you have learned, right?" Mush asked, indifferent to Nasir's humor.

"Correct."

"So, I will tell you a story. You will write an article. You are a respected man. You will report that a reliable source claims Amir Hamdallah is dead. You'll mention that you have spoken to people who explained how it happened and when," Sahi confidently concluded. "And what will happen after you publish this in Al Jazeera?"

"People will know he's dead," Nasir cooperatively provided the expected answer.

"No. Quite the opposite," Sahi smirked. "They will believe you have been fed a fiction. They will listen to every detail of your story and then dispute each in turn. They will ask for proof and when you give it to them, they'll tell you it's not real evidence of his perishing. When you fail to produce an arm, leg, heart or head, a cell from which his genetic code can be identified, the credibility of your story will fall like stock in America."

"And if my story crashes, what are you going to gain?"

Sahi leaned backward, spreading his arms and smiling widely as he spoke to an invisible audience. "It will make the legend of this great man even stronger."

"I'm not a stupid person, but I'll admit at times I'm confused by the reasoning of my fellow man. I don't understand what that will do for the dead man's reputation."

"It will be believed that he has eluded the infidels who have poured all their resources into killing him. He will remain alive in spite of the reality, that he is dead. His stature will grow even greater. Mr. Nasir, I'm sure you understand that our people wish their leaders to be chosen by Allah, thus to be special people; ones with no imperfections, ones with supreme courage and strength."

"Like movie stars, Hollywood big wigs? Man loves heroes," Nasir mumbled with a scent of sarcasm.

"Correct. Only Allah selects real heroes, not the ungodly, immoral types promoted like cartoon characters in America and shipped to our land to pervert our people. Amir Hamdallah, you should know, gave his life for his people and his faith. He made the greatest sacrifice a man can be called on to make. His wealth, his education and his mind were surrendered to Allah."

Nasir couldn't—yet at the same time could—believe what he was hearing. This intelligent soldier sitting with him bowed to the image of a man who in Nasir's mind could only be judged as a monster.

"Now that you told me this, what makes you think I'll risk damaging my credentials to publish a story I know is born of ill-intent?"

"You will because that's what reporters do, report. Besides, if you choose not to, how long do you think it will be before we find another esteemed servant willing to serve Allah's wish?"

"I'll do it, you're right," Nasir confirmed for Sahi.

For obvious reasons, he sought proof of Amir's death; he was willing to play the chump to get it. Besides, he reasoned if they were correct and Amir was no longer of this planet, than somebody else was responsible for the acts of murder committed and the threats being made to his stepson. It wouldn't answer whom, but it would weaken the proposition of a personal vendetta against me.

"If you would like to take a trip with me I'll tell you—and show you—the story of Amir Hamdallah," Sahi promised. "Then I'll have you meet Suhail Abdo, who will give you the final proof you're looking for." He then chortled, the sound of a braggart. "You have a duty to perform for us. Tell me, would you resist doing it?"

Nasir answered the question by following Sahi to the car. As they drove, neither he nor the man driving had an awareness that their every move was being monitored, that they were venturing off for a long, violent...and deadly afternoon.

Unknown to Nasir, Sahi was second in command to Suhail Abdo, undoubtedly the most sought after man in Syria by the Israelis. Abdo operated training camps that had recruited and groomed thousands of soldiers who fought as part of Hezbollah, launching missiles into northern Israel and repelling incursions by the enemy. He also controlled the pipelines that transported rockets, bombs, firearms and munitions to Lebanon from Iran. To find out about anything pertaining to terrorist activity in the central region of the country, Suhail Abdo was the man to see.

Sahi spent the afternoon taking Nasir on an orchestrated journey that included the places and persons needed for Nasir to document Amir's death. When he had finished his mission, he pulled off the road to make a call. It was brief, but as he pocketed his cell he told Nasir that it would be another forty-five minute drive to introduce him to Abdo.

The last several miles had been on a dirt road. The wind had kicked up and was blowing sand so hard it felt like needle pricks on Nasir's exposed face and hands. Sahi had draped his body cloth around his face to prevent breathing fragments into his nose and mouth. Nasir wore western garb but wished on this occasion he had come better prepared.

"We're almost there," Sahi informed him, noticing his discomfort. "I'll get you a Gutrah for the drive back," he kindly offered, never imagining this was a one-way trip.

As they approached their destination, Nasir eyed what he thought at first might be small conical-shaped grain silos. Yet as they closed the distance he noticed, like Indian teepees on an open plain, a cluster of high-beamed adobe brick structures.

"What are those?" he asked Sahi, still not aware the funny domes represented the terminus of their journey.

"We call them beehive homes," Sahi answered as he abruptly stopped the car.

He was about to embellish on the question but noticed as he was getting out of the vehicle that it was swaying. Nasir jumped out at the same time, both men aware that when their feet hit the ground the earth was shaking and rocking, the movement lasting several seconds.

"That was a good one" Sahi commented matter-a-fact.

"Earthquake," Nasir confirmed.

"Well, that's why we build this type of house here in the desert. That earthquake was not an unusual event here—we get a ton of them. This style of house, with the materials we use, withstands wind, earthquakes and heat better than any other. You've never seen it?"

Nasir had no opportunity to respond. Two events unfolded almost simultaneous to one another. First, a man in his sixties came out from one of the beehives. Nasir caught sight of him wearing a finely pressed shumaq, a red and white checked garment similar to the plain white version being worn by Sahi. He had a nicely manicured grey goatee. He casually raised his right hand just above hip level to welcome the guests.

As the arm was lowering, the second event began. It was a roaring sound from the west. Several jets were flying low over the desert floor. Rather than in formation, however, they trailed one another in a straight line. The noise was deafening…and intentionally so.

Following the last plane was a squad of helicopters, their blades spinning at near the speed of sound and collectively creating a shocking thump-thump-thump-thump-thumping. Within seconds, the rotors slowed, replacing thumps with whooshes.

The birds descended swiftly, heavily armed men jumping out in every direction but not before massive weapon fire reigned down on the structures and exposed personnel. Suhail turned to run inside. Soldiers bursting out of the caped houses bearing machine guns were firing wildly. Two were carrying hand held rocket launchers they wished to fire but never had a chance. All of the men were overwhelmed by far superior gun and manpower.

Sahi grabbed his rifle from the back of the jeep. As he did he glanced at Nasir, astonished by his likely presumption that the visiting journalist had set them up for death. He aimed at Nasir. He began to pressure his finger on the trigger. As he did he took multiple bullets in the chest, groin and neck. Still standing, the blood pulsing from his lower abdomen looked like a kid urinating red on the playground.

One of the soldiers pulled Nasir from behind by the collar of his shirt, nearly choking him. He then threw him to the ground behind the jeep, actually covering the reporter with his body.

The operation was over within minutes. Nasir was led to one of the choppers. It was the second time in a week he was aloft in a whirly bird. The first occasion unnerved him. Now, with bullets flying every way imaginable he understood terror; he was closer to the deadly reality of war than he had ever been.

25

AND THE SUPPOSED STORY OF AMIR

I'VE SEEN MY FRIEND Josea angry a few times. She's far from a physically imposing figure but I'll swear when she gets riled her brain swells and she swings it wildly like a bowling ball on a tether—that's imposing if you're in the same room and can't find a desk to hide under or a window to jump for safety.

I wasn't there when she met with Hazut after the Israelis pulled rank. They had fortuitously been backed into an optimal situation and acted accordingly.

Josea had been faithful all along, keeping the Israelis in the loopdiloo about every event or circumstance pertaining to Nasir. Therefore, when he emailed her excitedly that morning telling her he was certain he was about to get the scoop on not only Amir, but also Suhail Abdo (unknown to him to be the notorious enemy of Israel), she forwarded the good news to the Israelis.

They couldn't resist an opportunity they knew might not be present again for years. Hazut personally led the operation and was the butt of her rage, delivered to her ex-boss impolitely in front of Mr. Caplow, the American Secretary of State who was sitting in on the meeting.

"We had a deal," she shouted, breathing heavily. "It was trust. We sat right here and agreed that you would stay out. Nasir was nearly killed!"

Hazut had the answer to shut her up and knew it. He tried everything not to employ the trump card but she wouldn't relent. He remained calm throughout her tirade, finally sobering her with one statement.

"Josea, you would have done the same thing—I've seen you do it."

That was all he said and all he needed to say.

In the service of Israel, she had engaged in practices she wasn't proud to admit. Yet she knew they were unavoidable at the time owing to the damage to life and property that would have occurred had she operated with unblemished morals.

Calmed down, Josea turned to Nasir. "I think we'd all like to know what happened that afternoon when you were out with Sahi. Are you up to it?" Nasir had arrived only an hour earlier and had to be exhausted. "If you're not, we can wait... five minutes," she joked to Nasir.

"It is fine," Nasir responded.

He proceeded with a remarkable tale. He was frequently interrupted as questions cropped up.

"After Eppy secured Amir's passage to Syria under the new identity of Ashur Tayyed al-Atassi, you people lost track of him. What you might not have known is that he was far more treasured in Syria than even Pakistan. Sohail Abdo arranged for yet another name and accompanying identity documents. He was now known as Hisham Alhusen, which was the last known alias.

"He did everything exactly as you would have predicted him not doing. He stayed in Syria rather than fleeing further from Israel. All the time you were seeking his arrest he was closer in time from you than an average morning commute on a Los Angeles freeway.

"Settled in Syria, he dreamed that he would soon return out of exile to his beloved Palestine. He had a plan to make it happen; all he needed to do was reach one man.

"His brother-in-law, the same Dr. Efron who as you know had applied his scientific genius toward Jawiris' plan, had an assistant he held in the highest regard. It was Efron's opinion that this man would some day stand on the shoulders of the greats of science, making life-altering inroads in the fields of biological and chemical research.

"This may have been an overblown assessment but it registered with Amir, perhaps making it the catalyst for his vision of "The Final Solution" to the Israeli situation."

"You going to keep us guessing here, Nasir, who the mystery man is that Amir was so intent on meeting?" Josea questioned in a teasing tone.

"No," Nasir responded indifferently. "His name is Fadi Abbas."

Josea looked like she was sucker punched by a heavyweight boxer. The air expelled from her gut vanished and she forgot to replace it. Finally she gagged.

"Fadi Abbas is the man working for Nadine Street. Nasir, he's assigned to protect Zach!!" she shouted. Then after a few silent moments of contemplation, she spoke. "Nasir, before we do anything, let's get your story finished up," she instructed impatiently. It's best we have all the information before sending off a warning to Nadine."

"Eppy, the man in Pakistan, must have presumed that Fadi Abbas was in Syria because he was Syrian by birth, a fact unknown to Amir. Thus, he was successful not only in getting Amir to that country, but also hooking Amir up with Abbas. The relationship between the two men quickly became very close."

Nasir also interjected that Sahi mentioned to him that he wasn't surprised Fadi and Amir got on well. Both were very intelligent. Both had a strong commitment to their faith. Both had inexhaustible determination and drive. They even resembled one another in so far as they were built similarly; except their faces would leave no mistake they were not twins or even relatives.

"One of the stops that Sahi made with me that afternoon was to the home of Fadi Abbas' parents," Nasir continued. "Sadi had a need to verify every element of his story. I could tell that the mother and father were saddened due to the loss of Amir. The most remarkable thing they told me was that Fadi was mesmerized by Amir and idolized him. He would do anything to please his new friend and business partner.

"They explained that while they knew no specifics, Fadi was the only person to whom Amir confided every detail pertaining to the Jawiris plan; what it was, who was involved and why it failed. Amir had given Fadi a list of objectives to fulfill in the event something happened to Amir.

"As a loyal devotee, Fadi swore to him as if he himself were Amir, that every one of his wishes in the service of Allah would be fulfilled. The parents did not know what the commitment was but it definitely included revenge toward Zach and heaping suffering on the parties he held accountable for the oppression of Palestinians and abuse toward Muslims—America and Israel."

"So, are we to conclude Amir is dead?" Caplow asked.

"I'm almost finished," Nasir responded apologetically. "The temple in San Francisco where all the young people were drugged? That's the awful proof that what Amir sought from Fadi Abbas was accomplished. Amir envisioned after what he heard about Fadi that the young genius could create new forms of drugs that would act with severe and irreversible effects. These substances were intended to be the means to potentially poison millions of people. Simply stated, Amir was looking for a new type of nuclear bomb, one that could pass through airport security as easy as three ounces of mouthwash.

"Day and night they toiled in the laboratory Amir had built for them. Amir assisted as best he could, but it was all Fadi, inspired by service to Allah first and dedication to Amir second.

"None of the paper work for the research has ever been found. Fadi must have it with him. But according to the sources I talked with earlier today, they had guinea pigs lining up to try the new boutique drugs. Sadly, a number of them either succumbed to the effects of the substance or never recovered. Since that was the intended outcome, you might say they were successful."

The audience was entranced, yet impatient. Nasir dashed forward to conclude his orientation.

"One afternoon Fadi was at home talking with his mother. He mentioned a plan to come to America and attack the infidel on his own soil, indicating it was too dangerous for Amir to travel. An hour later, he left to go back to the laboratory. It was presumed that during the interval between when he left home and arrived at the lab there was a terrible explosion.

"Sahi explained that the facility was totally destroyed. Body fragments were undetectable but Amir's clothing and fancy jewelry—watches, necklaces, diamond studs, and rings that he refrained from wearing—along with quite a stash of money he kept hidden in the lab was found in the debris, the articles of jewelry mangled but identifiable. The police investigative reports determined that the human elements were from Amir's body."

Nasir now stopped to inspect the faces of each person present before pronouncing his verdict. "Amir Hamdallah is dead."

It was silent for quite some time before Caplow finally spoke. "So Fadi Abbas is pinch-hitting for Amir. He's proven himself to be equally as adventurous, cunning and deceptive, hasn't he?"

"We'll need pictures of this Fadi and whatever other information we can get," Hazut added while making notes on a pad of paper. "I'll have my people get working on it immediately. You didn't happen to see what he looked like when you were at the home of his parents?" he asked Nasir.

"I really didn't—"

"You're not getting it, sir," Josea respectfully addressed her old boss. "This man is in New Mexico right now. He works for a close friend of ours. That's how he's cleverly positioned himself to torture Zach and harm innocent people. This is over! We just need to be careful approaching him. Once we pick him up, he's finished, and this is history."

Hazut looked at Caplow, inviting suggestions how he wanted to proceed since Fadi Abbas would be arrested and tried on American soil under American jurisdiction.

"This is federal. I want to fly home…Josea, as far as you know is there any reason he won't stay put until I get back and have this handled flawlessly?"

"I don't think so, Mr. Caplow. He can't have a clue we're on to him. His attention has to be on when to strike next. Still, he'll want to have easy access to Zach, so I doubt we're taking a risk waiting a day."

"Settled. I'll meet as soon as I get off the plane with Horton at CIA. He'll have his top people take Abbas in."

The meeting disbanded, the four people relieved that Fadi Abbas, the stand-in for the dead Amir Hamdallah, would, in a few hours, be in custody. The world could then rest peacefully knowing that one more demonic character had been placed where he could no longer harm others.

It was agreed that until Caplow was home, and Fadi Abbas was arrested, no emails, calls or communications on the subject with anyone outside the room would be permitted—no exceptions, not even to tell Zach Miller that soon he could resume a normal life without further torment by Amir Hamdallah's servant.

All parties were celebrating the happy ending.

Amir Hamdallah is dead. Fadi Abbas is on his way to a life behind bars. Yippidy do da, yippidy day.

Evil on earth is coming to an end.

BOOK III
TAKING REVENGE

26

A BRIEF RESPITE FROM CRISIS

THE OTHER DAY, I was reading the newspaper. For those who have never heard of them, in the old days they used to print stories and current events on paper, and then sell them at newsstands or deliver them to subscribers' homes. It was a remarkable means of communication, one that is now reaching as close to extinction as a record turntable.

It's progress! Today, a cumbersome document printed on a daily basis with enough words that it would take an Evelyn Woods Speed Reading champ a week to plow through can be conveyed in seven words and digested in under three seconds: *Hate! War! President's a meanie. Go Dodgers!*—and you don't even need to take a grammar class to tweet it, nor to compute it.

I still preferred the long versions of stories. Yet I was wondering as I browsed through the pages of the Los Angeles Times on the very morning Nasir had arrived back in Tel Aviv after his adventures in Pakistan and Syria, if my hometown paper was repositioning itself, to become some sort of hard tweet; the text, hidden between advertisements, had shrink to near nothing. Relegated to the bottom of a page my attention was drawn to a simple statement: *Study conducted in Britain finds that people recover best after surgery when they believe they are loved.*

Now that's a real piece of genius, I sarcastically muttered through my chuckling. *Somebody conducted a study to prove what any moron instinctively understands?*

To prove my point, I asked Sousche, my little girl, if she thought the research provided a breakthrough insight. She also laughed, but harder than me. "Of course, daddy. But I don't want a sturgury." I was about to correct her pronunciation but thought better of it—was she making a joke, intentionally talking fish?

That single newspaper sentence did stimulate another thought. Would the principle apply to surviving a life crisis; would a person living moment-to-moment knowing their family might be wiped out do better under the circumstances knowing that others loved them? I had my doubts.

The sad reality was that during the three weeks plus that Nasir and Josea were on their trip, I was tormented. Many of the same symptoms I experienced while imprisoned in Israel hopped back into my life like they were jolly old buddies.

My gut was constantly tightening and I found it hard to hold down food. I'd have bouts where my heart would race uncontrollably and then thump until my chest ached. Headaches, backaches and neck stiffness—I had all of it and more.

Visions of Amir would invade my hours of attempted sleep, startling me to wakefulness. I'd then lay for hours shaking and unable to fall back to sleep. In the morning I'd be listless, then lack energy for the rest of the day.

Time became my worst foe. I cursed the sadistic, lazy, immovable seconds, minutes, hours and days. The human perception of time operates in lockstep with our emotions. Just ask any teenager. An evening out with her boyfriend whizzes by in a fraction of a second; waiting an endless five minutes for an email to be sent informing her if she was admitted to the college that's her first choice, turns her skin prickly over what seems to her to be a decade. I was pathetically trapped in time's gripping force.

I had earlier proclaimed that I wasn't fearful—by this point, time had mercilessly ravaged my defenses. I'll admit I was scared for myself as well as my family.

To put it into temporal perspective, the day Nadine called and asked me to talk, then driving up to Mescalero to see me, was about a week prior to Nasir and Josea taking flight to Israel.

"It's about Fadi Abbas," she had expressed with an urgency I couldn't understand. "Something seems different and I don't know if there is anything I can do," she shared with me when we were together.

"It must be important for you to come up here," I commented. "Is he not well?"

"I'm not sure. He's not a man who complains or asks for anything."

"Tell me what you notice and then let me see what I can make of it."

"I know he's alone. Zach. I'm not aware of a friend he has in the world. That may be part of it. He seems so...lonely.

That's it! He's always been in a good mood. I hadn't ever seen him otherwise until the last couple weeks. I'm not sure if I'm observing sadness or he's just preoccupied."

"Does he fail in his assignments?" I posed to assist in the analytical process.

"No. He's as reliable as ever. I have caught him sleeping at his desk a couple times," she deliberated, as if her words were uncovering a mystery. "Look, I'm sorry. Here you are with all these problems and I'm burdening you over nothing. It's likely all my imagination."

"Nadine. The last person I know who could be tricked by their imagination is you. There's a change and it's bothering you because you don't get what it's about."

"I do have a tendency to wrestle with loose ends, don't I?"

I smiled to let her know it was an accepted fact she was a freak about getting answers when something didn't make sense to her. That's what had contributed toward her being the best of the best as a detective.

"I don't understand why I'm saying this but, Nadine, my instinct this time is that you should dig into your feeling."

"Oh, you're always the one advising me to ease up and let some of my suspicions rest until they either die on their own or demand I address them. What happened?"

"Like I said, instinct."

I'll never forget the conversation. Looking back, that's all it was, raw intuition.

"I don't know, Zach. The more I discuss it, the more I think he's just going through a bit of troubled psychological waters. He has a right," she stated as a declaration to herself. "If I could find him a lady, I think he'd be back to himself."

"Do you know anything about his personal life? Does he have a girlfriend or ever go out on a date? Does he have relatives close by?"

"I wonder if it has to do with money?" she posed as if she unearthed a missing element, while ignoring my questions. "It could be cultural. Perhaps he needs a raise but can't bring himself to ask for it?"

I strolled close to her side while she mused about the situation. A moment later, she appeared as if she were totally satisfied she had made a proverbial mountain out of a molehill. When the weeks leading to the return of my stepfather and friend from the Middle East passed, we would all learn that sometimes we make a molehill out of a mountain.

"I'm going to leave it alone, take your advice this time—"

"You're not doing what I'm suggesting," I humorously declared. I was making a point we both knew well, that when it came down to it, Nadine Street would live or die by her own wits.

"No. If I see the pattern continuing in a week or two, I'll talk to him myself."

That conversation would never take place. A couple days later, Nadine would joyfully call me to announce she had been wise to not pursue the matter further. Fadi had been as relaxed and pleasant as ever.

Silly girl.

I will admit that the three weeks while Nasir and Josea were away were peaceful, which, of course, would seem senseless in so far as I've already described myself as deteriorating emotionally and physically. But the reality was there were no acts of violence against Jews anywhere in the country. There were no overt threats to my family or me. If nothing else, the murder of Platta may have crimped the operation that I was sure Amir was leading from thousands of miles away.

Then preceding the return home by Josea and Nasir by a few days, several events unfolded in rapid and momentous succession.

As Nadine was developing her investigative business, she had occasion to meet with many of the local law enforcement personnel in Albuquerque. She was beginning to earn a fine reputation. Along with her references from Washington, she was gradually being referred a greater number of cases.

On the afternoon three days before Josea and Nasir landed in America, she was on her way to a meeting with a detective from the Albuquerque Police Department. She was half way there when the officer called her, announcing he had to postpone them getting together due to a family emergency. Nadine had files she hadn't finished that were in the office and decided to head back.

When she reached the front door, she keyed it open as she normally would. Just before she left, she had sent Fadi on an assignment so she didn't expect anyone to be there. But as soon as the door was partially opened, she heard a rustling sound coming from her personal office; a second later, a startled Fadi came out. He was carrying a handful of papers.

"Nadine, I had to come back and check something on the Otis Riley file," he volunteered awkwardly. "I'm going to take off. I'm late." His rushed exit precluded her confronting him about why he had entered her space.

He left Nadine wondering if she had been the intruder in her own office. When this incident later proved to be worthy of telling, she explained that the material he alleged having gone into her office to get was already on his computer. Furthermore, they had an unspoken rule that they didn't enter each other's office without permission.

That was not all. When she sat down at her desk to address her own work, she noticed that her computer had been tampered with. She had left it in a sleep mode. Even if she had forgotten to do so, it was programmed to resume a slumber state after ten minutes of inactivity. The screen, however, revealed the cute orange ladybug picture she loved. Some-body had used the computer within the last ten minutes and it had to have been, Fadi.

Totally out of character, Nadine chose not to later confront the suspicious behavior by her assistant.

A second matter came up that Tuesday. A prospective client was scheduled to meet at the office on Wednesday after-noon. Both she and Fadi were to attend. However, late that Tuesday evening she found an email on her computer. The note was short: *How's Thursday at 3:00 instead of Wednesday?*

Nadine was tired and went to sleep, forgetting to forward the message to Fadi. It also slipped her mind the next morning. Then on that afternoon (Wednesday, when the meeting had originally been set) about five before three o'clock, Nadine remembered she had not informed Fadi of the change. When she looked into his office he wasn't there.

This time she violated the unwritten agreement and went inside, noticing on his appointment book that the meeting was penciled in. Knowing he was planning to be there, she wondered why he hadn't come back.

"Fadi, I guess you forgot about the appointment for three today," she mentioned casually as she spoke to him on the cell.

"No, it's Thursday," Fadi responded.

Nadine hesitated for a moment, collecting herself before delivering a calculated response. "I must have forgot I told you." To not arouse suspicion on his part, she made light of the situation. "See what aging does to you?"

She hung up the phone. There was no way Fadi knew the appointment was changed. She was absolutely sure that she had never mentioned it to him and the person she hoped would soon be a new client had already confirmed the new date with her directly—Fadi didn't know the person.

For the first time Nadine acknowledged there was a problem with Fadi—he was spying on her. The matter weighed on her that evening but she decided to approach the situation with counterespionage of her own. She reasoned that if she used the next few days to carefully monitor the activities of her assistant, she'd have an answer to his unprecedented actions.

The next day—one day prior to Caplow's intended date to arrest Fadi—her computer was acting up. A small tech repair store was located on the same block as her office, R & N Computer Services. She decided to give it a try, the one-man shop run by Rusty Nogales.

"It started acting strange this morning," Nadine informed

him. "I can't shut down my server and when I'm in Word it turns off arbitrarily in the middle of any function."

"Probably a bug," he surmised while bending over the machine to run a couple manual tests. "Odd. Anyone other than you use this computer?"

"Never," she stated emphatically.

"Somebody's logged into your accounts, I can tell you that. Have a few minutes, Miss?"

"What is it?"

"I want to check something. This is not a common virus." He still hadn't looked up at Nadine but was fiddling around pushing keys. "Do you have a cell phone with you?"

Nadine reached into her purse and handed the phone to him. Without a word, he took both the cell and computer and went to the rear of the store where he had his workshop. Nadine watched as he performed a few tasks. About fifteen minutes passed before he walked back to Nadine.

"I'm a bit of a freak about tech stuff," he smiled with his eyes aiming downward. "Geek I guess you'd call me. Anywho, does this number mean anything to you?

He handed Nadine a small piece of paper with a phone number. She stared at it, shocked and indignant, shaking her head up and down.

"Every message on your email, every call you get on your cell, every file in your computer is being accessed by whoever is at the end of that number."

"Does that person—"

"Sorry to interrupt, but did you know this computer is linked, like in a network, with another computer?"

"I have no idea what you're talking about."

"It's like you have two computers in one. Are you sure there isn't anyone else that had this computer?"

"It belonged to a friend, but right after she bought it she decided she wanted a different model and sold this one to me at a discount—I'm the only one whose used it in the last several months."

"Miss, I can guarantee you that every file on your computer can be accessed on the other computer owned now by whomever is your friend—get it?"

"Not really," Nadine admitted.

"Look, your computer and your friend's computer are now synced. The third party has access to both of your drives. I'll also tell you that the person who is monitoring your computer is likely as interested in the one that belongs to your friend— your computer is being used as a conduit also to get to that target unit. The reason everything started going haywire just now is that whoever was trying to break into the other person's computer just succeeded."

"So I can see everything that is on my friend's computer and the person with this number can see what is on both of our computers?"

"Right. I hope it's not an enemy," Rusty laughed.

"I'll soon find out," Nadine asserted. "How much do I owe you?"

"I should pay you. This is the type of mystery I love solving."

Nadine wrote out a check and left.

She went back to the office, knowing Fadi would be out for at least the next two hours. Her intent was to see if she could determine why he had been trying to, and finally succeeding in, monitoring her and Josea's communications. At a minimum, she already had the answer as to how he knew the meeting had been postponed to Thursday.

She sat at her desk. Her first task was to email Josea to warn her about Fadi. The message came back with an answer. Josea Roth was not available. She was in transit back to America. She'd return messages at the time of her arrival.

Her next task was to snoop into the messages on both her computer and Josea's in order to determine if Fadi had attained any important information. It took only minutes reviewing Josea's personal notes to understand that Fadi Abbas was the link to the dead Amir Hamdallah. He had come to America to make his mentor's dreams come true— Nadine turned white.

She wasted no time before beating herself silly for being such a fool. Nadine prided herself on being able to read people—more than pride it had been perhaps the most essential ingredient in the keep-myself-alive recipe.

After the history of Fadi Abbas came to light, she could be heard using terms like "mesmerized," "spellbound," and "hypnotized." She had dealt over the years with investigating serial murder cases involving monsters of unimaginable cruelty. But now she wondered if demonic spirits were for real. Had Fadi Abbas donned a satin cape with pointed jabot, vest and black gloves and used diabolic incantations to cast her into a trance from the beginning?

She took the deceit to heart, a dangerous part of her anatomy to let wander mischievously a betrayal of such magnitude. She was wired to respond in one way only, justice needed to be satisfied. I'd seen what she was capable of doing when threatened or violated. In fact, I had advised Preston from the start of their romance not to impale this lovely woman unless he planned to lick every drop of blood spilled.

Nadine now understood that if what Rusty Nogales had told her was true, Fadi was already planning his getaway. The only possibility of intercepting him would be that he knew he had until the next day before Caplow would be back to issue the instructions for his arrest. She reasoned that as far as Fadi knew, Nadine Street was ignorant of his activities. Still, she understood it would alarm him if she tried to get in touch with him.

Her desk had a set of two drawers on the left side. They were deep but the bottom one if pulled out all the way revealed a hidden section that could be locked. It was there where she stored valuables. On her keychain was a small key she used to open it. She pulled out her revolver, a Smith & Weston 38 Bodyguard. She placed it carefully on her desk.

She knew where this was going, what she had to do—Fadi Abbas was soon to die.

27

BUSY DAY IN EMERGENCY SURGERY

NADINE LEANED OVER HER desk, staring at the deadly weapon she knew was soon going to be put into service. She picked it up, removing the bullets from the cylinder. Then she held it outstretched in her right hand, the thumb pressing the release to be sure it was working correctly. She then rapidly pulled on the trigger six times.

As she did, a feeling she had experienced only once in her career returned. It was the sole occasion she had to use her weapon, the one time she killed a man. She had hoped it would never have happened, especially to the man she had no choice but to bring to an end. Now, however, she wanted to stop Fadi dead in his tracks.

Satisfied that it was in good working order, she reloaded it and reverently put it in the precise location of her bag where she knew she could grab it in an instant. She locked the office and ran to her car. It was just another manhunt, like the old days. Or was it?

It didn't register that she was not dealing with a common serial killer motivated by a personal history of hurt, fear and insecurity, and sated by the suffering of an occasional victim. Fadi Abbas was a unique beast intent on large scale mass killing.

Before she locked the office she went into Fadi's room. There was nothing for him to clean out. He had never brought in a single personal item. Except for the papers on the desktop, it looked identical to the day she hired him. *Odd*, she ruminated. I never saw him. *That's precisely as Fadi Abbas had willed it.*

She drove directly to his apartment. She had never been inside. Only once had she dropped him off. That was when what she had referred to Preston as "a pile of shit car" owned by Fadi had broken down and she offered to replace it for him. Staring at the slum of an excuse for a human dwelling, it all came together. Fadi Abbas had played her like a sucker to position himself close to Zach. He had to pay.

The afternoon was cool and clear. It wasn't necessary to wear the wool coat she had on. But it had the advantage of her being able to put her gun in the right pocket so she'd have it ready for use. Once she positioned it inside and rubbed her hand around the grip to feel its exact position she went to the front door. She followed the same path Fadi had led Platta on his visit weeks earlier. She found the number "6" written with a marker on the outside of the fourth door on the right.

She pulled out her weapon. Then she cautiously tested the door lock. It turned but as she used her left hand to apply force there was resistance. The answer why was visible by cursory inspection to the naked eye. The jam was so badly warped that it likely had to be near slammed to fully close. There was only one choice. Nadine took a step back, drew her gun, and kicked forcefully with her left foot, the thrust shooting the door open as her body flew into the room.

It was dead silent. The room stank from dishes with rotting food particles. The sun was close to blinding as it was seen descending at eye level through the uncovered windows. Inspecting the bedroom and bathroom, she noticed that all the toiletries and clothing were untouched—he had left in a hurry or had no need for the few possessions he had.

Satisfied that he was not in the unit, she went downstairs to inspect the parking area. The slots faced the street but she hadn't noticed when she arrived that his car was there. Now she approached carefully and looked inside. It was empty. She opened the trunk. There was nothing except for an airless spare tire and a tire iron flung toward the rear of the compartment.

She leaned against the trunk while facing the street, contemplating what her next move could be. It was then that she spotted a late model Mercedes coupe coming down the block.

"It had to be that the car was so out of place that caused me to instinctively slide into the covered space behind the car next to Fadi's," Nadine later reported. "As I peeked through the glass window, I noticed it was him. He must have forgotten to take something. He pulled up parallel to the parking area and in front of his own car. He was wearing a white sport shirt under what looked like a gold-colored cashmere sweater with blue jeans and white tennis shoes. I had never seen him dressed so fine.

"As he approached his car, he went directly to the passenger side. I was one car over, on the driver's side. I waited as he withdrew an envelope from the glove compartment. Then as he turned to go back to his new spiffy black Benz, I did just as I had rehearsed in my head, I raised my weapon with my right arm. I had no hesitation as I prepared to take him out."

That's when the story fell apart and she couldn't go on. After several attempts to splice together what likely happened, we determined that unbeknownst to Nadine, Fadi had by chance caught sight of her reflection in one of the car windows as he turned. She had only been able to lift her arm partially before Fadi swung around and fired. He was able to deliver two shots, one to her chest and the other to her left upper arm. No doubt he would have emptied his clip had she not dropped out of sight from the impact. Just at that moment, a man coming down for his car ran around the side of the building after hearing gunshots.

Fadi jumped in his car and took off, leaving Nadine either dead or soon-to-be.

The resident had a phone and called an ambulance. The man living in Fadi's building may have been poor, but he saved Nadine's life. By chance, he worked as a scrub nurse at the University of New Mexico in their Level 1 Trauma Center. More remarkable, in his country, Nigeria, he attended the College of Medicine at the University of Nigeria and graduated, but had never practiced.

Uwa Okoye came to America with the dream of furthering his training in surgical medicine. He was as black as the soil he was raised on was worthless. He got off the plane with enough money to beg a room to sleep and nearly starve for two weeks before finally landing his position. Unlicensed, he had no choice but to take any job he could get. He had been employed all of three days when he witnessed the traumatic shooting of Nadine.

Recognizing the point of entry had fortunately missed the heart, he also surmised that the bleeding would soon flood the pleural space and she'd expire unless a tube thoracostomy was inserted quickly to drain fluids—the left arm was immaterial and could be addressed later.

He had no instruments. As he waited with the bleeding body of Nadine beside him he prayed the ambulance would be quick and they'd reach the hospital in minutes. He did what he could in the meantime with CPR to assist her unsteady breathing until help arrived. She had already lost consciousness.

By the time the ambulance came blaring down the block, several other locals had gathered to observe the gruesome scene. The paramedics must have assumed that Uwa was connected to Nadine in some way, since he was bent over administering care to her. When he jumped into the rear of the ambulance, they said nothing.

Nadine was losing blood quickly. But more worrisome to Uwa was her breathing—or near lack of—and the assumed fluids that unless effused would likely expire her. Making the crisis worse, they jumped on Interstate 25 heading north to make time. Had the traffic been normal and there not been an accident that took place nearly in front of them at Gibson, they could have been there in less than ten minutes.

Stuck in traffic and desperately trying to find an opening, with the siren blaring, the paramedic glanced dubiously at Uwa, His message was clear: We're close to losing her. Uwa took over.

"Give me a scalpel," he commanded the technician.

When the man hesitated, Uwa shouted at him with his mud-thick accent. "I'm a surgeon. Now do what I tell you."

Uwa commenced with precision to make an incision in the left lower chest. His handling of the emergency inspired confidence in the attending technician who from that moment forward offered not a word of objection. He did understand what Uwa was doing and grabbed a piece of tubing that he handed to the surgeon who inserted one end into Nadine with the other dropping down to the ground where the technician placed it into a jar—a mass of liquid began draining.

"Call the hospital and see if Dr. Osmond is there," he instructed the technician. "If he's on duty, tell the secretary it's Uwa Okoye and it's an emergency."

When he was told the doctor was in The Center he took the phone and spoke directly to him, impressing Dr. Osmond with his brief but precise summary of Nadine's status.

Nadine was in surgery seven hours.

Her pistol was left lying on the ground next to her hand-bag. One of the locals thought nothing of a gun at the scene in a high crime area. She swept it into her purse and then kindly handed it to Uwa as the rear door of the ambulance closed. Thus they were able to identify the victim and get in touch with Preston, who was working on campus.

He called me just after he reached the waiting room. I was at Kuruk at the time. In the pandemonium of the moment, I ran out the door and raced to my car. In so doing, I unintentionally set off an alarm with Bernadette. She had been assigned as my security person that day—we still had round-the-clock protection. She jumped out of her car and scared the hell out of me as she screamed across the lot with her gun drawn for me to get down.

When I finally came over to her to inform her what happened, she wisely had me get into her vehicle and drove me to the hospital. When I arrived an hour later, Preston was sitting with Uwa by his side—it wouldn't be until after the surgery that Dr. Osmond would inform him that the stranger comforting him saved his fiancé's life.

The wait might have been more dramatic had it not been for the fact that Uwa served as a play-by-play commentator, periodically going to the surgical suite and getting reports on the progress. Normally, the family and friends of victims of trauma need heavy doses of tranquilizers to endure the waiting, but with Uwa continually reassuring Preston that all was going exceedingly well and she was going to make it, a couple burgers with fries and three donuts managed to do the trick. Even with Nadine's tutelage on healthy diet, he still had a proclivity to eat like a trucker.

When I first arrived at the hospital, I hadn't been told about the circumstances leading to her being shot. I assumed... nothing. Preston was told the shooting took place at the residence of Nadine's assistant, Fadi Abbas. However, he couldn't imagine that the man she had placed her trust in had tried to murder her. My friend surmised that Nadine had to go over to Fadi's place to pick something up. She was just unlucky to have been caught in the middle of a crime or a drug deal in a dangerous neighborhood.

I also had no reason to believe it was Fadi Abbas who tried to kill her, until I received a call from Josea. She had just arrived in Washington, D. C. with Caplow. It was rather shocking when the call came in: it was identified as coming from the State Department.

Josea was having problems with her phone and computer. The little whiz immediately was able to diagnose that she had been hacked. Unable to deal with the problem at the moment, she shut down and used Caplow's secured phone line. The reason she wanted to talk to me was because she couldn't reach Nadine. She panicked—rightly so. What she intended to do was warn Nadine that a crew of agents was about to descend on her office and to get out and stay away until Josea informed her that it was safe.

When I told her where I was and why, there was a long silence.

"How the hell did he know...?"

Then I could hear whispering and a second later, a male whose voice I recognized as Caplow's shrieking as loud as possible, "FUCK!"

"It was Fadi," she informed me as she came back on the line.

I had no idea what she was talking about but could tell by her voice that something was terribly wrong.

"I'll explain everything when I get home tomorrow. Is there somebody with Preeti and the children?"

"Of course. Why?" I questioned, noticing my heart thumping.

Bernadette had left with me but Preeti and the children were at her father's house. I called her immediately and told her not to leave until I called her back.

"I'll see you tomorrow." Josea hurriedly called out.

She hung up. Had she implied it was Fadi Abbas who had harmed Nadine? If so, how could Josea know that he shot her? My mind was going in circles. I had to have misread the message.

I wondered if I should share my unfounded concerns with Preston but thought better of it. What difference did it make at that point?

Trying my best to leave the topic of Fadi Abbas alone until I could get the whole story from Josea, I devoted myself to Preston. But then about two hours later another call came in, almost as odd as the one before.

"Zach, it's Jay," the man on the line informed me. "This is really strange so I want to give you a warning call before you receive the package."

"Package?"

"I'm not sure what it's about either. I'll have to wait until you open it and let me know what we're dealing with."

"I'm having big problems here—"

"I know. I talked to Preeti, but she said things calmed down a bit."

"Well, I have a feeling they're about to explode." After I said the word, I suppressed a thought I didn't want to address, but had to. "I hope it's not a bomb you've sent me," I said with earnest.

"No way," he assured me. "I had it checked. Nothing but papers."

Jay Weiner was a high-powered entertainment attorney in Beverly Hills. When I was investigating the disappearance of Stevie Green, the great musical icon, I had extensive dealings with him. It so happened that he and Stevie Green had a friendship not dissimilar to mine with Preston.

Owing to the wealth that had accumulated in the estate of his friend, most of Jay's time was devoted to managing Stevie's business affairs—his practice had become a single-client operation.

"If you have a minute, I want to give you the history on this."

"Jay, I'm sitting in an emergency room. One of my best friends was just shot. I'm keeping her fiancé, my best friend, company. Somebody wants to kill me and possibly harm my wife and children. The Center was burned to the ground. I have time, but what I don't have is a wish for more grief."

"This seems pretty innocuous to me," Weiner said in a soothing tone.

I can see how he reached that conclusion…but he was incorrect. The package was another method of tormenting me, a taunt. It was a clever way for my nemesis to inflict the highest doses of torture on me, and thinking of him laughing his fool head off didn't make the suffering any easier.

"Let me tell you the story," Jay continued. "You've heard of the Law Offices of Chappell and Weill in New York, I'm sure."

Who hadn't? They were probably the most prestigious entertainment law firm in the world.

"Lou Chappell called me the other day asking if I knew you. Of course, I said I did. He had no interest in our relationship but wanted me to carry out an assignment. Obviously, had it been someone of lesser standing, I'd have refused before even hearing him out. But I've known Lou since law school and over the years helped him with matters here on the West Coast.

"He was approached by a man named…I think it was Walli, or something like that…an Arab name that's difficult to pronounce. Well, this man says he has a document he wants delivered to a Zach Miller in Mescalero, New Mexico. The man said he didn't know anything about the content of the envelope other than he was told that Mr. Miller was to be informed it was a movie or stage play script that his client thought was perfect for The Center for the Performing Arts at Kuruk.

"Lou looked at him with puzzlement. He knew every major forum in the world but never heard of the one this man was requesting assistance in reaching. Before he could ask the man about the theatre, he mentioned that he wanted the package to go first to Jay Weiner, and then from Jay Weiner to Miller.

"This Walli fellow who made the appointment with Lou had paid $2,500 in advance just to meet with him for half an hour. Lou explained to this stranger that his firm wouldn't take on unsolicited clients and he knew I didn't either. He suggested trying someone else. The intermediary would hear nothing of it. He told Lou that whatever the cost would be, his client would be pleased to pay. He added that it was sort of a joke but the man he represented was so wealthy he could well afford the luxury."

I was listening, but in disbelief. It had to be something intended to harm me, another diabolical scheme dreamed up by Amir that was being executed by one of his agents. Yet I'll admit my curiosity was tweaked. I even began my own fantasy fair, envisioning Amir calling his harassment of me a gag and sending a let's-be-friends-again peace offering—I was dizzy.

"To make a long story short, Lou mailed it to me and after I confirmed there was nothing other than sheets of paper enclosed, I forwarded it on to you," Weiner informed me. "You have some odd friends, Zach."

"I don't think it's a gesture of friendship, but I'll let you know."

We said our goodbyes. I went back to Preston, my head fighting to keep above powerful rapids commissioned to sucking me under. Abbas shot Nadine? That had to be what I heard. My best friend was understandably out of his wits dealing with possibly losing the only woman in his life with whom he'd ever fallen in love. Josea called to find Nadine and didn't even ask how she was, after I said she'd been harmed. Amir was sending me his latest script, likely requesting I stage it at Kuruk. Wow! What a lucky guy I am.

Bernadette, my faithful bodyguard, had curled up in a chair and was fifty-two percent asleep. Preston was mute, manicuring his fingernails with his incisors. I called Preeti again to make sure all was well and reminding her absolutely not to go home yet.

As I sat, my mind journeyed in a direction guaranteed to get me into trouble. I began wondering what makes a man content. I knew I wasn't. Then in the midst of trying to unravel this absurd psychological circus, it hit me. There were three basic essentials that made for a good life. They were so simple, yet at the moment I had none of them. It didn't matter a smidgen how much of the time one possessed them in the past, take one or more away and the blues would set in.

I laughed as I contemplated my empirical finding: *If a person awakened after a good night's rest, enjoyed sex when they needed it, and performed a good you-know-what with regularity, they had no right to claim depression.* Ah! I'll call it the three S's—sleep, sex and…guess what four-letter word.

Everything that goes wrong in life manifests by assaulting one or more of the three S's. Your business is off twenty percent or you recently lost half your retirement in a stock market downturn. How can you sleep? Your wife is so tired chasing after the little toddler, the last thing in the world she's thinking about when you wake in the middle of the night with the blanket lifted eight inches off your abdomen are words starting with "S," unless it's sleep, which is what you need but only after the other "S" word pulsing your privates gets attention.

You left work an hour early to attend your son's soccer game and had to make up the time working—you passed on lunch. At the park you choke down a cheap dog with mustard, relish and a fat white bread roll with a package of chips. Then you come home and find your wife hadn't time after work to cook so it's off to the Big Mac for supper. An hour later, you're famished so you reward yourself for one hell of an effort staying alive that day with a bowl of ice cream garnished with two Oreo cookies. Before retiring, you pop a couple Tylenol to tame that eye-pulsing headache. By the next morning, an elephant would have a better chance tap dancing than you having a hearty bowel movement.

What was I complaining about? I didn't have any of those pressures. For me, it was just one lousy guy trying to kill me.

Dr. Osmond mercifully terminated my muse.

He was known as a top trauma man and in all earnest we were thankful that he was on duty that day. Preston went running up to him as he came out one of the doors that civilians are never allowed to enter. Like every surgeon after finishing a procedure, he was wearing a spiffy minty-green surgical gown. Osmond looked tired, and no doubt was. But more important to us, he was smiling. He informed Preston it would be a while but she would make a full recovery.

I doubt Preston heard a word after that, but the doctor explained how the bullet to the chest did damage her lung but he felt confident it would heal. No other vital organs had been hit. The doctor patted Preston's shoulder and took off back through the same doors.

Preston looked at me and I could see it coming, a flood of relief tears. They were the type that streams from the eyes in a solid rivulet that drips onto the lower lip that is extended in a smile of dissolved horror.

I politely allowed him his catharsis. I was jealous it wasn't mine. When would I get one?

When we left the hospital, I asked Bernadette if she'd mind running me over to Kuruk before going home. I thought of asking her if she'd just run me over, period, and save Amir the trouble. In the car, I was restless. The events of the day overwhelmed me, yet there was something gnawing at my mind. It was like a dream element I was trying to dredge from the residue of a prior night's sleep.

The more I dug, pulled, pried, pushed, petitioned and prayed, outright quit and then redoubled my examination of the fragments tenuously flitting in my mind, the images and associations dissolved into a mist of allurement beckoning me to come back for more of the same. I knew whatever it was I was trying to dredge up was urgent. I persisted, taking the bait like a sucker going broke trying to recoup his losses at a gambling table.

In the end, the frisky symbols that were insisting I keep searching for that elusive secret missing piece forced me to declare mental bankruptcy. Had I succeeded in hooking the big fish, I would have learned that what the dream-like element was intent on lighting up in my dreary mind was a grand mistake made by the master of deception, Fadi Abbas. If only! If only!

Sadly, the grandest and biggest mistake was mine—I blew it. Had I captured that one fragment of the whole, I would have been able to solve for myself a mystery that would not come to awareness until…

At Kuruk a package had been hand delivered and then placed on my desk. It was from Jay Weiner's office. I tucked it under my arm and went home. Forget all three of the S's, I'd be delighted with just one—I was exhausted.

28

THE SCRIPT

JOSEA AND NASIR LANDED in Los Angeles. She called immediately to tell me everything that she had learned on the trip. On the one hand, I couldn't help but be relieved that Amir was dead. Yet the offset was that Fadi Abbas had been trained to be the perfect duplicate of Amir.

Fadi had been programmed to carry out every piece of minutiae that Amir outlined to defeat his enemies. It made sense. Fadi Abbas had performed an act of psychological gymnastics that only psychotics could succeed at. The young man had transcended his personal identity and assumed that of Amir Hamdallah. For all practical purposes, he was Amir Hamdallah.

The more I dwelled on it, my thoughts left me no more comforted than had Amir survived. In fact, I concluded I'd have been better off with Amir on the hunt. At least then I would have the advantage of knowing him intimately so that I might sense his presence, smell the odor of his flesh, hear his familiar gait or see one of his habits like when he'd deliberate by unwittingly tapping his right index finger against the ridge of his lengthy jaw.

I had only seen Fadi Abbas on one occasion and even then never heard his voice, watched him walk or peered into what had to be his steel-cold eyes.

Early in the conversation with Josea—one that went on well over an hour—she informed me she already knew of Nadine's status. Caplow had been on the phone himself with Dr. Osmond, pestering for an answer as to when she could be debriefed. He did inform the surgeon that there would be FBI agents handling her security. Needless to say, Josea knew more about Nadine's condition than Preston.

She said that Caplow was irate that Fadi had outfoxed them. He had no idea at first how it happened but by the time Josea landed in Los Angeles she had figured it out. Through her computer, Fadi learned the whole story. Realizing he was a hunted man, he took off.

The plan to pursue Fadi Abbas now had to be revised. Initially considered was a full disclosure to the media with Fadi's picture. But Caplow reasoned that every Arab male in the country would be under suspicion and the authorities would be getting more calls than they could investigate. The hunt, therefore, in his opinion, had to be more focused, relying on specific agency personnel.

I said nothing to Josea about the strange parcel that Weiner had forwarded to me. Why should I? I hadn't even opened it. Furthermore, I must have been dealing with a massive force of avoidance in that I had ignored investigating the contents of the envelope.

After getting off the phone with Josea, I made breakfast for Preeti and me. Then I took my children out in front of the house and, along with Henry Higgins, we played for over an hour. Afterward, I went to Kuruk to talk with our manager about aiding a waitress who was struggling with an unwanted pregnancy.

The day went into a welcome gallop. The pace was noteworthy in that it contrasted with the agonizing creep my depressive state had been experiencing. It was after four, when I heard the phone ring. Preeti informed me that I needed to take the call.

"Hello," I voiced awkwardly.

"Zach, it's Jay. Couldn't help but wonder what the hell was in that envelope."

"I never looked at it, Jay. What do you think about that?"

"I think you should open it now." He seemed irritated. "I know you have other things on your mind but if this has something to do with Stevie don't you think out of respect for him we need to know?"

"I don't see how it could be. Jay, I'll open it soon and I promise if Stevie is involved, I'll call you immediately."

"Damn it, Zach. Open it now or I'll call Preeti back on the line and have her do it."

"Hold on," I grumbled.

I had left the envelope on my desk. When I reached my office there it was, looking peaceful as a napping infant.

I picked it up. That's when I felt it rumbling. Then the shaking gained momentum. First the walls of the room began rocking, creaking and pounding, after which the floor vibrated a billion cycles a millisecond while pulsing upward and downward. The room moisture heated like a furnace and the boiling air began to funnel as if being sucked into an invisible chamber inside the package.

I looked down at it. That's when I saw a thick, viscid substance effusing and dropping like molten lava. It was red and black and began spreading around the room, filling it like an aquarium. The soles of my feet were burning as the liquid rose gradually. The outpouring was intensifying, the goop now shooting outward and battering the ceiling with stony particles joining force with the heavy matter.

"Zach!!" Preeti shouted from down the hall. "Where are you?"

"I'm in here. I had to get something," I called out from my grotesque volcanic fantasy.

"Jay called back. You must have hung up by mistake."

"I'll get it, Preeti."

It was remarkable. I desperately wanted to avoid the evil that had to be contained in the package. By the time I had finally been forced to address it, I had worked myself into a state of panic. Yet responding to Jay on the phone, I was as composed as if I was telling him my little dog was licking my nose.

"I've got it right here, Jay. Give me a minute and I'll open the little devil up," my big man persona said flippantly.

Jay had placed the eight and a half by eleven-inch wax-sealed envelope in an outer delivery folder. I pulled the sealed package out and when I opened it I noticed a stack of unevenly positioned papers. They looked as if they were haphazardly shoved into the yellowish wrapping, a frantic act by a crazed mathematician who had mentally broken down after having taken 300 years to finally prove Fermet's Last Theorem. I peered down at the material—the horror I had lived through anticipating opening it had oddly allowed me to conduct the exercise with detached calm.

"It's nothing but a pile of papers," I informed him, pausing to thumb through the pages. "No, there's nothing here having to do with your friend."

"That's a relief, buddy. You take care of yourself and if you need anything let me know."

The top page confirmed what I expected all along, that I had just been delivered another stake of ominous threat no different from what Fadi had shoved into the soil of my front yard weeks earlier. But this one was not to be driven downward in a vertical trajectory—it was definitely aimed horizontally, and for my heart. In bold lettering it read: *TAKING REVENGE—GETTING IT RIGHT.*

"*TAKING REVENGE*" were the same two words written on the top of the document I pulled out of Amir's safe, an outline for the intended evil project Jawiris, Amir, and their backers had been working on. The words symbolized the beginning of trauma.

Typed two lines below *TAKING REVENGE* on the document I had in my hand, was the name Usetah Rima—I had no idea who the person was or why the name was there unless she was the author. I noticed many pages had typewritten material that looked like whole paragraphs, as well as sections that were dialogue.

It was time to read.

It began as I expected, like an allegory. A young Palestinian man, Saleh, by coincidence on his way home to his country, makes the acquaintance of a traveling American close to his age, Cameron. Saleh invites him to stay at his home and they develop a very close relationship.

Saleh has a sister, Yona, and Cameron falls for her mystical beauty. The siblings invite the guest into their private lives, which turns out to be what appears on the surface petty terrorism against the oppressor, Israelis. Cameron is sympathetic to their cause but in truth is discovered to be an agent of the Israelis sent to spy on the Palestinians.

Cameron's critical act of betrayal was to sneak into his new friend's room and then break into a wall safe containing evidence of a planned terrorist act involving Saleh. Owing to his perfidy and allegiance to the Israelis, the enemy was able to imprison many great Arab men. Saleh and his sister were forced to go into hiding. More tragic still, the sister, during an unexpected assault on a facility where they were suspected to be hiding, was killed.

The man assigned the lead role, Saleh, placed responsibility for this second tragedy on Cameron. He vowed to avenge the betrayal of the man he trusted like a brother. He also pledged that the aim of the project he had devoted two years of his life to with an associate would eventually be accomplished.

In his pursuit of this goal, he hooked up with a partner in Syria. This man was reported to be a genius in biology and chemistry. Allah had spoken to Saleh, ordering him to battle the enemy with any means possible, but especially to develop a new strain of hallucinogenic drugs that could be used to destroy the minds of millions of enemies, leaving them in an eternal mental and psychological opacity.

Saleh mentioned his communion with Allah to his partner, Fadi (the only real-life name used in the parable). His worry was that something would happen to him and with his passing he would again fail his God. He then tells the entire story of Cameron's deceit to Fadi and gives him instructions on what to do in the event he has to take over the project. Fadi swears to his God, the same Allah, he would not only seek revenge but he would achieve it.

The opening few pages end with a tragic explosion of the laboratory where the research being conducted to develop the new "wonder drugs" was taking place. Saleh was there when it happened and was killed. Fadi never buys the prevailing opinion that Saleh had performed an untoward procedure that lead to the chemical mishap. He believes instead that the Israelis had been given a tip and intentionally killed his dear friend.

He takes off with America as his destination. Owing to his devotion to Saleh, Fadi will punish Cameron. For his people, he will make the Americans, and later the Israelis, pay for their maliciousness. For Allah, he will serve by bowing to His wishes, and die, if necessary, to prove his own faith.

Then as I turned the page, it was mentioned that Fadi was in Albuquerque. I noticed that a large gap in time was missing, but had no idea if this void was intentional or an omission by error. Nevertheless, the tale was, in truth, simply a recounting of my relationship with Amir and Bahlya, through the eyes of Amir.

What had happened during the allegorical presentation between when Fadi left Syria and came to America, and ultimately to New Mexico—a period of several months? That question would eventually be answered but it would not be contained in the written notes I had received, ones that had been authored by Fadi Abbas.

Is there a better way to torment someone than to provide a preview of how they are going to be punished and then offer them no communication that might allow redemption? Knowing electrical shock is on the way, but not knowing when, is a worse torture than touching the electrode to the skin and experiencing the ramping up of the voltage. It was my initial thought that Fadi Abbas wanted to send the material to me like a big bully shoving a puny kid on the playground, then while the victim was lying backside on the dirt, issue warnings of what methods he'd use in the future to harm him.

From a college course in psychology, I recall studying schedules of reinforcement. The most damaging was a variable interval schedule. Firemen are frequently victims of this pattern. They rest not knowing when they will be called on next to risk their lives. Soldiers in the field learn the mental experience of battle fatigue and post-traumatic injury owing as much, if not more, to the unending anticipation of life-threatening events as opposed to the real conflagrations.

That's what Fadi Abbas had in mind for me, the cruelest

and most vicious means of keeping me alert and wondering—
he went to a lot of effort and expense to prove it.

Before I was able to get further along reading the pages
Fadi kindly sent to me, Josea called. The entire intelligence
networks for both Israel and the United States were at work
on the disappearance of Fadi Abbas. They had already pieced
together portions of his travel itinerary for coming to the
United States.

When she finished relating to me information, that
frankly I had no interest in, I picked up the remaining papers
and continued reading. It was as if Fadi had the power of
precognition. His next passage in the text reiterated what
Josea had disclosed, plus lots of other details.

He described his journey out of Syria and heading east.
Passing through Iraq, he then landed in Iran. He spent several
days there working on a project, the nature of which we would
learn through the *TAKING REVENGE* material. He then went
southeast into Pakistan, finally ending up where Amir and
Bahlya—according to the reporting of the Israelis and
Americans—landed after leaving Egypt, Karachi.

He then traveled by ship around the Cape of Good Hope
and Cape Town, before disembarking in Argentina. It was
an amazing journey, intentionally circuitous to make it more
difficult to trace in the event anyone were looking for him.

He then headed north through South America and
Central America and into Mexico. It was at this point, that
he took special precautions to complicate any attempt at
following his movements. Arrangements had been made for

Fadi to have access to the vast fortune Amir had left. He had various methods of gaining access to funds as the need arose. Thus, if a large payment was necessary to smuggle him past the border patrol to illegally enter America, it was no problem. In Mexico, he was able to attain passage on a cargo ship that landed in San Pedro, California.

According to the braggart's writing, he first walked on American soil on April 11th. He would reach Albuquerque, New Mexico on September 23 of the same year. On a separate page, as if at some point he had in mind writing a novel or screenplay, he vaguely addresses the span of time by using fictitious characters in dialogue.

"Fadi, what were you doing during the five and a half months between when you came to America and drove in your old clunker car to Albuquerque?" a fellow terrorist living in Denver asked, as he played his role in a script that had to be scribed by Fadi.

"Preparing to make total fools of the Americans. Eventually, I will meet with Cameron—"

"Yes, we will help you kill him," the other man promised.

"When he sees me, he'll be the first person to know where I spent the five months." Fadi had to be chuckling. "Then I'll give him all the time he wants to think about what can happen when you betray a friend. I want him to see the power of Allah…when I'm convinced he has, I'll kill him."

This was not going to be a good "S" evening. The reading material was worse than the nightly news…and I had only looked over a few pages.

29

FIXING A FILM FESTIVAL

I TOSSED AND TURNED all night. The last thing I wanted to do was get out of bed and surrender to the urge to read ahead. My instinct was to look over the material a few pages at a time. So I remained in bed, wondering how he planned to kill me, doubting that he would be so bold as to tell me in the upcoming story. Indeed, he had gone to a good deal of trouble to put the envelope in my possession, but surely he wouldn't ruin the fun by prematurely revealing his plans.

I still hadn't told anyone, even Preeti, what I was reading. When she woke up, she turned over and looked at me. I wanted her to see, to really see me. The hurt was too much to endure alone.

"We're going to make it through this. I know it," she whispered.

I touched her hair. Even before grooming it the strands spread like a thin golden garment over the top of the pillow. I loved seeing if I could gently slip them over my hand to feel the soft silkiness, but not upset their natural order.

We liked to sleep with the shutters open so on the mornings the children permitted us to rest in bed we could watch the sun being born. This morning I noticed the first beams of light glittered off her moistened cheeks.

My eyes were wet. I was stripped naked of the veil we humans can use for hide-and-seek.

"Zach, you have to keep your faith."

"That's my curse. I just don't have it."

"Yes, you do. You have it more than anyone I know," she insisted with such assurance it irritated me. "You have your own God, honey. That's what I love about you."

"I wish you wouldn't say that. The lucky ones have God—"

Preeti drew me close to her chest. "Hush."

The next five minutes were my only moments of peace for the whole day. I would have elected Preeti to be my God, but didn't have the heart to put that one on her.

After postponing it as long as I could, I finally sat at my desk, staring down at the envelope awaiting me. I opened it to jubilation, Fadi's. The sadist was celebrating his marvelous accomplishments that included brutally stabbing a Jewish actress, blowing up Jewish children, permanently impairing Jewish teenagers, burning down a wonderful artistic facility and embarking on a systematic plan designed to slowly toast the life of a man he once claimed to adore.

Then the narrative turned to dialogue. "How much more do you want to do?" A young man trained as a suicide bomber and awaiting the opportunity to fulfill his devotion to God was described as having posed the question.

"I WANT NOTHING." The all cap reply suggested that the antagonist shouted vehemently at the wayward devotee. "I do as Allah orders. Is it for *me* to decide?"

The young man was described as shaking, but Fadi wouldn't let up.

"You have shamed Allah. Pray for forgiveness. Saleh has given his life. He has lost most of his family. He did not ask how much, how much more."

Fadi's writing on the following page described an immaculate vision wherein he saw himself as a viper widening his jaws and about to inject a lethal dose of poison into the victim who was quivering in the corner of a glass enclosure. The reptile smiled as he slithered up to the terrified prey but backed off, repeatedly performing the act to prolong the fright.

Admittedly, I was quivering. I was also becoming irate over being the brunt of a bad gag. Once again, I had been tried and sentenced with no right to speak in my own defense. I wanted to pose to Fadi if it were possible to commit an act of betrayal when one's motive had been to obstruct a group of perceived madmen from killing millions of innocent people. I thought I might question him if one could be deemed heroic, honorable or humane for sitting back and doing nothing when they had knowledge that those same millions of sinless people were about to be slaughtered?

When the planners of evil are forced to abandon their scheme and run for their lives, should the party who brought the criminals to light be held accountable for collateral damages to accomplices or advocates? I yearned to shout those questions in his face.

But would I be given the opportunity? Amir Hamdallah, Fadi Abbas, and most of their type don't adhere to evidentiary procedures or rules of law. Why should they? They enter through the back door for ex parte discussions with their God. Decisions are rendered, but the accused party is never offered the opportunity to enter pleas, arguments or statements typically permitted in the refutation process of a legitimate courtroom trial.

Read on sucker. That was all he had written on the next page. Fadi Abbas knew I had bit and was reeling me in page by page. I was guilty; my sentence had been written.

There it was, *TAKING REVENGE—GETTING IT RIGHT*, boldly written on the next single piece of paper. GETTING IT RIGHT?! If at first you don't succeed…the wizard had delivered the proclamation that what went astray the first time was not about to be duplicated. He'd placed the declaration at the tip of my hand with a snicker and a sneer.

The document went forward with another dialogue, this time between Fadi and the character playing me in the fable, Cameron.

"I challenge my reader to turn the page," Fadi declared to what he knew was an audience of one, Zach Miller. "My mentor and friend accomplished great things in Syria, but you had to have him killed."

"He died by accident!" Cameron argued against the assertion of murder.

"Wrong! There is no error in death," I could hear Fadi countering like an arrogant professor scolding a college freshman. "It was made to look like an innocent mishap, but we know better. The Israelis, with your assistance, performed another vile act for which they will pay." Then on the next page: "We have more important affairs to address. Are you ready to go to the movies?"

I felt like I was an actor in a Kafkaesque play. Amir had been no existentialist, and I assumed Fadi would likewise eschew the label. But his document swaying from real to surreal might be emblematic of how some look at the pragmatic and experiential philosophy.

I turned one more page. There was only a single paragraph spaced in the middle.

By the award winning director/writer Jalal Bashi, a new short film entitled, Wonder Drugs. Winner of the esteemed Farhar Film Festival in Iran, it will be showing shortly at the Baht Iranian Film Festival in Montreal.

After reading the three lines my eye dropped down to the bottom of the sheet, where I noticed one final instruction.

"Don't go on until you've seen it," Fadi ordered.

I rushed to my computer and typed in: *Wonder Drugs, Iranian movie.*

It was exactly as Fadi had announced. The film was made in Iran and won the referenced award. More astonishing was that it had played the previous day in Montreal—I had to see it, but how? There was no way I was leaving Mescalero; there was no way I would be allowed to.

Fadi timed my receipt of the envelope perfectly. He knew I wasn't going to Montreal, but surely anticipated I would try anything imaginable to watch the short piece. Conveniently, he had placed it on *YouTube* immediately after it was featured in Montreal.

The total running time was thirty-two minutes. It played as it was, a documentary centering on a poignant political agenda. It began at a small laboratory in the Syrian Desert. Two men—a scientist and his associate—were experimenting with hallucinogenic drugs.

"Dr. al-Watan, what is it exactly you're trying to accomplish?" the narrator asked.

"Throughout history man has fought wars. It has been done to protect sacred land, to preserve culture and tradition, to safeguard treasures and to defend loved ones. Man will use any means at his disposal to win when he is desperate," the doctor explained. "The righteous always prevailed due to their perseverance and determination. A thousand years of resistance and battle is nothing when you are facing extinction by an un-godly enemy."

"Of course, but what does that have to do with your research?"

"The Arab world is at war. Put the polite political platitudes aside and what do you have? Hundreds of millions of people being oppressed, exploited and swindled. By what means can we fight? Our weapons are inferior. We cannot ask our people to go out with shovels and defend against machine guns," the doctor tittered at his funny. "So what can we do to even the conflict? We are inventing Wonder Drugs that will disable the enemy." al-Watan smiled for the camera. "Care to learn more about our work…see the remarkable outcome of our research?"

al-Watan began with a brief lecture, his enthusiasm worthy of at least a cameo role in a full-length film.

"Mind altering drugs are nothing new," the doctor stated while referring to a chart on the wall. "The Hindu's in their book, Rig-Vega, refer to 'soma' as a sacramental substance. The Chinese almost three thousand years ago also referred to hallucinogenic drugs. We know the Assyrians used cannabis not only in religious ceremonies, but also medicinally for diseases of the nerves and psyche. Eastern Europeans as recent as five hundred years ago discovered that *morning glory seeds* had hallucinogenic properties.

"These substances are readily available in nature. Psilocybin is found in mushrooms. From their dried fleshy tips, called peyote buttons, a blue-green cactus, mescaline is derived. Also from the Americas, in the Amazon basin, there is a plant they call 'yakee' and the bark of that specimen contains DMT. Similar mind enhancing chemicals are found in a variety of toads, specifically in their venom.

"It's only been in the last fifty to seventy-five years that new scientific methods have allowed us to examine these wonderful chemicals in more depth. In fact, it was in the late 1930's that a man named Albert Hoffman synthesized LSD. We might conclude that the modern drug era began as a consequence of his research. In the 1950's, the then Swiss pharmaceutical company, Sandoz, began researching the drug and during that same period the CIA in America couldn't pass up the opportunity to explore whether or not these substances might be applicable to mind control or chemical warfare.

"They were on to something, but the spread of the drug culture in the United States in the 1960's brought research to a sharp halt. Since that time, only a few isolated ventures have been funded. The considerations of greatest importance were left unaddressed. Could there be a place in society for drugs that could produce euphoric states, reducing depression and anxiety? Could these miracle drugs have value in medical treatment for various diseases by acting on specific regions and structures of the human brain?"

al-Watan stepped closer to the eye of the camera. He then grimly continued.

"What was never asked was if we might splice and dice these substances and create chemicals with precise, predictable and permanent consequence to human functioning. We know that the application of these hallucinogenic drugs can produce prolonged arousal, alter emotional sensitivity, change visual perceptions, modify self-esteem and self-image, and transform thought processing.

"They are also capable of producing what is called 'bad trips' resulting in panic reactions, terror, loss of physical and emotional control, social mistrust and isolation, as well as physiologic episodes of accelerated heart beat, excessive body warmth or cold, radical shifts in appetite and consumption of liquids, extreme hydration...that's the tip of the hallucinogenic iceberg."

The narrator now motioned toward a door at the rear of the room he was standing in. A man entered, accompanied by a woman who was leading him. He was in his twenties. There is nothing remarkable about his appearance. He seemed relaxed. He was well nourished.

al-Watan greeted the fellow by reaching out to hug him, but the man offered no reciprocal gesture to al-Watan's welcome; the doctor might as well have been embracing a sack of rice. al-Watan then smiled directly at his subject but the man's facial presentation was flat, not a muscle flexed.

"Can you tell us your name?" he addressed the young man as if he were his guest contestant on a game show.

"Firouz," he answered but still with no observable movement of facial features, with no indication of emotion.

"Now, Firouz, can you tell me what time you woke up this morning?"

"Seven-fourteen."

"What about your education? When did you last attend school?"

"I graduated college three years ago as an engineer."

"What type, may I ask?" al-Watan posed in the friendliest manner.

"Structural."

al-Watan now directed his comments to the unknown audience viewing through the camera lens.

"Firouz volunteered for one of our experiments. He was highly depressed and had attempted suicide on several occasions. As you can see, his depression has lifted," al-Watan reported with a smirk. "Perhaps we should say it has abandoned him. Quite frankly all emotion has abandoned him. Watch."

al-Watan walked over to Firouz and spit a wad of saliva in his face. Firouz didn't move and again was without visible response. The woman who led him in took a napkin and wiped his face. The doctor then motioned to the woman that she could take Firouz away.

"Perhaps one other example will help you understand the breakthrough research we have completed."

A few seconds later, the same woman reappeared with another male. He also presented as a nice looking man. It was noteworthy, however, that he was holding his hands over his ears. At the same time, his face was grimacing as if he were in grave pain. He was brought over to where the doctor was standing.

"What seems to be the trouble, Nouri?"

"I told you, it's the noise in my head," he responded pleadingly. "I can't stop it no matter what. Can't we do something to end it?" His frustration was bordering on anger.

"Did you have your medicine today," al-Watan asked unsympathetically.

"We keep trying, everything, everyday…but it won't shut up," he screeched as if trying to be heard over the noise of a roaring crowd.

"What is it you're hearing today?"

"The same thing. Loud music; my head is bursting and my eyes burn. I can't think straight."

al-Watan nodded his head to the woman to signal the purpose of the interview had been accomplished. She led the pathetic man off stage. al-Watan again addressed the camera.

"Nouri was also a volunteer. It's true he's in pain but he was facing a death sentence and in exchange for his life he was willing to risk whatever might be the consequence of the experiment.

"The truth is that for both of these men what you have witnessed is exactly what we were hoping to accomplish. I could have brought for your observation today over a dozen other examples of people with different conditions. Some have the sensation of not being able to get enough oxygen to breath comfortably. Others are overwhelmed with worry, anxiety or depression. Another group would have inescapable hallucinations, inability to concentrate, loss of appetite requiring tubal feeding, uncontrollable twitching, unendurable headaches caused by perception of intolerably bright lights, total loss of past memory, terrifying dread of death, or incapacity to locate prior identity.

"If I may add," the doctor noted with diabolic pride, "the symptoms these people are experiencing will never cease. Furthermore, the severity is life altering; or should I say, life shattering—these subjects will never appreciate what we would refer to as a normal, pleasant moment. Most remarkable is that no surgical procedure was done to any of these subjects. In fact, no medical procedure of any type was needed. Thus far, we are unable to find medications or techniques to alleviate the conditions—and we are devoting resources toward remediation."

al-Watan could hardly contain his excitement. His arms did a full sweep as if he was about to announce that his next visitor would be his Lord.

"Needless to say, the cases you have observed, as well as the numerous others I referred to, were all subject to one simple procedure. They were given one of the various wonder drugs we have created—a single dose! Once the breakthrough was made showing how the chemicals altered the neural patterns of the brain and we made the discovery regarding how to dissect the substances themselves into elemental parts, the next step in applying the results was simple. Grandly, the tests unfolded exactly as expected."

The program continued by adding political material. It was the intent to use what was discovered to engage the enemy in the next great battle, leaving them systematically disabled. As greater and greater numbers of people were rendered unable to fend for themselves, the demand on those remaining would be overwhelming and their ability to defend themselves lost.

"Not to worry," he assured those watching. "The formulas are all safely tucked away. Oh, and we can produce these substances in no time, anywhere in the world." His final parting words were delivered with bountiful laughter. "Who knows, by the time this little documentary is released the experiments might have begun."

As the video was concluding, I angrily threw the material from Fadi that I held in my hand, the pages floating like germs before slowing falling scattered on the floor. It was so vile it carried me beyond my own trivial concern of safety for my family and me. It was the same garbage over again. What a sap I had been to believe for an instant that there could actually be a final battle and the enemies would lay down their weapons and let one another live...in peace.

As much a pacifist as I swore to be, lines were being drawn and I knew where I stood. I would defend if nothing else my right to live in a godless world, or if so desired by others or me, a world of infinite gods. "Damn it!" I shouted to no one in particular. "Hate. It's all about hate."

"What is?" Preeti came rushing into the room. "You'll wake the baby screaming like that."

"Look at this," I suggested while I was scrambling around the room picking up the sheets I had tossed.

Preeti helped me collect them in random order and then began scanning page after page as if she was looking for the answer to a riddle. When she saw the title, *Taking Revenge—Getting It Right*, her voice squeaked out an objection.

"Oh, Zach, it's monstrous." Her eyes tightened in a look I sadly knew was hate. "He'll never get it right."

"But he'll die trying…and what if he hurts you or the children along the way?"

"He won't. Do you have trust in me?"

Preeti couldn't be distressed like I was because she believed it would all turn out well. "Worry after it happens!" she'd express to me time and again. My strategy? Worry yourself to death over every imaginable scenario before it happens as a ritualistic method of warding off evil spirits—a primitive but cogent "approach" whereby visualizing and rehearsing horror is used to prevent its occurrence in reality. I may have been on to something.

"Sure I do," I said to comfort her.

"Who is Usetah Rima?" Preeti asked, still perusing the page with the title.

"I doubt Fadi has a lover…the whole thing is bizarre."

"Did you start reading…that's why you're upset?" she surmised. "You better call Josea and see what she wants to do with this."

Preeti left and I picked up the phone. I still didn't want to let loose of the material until I finished, but I did call Josea. As the line was ringing, I recognized I hadn't calmed a bit—I was fuming.

30

HAVE PATIENCE

I CALLED ON THE home phone first. There was no answer. Then I called on Josea's cell. There was still no answer. I opened my computer and pulled up a Freecell game. I wouldn't admit to being addicted but if I had to confess to anything approaching an unbreakable habit, this was it.

I was into my second game when Josea called back.

"Did you see it?"

"What are you talking about," Josea responded with utter confusion.

"The damn movie," I yelled as softly as I could so as to not disturb my sleeping babes. "*Wonder Drugs*, they titled the monstrous piece."

"How do you know about it?" She sounded like a parent reproving a child for going on a porn channel.

"I was on the internet—"

"Haven't you been through enough? Stay off it until this is over, okay? Do yourself, and me, a favor."

"Just tell me what you know," I insisted, still withholding the truth about how I had discovered the movie.

"I may be leaving for Washington in a couple days. I'm going to have to go back to work for a while."

"Josea, you're still not answering me."

"A lot of resources have been dedicated toward tracking down what happened to the money Amir and Bahlya were left. It's near impossible the way they transfer funds over there. Then to discover what names it finally ends up under and in which banks? But what we did find out was that the film was made through a contract funded by Amir's estate. The Iranians claim no knowledge of it and probably really had no hand in it…though they didn't discourage its release either," she added sarcastically.

"The man who supposedly wrote it also directed it. We caught up with him in Switzerland. He was with a lady friend when a couple agents unofficially paid him an unannounced visit in the 'wee wee' hours of the morning—you'll get the pun in a second."

She described to me the scene and I laughed to myself. The director/writer, Jalal Bashi, was with a beautiful model. He was sleeping like a prince when the men entered the room. They locked his date in the bathroom, promising her that if they heard a peep from her they'd beat the snot out of her— she didn't test them.

Bashi was ordered to stand naked. The men opened the window. The air temperature was freezing and tunneled furiously through the room. It took about thirty seconds for his skin to look like a lilac patch. His teeth were chattering faster than a racecar piston and he made a "wee wee."

Within minutes, his jaw followed suit of the clattering teeth and Jalal started talking. He explained how he became involved in the project. A stranger had approached him about directing a film and putting his name to it as the writer. He related that the way it was presented to him, it didn't appear as much an offer as an order; and then with a fee of a hundred thousand American dollars after expenses, the project didn't seem like such a bad deal.

The reaction in Iran after being presented in the Farhar Film Festival was strongly positive. President Morooz boasted as if he had conducted the research himself. He was seen on Iranian television with his arm around Jalal Bashi, complimenting him on his courage in creating the controversial piece. He went further in touting it as exemplary of the innovative, free and fearless spirit of the Iranian people and the Iranian film industry.

Josea also pointed out to me another example of how money talks all over the world. At the Baht Iranian Film Festival in Montreal, there was objection to letting the piece be shown. After what happened in San Francisco, they worried about a backlash from religious and political groups from around the world.

But a contribution of half a million dollars to The Festival gave them a new point of view. They jumped on Marooz's theme like it was a pony. The public had a right in a democratic world to see the diversity of filmmaking from around the globe. What they didn't mention was that there were two hundred forty-nine other entries in the category of "documentary shorts" that couldn't afford to tip the administration, and were rejected.

Furthermore, proving that money could make the planet Mars out of cooked pasta, an extra quarter million dollars was thrown in to guarantee *Wonder Drug* winning as Best Film— shocking to every person attending the festival except the people putting on the affair and their bankers—it won in a landslide vote.

All of this invaluable history on the making and showing of *Wonder Drugs* was provided courtesy of Ian Jacobson, the chief administrator of The Festival. As a pathetic aside, Jacobson is a Jew living in Montreal. After a brief introduction by a pair of agents associated with those who were talking at the same time with Bashi, Mr. Jacobson explained how it came to be that *Wonder Drugs* rocketed to film acclaim—he was described as so cooperative that his visitors kept the windows shut, although they were wearing down coats just in case.

The truth was that within days of the picture's release, there was expected outrage from many voices around the world. Not surprising, however, the liberal Hollywood element, many of them Jewish, heralded the piece as a modern expression of science fiction. Clearly, these people didn't compute that these boutique drugs might end up being handed out in schools. A single dose might leave one of their children whistling *Mary Had A Little Lamb* for the rest of their life.

In fairness, the severity of what had happened in San Francisco was not properly conveyed to the public. As is the case with all fires, they eventually extinguish unless fueled by more combustible material. With no incidences after Phoenix and San Francisco, the public's attention died and the media saw no value trying to stoke yesterday's news. Instead, they moved on to rising star Juliet Rolli's baby shower and the fact that three men were claiming to be the expectant father, while Juliet smiled but refused to tell the truth.

Most importantly, few understood that the movie was a shot to the bow of freedom and liberty. There was a war being fought and the vast majority of those whose lives were in danger didn't want to see that the enemy was so cocky they were delivering their real game plan for the entire battle after only firing a couple rounds.

As Josea was recounting the history of *Wonder Drug*s to me, I was contemplating what other tasty treats were coming my way in the document held in my ownership. Up to that point I had done as told, not flipped past the instruction on the bottom of the page numbered sixty-seven. The funny part was when I counted, there were only twenty-seven pages up to that point.

In fact, it was only that page, number sixty-seven, that had been numbered. Then, curiously, every single page following the one supposed to be the sixty-seventh was blank. Then when I reached the last page it was numbered one hundred eight—interesting selection to me because I am aware that 108 is a sacred number in several Eastern religions and also refers to God in the Muslim faith. At the top of the page was one line: "Be patient."

One possibility for the odd pagination was that Fadi had comfortably composed the work, but then decided that it would be more thrilling if he sent it to me piecemeal. The blank pages might be filled in progressively over time. Another thought I had was that he hadn't finished whatever he was trying to accomplish, and then owing to having to unexpectedly pick up and flee, he settled on the clever idea of serializing whatever else he had to say to me.

"Josea, I have to level with you," I remarked as I was shuffling through the document and discovering its unusual order.

"This is not the time for heroics, Zach."

"No, it's not that. Besides, I didn't hold out on you too long—it's only been two days."

"Tiny lies, little white ones, big stinky ones—they're all lies," she chastised me humorously.

"If you have a chance, come over. I'll show it to you."

"What's Preeti making for lunch?"

"Baby food. I have an upset stomach."

"I'm leaving in ten minutes."

Josea arrived precisely as she promised. I had placed the papers neatly on the table in the living room. I handed them to her. We both said nothing, but I could see the neurons in her mind lighting up like a city that just recovered from a power outage. She scanned the pages, tossing them aside faster than a printing press.

"Did anyone other than you and I touch this?"

"I showed it to Preeti and…yeah, for a second she held it."

"I have to take this, of course, Zach. It is not likely but we'll see if we can get prints—you can never tell what we might learn. Can I have the envelope it came in also?"

"I don't need it," I assured her as I handed over both envelopes.

"You will get more installments," she assured me, flashing the blank pages in front of my eyes. "You need to promise me you'll let me know as soon as you do."

"Sure."

"I talked to Persky this morning. He has agents with Nadine round-the-clock. There's also going to be more people securing you. Bernadette has another man with her so you should be safe here. Just don't go anywhere alone, right?"

"You did," I teased.

Josea took me by the arm to the large window of my living room. It looked out at my front lawn and then further to an unpaved road leading to my home. I saw her dull green Range Rover in my driveway. On the street there was also a black unmarked Chrysler sedan with two men in suits seated in the front.

"Did I?" she laughed. "Until we bring him in, and we will, nobody is taking chances."

Josea rushed off, never mentioning the lunch Preeti was spooning out of jars.

About an hour later there was a knock on the door. It was Persky. I invited him in but he said he only had a few minutes, so we talked on the porch. I noticed that he was holding an envelope.

"Oh, I saw the FedEx delivery guy about to come to your house so I saved him a trip." Persky handed me the envelope.

I knew what it was but said nothing. I wanted to be the first to read it. "Do I still have the part?"

"What role is it you want? How about the Arab guy trying to kill me? Or would you prefer Zach Miller? I doubt Adina Bernard. I got it, the FBI agent who sits in his office and lets the whole affair unfold without him lifting a finger?" I jested.

"How about the FBI agent who at the last minute saves your life?"

"How about the FBI agent who does nothing because he doesn't need to save my life because I'm safe all along?" I countered.

"Boring. Unless you're about to die and I come in at the last second and rescue you, where is the thrill? Lordy be, Miller, the flick will run like the Godfather with Don Corleone teaching nursery school."

"I like boredom, Persky. I had boredom not long ago and I was content. I was sleeping, I was…let's just say things can be worse than boredom."

"All joking aside, I do want that role," he smiled, jabbing me in the rib with his finger. "You're going to notice some new faces around here so don't be shocked. We are paying attention to you."

"What's going to happen now?" I asked to be conversant.

"We need to find these chemicals and we need to find this Fadi character. The main things are the drugs. Once the science people figure out how to unlock the code, we'll have antibodies to counter the effects. Then the game will be over."

Persky was an eternal optimist. He had no doubt we were going to win. He had no doubt he was going to be famous. He could be wrong a hundred times and still believe the next time he would be vindicated. He was a damn fool, but perfectly tempered for the role of wanna-be actor.

Before I could open the package containing what I assumed would be more scenes from a scary movie, the phone rang. It was Josea.

"Nadine is awake."

"Josea, I know. I talked to her this morning."

"No, I mean she's alert."

"She sounded like it to me," I responded, sensing she had more to say.

"We have a problem," she hesitated before going on. "We were able to follow up on Nasir's visit to Syria and get pictures of Fadi Abbas from his family. One of the agents working on the case just left Nadine's room. She's positive that the pictures of Fadi Abbas taken from his parents—and confirmed to be him by several neighbors—are not the Fadi Abbas who worked for Nadine. Zach, she looked at the photos and showed no recognition."

"Then who was it that was working for her?"

"The situation is getting more complicated by the minute. We don't even know who we're looking for."

"I can barely describe him myself—I only met him once and that was for a glancing second," I informed her. "I wouldn't be much help. Can Nadine assist with a drawing?"

"She trying to do it as we talk. But I have another theory." She continued with a premise that she was hatching as we talked. "What if Fadi Abbas, the real Fadi Abbas, after learning of Amir's death, decided it was too risky for him to come to America? After all, if something happened to him, the whole effort would be for naught. So he stayed in Syria—just like Amir would have had to do if he lived—and then moved on to take hiding in…Pakistan, Iran, Somalia, wherever, not even letting his family know. Then he sent someone else on the mission Amir assigned him, and gave that person the identity of Fadi Abbas," she posited.

"If that person is uncovered, it's like losing a third string reserve player on a football team," Josea continued. "The starting quarterback can call all the plays from the safety of his homeland and have access to all the funds that he can now transfer with ease to any party he wants, anywhere in the world—for laboratories to produce the substances he's developed, to sign new quarterbacks, to enlist explosive makers, to make movies for film festivals…anything needed to help the team win. What do you think?"

"I never would have figured you to follow football."

"Every geek has a jock programmed into their hormones. I'll bet you don't even know who won the Super Bowl last year," she poked at me.

"I don't," I admitted. "How many points in a touchdown?" I challenged.

"Six." She proclaimed proudly. Then she continued in a grave tone. "We're down at least one touchdown. Zach, this is not a game we want to lose."

"For whatever its worth, I like your thoughts on what might have happened. The big problem is if you're right, it makes Fadi Abbas near worthless in the long run. Sure, if he's found he can't hurt me but the real Fadi will send another and another to do his work," I reasoned.

"Zach, the Fadi Abbas who worked for Nadine is likely already out of the country."

"And for all we know, the real Fadi is already implementing his next move," I said dreadfully. "Besides, what could the Fadi Abbas who worked for Nadine even tell us? If you're correct he only knows what he was told to do. The master chess player is likely thousands of miles away."

"We need a fumble, an interception—a turnover," she exclaimed solemnly.

"Wow. Football junkie." I was amazed.

After she hung up, I had one of what had become recurrent moments when I would dwell on the nagging piece of information I couldn't recover after Jay Weiner called to inform me he had sent me the envelope. Each time I examined that precise instant when I first had the sense that something crucial was being revealed to me, that point in the conversation when I had an awareness that an error had been made by Fadi, and I came away empty.

Wasn't there a way to capture what had been so evasive, a sure fire method of retrieving awareness that would bring that mere fraction of a second of time into focus? I thought of using a mallet to pound on the exposed surface of where I was sure the insight was housed in my brain. Would the answer I was seeking spill out if I were able to crack, split, burst, fracture or rip open my skull. Not exactly Freudian methodology…but I didn't have years for that anyway.

My efforts proved futile, often leaving me, as they did on this occasion, spitting, foaming and grunting like a lunatic. What I was looking for had buried itself deep in my psyche and I sadly lacked the analytic flame to back it out like a sucking tic. Damn! Double damn!! It was that big.

It was about Fadi Abbas. It was about his mystery.

I just wasn't approaching the problem through the right prism.

Perhaps I was too irate, at a point of emotional jumble where my affective experience was causing reason to go berserk.

As I thrashed about in the eerie and dangerous predicament I found myself in, I noticed those same feelings of hate raiding my nonbelligerent persona. That unpopular emotion dared me to strike back and hurt somebody.

I sought revenge, wrathful, vile revenge against Amir's protégé, the real Fadi Abbas. Worse still, I couldn't imagine any human being feeling other than I did. Would I kill Fadi Abbas if given the chance? That was a big question that I wouldn't be able to answer until placed in that situation.

I didn't want to be put in that position. However, I also knew that I could be.

31

TINY NUKES

BIG DOLLAR QUESTION: WHAT do countries pay billions of dollars to develop and maintain, yet know they will never use?

If you're answer is a pencil sharpener that doesn't bust lead you would be incorrect. For the winning reply, you might consider taking a course in the history of modern warfare. The correct choice is nuclear weapons.

The theory behind the frenzy to amass more of these devils than your closest neighbors is deterrence. If you have them and everybody knows it, then the prevailing belief is they won't attack you because of the calamitous consequences to both parties of the conflagration.

So close to absolute truth is this maxim that no country worth its salt, sugar, oil, gold or Juicy Fruit Chewing Gum would choose to shame itself by showing up at the United Nations without being able to brag about its short, medium and long-range missile program. Those member countries without at least a couple frightful atomic treasures clearly have to have an inferiority complex...and a burning desire to get their hands on these deadly toys.

The United States is the acknowledged leader in this category of super firepower. My nation has submarines with enough nuclear muscle to blow up the entire earth multiple times over without emptying its full load. I love my country.

I'll admit, though, to getting a little nervous when on occasion I think about all that power in the hands of people with a what-the-hell, I-have-lots-more-lives-in-the-future-anyway belief. I'm not complaining, I just hope those who can put their fingers on launch buttons consider the few people who periodically find that predictions for the future, especially on issues like reincarnation, can turn out incorrect.

That said, could we blame the sad sack members without these dandy deterrents for feeling left out? Likewise, can we blame Amir, along with his sidekick, Fadi Abbas, for wanting to rewrite the rules of engagement by creating a new strain of little nukes, the microscopic type? Not unless their intent was to use them not as a deterrent but as a weapon of aggression.

Somewhere out there was a man whose true identity nobody knew, but who was worthy of attention in that he was armed with enough of these mind destructive explosives to do what he professed to be his aim.

When I finally sat down to read the latest delivery Persky had handed to me, I thought I was prepared for anything. I'm not sure I'll make that mistake again.

There were only two pieces of paper. On the first page was the precise question I just posed: *What do countries pay billions of dollars to develop and maintain, yet know they will never use?*

My eye cheated ahead to the answer. Absolutely, I had it right. On the opening page, Fadi Abbas was lecturing on the subject of power politics, seeming to love the word 'deterrence' because he used it several times, mocking what it stood for.

"What if the enemy will not be deterred?" he posed. "Then will there be an adversary with the faith in God to give up life today for the promise of freedom and liberty when Allah proclaims them worthy?"

Fadi then issued a challenge to the brave, and a warning to the weak.

"Nuclear weapons are fossils deluding their owners into a false sense of safety. These so called destructive devices are irrelevant. Wars are fought with minds as the trophies for the victors. One child with his pocket full of magic can do more damage than all of the bombs on earth."

Fadi described himself taking off the robe and head covering he was most comfortable wearing and clothing himself instead in a sport shirt, jeans and tennis shoes. He boasted. "Don't believe it? I can be anyone I want at any time. I can blend in like a brushstroke. Watch!"

On the second page, there were only three words: *Sinclair Kosher Water.*

I quickly typed the name into my computer and found it located in Tacoma, Washington. I knew I had to get the material to Josea but decided to at least read about the company and see if there might be some reason he was drawing my attention to it.

Their website indicated that Avril Sinclair was the owner of the company, a family business that had been bottling sparking and flat kosher water for over a hundred years. They made no claim to sell only to Jewish establishments. Instead, they were proud that their products were marketed internationally. One could find a bottle of Sinclair Kosher Water in outlets ranging from Indonesian and Chinese markets to traditional American stores to Orthodox Jewish establishments.

What they were selling was tasty, fresh, pure water that had the rabbinic blessing to assure its customers that no compromises were made in the procurement, transporting, processing, storage and bottling of the product. People were buying. The company was posting steady gains in sales since a revival in the eighties, prior to which they nearly had to file for bankruptcy protection.

I was impressed. Enough so that I was contemplating featuring it at Kuruk when the phone went off again. It was Josea.

"I was just getting ready to fax over to you two pages of material that I received in a FedEx envelope from Fadi."

"Just tell me, Zach. Is it something to do with water?" Her voice was tentative, hoping for a negative reply.

"How did you know?"

"It hasn't even hit the news yet, but there's a kosher water—"

"Sinclair," I confirmed.

It was a life tragedy unfolding in real time—Fadi was showing off. There was no other reason to send the papers.

"It's impossible to tell at this point but they definitely shipped thousands of cases," Josea informed me. "Unfortunately, that run was delivered to local outlets and much of it went on shelves almost immediately."

"How bad is it?"

"Hard to tell but we have hundreds of reports so far of people experiencing regressive behavior. They're balling up in fetal position and crying. The emergency rooms are doing their best but nothing is helping."

"Sounds worse than San Francisco," I commented dejectedly.

"He's an asshole. These are not only Jewish people. There are more non-Jewish people buying kosher because of the purification issue."

"I know. I was just reading about the company."

"It's a tiny business—they're ruined," Josea, a true champion of the individual entrepreneur, cried out.

"I'm sure people working there are identifying who are responsible—I mean we know who but aren't they getting more details?" I queried.

"Yeah. It'll take a while to get this sorted out but we already have some information."

"If the man who did this is the same Fadi who worked for Nadine, then he didn't leave the country. But, Josea, if that's the case, why would his superiors allow him to keep operating when he is going to get caught?"

"Good question. Renegade? Empowered with the drugs he possesses and believes he's doing God's work, so he refuses to be called off? Then again, we might get a totally different visual picture of the man and conclude it's a different person. Mr. Sinclair, the owner, did report that the man they hired went by the name Jib Hassani. They're an equal opportunity employer and they had no issue with hiring an Arab. He held a responsible position," Josea explained. "He had to take samples of water from the tanks and then test for impurities before it could be bottled."

"How could they hire him for that type of job? Don't you have to have training—?"

"Mr. Sinclair happened to be there when this Jib Hassani applied. He personally hired him. The resume he presented outlined background in chemical analysis and laboratory research—no fibbing there, right?" She waited for a reaction but I had none. "He had full identification papers. One of Sinclair's inspectors had been in an accident and they needed a fill-in quickly: the HR department had listed the job only 24 hours earlier."

"I guess you want the originals of this latest delivery? Josea, it's only two pages," I informed her.

"I'll come by later to get them," Josea said softly as she hung up.

It would not be until the following day that there would be confirmation that the man known briefly as Jib Hassani at Sinclair Kosher Water was the same man pictured in the rendering made by the FBI artist based on Nadine's description. Also of interest was that the FedEx package I received had been picked up in a FedEx drop-off box a short distance from Sinclair Kosher Water.

Those two pieces of information raised questions for me that I knew the FBI was addressing. Why would this man who had been identified, who had to be caught eventually, not have exited the country but instead stayed and placed himself in danger? Before I made too much of the matter, I recalled studying the mentality of the suicide bombers. The glory was dying for the cause. Nothing could be deduced from his continued presence except he was following what he deemed God's plan.

This Fadi Abbas believed—and did so without a single doubt.

32

PROTÉGÉ OF THE
REDHEADED REDHEAD

TYPICALLY, STATISTICS BORE ME silly. Usually they're inaccurate or misleading, and almost always collected with the purpose of proving a point serving the financial interests of those funding the project. That said, once in a while I hear a figure and it will astonish me.

I couldn't help thinking about this one as I reached this juncture in the demon-themed ride; it related to male auto-eroticism. The staggering figure that stuck in my brain was forty billion. I might explain the significance of this huge number and how it was derived.

It was estimated by the writer of the study, Evan Cram, Ph.D., that there were approximately a hundred million men in America between the ages of fourteen and sixty-four—a conservative estimate. Based on the numerous research articles that Dr. Cram reviewed, it was assumed that each of these men practice masturbation about twenty thousand times in their life—that was calculated by taking the number of days between the ages of fourteen and sixty-four and multiplying by 1.5 (the number of times per day the average male masturbates; based on several research articles).

He then divided that figure by the length of the lifespan it was assumed men were active in the exercise of self-stimulation, that being fifty (again, between ages fourteen and sixty-four). That produced the number four hundred. From there it was a simple act of multiplying four hundred by one hundred million to calculate forty billion acts of masturbation *per year*—only in America.

My point is not to intentionally sneak into this story racy material. Rather, it is to highlight that the sexual drive in males may vary in intensity from one man to another, but not in its universal existence for all men. Every man has the drive and it's a fair argument to make that very, very, very few don't at times engage in autoeroticism.

When Nadine Street first came to me about writing her story, she mentioned a lady who had been a prostitute on the East Coast. She was a bright and entrepreneurial woman who was able to parlay her sex business into a thriving bar with her name on the bright red outdoor sign, *Red Hot Redhead*.

One of the girls who worked as a barmaid for the red-hot entrepreneur admitted that she took jobs on the side selling an item even more popular than beer and pretzels. While she was reputed to giving the best head in the city, she had no shame letting those who cared to know her that she also had one of the smartest heads.

She was very young when she came under the tutelage of the Red Hot Redhead. Astor Philipe listened like a dedicated student to the instruction of her mentor. By the time that she was twenty-one, she had saved enough money to set up her own business.

Her family lived in the San Francisco Bay area. They were poor people, but kind. Sadly, her father was bedridden from a serious construction accident. The attorney who had settled their case had shafted them. Somehow he had given them only a small portion of what was paid by the insurance carrier and then absconded with money from several of his clients. As a consequence of that misfortune, when Astor was working she would send money home. She also felt a force pulling her west from east.

Shortly after her decision to move back to her hometown, she set up shop. Astor had been schooled on the number forty billion by The Red Hot Redhead. Ms. Redhead had calculated in her simple brain one afternoon what Dr. Cram took months to verify. From her perspective, she recognized how ridiculously successful she could be capturing a tiny portion of that market—she later shared her finding with her understudy, Ms. Philipe.

It didn't take a degree in mathematics for Astor either to figure out that San Francisco alone had to be worth hundreds of millions of acts of self-satisfaction and that a portion of that huge number historically couldn't resist on occasion substituting real sex for the imaginative version.

It was not her thought to work on her back forever. She took her cue from the Red Hot Redhead. Her goal was within two years to be making her money off the sweat of other girls less capable of running a business.

She used every penny from what she had been able to save as a down payment to purchase a small building in a trendy area of the city. The renovation went smoothly and in no time she rented suites to other girls. She didn't want to run their businesses except she did insist that her "tenants" not have pimps and not be on drugs. She would take care of police protection and offer medical services in exchange for higher rents and a percentage of their revenue.

Astor had a way with people, especially the local police. Offering sex in exchange for being ignored by the authorities would be far too expensive. She reasoned the answer that best suited her situation was to pay off with plain green cash. It was the old fashioned way of doing business, and it worked.

I'll admit that after this fiasco with Fadi started, I sometimes wondered what a man like him did to satisfy his sexual needs. Did he have girlfriends? Did he buy dirty magazines and sit home beating off? Did he visit whores? Was he gay? Or, was he a member of an elite and likely highly pathological group successfully abstaining from satisfaction of a need as vital as eating for most men?

All this sexy talk sets the stage for the next big event in the story. Over the course of the following week, I received three more envelopes from Fadi. They were all single-sheeted and with taunting statements: *"Don't worry, Zach, I'm coming for you." "Hold on. Big things are in the works." "Allah loves you."*

Nothing actually happened during this brief span of time. The FBI was able to chart the progression of his travels based on where he was dropping off envelopes. His route out of

Washington State took him directly to Oregon, first Portland and then inland to Bend. From there he went to Redding, California before arriving in San Francisco, where at last he was scheduled to meet his fate.

Here is where the forty billion lead in, and dear Astor, comes into the picture. Fadi was having so much fun killing, maiming and terrorizing it gave him an irrepressible erection. Upon arriving in San Francisco, he took a room interestingly at the Astor Hotel—no relation to the budding entrepreneur. After a generous tip handed to the bellman, Fadi requested an evening of entertainment. The call the hotel clerk made was to a friend, Astor Philipe. She instructed the bellman to take the fee of $500 in advance and then send Fadi over.

Cleanliness was a big issue for this self-employed lady. She ordered the man who had worked for Nadine as Fadi Abbas, a fellow now presenting himself as Mr. Hakim Soorani, into the bathroom for a thorough wash. Perhaps owing to the line of work she was in, Astor had a good sense about men in particular. She noticed that she didn't like Hakim. There was no explanation for her reaction to him other than she plainly didn't like him, an impression she rarely had toward a client.

While he was doing his service to hygiene, Astor was sifting through his pockets. In his wallet was a driver's license with his name and a large collection of hundred dollar bills. Also in the money section was a piece of paper. When she unfolded it she noticed a drawing. It had been printed off the internet. Written in at select locations were notations about explosives. She replaced it in the wallet and in turn the billfold in his pant pocket, just as he was coming out of the bathroom.

She described him as the nervous, insecure type who performed like he was in a mad rush to prove something. It was her opinion he was, or had been, gay. Further, she had the impression that his homosexual impulse was one he was attempting to purge through forced experiences with females. After quickly doing his perfunctory duty, she watched him dress and sent him off.

As he walked out, it immediately began to burn on her consciousness that the whole time she was tolerating his penetration she wanted more information on who this man was. Assuming it would be too risky to follow him and see if he were driving a vehicle, she decided instead to wait a while and then go over to the Astor Hotel and see if her friend might be able to find out if a vehicle was parked in their lot that was being driven by Mr. Soorani.

What she discovered was that he was driving a 2011 535i BMW, California License 6PSY443. She took down the information and left. A born snoop, she wandered into the parking area and found the car. She looked in and noticed several boxes in the back seat but nothing suspicious. It was late and she decided that in the morning she'd call the police, just in case her assessment that he might be up to no good was accurate.

She didn't wake until almost ten but made it her first order of business to call the local police station. Hesitant to announce to the officer on the phone her career and how she came to her suspicion, he seemed disinterested. He did say that if she cared to, she could come down to the station and file a report.

Perhaps it was the thrill of espionage—a diversion from her typical day's work—that excited her fantasy that the man who purchased sex from her the evening before might be a terrorist. That thought played at an increasingly loud volume, expanding her imagination to the point she was convinced at any moment evil might be happening that could possibly be circumvented if she were to act immediately.

She decided to go in person to the FBI office. It was located on the 13th Floor of a building at 450 Golden Gate Avenue. Had she known she could have contacted the office 24-hours a day, she might have put an immediate end to the reign of terror by Mr. Fadi Abbas. Instead, by waiting, her efforts had a far different consequence.

The FBI was a great deal more receptive to her than the local police department. They showed no prejudice toward her when this time she disclosed her profession. In fact, the intake officer was so aroused listening to her he drifted into a fantasy of his own, one he couldn't wait to whack off to that evening after his wife went to sleep. When he did calm himself down enough to ask a few basic questions, he realized there might be serious business to attend to. He made a call to a superior.

A moment later, Astor was ushered into an inner office. Special Agent in Charge, Stephanie Dodson, interrupted a meeting with several of her agents to talk with Astor. She had no fantasy to dispel upon meeting Astor, but did notice that personnel, both male and female, were sauntering past where she was sitting in an unusual number.

"Tell me what you have, Astor," Ms. Dodson, a spindly figured woman in her fifties, ordered. But before she could answer, Dodson displayed irritation with the juvenile behavior of her crew. "Steve, close the door," she barked at her assistant. "Go ahead, Ms. Philipe."

"Here," Astor responded by handing a piece of paper to Dodson.

She had written down the name Hakim Soorani, license number of his car, hotel information, crude description of height and weight as well as facial features, and with amazing precision a replication of the drawing she had taken from his wallet.

While Dodson was looking it over, the door opened and Agent Mike Templeton stuck his head in.

"Boss, sorry I'm late but I—"

"Mike," she curtly instructed, "as long as you're here bring me that rendering of Fadi Abbas, will you?"

A minute later, Agent Templeton returned, handing the picture to his boss. His eyes focused first on the five-foot nine, buxom brunette who, even dressed in civilian clothing composed of a plain orange blouse and blue jeans, oozed sexiness. He then looked at Agent Steve Garcia who was in the room as well. He also had his eyes on their guest. Dodson placed the item on the table in front of Astor. Her eyes and mouth opened. She might have been staring at Star Wars' Darth Vader in real life. She pointed and nodded before a word came out.

"Definitely. That's him!"

"Steve, not a word to anyone until I reach Washington," she sternly ordered to her assistant before addressing Astor. "This is very important. You've done a great service to your country. Now I must request you talk to nobody until we can address this. If it wouldn't be too much trouble, just to make sure you're safe, I'll have one of my people with you for—"

"Is something going to happen to me?" Astor asked, fearful her Good Samaritan act might backfire.

"You're in no danger, I promise. If by chance he can't resist coming back for seconds, I don't want you alone with him... then you could be in trouble."

Dodson had one of the female agents babysit with Astor. In a second, Dodson was on the phone to her superiors in Washington. The input by Astor had given them a definite identification of Fadi Abbas, who was using the name Hakim Soorani and presenting with his head shaved bald but with a short full beard. With the license of his car, they anticipated that within hours the arrest would be made.

Unfortunately, by the time they reached the hotel, the car was no longer in the parking lot. Soorani had fled. By early afternoon, the vehicle was spotted outside a small boutique bed and breakfast in Oakland. Dodson and seven of her top agents took on the assignment of taking Fadi in, hopefully alive.

Four FBI vehicles parked down the block from the building. Three of the men carried rifles and the rest of the team, that included Dodson and one other female agent, were with handguns. The clerk at the front desk confirmed that the man in the picture being shown to her was Mr. Hakim Soorani whom she had put in Room 8 on the second floor. She believed he hadn't left since registering only hours earlier, at least he hadn't walked past the front desk. She explained that there was a back door through which he could have exited unnoticed.

Two of the agents posted themselves outside the back door and two in the lobby while the other four ascended the stairway to the second floor. When they reached the door they heard the sound of the television, tuned to an Arabic station. Dodson pointed to Steve Garcia. In an instant, he kicked in the door and the foursome rushed in. A quick inspection concluded Fadi Abbas was not there. In fact, none of his personal belongings were in the room.

The clerk checked the record. The room had been paid for in cash, for one night only. The guest hadn't required help with his baggage but she recalled he was carrying a small suitcase.

The agents met outside by the front entrance and huddled.

"Why would he register, pay for the night, and leave?" Dodson wondered out loud. "That Astor girl had to talk with someone when she went to his hotel...or by chance he saw her snooping around his car?"

"Want me to check on it?" Templeton asked.

"What if he's just rattled, knowing we're close to him now? So he's running in circles," agent Brourman mentioned.

"Let's hope so," Dodson muttered. "In the meantime, Morgan and Winnick, you'll stay here in case he comes back. I have to call Halstrom (Director)...this is not going to be a pleasant conversation."

Dodson and her five agents entered their cars. The three vehicles took off, leaving Agents Morgan and Winnick to handle monitoring the building.

Within five minutes, three explosions occurred which killed the six agents. The blasts were so strong that scraps of metal were found two hundred yards from the point of detonation. Fadi Abbas had placed the time-delayed bombs under the frames. By the time the destruction had taken place, he was making his way to a used car lot where he paid cash for a late model black Toyota Avalon.

His first order of business might have been to head back to Astor's place and after killing the agent assigned to be with her, enjoy a freebie before serving the girl a dose of one of his "wonder drugs." But business was calling and he'd have to postpone that revenge for another time.

Killing six FBI agents wasn't enough pleasure for one day for Fadi Abbas. The man was a pig. There was no other way to state it.

33

FADI, HEAVEN OR HELL?

THE FBI HIGH COMMAND was in pandemonium, not a comforting place for citizens to contemplate their top internal intelligence and defense network personnel being.

My best recall was Pandemonium being located deep in the underworld. It was a palace that was ordered to be built by the toughest, cruelest, vilest, most terrible, horrendous, evil, wicked and deplorable dude ever known to man, Satan. He wanted Hell to have its own capital, and damn the God of Goodness if the God of Evil's domain wasn't going to be the most wildly disordered, loud, ugly and hot place to ever exist.

It was his belief that the lowly humans descending to live their eternal existence under his authority needed a quick orientation as to what they could expect. The best atmosphere, he reasoned, would be one of mass confusion and hysteria.

He wanted no misunderstanding that those under Satan's command would have to take their smoky dreams, with visions of maidens escorting them to Houses of Song where they awaited purification for a world free of evil, and dispose of them in fire before entering his domain. Those anticipating singing and rejoicing in 1,400 square foot enclosures with 200-foot walls to protect them from bad were in for a real shock.

What about the freshmen looking forward to gardens where they lounged in green silk and brocade robes on couches in a climate-controlled environment where they were surrounded by "bashful, dark-eyed virgins"? Let them dream. There were also the lunatics thinking they could escape the endless cycle of life and death by simply attaining awareness of themselves as Brahman. What a surprise he had for them.

They better all buckle up for a long teary session with a wicked badass who had no sympathy for whiners.

"Pandemonium, dude, is eternal burning and punishment," Satin lectured to a new crop of inductees. "Fire? That's the beginning. Shout out in torment and then the fun begins. Your skin gets sprayed with water as hot as molten brass, 'in your face' ha ha. Then expect the lashing with iron rods. And you Jews arriving with passes expecting a maximum of one year, ha ha ha ha ha, whatever you paid you got 'Jewed' ha ha ha—I don't honor those complimentary tickets...and don't argue with Satin!"

The amazing thing was that I know for a fact Amir, before his death, was at peace knowing Allah was dispatching a crew of angels to take him to Heaven when his time arrived. I had to believe Fadi Abbas was expecting the same. I know these angels are not granted the right to operate on their own free will, but that doesn't mean they have no conscience. If transporting demonic figures like Amir and Fadi was too duplicitous for them and they banded together and threatened to strike, God might listen. I wouldn't be so smug if I were Amir or Fadi, but then again I don't profess to have the direct communion with a higher power they did.

After the FBI fiasco, it was as if Satan had entered the boardroom of The Bureau. They lost six people and were grieving. They lost Fadi who was practically in their grip. They were about to lose more. Director Halstead was in a furious mood.

Top officials at The Agency couldn't begin to understand how Fadi had pulled off his last-second escape. Templeton later determined that nobody at the Astor Hotel tipped him off and surely Astor herself didn't. Was it possible he was gazing out the window and saw the vehicles pull up and crafted his counterattack on the spot? It was not feasible since his room faced opposite to where the cars parked. Blind luck? Did he happen to walk out at that moment and witness men and women that he somehow recognized as special agents of the FBI? Even then, how could he have planted the explosives so quickly?

While they were deliberating where things went awry, Fadi was working. He had lined up a job for that evening and his swing shift was to begin at five—the only remarkable thing about the new position was that he was the only one who knew he had been hired. His sole worry was the possibility of being rained out—curses to San Francisco, The Rainy City, for troubling the man with uncertainty.

AT & T Park is the home of the San Francisco Giants. Fadi was no fan of baseball, but that evening he was singing, *"Take Me Out To the Ballgame."* The Giants were playing the

Dodgers, a cross-state rivalry sure to pack the stadium with riotous, hungry, and most important, beer drinking, people.

The fellow who was bringing in a truckload of kegs of Coors was on his way to make the delivery when he had a slight mishap; somebody had hid themselves in the back of the truck and when Bobby Cotts stopped for a streetlight he was injected with a solution that instantaneously put him to sleep. Fadi Abbas shoved him aside and took the driver's seat himself.

He had to make a detour to dispose of the drugged Cotts who wouldn't wake until long after the game ended; and then he'd wish he never did. While stopped he also used a syringe with a long needle to modify the formula in the beer containers. Fadi then proceeded to the South Beach Park area and into the stadium parking lot to unload his goods.

When he arrived, the guard at the gate greeted him with a smile and began to wave him in. But then he hesitated, moving from his kiosk toward the truck.

"Where's Cotts tonight," he posed to the driver.

"Called in ill," Fadi responded.

"That rascal," the guard laughed. "Does this all the time so he can shack up with his girl."

"He might have the right idea," Fadi joked.

"Well go on ahead. Don't want to hold you up."

Fadi proceeded. He made several stops to drop off the containers at their proper locations. He then went back in the truck, drove it about a mile, and got out. It was an alley where he abandoned the vehicle. He walked to the street and then south about two blocks until he reached a black Toyota Avalon parked on a side street. He opened the door, entered, and drove off, heading east toward the San Joaquin Valley.

That evening several thousand people would have the mother of all hangovers. Each would have near identical symptoms of paranoia and panic. Emergency medical teams would be called to the area to assist with treating a condition they had no remedy to relieve.

The following day, I received a delivery. It was a one-liner: "Wait until tomorrow."

He must have thought he would excite me. Whatever this viper had in mind was not what I was interested in finding out. As it happened, it didn't involve me. A story appeared in the *New York Times* about the FBI investigation, sternly chastising The Bureau and demanding that the public be informed of the risk they were facing. I'll provide a portion of the piece.

Most impugning is a statement by an individual who claims to have inside information that the FBI has had a confirmed description of the man responsible for these acts but has withheld releasing it to the public. Their rationale has been that because the man is an Arab, racial tensions will be stirred up.

Most remarkable is that the refusal by The Bureau to level with the citizens might have cost the suffering of thousands of innocent people. It's this type of reckless disregard for the public's safety that brings into focus the prevailing attitude of law enforcement personnel around the country. We must not forget that as we lean ever more in the direction of secrecy and nondisclosure, we sacrifice our precious freedom and liberty.

Talk about hell. Director Halstrom of The Bureau was irate. It wasn't only the billboard style upbraiding by the press—a not uncommon public relations issue that could easily be dealt with in a slip-and-slide manner. Far more distressing, and leaving The Bureau command station similar to Pandemonium, was the fact that they were entertaining the unpleasant consideration that a traitor had infiltrated The Bureau.

"How else is this slime ball, worthless piece of rancid rat turd, sociopathic vile, venomous vermin slipping out of the noose every time?" Director Barry Halstrom shot out as he paced around a large conference table where his top executives were seated. "Ace, this one's on you. The son-of-a-mother-fuckin'-ass wipe is getting fed a steady diet of highly confidential material—no other answer."

"I'm working on it, sir," Ace Reynard, Associate Director of Technology and Communications, answered back obsequiously. "I have a couple of ideas."

"Ike," Halstrom called out to his Chief of Personnel, "you'll work on this with Reynard. I want every damn person with knowledge of this investigation swept so clean my wife wouldn't be able to find a molecule of dust—and I mean everyone in this room, including me."

While the FBI was trying to sort out who might be the traitor, the Israelis were hunting for drug manufacturers. They were working feverishly to get a jump start on how to treat the effects of the substances they were certain would eventually be brought into Israel with the same intent as was taking place in America.

They were confident that with samples of the hallucinogenic drugs they could develop antibodies. In fact, blood samples had already been forwarded from victims at the temple in San Francisco and AT & T Park, and those who drank the tainted kosher water from Sinclair, to Israeli laboratories. So swift were the scientists that a couple of test runs of potentially helpful treatment drugs were sent to America to be tried on the youths at Mogen David Temple.

Still, they were aware that multiple forms of poisonous drugs existed and others could still be in development. It was their goal not only to learn how to neutralize the substances, they also sought to attain the formulas that created them, as well as the supporting research identifying how they might operate on particular brain structures.

Their first break came close to the time that Fadi was putting on the post-game show for the fans that attended the Giant-Dodger battle, at least the ones who could afford the $8.75 a pop for a beer. The Israelis never disclosed their sources but they even had friends in Iran…especially in Iran. They had put out the word they were looking for pharmaceutical laboratories that might have been involved with testing new drugs. One of these informants was able to ascertain that a small laboratory some weeks before had manufactured a new strain of drugs. The report went to the Israelis.

A few days later, two Iranian men raided the facility. They were able to secure the two drugs that had been produced along with the supporting records disclosing the formulas used to make them. They also determined who had placed the order, but there was a notation that the product was picked up and the "enormous" payment made upon receipt.

The Israeli scientists were quick to replicate the drug. With the information and samples from America, they were able to determine that the two drugs made at the Iranian facility were not the ones used in any of the incidences already recorded. They reasoned there were likely several laboratories that had been used to produce the drugs; it might take months to find each of them. There was also still no documentation addressing precisely what the chemical reaction was that was occurring in the brain to cause the conditions being produced by the drugs.

Two days after the raid, I received another letter from Fadi Abbas. It was a sick statement by a head swelled with conceit. *"The Israelis might think I'm stupid enough to have only one source for my supplies, but the truth is I can get that same line from any of my other labs. Tell your ex-employer (inaccurately concluding I had worked for the Israelis) to watch what is happening in America carefully because they're next."*

As I did with all the letters I was receiving, I passed this doozie on to Josea. This most recent communication from Fadi was more troublesome in that it raised further concern for both the Americans and Israelis that they had serious security issues.

Fadi Abbas knew what they were planning and thinking almost as soon as they did—the FBI had sprung a leak, a real gusher.

Fadi was having a knee-slapping good time, merrily shoving feces in his enemy's faces.

34

SPIES—WORSE THAN LICE

ESPIONAGE MIGHT BE DEFINED as an activity aimed at accessing a place where privileged information is stored or the people with that knowledge who through some form of subterfuge can be enticed to divulge it. The modern version of this practice seems to have evolved as a result of governments either trying to attain knowledge pertaining to what a prospective or existing enemy is planning, or needing information on a prospective or existing enemy that can be used to plan an action against them.

Essentially, spying pertains to vital material that a government could use to its advantage for defense or aggression. While initially simple agents dominated the field—individuals recruited by their governments and sent on missions into other countries to seek cherished information—as time went on the profession became more complex. For example, what might happen if an agent for Country X were to be discovered as a spy by Country Y? The obvious answer is the person would be tried and executed, or in many cases killed without due process. But that strategy eliminated a host of more advantageous options.

Why punish the person when once they have been identified they might have greater worth left unmolested? A strategy far more advantageous might be to stuff the exposed agent—unbeknownst to them—with false information they can then take to their employer. Now, by utilizing misleading data the enemy is prone to incorrectly implement a program or act so as to commit an existing mission to doom.

In actual practice, this approach proved amazingly successful in defeating aggression by an enemy, and at the same time potentially embarrassing them in the international community.

But the game didn't stop there. Recognizing this eventuality as a possible shortcoming of their espionage operations, Country X might anticipate the hoax. Their anticipatory counter move might be to send the same agent back into the same field of operation with instructions to contact their source and confirm that not only has the deception been received by the enemy but is being used to implement a particular operation—the intended outcome being to entice Country Y to respond in a matter harmful to themselves. More specifically, the anticipated action of Country X never occurs but instead a totally different scenario is implemented.

These poor devil spies that signed up out of devotion and loyalty to serve one master might find they were being pinged and ponged across oceans and landmasses, and eventually have no idea who they were working for or what aim was being sought through their activities. Single agents became double agents and then could be re-birthed as re-doubled agents. Eventually their goal became to pump enough money into a foreign bank so they could eventually retire.

The point is that espionage can be practiced by any group or entity today that has enough money and is willing to spend it on a pet mission—even corporations love it. Fadi Abbas had all the funds he could dream up. He also had a mission. True, no sane person would get close to his pet project but Fadi Abbas was a maniac looking to recruit people such as Bernard Platta, and there were plenty in that category.

It was a chance incident that brought Clarence Baxter into Fadi's life. Baxter had been second in charge of the FBI Data Command Center for over a decade. He was indisputably a wizard when it came to technology. He had worked his way up through the ranks over a period of twenty-five years with The Bureau.

He was a tall, lanky man with light, sandy brown straight hair that was just long enough to constantly be falling down onto his forehead, so maddeningly that he developed what appeared to be a nervous habit of flipping the strands back atop his crown with the fingers of his right hand. Anyone observing him over the course of a few random days would have had to conclude he was irritated by the visual inconvenience of hair blocking his view—his ocular defect must have been blinding his psychological clarity for what other explanation could there be for him not considering a different hairstyle or a hair balm?

Generally he wasn't an excitable type. When confronted by a problem he couldn't immediately resolve, his face would take on a doleful appearance that would affix itself until he was able to correct the matter, but he'd never lose his temper. He was considered an ideal employee who would work through the night if necessary to fix an irregularity.

Clarence had one problem, an addiction. It wasn't gambling, drugs or alcohol. The poor man was like so many geeky types. He wasn't the hottest looking male on mother earth and what appeal he did have he hadn't a thimble of confidence he could use to attract a lady. He was also ignorant of the fact that most women are far more interested in the characteristics that he was rich in, including reliability, earning capacity, devotion and loyalty.

Through an act of immaculate self-destruction, Clarence drew into his life an exception to the principle just mentioned regarding what most women actually value. This was a lady looking to seize on a prey who was desperate, weak and insecure—and then as could be predicted for a man of Clarence's fragile ego, he fell madly for her, so much so that in no time he married the schemer.

Therise Baxter was one of a rare breed of cunning women who most men would have had the good sense to dismiss as the duplicitous being she was, in spite of her attractiveness. But women like Therise don't care how many men label them pejoratively. They're on the hunt for that one moron who is so hopeless about finding a woman interested in them, they'll rationalize away the most evil and repugnant characteristics.

Therise had a treasure chest of unworthy traits. But the key issue she sought to satisfy through Clarence was fulfillment of her addiction. Her weakness was not complicated, unusual or harmful—she loved spending money, all she could get her hands on.

Clarence's vulnerability was equally uncomplicated, equally harmless and equally usual—he lusted for sex, wild, forbidden and juicy sex, all he could get of it. Brought up with a strict Christian code, his profile was a downward weighting of the statistical model for autoeroticism; it was a behavior more humiliating to this weakling than arm wrestling. This left him hopelessly dependent on women. Handing this knowledge to a lady like Therise was equivalent to letting a pre-teen boy take a test drive with America's nuclear arsenal.

She demanded a steep price for her favors. Clarence would do anything to afford her fare, even commit treason against his country. His venture into treachery began benignly, as is generally the case. He met a man who needed a consultant for a tech project. Hearing that on occasion Clarence Baxter would moonlight for extra money, he approached him with an offer.

The deal was too good to pass up—it was also too good to believe. However, Clarence was not thinking with the brilliant mind he possessed. A retainer of ten grand per month for making sure a simple internet system remained fully operational could be turned into tokens with Therise that would earn fetish gratification on demand.

What he was not savvy enough to recognize from the onset was that he was being set up. During the first six months, a period during which time Clarence was the most content he had been in his entire life, he was routinely handed his cash payment for doing near nothing. (Incidentally, for

Therise, surprisingly, it was the worst in hers in that while she loved the money, the loss of power as her dependence on Clarence increased put her in a state of insecurity bordering on frenzy.)

Then the bait-and-switch game began. The employer asked if Clarence might do him a small favor. It wasn't much. He knew the man worked for the FBI. If Clarence could get him a couple pieces of information—in reality near worthless and inconsequential—there would be an extra ten thousand that month. The man also subtly let him know that if he didn't want to cooperate it was fine...except that they might seek another computer man to handle the job Clarence had been doing for them.

With that single request a spy was born. For each month thereafter, "benign" items with increasing value and relevance were requested. Soon Clarence was sneaking out of the office with discs and flash drives shoved in his shoes, under his armpit, swallowed in his gut or taped to his chest.

It so happened the man who was the contact dealing with Clarence was working for an organization called the Pakistani-Kashmir Freedom Federation. Their mission was ostensibly to raise consciousness around the world regarding India's illegal incursions into a land Pakistan believed was theirs. But they had other objectives. The main one was integrating terrorist sleeper cells deep into American culture to be called to life when needed.

Interestingly, the Pakistani-Kashmir Freedom Federation was fully funded and operated under the same organization that had helped Amir Hamdallah, the Al-Sulah Trust. That

Amir Hamdallah was dead did not mitigate in any way their allegiance to his mysterious myth, and thus the Al-Sulah Trust offered full support to Amir's chosen protégée, Fadi Abbas.

In fact, it was through this group, with its collection of loyal followers, that Fadi was able to attain explosives, and arrange the manufacture of any substances he needed. It was also through Al-Sulah that Rasul Zatif, their representative who had been bribing Clarence Baxter, was being instructed on behalf of Fadi Abbas.

Clarence's employment through Mr. Zatif was smooth, without Clarence needing to question why he was being rewarded so generously. But approximately three months prior to Fadi's first act of evil with his accomplice Bernard Platta, the moment of truth arrived.

Clarence was given a once in a lifetime opportunity. He could cooperate by providing the information being requested, in which case his monthly stipend would increase to fifty thousand, or he would be exposed to his employer, and then be tried for the worse of all crimes against the state, treason.

There was one stipulation placed on the huge monthly payment, that Fadi Abbas remain alive and free. As long as that was accomplished, the money would keep rolling in. But Clarence would now be working directly under the authority of Fadi Abbas, and in the service of him outwitting law enforcement officials so he might continue to function unmolested.

The numbers Clarence was playing with were astronomical. If he could stash the tax-free funds (which he had already started to do in an offshore account in the Cayman Islands) for another year or two, he would be able to disappear to a land where he could satisfy his puerile fantasies for a fraction of what he was paying out to Therise. He had come to despise the woman.

In fact, with the massive inflow of money, his confidence elevated. He began turning the tables on Therise, criticizing and belittling her for every flaw—and she had a closet full from which to choose. He'd come home late and smell of perfumes from women he had taken out to dinner. When she protested, he told her to get out.

None of this change of personality by Clarence was brought into the workplace, nor was it registering on the radar of the employer's security procedures—most of which after having been with The Bureau over two decades he knew. He was knowledgeable about how to keep the enormous amounts of money he was hoarding undetected. If Clarence took out a date or visited a hooker, it was all with cash—nothing visible in his lifestyle was altered.

Therise was placed on a limited "allowance." While she'd spend it impulsively on jewelry or waste it frivolously on fancy lunches with friends or afternoons having massages and facials at trendy spas, the amount was small enough that she'd run out of funds quickly and not have the opportunity to cause scrutiny of their finances.

Understandably, once Clarence was connected with Fadi Abbas, his account balances swelled. He had outlined what steps he'd take in the event he were discovered and needed to make a quick escape. He assumed he'd be able to outsmart the system because if anybody would know if he were under scrutiny, it would be him. Plus, the wily gentleman vowed to his God that two years would be the maximum he would continue the role he had magically fallen into.

His Director, Halstrom, was no dummy, but was about to be made the biggest dupe in the history of The Bureau. Where Halstrom screwed up was underestimating Fadi Abbas. In so doing, he found himself in the position of becoming the first in his bureau to ever serve as a "blind agent," a newly created category defined as a legitimate and loyal official of a governmental agency who unbeknownst to them becomes an agent serving the interests of the enemy no different than if they were being paid as a traitor.

How it happened was that Clarence was not quite as brilliant as he thought himself to be. Ace Reynard, at the direction of his boss, began checking outgoing and incoming communications for the tech people with access to the Fadi Abbas manhunt. To make an extraordinarily long story short—a tale that would surely bore any person who freaks out trying to understand how to operate their home entertainment system—Ace performed some technological tricks of his own and was able to single out Clarence as the traitor. As soon as he had confirmed his finding, he went running into Halstrom's office.

"Sir, I have an answer for you. It's one of my people, Clarence Baxter," he said, still catching his breath. "I'll have him brought in immediately."

"Don't do a thing," Halstrom roared, realizing he now had at his disposal a sure-fire strategy to defeat Abbas. "For god sakes, we just hit a jackpot."

"I don't understand, Mr. Halstrom," a dumbfounded Ace responded.

"You leave this to me. And not a damn word to anyone," he emphasized by rising imperially from his chair.

Halstrom was a large man, known best for having been a power forward on his college basketball team. His fame was that the school made the NCAA final eight, but they had accomplished that great feat three years after Halstrom graduated. However, the man did have legitimate credentials. He had served two tours as a Marine in Viet Nam and been awarded the Medal of Honor for his heroism in an operation during which he saved over a dozen men. After the war, he attended Columbia University Law School and then went to work for the State Department and subsequently for the CIA.

He was a take-no-bunk-from-anyone type leader. If a subordinate tested him, they could be sure to be invited to a fight to the death, as opposed to being offered the more advisable option of termination. Halstrom wasn't a bully. He chose the form of warfare not out of experience but fantasy. He imagined himself a medieval swordsman, though he had never had a lesson nor practiced the sport.

He simply loved fencing. It didn't matter if the person were man or woman. If they challenged his authority, they could expect to be suited with fencing pants, jacket, mask and gloves, and a foil. He stored these items in his office and the performances would be put on by announcement in the bureau gym. Halstrom didn't care if the person was skilled or had even picked up a foil, they were going to defend themselves.

The craziest part was that after the encounters during which most of the opponents would have been slashed literally to pieces if not for the protective armor, in front of the entire audience (attendance was mandatory for these spectacles), if the person put up a gallant fight Halstrom would hear out their entire argument and agree to a full debate on the merits of both sides of the disagreement. Following that procedure, the topic at hand would be bantered by the entire group for hours until the best conclusion was determined.

There was to be no opposition by Ace, who typically didn't get involved in the punishment or interrogation of employees. Furthermore, he had no inclination to be thrashed by his boss in front of the entire Bureau. The Man said he'd handle it and that was it. It was too bad because it was one time Halstrom may have been saved had he taken the matter under advisement with his troops.

His plan—which made perfect sense—was the only rational thing to do. They would eliminate Clarence by secretly imprisoning him. But the zinger was that Halstrom himself would become a blind stand in for Clarence, continuing to feed Fadi Abbas instructions, presumably from Clarence that would lead to the madman falling into a trap—he was convinced that Fadi Abbas would be in custody within two days.

When he arrived at the office the next morning, he called in Nico Alexander, one of his key advisors and strategists. Together they went over the proposed intervention and concurred that it was flawless. That afternoon, the rat Clarence was to be furtively ushered to a meeting on another floor. There, two plain-clothed officers would take him into custody and place him in a maximum-security facility until Halstrom could deal with him.

The termination of Fadi Abbas, as anticipated by Halstrom, was not going to follow the ordained timetable of the FBI leader. There was to be another incident of pure bad luck for The Director. He had outlined the initial communication he was going to send to Fadi Abbas. Before doing so, however, he wanted to officially detain Clarence. The problem was that the snitch had taken off to spend a couple hours at the apartment of a new girlfriend nearly two decades his junior.

One of his associates, Brian Colton, noticing that everyone was asking for Clarence took it upon himself to call his co-worker and let him know he might want to get into the office because there was quite a commotion about his absence—the untoward independent action by the associate would earn Colton more than a mere fencing experience.

Clarence panicked, especially when he tried to log on to his personal computer where he had constructed a special private connection to keep Fadi up to date on developments of his case at The Bureau. He knew how his employer operated. You had a little problem if your boss threatened to fire you, a bigger problem if you were called to meet with Halstrom, and the biggest problem if you were technologically shut out of The System.

Clarence was out of the country by that evening. He landed unmolested in London with a phony passport and corresponding identification. He never left the airport, flying immediately to Madrid. After spending a week partying in Spain, he made his way to Italy.

His intent was to get to Syria, where the idiot believed, based on promises made by Fadi, that people would be eager to help him. But it was at the Turkish-Syrian border where the Syrians stopped him. One of their border patrol recognized Clarence's picture from a recent Interpol release. Once detained, he anticipated that due to the poor relations between Syria and America he'd be released. He had no judgment when it came to politics.

The Syrians didn't care a speck about America. However, they didn't want to have to deal with a fugitive. A day later, he was escorted back to the border and turned over to the Turks who immediately passed him on to the awaiting arms of two CIA officers. He had never contacted Fadi because he feared doing so would give away his location.

Countries have never treated convicted traitors with much mercy; Clarence would be no exception. Fadi Abbas was considered an enemy of the state and Clarence Baxter had given him aid, but not comfort. Still, his treachery was of the highest order in that it directly succored in the death and impairment of innumerable innocent citizens. Clarence would be punished with life imprisonment at hard labor in a federal facility without chance of parole.

Therise Baxter would get off easy, not that she was accused of wrongdoing or that she had a clue what her husband had done. Nevertheless, after The United States Government confiscated the funds hidden away by her husband, she was left penniless.

Halstrom was delighted knowing he had now taken over the voice and function of Clarence. This would allow him and his people to spoon-feed Fadi instructions that once acted upon, would lead to him being at last apprehended. That was the plan. But Fadi, from the beginning of his association with Clarence, had built in fail-safe mechanisms to protect himself against precisely the type of situation he was now about to face. He had learned this level of caution from his mentor, Amir, who in turn was schooled by Jawiris.

Fadi Abbas had integrated codes into the communications that were coming to him from Clarence or being sent by him back to the inside man. For example, after the third word of any line in any correspondence there had to be a double space. If that was not there, it meant that somebody else was sending the message.

As soon as Fadi received a note with no spacing after the third word, he knew there was trouble. Then when he had one of his associates from the Al-Sulah Trust make an inquiry at Baxter's home and at the office, discovering that the man had vanished, he understood that his treachery had been uncovered and he himself would for some time be flying solo, with no idea what strategy the FBI would be implementing to find him.

For sure, this had to be troubling news to Fadi. However, he was a bright fellow. He had to soon realize that all he had to do was follow his own format for responding to Baxter and there would be no suspicions on the part of the FBI that he had realized Clarence had been removed. The benefits to him had to be huge.

First, and of relatively little consequence, what was costing fifty thousand dollars a month he could now have for free. Second, and most delicious, was that as the communications came pouring in, he would know they were all designed to trap him. In essence, he'd still be able to avoid the dragnet because if whatever information being sent to him was directing him toward capture, then if he did the opposite he could travel like any tourist.

All the while, he could have associates plant clues that he was in the general vicinity where the FBI was looking for him. That would leave him comfortable to conduct the remaining business he had planned in America before heading back to the Middle East to focus on Israel.

It was too good, way too good to believe. But it was one of those rare occasions where "if it's too good to be true, it's not," is wrong. Fadi was getting all the luck and Halstrom was getting one of his foils shoved up his directorial rectum.

Life is not fair. Good guys lose. Bad guys go on doing bad things.

Fadi Abbas was bad to the bone.

I received a letter from a FedEx box near Modesto, California. Then the correspondence from Fadi stopped. That's when my worries increased, if that's possible to believe. It was a sense I had that I was on his radar. This was contradicted by information coming out of the FBI, concluding that he was in another region. They were absolutely certain that by this time, he was focused on running for his life rather than planning harm to others.

I would not rest easy until Fadi Abbas was dead or in prison. I also needed to be sure that there were no other Fadi Abbas look-alikes waiting to step in to replace him. It wasn't only sleep that I lacked. I was missing all three of the "S'"s.

35

SLIPPING THROUGH THE CRACK OF AN EARTHQUAKE

I HAD HEARD A tale at some time in my life about how cats were granted nine lives, something about a God, Atum-Ra, bestowing this privilege after his pet cat, Butch, displayed valor and bravery in serving his master. It registered to me as a cute myth, but as I became increasingly obsessed with the idea of Fadi Abbas being a cat, I started to wonder if there was some truth to the story—and that my nemesis was a rare breed of cat with more than nine lives. Halstrom didn't care how many times Abbas could escape his vice, he was going to terminate him.

Since the Director was aware that Abbas' last contact with me placed him in the Modesto, California area, Halstrom's intent to nudge Abbas further toward the West Coast and then south to San Diego. Thus, what Fadi would be learning from the communications presumed to be from Clarence was that the highways, railways and airways leaving the San Joaquin Valley were under heavy patrol. Fadi was sternly advised to avoid them. His best route was to head directly and immediately westward, toward the coast.

Of course, Fadi knew this to be incorrect. He was fortunate to still have the full backing of the cells loyal to the Al-Sulah Trust, an asset of enormous value he was continuing to spend willfully—their cooperation allowed him to delegate functions to individuals within the geographic areas he was being sought, so as to give the impression he was exactly where the FBI wanted him to be.

As a result, the next day I received the first letter in quite some time. The correspondence came from a Sacramento FedEx box. It was another vague note: I have some business in California. Watch the news.

I did watch the news, making sure I honed in to a broadcast coming from the Bay Area. The FBI had changed strategy and decided to release regionally the rendering of Fadi Abbas to the press, asking for the public's help in locating a man described as "exceedingly dangerous." It was a two-pronged approach: first, have Clarence Baxter tell Fadi to push westward, and second, expand and concentrate the search in that area to bring in the fugitive.

It was a great plan. The only problem was that Fadi Abbas was in the mood for a long scenic relaxing drive. After leaving Sacramento, California, he was looking forward to traveling east to pick up Highway 395. From there he'd have a beautiful trip along the eastern edge of the Sierra Nevada mountain range. Finally he hoped to hook up with Interstate 40 and head east, moving toward Arizona.

As he was just beginning this portion of his journey, there was a breaking news story out of San Jose, California.

Kramer-Katz, by far the largest manufacturer of Jewish food products, headquartered in Boston, had plants throughout the U. S. In fact, the largest was in San Jose. The plant boasted that if they were to pile the sheets of matzos they produced in a week along the U. S—Mexico border they could stop illegal immigration.

While the graveyard shift was on break, at three-thirty in the morning, four concussive explosions shook the facility so hard the waves of shock were felt over a mile away. One might think Abbas was losing conviction, opting to inflict evil at night rather than during the day when more employees were working. The truth was that the plant was at full production, all shifts equal. As it turned out, the death toll was eighty, with over eight hundred seriously injured.

The FBI reaction was mixed. The horrendous tragedy couldn't be measured in terms of human loss but if there was a silver lining it was that Fadi had taken the bait and headed west. Much later it was uncovered that two employees of the company were sleeper terrorists who received their wake up call.

Later that morning, one of them would type a note addressed to me, dropping it in a FedEx box in San Jose. The parcel was prepaid for same-day service. I'd receive it that evening. It read: *Zach Miller. You must pay for your sins against Allah.*

Shortly thereafter, another unbelievable event would take place. It meant another life chalked up for Fadi, a cat I was certain by then was setting records.

Most winter skiers and summer outdoor recreation enthusiasts coming to the Mammoth Lakes area know the City of Bishop. I recall passing through on many occasions and looking forward to some of the best squaw bread imaginable. More recently Bishop's claim to fame had become a thriving business in prostitution.

The little town was prospering so well with the new industry that Police Chief Maxwell Reddick had his hands full trying to control the illicit activity. Personally, it rankled him. He would have driven every one of the whores out of town if it weren't for the fact that the shopkeepers, hotel owners and leisure industry businesses were thriving on wealthy customers from San Francisco and Los Angeles.

He did decide one afternoon to instruct his officers that they needed to make a couple of arrests. He knew he couldn't do as he wished by crushing the whole disgusting business, but he could force it to go deeper undercover. One of his female officers had agreed to pose as a prostitute. She was instructed to wait until she was propositioned and then make the arrest. Reddick assumed he'd book the person, scare the crap out of him, make him pay a fine, and then release him.

It so happened that Fadi Abbas landed in Bishop on his way southward before intending to head east after reaching a more southerly California location. Stopping for gas, he happened to notice a young lady smiling at him. Fadi hit on her: if Astor Philipe's impression was correct it was to be another attempt to sort out his sexual preference issue. Before he'd have a chance to address that, he was arrested. At the station, he was booked under the name Hakim Soorani, the last known alias the FBI had record of Fadi Abbas using.

Here is where the tale has another bizarre twist. The intake clerk typed in the name and immediately the arrest went into a computer network that could be accessed by other law enforcement organizations—if this individual was wanted in another location then his legal status might change.

Fadi was instructed to take a seat while the clerk was processing paperwork. It was about ten minutes later when the female employee noticed something come up on the screen pertaining to the name Hakim Soorani. She stood up and was on her way to The Chief's office.

At that instant the building started shaking terribly. Two of the officers were thrown to the ground and literally every item on the desks and shelves was tossed asunder. The clerk was walking next to a bookshelf and fell backward so that her head hit the sharp corner and started gushing blood.

The shock waves pounded and rocked the structure for almost a minute. In the chaos of the moment, Mr. Hakim Soorani ran out of the office and jumped into a police vehicle parked in front of the building. He drove two miles before abandoning it in front of a strip of stores. The area had sustained severe damage due to the size of the quake. The people's preoccupation with the chaos left Fadi Abbas free to flee the area in a stolen car. He had plenty of time to stop later and purchase another vehicle.

He did change his itinerary, heading east immediately out of Bishop on Highway 6 and then catching Highway 95 to Las Vegas before proceeding to Arizona.

Phone service was interrupted for some time but the police office was online and able to communicate within minutes of the quake. The first call was from FBI Director Halstrom.

"Let me talk with your chief. This is FBI Director Halstrom," he ordered militantly.

A second later, The Chief grabbed his phone. "This is Reddick. It's an honor, Sir. What can I do for you?"

"You're holding a Mr. Soorani—"

"Hold on. I don't know if you heard but we were hit with a hell of an earthquake. It was at least an 8 plus. It's a damn war zone here."

"I don't give a shit what it is, don't let that man out of your sight. My agents are on the way in a helicopter".

There was silence for a minute. Molly Deets, the clerk who had been in the process of booking Soorani, was being administered to by one of the officers.

"Molly, where's that asshole who tried to proposition Maldonado?"

Molly looked around the room but noticed he was gone. "I'm sorry, chief. I was just coming to let you know there was some sort of alert status on the name when the quake hit. He must have run out."

"He's gone. He must have fled in all the excitement," Reddick disclosed to Halstrom. "The guy was trying to get laid. It wasn't like murder or anything serious."

"It's mass murder, damn it," Halstrom shouted. "Get every officer you have out looking for him. Call every neighboring station. Get them a description and let them know that this man is extremely dangerous," he barked out as he slammed down the phone.

The earth was shaking from Syria to Bishop, California.

That same evening I was in the front yard when a vehicle I recognized as likely belonging to an FBI agent drove down my road. I was correct. The agent parked and strolled up to me. He took out his badge to show me his identification. His name read Arthur Ortega. His skin was dark, but not the tone I typically associated as Hispanic. It may seem odd that I would focus on such a vague feature, but being around so many ethnic groups other than Caucasian had tuned me to certain subtleties of differentiation.

"Mr. Miller, I'm Agent Ortega. How you holding up?" he asked pleasantly.

"Not real well, to tell the truth," I candidly responded.

"Just wanted to let you know we'll be around. Persky wants to be sure we have agents up here all the time."

Ortega looked to be in his late thirties, only a few years older than me. He was a couple inches over six feet, which was close to my height. However, his build was broader, reminding me of the presence I imagined Al Capone had as he intimidated people with his powerful figure. I decided right then that if Fadi Abbas were to ever show up, Ortega was the man I wanted intervening on my behalf.

Agent Ortega, during the course of the next few days, would patrol the area for a few minutes and then wave before disappearing. At this point, it wasn't unusual to have unmarked cars in and out of Mescalero and they were so familiar that most of the locals thought nothing of it.

One afternoon Bernadette had dropped me off at Kuruk. I had a couple of personnel issues to go over with our manager, Soeze. One of our waitresses wanted a raise and a chef assistant needed a loan. Routine matters that I assumed I could deal with in an hour.

When we finished, I noticed Agent Ortega come in.

"I couldn't help stopping in and trying the food. I've heard so much about it," he smiled.

"Well, the rule is half price for officers." I informed him, in case he wasn't aware of my policy. "I'd advise you order up."

"What are you suggesting?"

"My favorite on the lunch menu today is the tandoori Indian braised beef sandwich on naan. My chef has this fascination with Indian food. Some time ago I bought him the best tandoori oven on the market and if it wasn't so heavy I'm sure he'd take it home every day to look at it. Any dish you can imagine, he tries to make it in the oven. I presume you're Hispanic?" I questioned.

"Part, yes. I'm a little of this and a little of that."

He swallowed and glanced away from eye contact for a second as he answered. I could tell he was uncomfortable with the personal line of inquiry, so I dropped it.

"The point is I've had Mexican burritos, Italian pizzas and pastas, Chinese eggrolls, American burgers and Middle East shawarma sandwiches all made tandoori style right here by our chef," I laughed. "But I'm sure you didn't come to talk about food."

"I didn't come to talk about anything in particular. I just wanted a reasonably priced meal," he joked.

"Well, that you'll get."

The waitress came over and Ortega suggested that I order for him. We sat and talked while waiting for his lunch.

"You must be feeling a little bit more comfortable," Ortega mentioned, seeming uncertain if he was posing a question to me or making a statement.

"How can I be relaxed when someone is out to kill me?"

"No, of course. But I mean now that we know Abbas is on the West Coast, it's more reassuring to you I'm sure."

The "I'm sure" at the end of the statement irked me. It was easy for him to sleep soundly believing I was at peace knowing Fadi Abbas was hundreds of miles away and about to be arrested. I had no faith in the FBI and their investigation. I still had Fadi ahead in his duel with Ortega's agency.

"I have private investigators hovering over me and my wife around the clock. Then there's law enforcement people like you snooping in on us," I voiced wryly. "Does that sound comforting to you?"

He shook his head to acknowledge my point.

"Listen, you enjoy your lunch but I have a few matters I still haven't addressed." My smile was forced as I stood up to dismiss myself.

I was about to leave when he did something strange. He stood up and took out two Sees suckers from his coat pocket. One of them was caramel and the other was chocolate.

"Take your choice," he offered as he held them out to me. "Go ahead, it's a thanks in advance for lunch."

"Should we cut it in half?" I jested.

He looked at me flatly, clearly not getting my humor.

"I give you half price for lunch, it's only fair I get half a sucker," I explained.

"Okay, funny man. No, you get a whole sucker."

I took the chocolate and walked away from Agent Ortega. I had an odd sense of dislike. The best I could put to my feeling was that I perceived him to be ingenuous, but in fairness my condition was not favorable to a reliable estimation of a stranger's character. He had actually done nothing either time I had interacted with him. My quick and unjustified offense toward a man who might be the one to save my life left me feeling ashamed.

The dragnet was closing in on Fadi Abbas. That was confirmed when for the first time I received two deliveries on the same day. When I arrived home early that evening, like twins they were waiting for me. Both envelopes contained only what was becoming the standard single sheet of paper with a few words typed on it. The first read: *Don't get hit by a truck before we get together.* The second was equally brief: *Southern California is getting a little too hot, if you know what I mean.*

What was the purpose?

Josea answered the question when she called the next day.

"We were worried he was dodging inland. We almost nailed him near the Sierras. But those last two envelopes confirm he's now following the instructions perfectly," she said confidently. "He's moving like a hunted animal. At last, he's scared. The first letter was from Valencia, California and the second from San Juan Capistrano."

"Damn it, Josea, I don't believe any of this. He's screwing with all of you," I shouted. "He's that dumb to be giving the FBI a map of where he's been and what direction he's traveling?"

"It has nothing to do with stupidity. I told you, he's trying to elude what he believes is a net being drawn around him."

"Then why send letters that can be traced? He knows they're going directly to the FBI," I argued.

"Zach, I understand you're having a tough time with this. But think about how he's behaved. Bravado. He can't help it. All megalomaniacs have the same weakness, arrogance."

"I think you're the one losing sight of the obvious." My tone was confrontational. "You know the mentality of fanatics like Amir and Fadi. They subordinate to their belief in Allah. As he engages a mission like this, he becomes more humble."

"I think within two days you're going to be proven wrong. I'm so sure, I'm leaving for San Diego this afternoon."

"Fine. But don't forget to take your bodyguard," I shot back angrily.

"Just hold tight, okay," she encouraged me. "You've done great so far."

Her compliment didn't register. I knew this was about to come to a boil and it would never finish as Josea or Halstrom envisioned. One way or another, Fadi Abbas was coming to meet me. Amir Hamdallah, his idol and mentor, had ordered it. Everything he had done since arriving in Albuquerque to work for Nadine was preparatory to a final showdown with me before he planned to take off for the Middle East.

Josea had been working directly on the case. Caplow had insisted to Halstrom that Josea be briefed on every aspect of the operation. She had to believe what she was doing was correct, but I didn't.

I had been through so much during the past weeks that I was almost looking forward to getting it over. Had I believed he was going to end up in San Diego, I might have escaped my guards and run down the streets of that city yelling for Fadi to come out and shoot me.

Fadi Abbas was coming to Mescalero. I was certain of that. I doubted there was anyone in the world that would believe me. I was right on that point.

The more worked up I became that Fadi was on his way, the more I was written off as being irrational. In fact, Josea called back to assure both Preeti and me that they now had reliable witnesses reporting they had sighted Fadi Abbas in locations on the West Coast.

"Zach, you're not paying attention to the facts," my wife tried to reason with me. "We've made it this far and now it's nearly over. I understand why it's getting worse."

"Preeti, this is one time you don't understand," I retorted as I took the rifle I kept loaded. I checked the bolt action. "I want to be ready."

She looked at me with her almond eyes, a thin sheen of moisture refracting light beams directly into my equally moist lenses. We would have been in perfect synchronicity except her forming tears were out of pity for my foolish suffering and mine were frustration owing to the fact that I was being labeled as hysterical.

"Are you suggesting the man has outfoxed the whole FBI, and our friend, Josea?"

"Yes," I responded emphatically.

"Even if he has, and he were to try and get to us here, we're being protected," Preeti countered irritably.

"Don't leave this house without me for the next day or two," I ordered like a tyrant. "I'm serious, Preeti."

My voice was threatening. Even I could hear it. I never spoke like that to my wife, but a never ends where a first begins.

"Yes, master."

"You know where all the papers are if anything happens to me. Your dad will help you with any of the legal stuff, but it should be fairly straight—"

"You're scaring me, Zach. Don't do this," she screeched angrily. "Is this what you want? You want to torture me like he's doing to you? You want to break me? That's the only thing that could destroy me, losing you."

"Not fair, Preeti," my assertiveness halting her. "You have two children—"

"We have two children! And they're not growing up like you did, without a dad."

I was shocked. It was the worst fight we ever had. All I was trying to do was prepare her for an eventuality that I figured was likely. I was counting on her not crumbling so she could be there for the children. Perhaps I became a bit too carried away with my fantasy of being killed, but it seemed a fait accompli as we were arguing.

"I'm only going over the possibilities, Preeti. We have to be ready," I explained, trying to ease the tension that she was just beginning to take to a new level.

"I've been ready since the moment Jivin brought you into my life," she bitterly shot at me. "People like you can't give up their traumas. You fall in love with them."

"That's terrific. Now I'm a martyr? Like I'm enjoying my past torments?" I jumped up and put my face up to hers. "I'm making all this up, am I?"

"You're just too enraptured with pity."

Her words were soft, tactically muted to draw my attention from the loud harshness we were inflicting on one another. I knew I had an issue with feeling sorry for myself. It was a silly privilege I permitted myself after Israel, but for the most part thought I had given up.

Preeti wanted me to fight, for myself, for us, for our family—not against each other. Any sign that I might fall short of giving my life for that achievement was betrayal. There was no middle ground for my wife. You're all in or all out. No hiding behind fear—rational or neurotic.

"I guess you're right," I conceded. "So what should I do?"

"Let the love we have for each other get us through this."

"It sounds easy. But I guess as much of a pathetic excuse for a man as I seem sometimes, I am a male. I can't hide under your skirt."

"Zach, have you ever seen me wear a skirt?" she laughed.

Come to think of it I never had. It was only pants.

"You don't have to hide. Just be courageous—have faith."

That did it. My emotions got the better of me once more. It was the same challenge that kept coming back to haunt me. Faith. Faith. Faith. Why didn't I know it like she did—like it seemed most of mankind did? She should ask me to have an appetite, a stamp collection, roller blades, a ticket to a concert, or a smile when I'm happy. Any of those I could touch, see or experience. I had words to explain them. Faith? That was a different animal.

I lay on the sofa that I had fallen into. In all my years up to around thirty, I cried less than a president admitted wrong-doing. Since then you could dress me in a skirt, take me to a movie, and pass me off as Brenda. Yuck. Tears were flowing again. Was that a show of faith?

"I'll be courageous," I promised. "That's half of what you're asking."

"If you're courageous, don't worry, you'll have the other half…faith."

Preeti came over and hugged me. I felt like a child whose mom was kissing a sore—I wanted to be a child, but I had been called to be a man, to have courage.

36

PUTTING ALL THE DUCKS
IN ORDER

THAT EVENING WE WENT to the hospital. I had talked to Nadine almost daily. Josea had kept her informed regarding the manhunt for Fadi Abbas. Her condition was progressing, but slowly. The medical people were telling her she had another week in the hospital and she wouldn't be back to work for a good three months after that.

The worst part was that Nadine hadn't objected once to the treatment or the prognosis. It's known that the best sign of recovery is the return of the dominant personality, which in this case would be a lady laughing in the faces of her doctors. But she had been shot in the chest and while blessed that more damage had not been done, the emergency treatment by Uwa in the ambulance followed by the lengthy surgery left her depleted.

I insisted on driving my own car. Preeti was shotgun. Bernadette sat in the backseat. As I glanced in the rear view mirror I noticed Bernadette holding a shiny steel knife. She was wiping it with a cloth. I had never seen it and for an instant wondered if she was about to announce she had taken employment through Fadi and was commissioned to carve me into pieces.

"What is that for?" I questioned tentatively from the front seat.

"It's my just-in-case-last-ditch protection."

Preeti had turned around to see what was the topic of my inquiry was.

"That's a beauty, Bernadette," Preeti complimented.

Bernadette treasured it. The rest of the way to the hospital she excitedly explained the details of the weapon.

"Grohmann Knives are the best in the world. This baby here is a D. H. Russell model. It'll slice a hair floating in the air in half just by landing on the blade."

"So you carry it all the time?" Preeti asked, intrigued more than I can say I was.

"Never leave home without it. Preeti, it saved my life," Bernadette disclosed, preparing to tell her story. "I was on a job about a year ago down in Las Cruces. Just like here with you people. The man feared an ex-business associate wanted to kill him. I was patrolling his estate. All of a sudden, I hear a click sound I recognized as a pistol cocking. In a split second I caught sight out of the corner of my left eye an arm raising a gun toward my head. There was no way I could retrieve my firearm, then aim and fire. So in one sweeping movement I grabbed Russell here and as I came across his wrist the knife went through easy as cutting butter."

We sat quietly for some time. Somehow these stories were not arousing higher levels of courage for me.

"Daddy wanted me to follow in his footsteps and be a big surgeon. Well, that was my first operation."

"Why do you do this, Bernadette?" Preeti asked. "Why risk your life?"

"I had an analyst when I was growing up. He kept telling me I wanted to be a man because I hated my father and needed to defeat him," Bernadette smirked. "I never hated daddy. I hated dresses."

"You have a man?" Preeti kept up the inquiry.

My wife loved hearing about people's lives, the more lurid, sensationalized or adventurous the better. This young lady, for all practical purposes role-playing as a male, was captivating to Preeti's imagination.

"Sure I do," she responded matter-a-fact, surprising both of us. "I've been with Sprinkles for three years. Some day I'll settle down and have a child."

Sprinkles? At least it wasn't Liberace. I couldn't wait to hear what kind of fantasy that dished up for Preeti. Sprinkles? There was no time for more details about her lover but we were sure we'd get the unabridged version of the story on the way home.

We arrived and parked in the lot near several vehicles that I was sure were FBI. As we walked toward the entrance, Bernadette was on duty, scanning every direction to see if she might get the opportunity to follow in her father's footsteps one more time.

When we arrived at Nadine's room, the agents outside frisked both Preeti and me. This was not my first visit, so I was used to the routine. When we entered, Nadine looked up and began crying. Preeti ran over to her and hugged her. I went to the opposite side of her bed and took her hand.

"What's wrong," we asked in unison.

"Preston didn't come tonight. He comes every night," she said breathing heavily. "He called an hour ago."

"I'm sure he just got delayed. Or maybe he forgot to tell you he had to stop at home first," Preeti reasoned.

"Preeti, he always comes right over."

This was not the Nadine that I knew. She had come way too close to death and was still traumatized—I recognized the signs. She had no tolerance for the unexpected. The slightest deviation from the norm might send her into panic mode. It actually sickened me to see her weakened. Nadine Street could bend, but would never break. I hated Fadi Abbas for hurting her. Her compromised state strengthened my resolve to survive him.

Nadine's hair had been combed and she had been able to put on makeup. She actually looked good, but her face was lacking the slight puffiness that made her appear healthy and robust.

"Zach, I called him a few minutes ago but he didn't answer." She was still agitated. "Will you try him again, please?"

I took my cell and pressed his number. He answered on the first ring.

"Where are you?" I shot at him, unwittingly aiming Nadine's angst like it was mine. "Nadine's worried sick."

"What are you talking about? I told her I was going to the gym and would be there after working out."

Working out? A workout for Preston had always been defined as scoring with one of his ladies.

"She didn't hear—"

"He's okay?" Nadine called out to me.

"Forgot to tell you he went to the gym. He's on his way," I hollered to her.

I could hear Preston on the line laughing delightfully.

"Why did you tell her I forgot? She'll kill me."

"Trust me, Preston," I said in a whisper, standing at the opposite side of the room. "She's in no condition to kill you and you'll do her more harm by letting her know she isn't hearing right."

"It'll take her a while, won't it? But you know she's a tough lady. Damn, I love her."

"Look, just get over her."

I hung up. Preeti signaled she'd be right back and left the room. I sat in the chair to Nadine's left.

"Zach. Something's been on my mind and I can't get it off."

"Go ahead. I've got nothing but time to listen."

"That's the problem. I can't recall what it is. It drives me nuts when I can't remember something. It's killing me."

As she said the words, it happened again for me. The name Jay Weiner jumped out at me. What was it about Jay that was eating at me? Nadine didn't know a thing about Jay, so it was not possible that what she was referring to was related to my issue.

"So happens I'm having a similar problem. Unrelated, I'm sure. But the feeling has to be similar."

"Zach, stop placating me, will you," she rifled back at me. "I'm not crazy and I don't appreciate being patronized, especially by you."

"Then you'll understand that's the last thing I would do to you. There's this man I know, Jay Weiner. He's the one who first called me about the package that was being delivered. Nadine, I had this queer sensation after he called but I've never been able figure out what it is. It's like an association between him and something else but I can't get the other end of the relationship. As you said, it's killing me."

"I'll figure mine out. It has to do with Fadi. I know that for sure," Nadine went on, narrowly taking in the essence of what I had said to her. "I've tried to spell it all out for the FBI people but I can't give them this one piece of data. Sometimes I lay here in the middle of the night for hours racking my brain. It won't let go of me, but it won't come into awareness either."

"If you want to believe it or not, I truly understand your distress."

"I wish I could help you, Zach."

"As a matter a fact, I think you can. You could get your lazy rear out of that bed and go kill Fadi Abbas for me," I joked.

"Ask me for anything else...," her voice took on the sound of a mobster.

Preeti had just walked back in the room and knew her line. We all loved talking about our favorite movies and specific pieces of dialogue fascinated us; we'd enact them, and this was a perfect time for comic relief.

"My husband doesn't request a second service when he's been refused the first," Preeti voiced like the family consiglieri in The Godfather.

"Okay, I'll do it, Nadine responded. "Just promise I'm not waking up tonight with a dead horse's head in my bed."

"It's a deal, Nadine. Just kill that bastard for us," Preeti requested with unmitigated zeal.

"At a minimum, terminate his command," I added, steering off from The Godfather to another movie the name of which I couldn't recall.

It was a nice fantasy, but Nadine didn't appear to have the energy to swat a fly.

Still, the three of us enjoyed the few moments of play. In a few minutes Preston arrived, a bouquet of flowers in his hand serving as a peace offering for having forgotten to let her know he was stopping at the gym—the kid had always been a fast learner.

We all talked for a while. Then Pretti called Bernadette—who was resting in the car—to let her know we were ready to go. She came and escorted us back to the car and then to our home. Len Cloud was in the house watching over the children.

He refused to allow anyone to be there with his grandchildren when Preeti or I was not home. Len Cloud was far more comfortable with a rifle than I was. In fact, we found him dozing on the living room sofa, the weapon resting across his lap. We woke him and a few minutes later he left.

I noticed the house frightfully silent. Everything was in order. My pet was laying on the floor in the living room and Preeti was preparing tea for us. Outdoors it seemed still. There was no wind and looking out from the bay window on to the front area of my property, the only movement I witnessed was a star that shot like a missile across the horizon.

I was sitting in the silence, pondering how a person acquires courage. Could I purchase it online through Amazon? I turned on the computer and typed it in; it wasn't for sale anywhere.

"Preeti, where are you?" I called out. What was taking her so long? Water was known to boil eventually, I thought.

"Did you forget the lemon pie I baked?" she answered back.

She had prepared it that morning. Of course, she was cutting us a slice to share and then wrapping the rest to put back in the refrigerator. The thought of that sweet tart taste helped me swallow the meaningless mental chatter about courage.

Then as I sat back gazing out the window waiting for the late night treat, a figure came into view I couldn't believe I was looking at. It was a huge male mountain lion. On a couple of occasions I had seen one but for the most part they're highly private and solitary animals. They do their hunting in remote areas of the forest at night.

Len Cloud had shared with me Indian legends about many subjects but my favorite was about the mountain lion and how the animal became so long.

"The Indians saw the mountain lion as a thief," Len laughed. "We referred to him as a rascal." My father-in-law always fused his tales with valuable and interesting information. "It's a fact well known to the Indians that this species kills for the sake of killing, and will put a dozen sheep to death while consuming only a portion of one. Well, one day an Indian brave came upon a lion that had killed a shameful number of deer. They were scattered in an open field.

"Now this brave had been raised in the tradition of a modern day ecologist. The cavalier attitude of the lion irked him. So he went up to the lion—that was smirking at all the mischief he'd done—and confronted him about his avaricious appetite for senseless killing. 'Why did you kill all these deer? You can't eat but a tiny bit of them.'"

The lion stared back with that deer-eating grin. "I wanted to," he responded vacuously.

"The brave lost his temper. He grabbed the arrogant fellow and threw him to the ground. Then he put his foot behind his head and held the tail. Now with all his might he began pulling and tugging. The beast yelped like a kitten, but the angry brave kept on stretching. Once the mountain lion was elongated to where he near ripped in half, the Indian took the tail and yanked on it until it was nearly as long as the body.

"Not fully content that he had taught the animal a worthy lesson, he put words to his act. 'From this moment on, all cats will look like you. They'll all have long bodies and tails.' Proudly he let the animal loose. It was a valiant effort, but did nothing to deter the mountain lion from his habit of gluttony."

"What else could he have done?" I loved pestering Len with unanswerable questions he loved answering.

"Nothing. Zach, you can squeeze a lemon as hard as you want but it'll still be sour."

He was right. There's no escaping the elemental instincts and characteristics that differentiate species from one another—the brave was wise enough not to try and fiddle with the beast's privilege of nine lives.

This rascal in my view—from where I sat in my living room—was definitely a fully developed male. He had to be eight feet long and as heavy as a large grown man. With vanity he stood. I would swear to this moment that he was looking directly at me. A small deer was hanging from his jaw like a rag. Then his right eye winked. It might have been a reflex except he was smiling devilishly.

This was not common behavior for a mountain lion. They'd never approach so close to my home. Yet there he was. What he did next sent a shiver slithering down from my cervical spine to the coccyx. I felt a sensation of cold trapping my body like all my flesh and bones were enclosed in an iced cellophane wrap. He dropped the prey, haughtily cocked his head, and ran off leaving the dead deer as a gift.

I interpreted this unusual experience as Fadi was coming to get me, and with a single clench of his deadly jaw on the back of my neck intended to kill me. Then, like a worthless item, he'd drop me to rot.

That mountain lion was the messenger. He was the incarnate of Fadi Abbas, a beast killing for the sake of killing while rationalizing his sickness as an act of devotion to a supreme force ordering him to do so. No amount of evil would satisfy his appetite. He'd go to any extreme to harm me in particular, even lowering himself to assume the body of a lion to tease me about the final solution he had planned for me. No other way to look at it, Fadi Abbas was insatiably hateful.

He was not, as the FBI was cock-sure, about to be arrested in San Diego. He had responded that afternoon to a missive the FBI assumed he thought was from Clarence Baxter with a brief acknowledgement he had received the warning and was heading south and would be out of the country via Mexico by the following day.

Every conceivable method to legally and illegally cross the border or leave America to any other destination was covered. The following day, Fadi Abbas' distinction as Public Enemy Number 1 was going to be declared ended by the FBI. The maximum-security facility where he'd be housed in the event they were successful in taking him alive had already made preparations with a sterilized setting precluding him from taking his own life.

You're dreaming. Those were the exact words I related to Josea when she called to see how we were doing earlier in the evening.

How could I know for sure the enemy was closing in? I knew; he had already arrived dressed in the skin of a lion.

The truth was that while I was visiting Nadine at the hospital, Fadi Abbas was a short distance away in a fancy home on a large parcel of property in the North Desert area of Albuquerque. He was preparing his lair to entertain guests.

He had planned every detail of the entire affair, from the flowers and music to the camera and recording. He was so thrilled about the upcoming event that he was making it into a full feature film—probably the longest flick ever produced. He slept like a lamb.

When Preeti finally came in with a tray with two cups of tea and two slices of lemon pie, I didn't mention the mountain lion. In the morning, we could deal with it. Hopefully some other animal less efficient in hunting would cart off the deer in the night.

I looked at my wife. She was a knockout. No doubt, in my mind, if something happened to me she'd be fine. For some reason, I refused more and more as time marched forward imagining anything happening to her, even to my children— it was a foolish mistake I could only attribute to selfishness. I was convinced I was to die, and tomorrow would be the day. That I might be the one to be left alone, widowed, seemed a taboo subject.

We chatted, trying to avoid the plight of our life together. I would have expected her to bring up Jivin, but she didn't. If he could save us, he would. But there was no value wondering about it.

"Things have been going great at Kuruk," I mentioned to make small talk. "The chef has a ton of new menu ideas."

"How is business at the other Kuruk's Kershaw's operating?"

"We'll never have a money problem," I giggled.

"Zach, you're distant. You know that."

"After tomorrow I'll come back," I promised like a lion-hearted brave.

"You're really stuck on something happening tomorrow, aren't you?"

"Something will happen," I responded while forking a taste of pie. "This is outstanding, Preeti. I don't know how you do it but every time you get better."

"You know how I do it. I just don't know how you do it."

"Do what?"

"Persist in your gloom," she smiled, tickling me gently. "For better or worse, it's not your top trait."

She wanted to lighten the mood, but I knew it was impossible. It might be the last night we would ever spend together, whether she wanted to believe it or not.

"Let's get some rest. Tomorrow's a big day," I finally suggested.

We went to bed and I pulled Preeti close to me, making heroic love to her—if love can be heroic. Then I slept, to my astonishment, with amazing peacefulness. When I woke, I went to the bathroom and enjoyed…I was ready to die. How would it happen; how would I handle it? I really didn't want to be there when it happened.

37

LET'S DO IT

ENDING STORIES IS NO easy business. The structure and mechanics are not too difficult. It's reliving the trauma. Every fraction of a second, every impulse, every thought, every event, in perfect chronological order, has to be revisited over and over. It hurts…but let's have at it.

Shortly after I awakened on this late spring morning, the calm of my sleep hitched a ride out of town and left me no better off than I had been the day before. I looked out the front window and I noticed at least one wish had been satisfied. The carcass of the deer was gone—and no, I had not thought that the whole mountain lion business had been a bad case of imagination gone wildly ungovernable.

Then I noticed Agent Ortega had paused his vehicle in front of my place. I opened the front door and waved to acknowledge his presence, at the moment wondering why I'd do so except to hope my gesture would send him on his way. To my relief, Ortega did move on after he saw me.

The rest of the morning was uneventful. I didn't want to leave the house. I wanted the family together. We did chores in the house and played with the children. Occasionally I'd look outside for lions on my property, mostly the human type. But with the exception of a couple of insignificant business calls, it was deadly quiet.

After lunch we put on my daughter's favorite visual stimulation, videos of Angelina Ballerina. We watched Nutcracker, Shining Star and Dreams. I was so bored that I was looking forward to Fadi showing up.

It was near three when out of the inanity of Angelina Ballerina I produced a breakthrough on the Jay Weiner matter. I was right. Fadi Abbas had made a huge mistake, but it might not be too late to capitalize on it.

I dismissed myself and went into my study. I tried to call Josea but she didn't answer. It was urgent. I began leaving a message.

"Josea. Whatever you're doing, call me right back. I finally figured it out. Fadi Abbas couldn't know who Jay Weiner was unless…"

My message was interrupted when I heard a screeching sound toward the front of the house. My heart leapt into sprint mode and my legs followed by running the short distance from my office into the living room to investigate the racket. I never put the phone back because…I guess I assumed I'd finish my message to Josea in a moment, or I was plainly too alarmed. Still, after I understood what the sound was about, I ran back and quickly filled her in. "Agent Ortega just pulled up in a hurry. I'll call you right back." I hung up.

From the living room, a car I had recognized as the one driven earlier in the morning and belonging to Agent Ortega was stopped at a random angle in the front of the house. Ortega had already exited his vehicle and was on the porch when I reached to open the door. His weapon was drawn and he was anxiously scanning the area.

"Get Preeti and the kids, now," he ordered to me in a frantic tone. I hesitated, but he offered no time for thought. "We're out of here. Fadi Abbas is in the area."

That I had been right all along was no comfort to me. I had no idea what to think but called out to Preeti who was already standing behind me. She packed up the children in under a minute and we were in the safety of FBI Agent Ortega. He swung around the car and skidded down the driveway until he reached the road leading to the main highway.

Preeti and I looked at one another but said nothing. She didn't want to address the fact that I had been right all along

"Where are you taking us?" I yelled out to Ortega who was sitting next to me.

"Where you'll be safer. They want you down in Albuquerque."

Strange, I thought to myself. Bernadette's car was parked in eyesight, but she wasn't following us.

"Does Bernadette know where we're going?" I asked him.

"Persky called her."

"But she would have come in, if he did," I argued.

"He probably called her just as I was pulling up," he responded with a sound of irritation.

The weather was mild. I was wearing a white t-shirt with faded blue jeans. I rarely sweated but noticed I was drenched under my arms.

We drove about five miles toward Ruidoso. The car started

to sputter and then lose power. Ortega pounded his foot on the gas pedal to try and offset the engine's inability to suck in fluid. Cursing, he pulled the car over, coming to a stop only a couple hundred feet along a dirt side road leading to private homes. Before setting off the motor, oddly, he opened the front and rear windows, an act I thought nothing of at the time.

"Don't move, do you hear me," he commanded. "Let me see what's wrong."

I watched as he inspected the car, his right hand now holding a cell phone. I heard him shout while at the same time waving a comforting gesture to me. "Get us some back up right now."

At that second, a vehicle I assumed was another FBI car pulled up behind us. Then things moved so swiftly that I really had no time to process what was taking place. All I knew was I glanced to the right and rushing toward the car was a male figure. He was holding an object in his right hand and reached through the window. I felt a prick, but that was my last recollection until...

I will now fill in a couple of details. Later that afternoon, Agent Ortega's vehicle would be discovered. A man who would later be identified as Ravi Sameed—a bartender living in Albuquerque who had spur-of-the-moment quit his job about two weeks prior—was dead in the trunk. The car was swept for prints and it was quickly confirmed that the four of us had been abducted. There was no indication where we had been taken, or if we were alive.

Sadly, Bernadette Raymond was sitting in the front seat of her vehicle. There were three bullets fired at close range from a .45 caliber handgun that shattered the rear window before bursting her head into pieces.

That afternoon when I had called Josea she happened to be on a potty break. It was only five minutes later when she attempted to reach me. She tried my line in the house and the cells for both Preeti and I. She knew that if I had left an urgent message, I had to be waiting for her to get in touch with me, especially since my call had only been made five minutes earlier. She knew something was wrong.

Still in San Diego preparing the final arrangements for Fadi's arrest, she noticed a sick sinking feeling. She called Persky.

"Zach placed an urgent message to me but I can't get back in touch with him."

"Don't worry, he's safe. I'll get in touch with one of my people up there right now to give me the status," Persky assured her.

"He said on the phone Agent Ortega was there," Josea shouted.

"I don't know what you're talking about. I have people up there constantly monitoring around his home and the restaurant…but there is no Ortega in this office."

"What? There's no Ortega? Get yourself up there now and have every law enforcement person in the area set up roadblocks coming out of Mescalero."

She hung up and made calls to Caplow, Halstrom and Preston, in that order. She briefed the first two and announced she was arranging a private flight immediately back to New Mexico. She had agents and other personnel in San Diego to handle the last minute details. She was still convinced Fadi would be arrested in San Diego. Yet at the same time, she recognized that the master demon could have had someone else take Preeti, my children, and me and be holding us captive, possibly for a huge political ransom. She refused to entertain the greater likelihood that we were about to be killed, or had already been.

"This is a rotten mess," she unabashedly stated to the American Secretary of State.

"Halstrom is confident we're taking him today near the Mexican border." Caplow expressed. "But you're right. We really don't need you there now that we're close to wrapping this up."

She had a different motive for calling Preston.

"Something happened to Zach, Preeti and the children."

I've mentioned that Preston had always had a protective attitude toward me. It might have stemmed from me not having a father and he subconsciously trying to fill the role, though my take was I was his best friend and loyalty was a big one for him—devotion to a friend would bring out the warrior in him.

"I'm on my way up there—"

"No. Don't do anything like that. I'm calling you because of Nadine. There's going to be more activity around there today in terms of her security. I don't want her to find out about what's happening with Zach and Preeti in the wrong way. You need to go see her now and be with her until I get back to you."

"Are they okay?"

"I don't know anything yet. Just take care of Nadine and I'll call you. I'm flying back now."

She was busy in the limousine on the way to the airport. Her mind was deliberating what I had mentioned about Jay Weiner calling to inform me that the initial delivery of the FedEx envelope was coming. Since it was from Fadi Abbas then there was no other way Fadi would have known about Jay except with respect to the Howard Medical Clinic.

I have to call Jay, she instructed herself.

The Howard Clinic was a unique medical facility intentionally located remotely in Topeka, Kansas. For the last decade, it had served as an escape for kings, princes, magnates, presidents, industrialists, A-listed entertainers; you name it, the most powerful, wealthy and renowned people in the world and their loved ones had come when they were having identity issues.

The common slob-of-the-world peon suffers their issues of self-esteem through drugs, alcohol, gambling or silence. Another massive category of mankind might purchase visits to a therapist to try and heal their bruises, or they may buy up prescriptions for exotic substances promising to ease mood, anxiety and a host of other "disorders."

Those are not the clienteles finding their way to The Howard Clinic. This facility is for those who demand The Full Monty, and can afford it. To say it's not cheap is platitudinous. It's intended to be obscenely expensive. To have what distresses you stripped away and replaced with a more satisfying presentation is no small order.

Don't like your tits, or your lover or husband doesn't like them? Dr. Howard will fix you up a pair of breasts that will earn you a centerfold shot in *Hustler*—at fifty years old if you like. Ass sags, eyelids droop, chin drops, forehead wrinkles, arms flabby, vagina too loose, anus stretched from gerbiling too many times, supraorbital process protrudes too much, mandible too straight, just tired of not being the prettiest girl in the harem—your wish is Dr. Howard's command.

Hell, if you want a full makeover he'll arrange it so your friends won't even recognize you. Tired of straining as a soprano? How about mezzo-soprano instead? Dr. Howard can fiddle with the trachea and larynx like a violinist with his strings.

If you don't believe he's heads above his competitors in terms of talent, just ask him. Arrogance is free. But the knife is more expensive than an ocean of oil. In fairness, he is likely the best. And he offers an extra that his customers will pay anything for, a sacred commitment to confidentiality. While the clinic has been in operation for over a decade, its most remarkable characteristic is that to the outside world it has never had a patient. As far as the doctor and staff are concerned no human identity corresponds to a person when they arrive, or do they have one when they leave.

Clients have been known to spend months at the clinic, never see another patient, and leave knowing the visit will never be discovered by a snoopy cousin or girlfriend. Dr.

Howard pays his staff excessively and they understand the rules. Never—never under any conditions are they permitted to discuss customers coming to the clinic outside of the facility.

That's what I couldn't put together. Stevie Green's best friend is Jay Weiner. Stevie Green had an association with Dr. Howard. Nobody other than Stevie Green, Jay Weiner, Josea Roth, Len Cloud, Preeti and myself were aware that I knew about Stevie Green's connection to The Howard Clinic. Therefore, for Fadi Abbas to connect me with Jay Weiner meant he had to know about Stevie Green and therefore know about The Howard Clinic—and he was letting me know it.

It was a circuitous set of associations to connect. No wonder it baffled me, especially given I had no reason to think along that path—Stevie Green had veered into and out of our life some time prior. What was meant by Fadi Abbas revealing the association I couldn't be certain, but I know when I called Josea I had the most vile taste in my mouth.

Once it was certain my family had disappeared, an all out effort was expended to find out what happened to us. Anticipating this, Fadi Abbas moved us from one vehicle to another. Thus, nobody could find evidence suggesting where we might be. Later that evening, part of the mystery would be solved. An email was sent to Clarence Baxter—intended for the FBI—stating the following: *Not in the mood for theme parks. Decided against San Diego. Where is Clarence?*

Fadi was a fierce competitor. As far as he was concerned, this was only the final inning of one big game in a long season.

He took my family to a house in Albuquerque. It was a large home, but best of all it was isolated. The lot was several acres, allowing for separation from neighbors. He had obviously spent a great deal of effort preparing for houseguests.

I woke up in a fog. It took quite some time before I perceived my senses returning to near normal but I had no idea how long I had been out. I was gagged and my hands were tied behind my back. I was able to get on my feet. The room was dark except for a sunroof that seemed to be covered from above with cloth that allowed filtered light to scantily illuminate the space—I could tell the sun was strong and I concluded I had to be out for the night and it was now the next morning.

There were two doors. I tried both with my bound hands but they were secured. Portions of the wall were covered with what looked like cheap plywood nailed over what I had to assume were windows. I didn't hear any sound. After about an hour, I started making noise. With the tape over my mouth, I wasn't able to produce much volume but I tried. It was hours before I heard what I thought was a key unlocking the door.

A second later, the Fadi Abbas who had been working for Nadine was facing me. He said nothing. His eyes narrowed. His hateful glare was dicing me horizontally into sections, exactly as I assumed he would dispose of my remains. The entire time I had been conscious I had been thinking about Preeti and the children. Where were they? Were they okay?

I wanted to ask but all I could do was produce howling, grunting or snorting sounds.

He stood immobile like a statue, staring at me. I was standing also, looking back at him when he smiled. Then he did the unimaginable. He walked up to me and put his arms around me, successively kissing me first left and then right, two times on each cheek. I noticed as he let go of me that his right hand gripped firmly for an instant on my left upper arm—his impulse registered with me, symbolic that he had no intention of letting me go.

He then stepped back and smiled again. It was the most peculiar experience because the longer he stood in front of me, as if he were there for no reason other than for my inspection, the greater became my sense of recognition. Then he spoke for the first time.

"You look at me as if you've known me from a prior life."

He was right. But I knew the man in front of me had worked for Nadine Street and had named himself Fadi Abbas.

"You are correct. You have known me…and it was a prior life."

Fadi's faith was Islam. I knew that Muslims didn't believe in reincarnation. Yet here he was talking about us having known one another in a distant past time. I concluded he was trying to mess with my mind. Had I allowed myself to go one step further with my thinking of Jay Weiner, I might have considered alternatives, but I was mentally impaired, madly worried about my family.

"Your family is well," he offered, anticipating my concern. "In fact, they're right here as guests in my house. You're going to see them again, one more time before they go to Allah. You are going to watch me kill them, one at a time," he informed me as if he were inviting me to share his box at The Metropolitan Opera. "We'll get to that soon enough. In the meantime, we have lots to discuss."

I tried to scream out a word but he grabbed my mouth with both hands and pressed the tape firmly.

"I'll return, Zach Miller," he informed me with a sinister nod. He walked to the door and opened it, glancing back at me. "We don't serve maqluba here."

After he made the bizarre announcement, he kept peering at me.

"We won't be serving anything. Americans have a foolish tradition of giving a man about to die a last meal," he chuckled. "Why waste the food when I'm going to kill you before you could digest it?"

Maqluba. Amir must have packed Fadi with every detail regarding the time we spent together. Maqluba was my favorite dish at the Hamdallah home. It was a casserole made with eggplant and rice, heavily spiced and heated with cayenne to bring out a sweat. The cook at the home was a dream of a woman who treated me to my favorite meal every chance she had. Hearing the word from Fadi, caused my scalp to drip.

About an hour later, he returned.

"I see no reason to prolong this. Before we address your beautiful wife and children, we have to get reacquainted. Isn't that what you've been looking forward to? Bring each other up to date about what's happened over the last few years."

It was a one-way dialogue. I would never be granted the opportunity to say a single word in my defense. Guilt was a foregone conclusion. We were not in the deliberation phase of the trial; we were addressing penalty. Fadi wanted me to understand that the punishment was just and mandatory.

If one could believe it, Fadi over the course of the next twenty-four hour period rarely left the room. I presume when he did it was to either eat or look in on Preeti and the children because he was gone for only short periods. I was aware of the length of time by calculating the movement of the sun.

He began with the evidence he had amassed that in a real court of law would have been used for my indictment—it was indisputable, in a rational court what he presented would have lead to charges being thrown out. It was a rambling several hour tirade that included the obvious issues of my dishonorable and deceitful behavior, the only legitimate offense being my sneaking into Amir's room and finding the safe containing among other things, the details of the upcoming project called, Taking Revenge, the payback against Israel and America.

He never allowed me even a bathroom break and by part way into what I'll call Chapter One I urinated in my pants— it was a combination of not being able to hold it any longer and terror. It happened, in fact, just past what I estimate to be the half way mark. Fadi was discussing my wickedness. I had come to the Hamdallah home knowing I was a spy for the Israelis. I listened to his untiring barrage but then when in rapid succession he three times used the word "my" it stimulated the enuresis.

"You are responsible for *my* sister and *my* father's deaths," he shouted. For the first time I witnessed emotion in his icy eyes. "Zach Miller, you killed my family."

My. My. My. What was he talking about?

I was going to find out.

He was about to unlock the safe within the safe's safe, taking me deeper into the phantasm of a madman exceeding any I had read about or that likely ever lived.

"I am Amir Hamdallah! I am the man you tried to kill! I am the man of Allah!"

My eyes watered. I wanted to tell him so many things, especially how much I adored Bahlya and that I still grieved her dying—that I had nothing to do with it.

He wouldn't permit a word. He stared at me, at my tears of pain, exactly as the Israelis did when I was in their prison. The more their false beliefs hurt me, the more convinced they were of my guilt, that I was expressing remorse for my sins. But it was different this time. I had a wife and children and this demented monster was going to kill them as part of my punishment. It was payback. My wife and children would equal the loss of his father and sister.

He then went on for hours, bragging about how he'd out-gamed the American's and Israelis, how he developed the drugs, how Fadi Abbas had been killed—not Amir Hamdallah—in the explosion and how that permitted him to take the other man's identity and leave Syria with the substances. He even recounted how he had invented the name Usetah Rima.

"Who is Usetah Rima? Didn't you want to know?" Of course, there was no reason to wait for an answer since I couldn't speak. "Turn the letters around. It spells, *Amir Hates U*. Childish? Everything about truth is childish," he giggled.

He was indefatigable as he detailed every event that occurred after he left Israel with his sister to go to Egypt and up to the moment we were together in this room, a chamber I was certain was my death cell—I owe to his inhuman perseverance in imparting every essential fact, feeling and thought of his journey to me, being able to provide as complete an accounting of the events comprising this story as I have.

Finally, he paused before proceeding to the part of the tale I couldn't have imagined to be the case, especially since I was certain Amir was dead. Again it was that detail regarding Jay Weiner that had tormented me from the moment Jay mentioned sending material to me. Amir assumed that when I had the chance to inspect him carefully, I'd be the first to recognize him as Amir Hamdallah. But he was wrong—I honestly couldn't see the resemblance. Dr. Howard had exceeded himself. His accomplishment during the several month period of making over Amir resulted in a seamless and undetectable transformation, so immaculate that his own mother might not recognize him as Amir Hamdallah.

Fadi Abbas had gone immediately to The Howard Clinic after arriving in the United States. For over three hundred thousand dollars, he had his face reconstructed and his voice permanently remodeled. He tormented me by describing the unimaginable pain having his jaw shortened, perhaps the most distinct feature making him entirely unfamiliar to me.

He also explained the mystery of Jay Weiner. The evening after the morning he left The Howard Clinic, he broke into the sacrosanct record room. It was his intent to make sure in the event the unimaginable were to occur—an FBI raid—there would be no mention of Fadi Abbas being a patient, nor any of the pictures showing before and after shots he was sure were kept in the records.

During his stealth operation, he came across the name Stevie Green. He read through the file of the famous entertainer and put it back, disappearing with his own material only. It was not, however, Amir's intent to give me this vital clue.

The mishap speaks to the near impossibility of executing the perfect crime. The evil mind always has nestled deep within it the seeds of self-destruction. Typically it's greed, hate, revenge, arrogance or some similar adverse motive that produces the defect with the potential to bring down the criminal.

For Amir, it was the irrepressible need to tease and torture, a mean spirit running out of control. He wanted me to know he was on to the Stevie Green matter, that he had figured it out and would use it to topple the man. As he explained while preparing me for death, one of his last pieces of business before departing America was going to be exposing the imposter.

"Sadly, Zach, you won't be with us to watch it unfold. Then again, I won't either. But I'll read about it in the papers," he smugly reported. "I know exactly what you're thinking. You consider me deranged, cruel…mad…is that right? Well, I'll tell you. Those words better describe you, and in a more global manner your country. It is America that brings evil to the world. It is Israel and the Zionist oppressors who cruelly murder and humiliate my people."

I had heard this bias political lecture many times. My sympathies rather than with causes or select interests rested with the incurable illness of the human condition and the state of nations—I had matured beyond believing there would ever be a remedy to war and hostility so long as the species, man, lived. I had been forced progressively to accept the atrocities that were inevitable between mankind, and that is no easy pill to swallow, let alone keep down.

Amir hadn't accepted anything other than there was good, and then there was bad. It was his mission to punish those on the side of wrong—defined as not being aligned with his beliefs. His hatred for America was as great, or greater than that of Israel, and that says a lot. At one point, he went into a rather remarkable discussion, one I had wished I could have bantered about with him.

"You wonder why I hate America? I never once mentioned this to you when you were at my home. The reason speaks to the heart of the matter—I wanted to be sympathetic to your feelings. That is the problem. Your country has neither sensibility nor sensitivity when it comes to the traditions, customs and habits of foreign people.

"It's not only their disrespect of the Palestinian people that demands their being humbled. It's the whole of the world that doesn't adhere to their values. I studied in your country for four years at Yale. I know the thinking of Americans. It's their arrogance, pompousness and self-righteousness that galls.

"You want an example," his voice rose angrily. "I saw a movie recently about the castration of females when they're little girls, throughout parts of Africa in particular. They used one lady—a model who as an adult had become a huge success in the Western world—as a voice to speak their disgusting conceit masquerading as tearful empathy for the poor women of backward nations around the world.

"Do I favor the practice of what was referred to as 'mutilation' of females? I am not a sadist so, of course, the senseless suffering of these young girls would not be something I would approve. But if there were a historical precedent—perhaps relating to survival for these people—that necessitated the behavior that was being chastised in the movie, then I would entertain, and if required, employ the technique. The point is that the matter was a cheap and ignorant attack on a culture, all from the American point of view.

"Imagine the audacity your country has. Americans eat diseased and chemically indigestible food, recklessly poison the ecosystem, live on drugs, smoke excessively, suffer terrible depression and other mental disorders, and create a never-ending cesspool of music and movies honoring perversion. All this they do knowing full well there is a healthier way to live, that they are harming themselves, the people they claim to love, and the environment. What could be more ignorant?" he shouted as loud as I recall his sister when she was railing about Israeli oppression of the Palestinians.

"The nerve," he bellowed. "America has the insolence to step in like a savior, attempting to use shame to influence people to cease a castration behavior that had to have been at least at some point in their past required and adaptive, crucial for their existence as a people? While indeed there may be an element of ignorance for these people now that advancements in science have been made, that does not mean that those committing the condemned practice understand that; they do not deserve to be condemned.

"Yes, I met the top American filmmakers when I lived in your country. I talked with the liberal generals of the movie and entertainment industry. They're out to sell tickets in theatres—their sensitivity toward culture is like a tomahawk missile. They parade themselves like gallant emancipators and their fans clap their angelic little wings to applaud the great efforts to liberate the oppressed and unenlightened of the world. The message is simple: 'We have all the answers and we are right.'

"That's why so many countries fears and detests America. Sure, most of the world's leadership capitulates—they're scared to speak out. But look around at the rebellions and civil wars rocking the regions of the world. It's the people who are not afraid. It's the people who have courage to stand up and die for their right to retain customs they believe they need, traditions that are their pride and glory.

"The movies, the music, the fast foods, even the trained habit of assuming excessive debt so as to enslave people—those are the spearheads being marched like columns of warriors into the lands of the downtrodden for their re-education. But the sharpened dagger points will be melted into piles of molten metal, left to dry as steel statues of an extinct civilization.

"Think about it. It's called dignity. That's the first pillar of freedom. Dignity for a human being is as elemental to his existence as air. Take away man's pride, esteem and respect and a slow process of asphyxiation sets in, leading to death.

"America and Israel have assaulted my people, and people in regions around the world, by attacking their dignity. Neither country has an antidote for their demise. They will be stopped. I am only doing a service to these sick and doomed cultures."

I wanted to reject his entire diatribe. He was a hardened man. His hatred had clouded reason. Even if I could have spoken, what was there to gain by refuting his ranting single-sided assault? Sure there were points worthy of consideration. The ice skater wins the Olympics but she doesn't do it with perfection; every victor is a work in progress trying to improve, and the culture of America was still evolving.

Amir with all his education and intellect was a fool in the hands of unrelenting hate. What would the world be like if he and his associates were empowered? Would abuse, corruption, killing and slaughter, greed, oppression and war disappear? I had covered that line of thought long before and resolved there would never be the satisfaction he sought.

How many Zach Millers could he kill? When it comes down to it, if there was a single individual left on earth alive, hate would have only one friend, the hater himself. If there were nobody left on the planet but Amir and his sister, he would murder her out of hate. She would at some point betray him, fail to gratify his imagination or disappoint his expectations.

Then Amir would stand with his only companion, hate dwelling within his own soul

How lonely. How tragic. Shortly he would find fault with himself. That would be the moment he would confront his God face-to-face and stand naked in His eternal light. Amir Hamdallah would be asked to rise and to accept a verdict of guilt. His Creator would seek his penance for having violated His highest order, the glorious marriage…of love and hate.

Seeking eternal salvation. Seeking an absolute right or wrong. Seeking an unequivocal truth. Seeking the ultimate faith. Seeking something to believe in—doubtlessly. Each of these enterprises ends in the purification of hate.

But then there is love. Love excuses mankind for living in the space between forgiving and forgetting. Love delights in mankind laughing at his ignorance and weeping over his impossible curse of reason. Love proves in the end to be no more, and no less, than the repellant force to hate.

Miraculously, love and hate push back with equal fury upon one another, both seeking union with each other, knowing there is no survival on one side only of the pulse of a human heart.

Amir Hamdallah needed a wedding.

As Amir continued railing on other pet themes, I noticed pauses signaling he might soon wind down his revilement. During those lulls, I recall thinking that events had to be taking place at that moment to rescue my family and me. Law enforcement resources throughout the State of New Mexico, along with personnel from other locations, no doubt were canvassing every imaginable place we might be. Sadly, however, those sorts of operations are usually futile in that it is in the imaginable places where secrets are hidden.

When the slowing of his pace of delivery became more certain, he began referring more frequently to Preeti and the children. He'd graphically describe how he planned to torture Preeti first, in front of me because Allah had ordered I pay "appropriately" for my sins. Then he'd focus on the children.

I could tell it was late. The sun was sending goodnight greetings as it arched westward on a cyclical journey I'd never enjoy again. It would only be minutes before it would be dark.

At that instant, Amir did something that alarmed me. For the first time, he bound my legs and used another rope to tie my arms that were already secured behind my back to a pipe sticking out of the wall. I had no ability to move more than inches from where I now sat.

He walked out of the room. A minute later, I could hear the sound of irregular foot movement. It was Preeti being pushed into the room where Amir had locked me.

She was dressed but her silky hair had wisped together from sweat and tears. Her face spelled terror and she looked at me to do something. I had but one act of courage to offer, and I executed it like a hero. I stared at her and never looked away. I made her fix her eyes back on me and never break the connection they accomplished for us. Whatever we had left of life it was going to be together.

Amir positioned her at the opposite end of the room.

"I'll bring the children in next," he informed us.

He then took out a revolver. He spun the cylinder freely several revolutions, fondling the weapon. I noticed a change in his attitude. He seemed to divorce himself from our presence. He had a chore to do no different than pealing a potato.

I refused to glance his way as he began walking out of the room to get the children. My eyes remained connected with Preeti's and she was of similar mind's eye as she peered imploringly at me. I thought of Jivin, the boy mystic, deceased son of my wife, the "little dude" who set my life on a journey of intrigue, danger, mystery…and finally love. I felt comfort knowing Preeti was thinking of him as well and that he had to be looking over us, awaiting us—after all my agonizing I found a morsel of faith in a ten-year-old boy who I knew was gloriously traveling in universes never discovered and who had showed me the birthing of stars and galaxies.

Amir must have had a sudden change of mind regarding the order of execution of my family. It was likely that he sensed the bond of love between Preeti and I that he could never break, for suddenly he came rushing back into the room.

I caught sight of him out of the corner of my eye. I noticed the movement of Amir's right arm as it rose, holding the gun, aiming it at my wife. I would see the tightening of the muscles in his right index finger as it was about to discharge fatal shells into Preeti's head. At that exact instant, my courage must have deserted me for I sealed my eyes shut. I heard three distinct shots. With each bullet, my mind exploded.

Bang.

Bang.

Bang.

Fragments of neural matter seemed to be bursting out of a black hole. Spheres were pulsing and whirling as they were attaining speeds beyond the movement of light. The material I once understood to be my brain was reaching the outer dimension of space, and then propelling beyond, seeking and searching. Would I ever find my love again in the vastness of eternity?

Preeti, I heard myself shout. It was a sound vibrating a billion cycles in a billionth of a billionth of a second; I might have repeated the iteration that many times . . . . then there was silence.

I had no capacity for thought, but what seemed a sensation of timelessness, weightlessness and nothingness slipped away as I felt two arms grabbing me. There was hair falling in my face. It smelled like coconut with cinnamon and I recognized it as a familiar scent; my mom wore a similar fragrance. I recalled also many times when with Nadine I'd catch a whiff of the same essence.

I felt my arms being loosened from the binding rope and tape. Then what was stimulating my nose very gradually evaporated. The sensation of smell was replaced by sound. I thought I heard someone being unbound as I had just been.

I sat still. A moment later there was another embrace. Silently, arms grasped me tightly, and a head burrowed into my lap. I knew the body odor.

"Where are the children?" The words wept out of the darkness that was sheltering me.

I recognized the voice, but couldn't believe she was there in the room. It was too confusing. I had no ability to produce vocalizations or to explore the space around me. A minute later, I heard more sounds. They made me cry—they insisted I open my eyes. I couldn't imagine doing it. It seemed impossible. I had to find the courage to do it. Finally, I peeked outward.

Nadine, holding my two children in her arms, stood facing me. Preeti had wrapped herself around me, blanketing me while at the same time being enveloped; we were entwined as one. Amir was on the ground, blood freshly dripping from his head and chest.

EPILOGUE

LIFE IS A BIG racket, sometimes we're pounded and beaten, other times we float merrily. We seem to have no influence over which way an event is going to work out but we are addicted to trying to alter the course of history. When the outcome is to our liking, we invent fictions to convince ourselves we did it. However, when things go sour, we're more likely to blame bad luck.

Is it destiny that controls the path of our life, or do we as individual human beings use our ability to reason and act so as to chart our own course? We smack the question back and forth seeking a final conclusion, but we never achieve resolution.

I recall after coming back from Israel being tormented by the topic. One day before he died, I discussed it with Jivin.

"You always have to have it one way or the other, don't you?" he scolded me. "Did you ever think it might be both?"

He then explained that we are responsible for many aspects of our life, yet at the same time there are elements that are part of what he called "a deeper destiny," matters we have to live out irrespective of our own volition. He added that each category is equally important.

His final statement on the subject emphasized his point, and went as far as humanly possible to get a working perspective on the matter.

"Life is not about using fate to absolve ourselves of duty and obligation."

My "deeper destiny" had just served me a big win. I was to live. At the same time, my duties and obligations were to continue. I was in the infancy of my roles as husband and father—after the cumulative traumas of my life to that point, I prayed I'd be fit to fulfill them.

What happened to achieve the destiny that did unfold? Well, it was close to the same time that I had the epiphany about Jay Weiner that Nadine had a breakthrough for the piece of information that had been eluding her. It was after she met with Preston, only minutes after Josea had called him. When Preston informed her that I was missing and then added it was presumed it had something to do with Fadi Abbas, that we had been abducted by him, a single instant from early in her association with Fadi came to light.

Fadi had kidnapped Zach Miller, his wife and children and was sure to kill them. She knew where they would be. How she knew, she couldn't explain at the instant it came to her awareness. Trying to account for the experience after the fact, she could be heard uttering statements like, "I saw it" and "I knew what I had to do."

Nadine was lying in her hospital bed when she realized she might have a chance to save us. At the time, she had enough security personnel outside her room to protect her against an assault by a full infantry, sufficient also to keep her imprisoned should she have decided to leave.

She had no explanation as to why she didn't call Josea. Likely the detective in her awakened and she went into spontaneous action mode. It was foolish—and reckless—to do what she did, especially as weak as she was. She sent Preston on an errand, asking him casually before he left where he had parked the car. His keys were on the seat with his computer. Her room fortuitously was on the first floor. The window was sealed but she noticed the glass held in place by six screws. She used a dime in Preston's bag and unscrewed them. She slipped on the only pair of pants she had in the room, removed the plate glass, and climbed out the window.

She drove home. In her desk, was a piece of paper with an address. Her handgun was in one of the drawers. She took both items and went back to the car. It was a three-mile drive to 427 N. Willow Road. She parked a distance down the block from the house and slowly made her way up to it. The front door was locked but she had no trouble opening it. As she crept down the hall, she saw Fadi with his arm reaching out with his handgun aimed at Preeti's head. It was the second time she had fired her weapon with intent to kill, and the second time she had shot a person to death.

It was obvious to her that there was a high risk of failure trying to take Fadi alive. Had she called out for him to stop, he might have shot back at her or possibly fired randomly and killed Preeti and I. Still, when I asked her why she didn't try she answered.

"Any sane human being would have wanted him dead. I saved the courts having to deliberate the matter."

How did she know about the address? I asked her that too.

"I had a client whose house I had to visit on occasion, just about a half mile further on North Willow. When I was coming back one time I noticed Fadi's car pulled up to the house at 427. It's a beautiful neighborhood and I assumed he was visiting someone. But when I went back to see the same people early one morning before going to the office, I noticed that Fadi's car was there again.

"I thought maybe he had a lover. I checked the deed for that property and it had just been purchased but was registered to a Mr. Aboud. Still, I wrote down the address and kept it. That was it. I knew nothing about Fadi's personal life—that was my only connection to something pertaining to his life outside of business. I didn't know it was his property nor why he had purchased it until I entered the house."

Later the formulas used for the drug manufacturing, along with records disclosing every laboratory that had been involved in producing them, was found inside the home. Virtually all the contacts Amir had brought with him from his region or had made in America was attained either through documentation in his possession or by accessing computer and phone files—lots of people were to be arrested and tried, in America and around the world.

By the time we were taken home, it was late in the evening. Henry Higgins had been looked after by Preston. When we opened the door, he jumped out of the chair he had claimed as his own in the living room and ran to the back of the house. We called him several times but he refused to come. Finally, I hunted him out and carried him where we could all drown him in love.

"How come the whole family goes off on vacation but I

get left behind?" All of us heard him say it; the dog had a way of speaking.

"Henry, my boy, be grateful you had to stay home," I advised the little pisher.

It was a scene getting the children to sleep but we finally did. They were inconvenienced but thankfully not harmed. When they were secured, I unloaded the bullets from the rifle and put it away. Then I went to the refrigerator and took out the remains of the lemon pie. Preeti and I sat in the kitchen— she was the second partner I could laugh and cry with. We did that, as we devoured every last crumb of Preeti's baking.

"Preeti, I want to get in bed."

"You must be exhausted."

"No. I want to satisfy one of my "S" needs right now."

"What?"

"Preeti, just come to bed."

The next morning, we had visitors.

Josea was the first to arrive. She cried. Then, she unmercifully flagellated herself for having not believed my gut instinct about Fadi. She had to touch us several hundred times to be sure we were alive.

Kershaw flew up from Los Angeles to offer moral support— I was genuinely moved by the gesture. He also hand-delivered another giant royalty check while informing me they were opening a new Kuruk in Atlanta.

"What am I going to do with all this money?" I posed to him like an ultimatum.

He had never physically embraced me in the past but he

came over and hugged me, whispering in my ear at the same time. "The way you invite crises, you'll need it."

"Very funny. Won't be much use to me if I'm dead, will it?"

"You'll be fine." He unwittingly parroted the words Jivin used to assure me that regardless of the danger I faced I'd survive. "You're the man with nine lives."

"Are you counting?"

"No. But, Zach, you've got a long way to go."

What baffled me was that I knew it to be true. I had...well, I had something that convinced me my time was not near expiring. Still, I recognized a faint sensation deep in my being telling me I was emotionally overdrawn.

While Kershaw and I were talking, Persky stopped by. The two FBI men had known each other professionally and greeted one another kindly.

"Zach, I'm here to collect," Persky commented in an earnest manner.

"Collect? You don't even know when a counterfeit agent is hustling you."

"Be nice to him, Zach," Kershaw injected. "He's coming to L. A. and we're going to make him a star."

"Okay, I'll write it. So, what role do you want?" I asked the agent-soon-to-be-star.

"You."

"I'm warning you, don't do that to yourself."

"I want the whole tamale. I want top billing," Persky said with a glint in his eyes.

"You really wouldn't make a good Fadi Abbas...well, in appreciation for the sincere effort you put out, you may play me. But we are going to have to get rid of that limp," I poked at him.

"No fair. You're teasing me."

Our home was like Grand Central. Preston and Nadine visited later that morning. It was another leaky valve affair; there was so much to celebrate the emotions was as unsteady as at a funeral—but we were all alive.

When the scene calmed down, we were informed that Preston and Nadine were getting married—big surprise. They wanted to have the ceremony at Kuruk—another big surprise. They wanted it soon—oh, what a whooper of a surprise; the glowing smile on my savior's face left no doubt she would deliver a full-term baby eight months after matrimony—she deserved it.

A month later, we attended a wedding.

Within that same month, between when Nadine terminated Amir Hamdallah and Preston and Nadine married, the Israeli scientists—with the assistance of American researchers—had developed chemicals to combat the effects of the drugs used in San Francisco—both at the temple and ballpark—as well as those affected by the tainted kosher water. The victims were all partially on the way to recovery.

The afternoon one day before the wedding, Josea was visiting my home and took a call from Caplow. He was trying to entice her to return to work for the State Department. One of his lures was that the chemists were making rapid progress duplicating the scientific findings of the real Fadi Abbas.

Excitedly he explained that they were studying the new "weapons" to consider their applicability for the "limited action warfare" program (LAW)—the only major hurdle left to be overcome was finding a suitable acronym for the substance operations section that now incorporated the newly researched drugs.

Initially they had settled on (DOW) for "drug ordinance warfare" but Dow Chemical caught wind of the proposal and threw a fit, arguing that somebody might mistakably recognize the truth, that the giant chemical company was going to be the biggest name involved in developing more advanced versions of these new nuke-like substances.

We laughed until we near gagged—then we arranged to have the food and drinks at the wedding lab tested before we served them.

Then, after the wedding, when most everybody had left, Preston came up to me.

"So, can you tell me now, what's the big secret about the honeymoon?" I asked my friend.

"Tokyo."

"Preston, that's terrific."

"You have to hear the whole story. I received an invitation to compete in the World Cyber Cup."

"Video games; but you haven't competed for over a year."

"I know. I think it was just a courtesy but Nadine is so excited. Anyway, the guy I'm up against in the first round, a kid named Jason, is the best in the world so I'm over in a day. Then we'll travel a few weeks both in Japan and China."

"I'm excited for you."

"There's more. I've known this Jason for a while. The other day, he called me...out of the blue. Last time I saw him, we were talking and I told him I knew you—he's read all your work and loves it. Anyway, when he called, he said he had an idea and wanted to meet you. The guy has an imagination. He's got this story—"

"Stop it right there. No stories. No more adventure."

"He just wants to meet you," Preston eyed me with a pleading look.

"Preston, you're my best friend. I know you love me. But I wonder sometimes if you don't have a hidden wish to do me in."

"This is nothing, I promise. Straight adventure."

We grabbed each other for a huge hug. I kissed him alternately on each cheek, twice. He looked at me dumbfounded, not used to the Arab male in me.

It's a wild, wild, wild world out there, but I sure am beaming-from-head-to-toe joyous to be part of it.

Until next time…

*****

Upcoming Next:
Book 3 of the Zach Miller Advenure Series
Mescalero Blood

As far as an introductory note on *Mescalero Blood*, Zach Miller will swear that he is not an investigator of corruption, murder or missing persons. Yet within a span of a few weeks he's got his hand in all three. Making the tale all the more damning is that the triad of discreet circumstances proves to be intricately entwined. By the time each of the dramas unravel, Zach will be making new friends, relatives and enemies.

Look for *Mescalero Blood* to be published late summer of 2016.

As always, I'd love to hear from you and feel free to visit my website:

dennisnehamen.com

See the following page for a preview of *Mescalero Blood*!

MESCALERO BLOOD

By

Dennis A Nehamen

PROLOGUE

THE STATE OF NEW Mexico hadn't seen anything like it since it served host to the Manhattan Project and the development of the first atomic bomb. You might have thought Einstein had been reborn and was visiting. Instead, it was Stevie Green of LIVE.

For the past seven years, the iconic leader of his band had owned the world of music; he was the world of music. It was all about Stevie, as much a wonder as a new planet never before discovered. Then, to top it off, he was playing a one-night-only show in Albuquerque at Isotopes Park—he was an isotope, a divined element recently greeted into the periodic chart that had his fans dancing ecstatically to the magic and spirit defining the miracle.

This genius had literally branded a novel movement in sound. He borrowed from his training as a classical composer á la Beethoven, infused it with hip-hop, and then bestowed it with as revolutionary and energetic a pulse as Presley did for rock and roll.

Thanks for a father-in-law who was eager to babysit. My wife, Preeti, and I were enjoying a night out in heaven. It's doubtful that one more seat could have been packed into the stadium. The stage had been temporarily constructed in the center of the area, what would normally be the territory of a deep-playing second baseman if the field were being employed as it typically was, for baseball—an actual theater in the round.

We were sitting high up in the bleachers above the right field line, which were ideal seats that a friend of mine had acquired by way of her special status at the University of New Mexico, where the park is located. All was going well and the group was halfway through what they usually perform as a twenty-minute piece, "You Can Do the Same Thing Too." Then, the unexpected happened. The forecast for the early spring evening had called for a few clouds with no rain, but the weatherman must have had plans to attend the concert and suffered from an unforgivable case of wishful thinking— it started to pour. Most everyone has been in a rainstorm, but this was a New Mexico deluge, a genus unique to the region. On this evening, the act featured an unthinkable array of luminosity.

Lightning bolts, so dense and thick they might have passed for brightened torpedoes, struck like warriors' weapons on the sky's breast. Gods hurled exploding light patterns mimicking upside-down trees pointed at the earth like spears. Then, dancing stick figures of persons and animals stepped on stage, replaced by broad panoramic views of a globe outlining the borders of continents and countries in white—all electrical activity showing off its immense power.

But that was not the main attraction. Rather, it was that the rainfall had a mind of its own, splitting the stadium laterally from just behind the infield such that it heavily soaked the half with the playing field and all the boxes, booths, and seats wrapping around from the first base line to home plate and to the third base line. There were fans sitting literally two seats from me getting drenched while my wife and I were dry as unused Pampers.

The band was facing home plate and Stevie was in front, receiving his full share of the rainfall while the musicians standing behind him could have been dying of thirst. Remarkably, the legion refused to acknowledge the unexpected act of nature and went on singing, sopping up water like a gutter. In fact, Stevie was entranced, seeming to be brought to an unimaginable outpouring of emotion and energy, as if the heavens above were breathing through him.

To make matters more bizarre, there was no wind and the storm idled for almost a half-hour in one spot. Then, just as Stevie was finishing another piece, "Boo Hoo Bitching," the tempest exhausted itself, the beast packing up the show as if it had been waiting for its limousine.

Most of the concertgoers who had the misfortune of being seated in the downpour left to seek shelter. Their wet clothing and the coolness of the air precluded many from returning. The second portion of the program was viewed by about half of the beginning audience, but the star never mentioned a word about it.

While listening to the rest of the music, I couldn't help thinking about the incident, especially how life has a way of randomly slicing and dicing, cutting and lacerating, severing and disjoining, slitting and splitting, fissuring, parting, abstracting, divorcing, segmenting, subdividing, and fracturing us along an infinite number of planes and angles.

The wrong side of the tracks, the right side of the law, the right side of an investment, the wrong side of bed; we wake to uncertainty, live it out every minute of the day, and go to sleep, never sure if we're about to find ourselves on the wrong side of life when we rise the next morning.

A sick child, a spouse seeking love in the arms of a stranger, a lost job, an accident killing an innocent person crossing the street, a freak murdering for joy, a sad soul preferring suicide to facing another disappointment, winning a lottery, moving into a new dream home, making the basketball team, finding a new best friend, falling in love for the first time. Every second of every day we're turned like flapjacks on a griddle…one side cooling while the other burns.

That night, I, Zacchaeus Miller, known as Zach to my friends, was on the right side of the stadium. I hadn't always been as fortunate as on this concert night and wouldn't always be in the future.

The worldwide following of this man of unparalleled musical greatness was going to be on the wrong side of the news the next morning. Stevie Green's career slithered to a dead stop that evening and with it went the man himself—never to be seen or heard from again.

What happened? Well, that's the question hundreds of millions of people were trying to answer. It's also the mystery I was called on to investigate—and I begged not to take the job.

I will divulge that this adventure I'm about to scribe speaks to destiny's mercurial trickery and how human will is contested by folly. It seems that things just don't always turn out the way man plans. Some people get lucky and in the end find their way home safely. Some aren't so fortunate, and the load of dung they leave along one of their past roads traveled turns up at the most unexpected time and place— and stinks worse than a busted sewer pipe. This story speaks to the magical and maddening power of fate; one of life's inevitabilities that bullies you…more so if you try to toss it in the trash.

Welcome to Mescalero.

ABOUT THE AUTHOR

Dennis A Nehamen, Ph.D. is a forensic and clinical psychologist who has authored novels, screenplays and musicals, including the award-winning musical wrapped. He lives in Los Angeles with his wife and has two adult children.

www.ingramcontent.com/pod-product-compliance
Lightning Source LLC
Chambersburg PA
CBHW030536260626
47157CB00006B/2061